ALEXANDRA

A CHRISTIAN NOVEL

PAULA RAE WALLACE

Order this book online at www.trafford.com
or email orders@trafford.com

Most Trafford titles are also available at major online book retailers.

Scripture quotations marked KJV are from the Holy Bible, King James Version
(Authorized Version). First published in 1611. Quoted from the KJV Classic
Reference Bible, Copyright © 1983 by The Zondervan Corporation.

Print information available on the last page.

ISBN: 978-1-4907-5888-6 (sc)
ISBN: 978-1-4907-5890-9 (hc)
ISBN: 978-1-4907-5889-3 (e)

Library of Congress Control Number: 2015906115

Trafford rev. 04/24/2015

 www.trafford.com

North America & international
toll-free: 1 888 232 4444 (USA & Canada)
fax: 812 355 4082

ACTS 4:16 AND THEY SAID, BELIEVE ON THE LORD JESUS CHRIST, AND THOU SHALT BE SAVED, AND THY HOUSE.

TABLE OF CONTENTS

CHAPTER 1: GUILTY

"Get up! Stop that! Pull yourself together! Chopper's spotted us!" Brad Maxwell's tone was a cross between disgust and panic! He bent, jerking Alexandra Faulkner to her feet and rearranging her clothing! So much for their, 'No one will ever know', rationale! But still, what were National Parks for? Forestry guys must witness all kinds of goings on! And he and Alexandra were both of age!

"Remember whose idea this was," he hissed savagely as he urged her toward the settling craft!

❧ ❧

Daniel Faulkner bore down on the accelerator of a rent car! A successful Geologist from Tulsa, Oklahoma; but maybe he should keep both an apartment and a car in Durango, Colorado! His daughter, Alexandra's, scrapes were getting expensive! Panicked thoughts raced through his mind! Not that any expense was too great where any of his kids were concerned! His handsome features furrowed with annoyance! The washed out road above Silverton was still far from being repaired! Which meant he would be forced to take the narrow, crowded detour up beyond Al's mine, and then back down around! He grabbed his phone when the light displayed, before it had time to ring!

"Hey, Trent! What's up? Any sign of her?"

Trent Morrison, the USDA head of Forestry Law Enforcement's, voice seemed forever in coming!

"Yeah, yeah, she's okay! ~Er~mostly! Brad Maxwell~"

Daniel waited impatiently! Sat phones weren't supposed to break up in remote and mountainous areas! His worry was that the connection was fine, but his friend was too choked up to continue!

"What about Maxwell? He just happened to know where she was? Again?" Frustration at Brad's always being the Johnny-on-the-spot-hero, gave way to a deeper dread! "What~what~"

"We're about forty minutes out from her ranch!" Trent's clipped, suddenly authoritative voice! "We should arrive about concurrently with you! Remember, it's not the end of the world! Keep yourself under control! He's not worth going to jail over!"

"Right!" Daniel couldn't remember ever having worked so hard to squeeze out a one-syllable word! "Right," he mumbled again under his breath as he disconnected!

Another phone jangle reverberated up and down his ravaged emotions! Diana! Pressing the answer button, he forced himself to sound normal! His wife was a hard one to fool, but he didn't have any solid facts! Just that the Forestry Service had found their missing child, and she was en route to her ranch! Answering, he reassured the best he could! Forestry had found her! He was on the way to meet her! Beyond that, he couldn't supply any details! Breaking the connection, he scoffed at himself for continuing to reference his daughter's Colorado acreage as a ranch! With the loss of her seventy-five head of cattle in the spring flooding, the place was more accurately a fledgling silver mine!

'That's right,' Faulkner', he mocked himself! 'Focus on trivia to keep your mind from~' The implication in his friend's voice was tough to ignore!

"Not the end of the world! Try to keep from killing Brad Maxwell when you get here!"

Pounding the steering wheel in rage, he slowed behind an impossible line of traffic! His emotions swung wildly from white hot anger to tears springing up from depths he didn't know were there!

≒ ▷

Furious, red-rimmed, gray eyes bored into Trent Morrison's back! Alexandra couldn't hear his phone conversation above the racket of the rotor! Surely his job description didn't involve tattling on grown kids to their parents! Obviously, though, he was no fool in perceiving~Of all the worst people~of all the worst times! She tried to find comfort from

Brad~but he sat, studying his class ring, lost in his own world! Still, they loved each other, and they could~go get married~she studied his thick, close-cut, dark hair, his muscular neck and shoulders~

She hurt everywhere, wondering if she could hurt worse had she tangled with a Mack truck! Brushing back wisps of flaxen hair, she fought tears! The worst pain was her upperback! Gingerly, she probed the area, and the pain drove deeper! Glass! She pulled her hand back! Blood! Whoever said it was impossible to feel pain in multiple places was wrong! Morosely, she wished~not that she hadn't arranged the clandestine meeting with Brad! After all, they were adults and they were deeply in love! She wished that Norma Engel's ranch house hadn't washed away~and also that the elderly woman hadn't perished shortly after from a massive stroke! She could use the house to clean up and hide the guilty evidence! And Norma, with a big soft spot for her and Brad, could create a buffer! She tried again to catch Brad's eye~for any reassurances~any moral support!

Trent Morrison tried to corral turbulent thoughts! He was just here doing his job! Well, actually, he usually did his job from the Sidney R. Yates Building in DC! But a stubborn criminal entity in the San Juan National Forest kept cropping back up, necessitating his returns to southern Colorado! He turned in his seat as one of the Forest Rangers in the rescue party approached him.

Nervous, Alexandra eyed them! They were talking about her~she shivered! The wound in her back throbbed! She mulled over her options! Somehow, she and Brad needed to steal into her modular home at the edge of the mining village! They could shower, and he could pull the glass out! Band-aid! Voila! She dreaded meeting questioning gazes of friends, associates, and relatives who populated her little makeshift town!

Suddenly, Mr. Morrison loomed over her! "You're hurt?"

"N-n-no; I'm fine!" She gasped!

"Maybe we should check with someone else about that!"

She flinched when he opened a huge knife! "Hold still! I'm cutting some of this fabric away!"

"Okay, hold it!" A member of the search party halted him, pulling a pair of latex gloves free and offering them! "Never deal with blood without gloves!"

Trent nodded. His agency's rules, as well! Pulling the gloves into place, he continued with his plan!

Alexandra cringed! For one thing, the jostling drove the pain to the top of the 'one to ten scale'!

A talk from her youth director played in her brain from out of the blue:

Sin takes you farther than you want to stray; it keeps you longer than you want to stay; and it costs you more than you want to pay!

She thrust the voice aside! That was just their scare tactics to keep her from embracing life and love! She shivered harder, fighting sudden nausea and dizziness!

⚜ ⚜

Trent stood indecisively! His coworker thought Alexandra should be taken to an ER to be checked out! Not being able to determine how invasive the glass was, the concern was that pieces might be driven deeply into the flesh with the remote chance of doing spinal cord injury! Trent was also concerned about how consensual the incident really was! The entire scenario shook him to his core! He fought his own emotions, praying for wisdom! His concern was that deciding to have medical personnel examine Alexandra's wounds, might enrage Maxwell in the confines of the small craft!

"Alexandra, there's a lot of blood here, and we can't tell where the glass is, exactly, or how deep it's lodged! We're bypassing your ranch and heading toward the Durango ER!"

As expected, Maxwell's head shot up, a mixture of wrath and fear contorting his features! "She's fine! Just pull the glass out, and apply a little bit of pressure to stop~"

"You're a doctor? How do you know, 'She's fine!'?" the ranger's retort sprang up before he caught Trent's warning look! Although not under Morrison's actual jurisdiction, he still held respect for him! And he was right! No point in antagonizing the guy!

⚜ ⚜

Daniel wasn't the only one making a u-turn in frustration at the traffic jam! Fresh panic clawed at him! Viewing Morrison's photo of his daughter's injuries, he raced back toward Durango to meet the chopper at the hospital! Arriving earlier than the rescue chopper's ETA, he guiltily called Diana!

"Glass in her back? From what? Forward the picture to me!"

Hands shaking, he complied, wondering the same thing!

⊰ ⊱

Alexandra was in pain; and scared! No longer did she feel like an adult woman firmly in control of her life! Tearfully, she wished Brad would show more concern toward her, both for her own peace of mind, as well as making a better impression on the Forestry rescue personnel! Again, she chafed at Trent Morrison, a family friend's, being the one to lead the rescuers! Who sent for a rescue party, anyway? Humiliation and pain rode the merry-go-round in her brain!

⊰ ⊱

Diana Faulkner fought feelings of total impotence and defeat! 'How could Alexandra have purposely~ Had they not taught her the serious consequences~'Glumly, she took the blame! Hadn't she done the same thing~when handsome Daniel Faulkner appeared on her bleak horizon? Well, that situation was different! And yet, eerily the same! Was that Alexandra's befuddled thinking? That she could tangle with Brad Maxwell, get him saved, and turn him into a stalwart Christian, as Daniel had grown into? But, when you disobeyed God and His Word like that, there were no guarantees for a good outcome!

On her knees, she poured out her fears and pleas to her heavenly Father! Then, on her feet once more, she wiped the tears away, repaired her makeup, and reserved the earliest flight to Denver, where she would connect for the small Western Slope town of Durango! She didn't like glass! As a nurse, she was aware of the scope of danger it presented!

⊰ ⊱

Emergency personnel met the chopper with a stretcher! Then frowning, the ER nurse, Megan Green, opted for a wheel chair to evacuate the wounded passenger!

Alexandra couldn't figure out what the problem was! She knew Brad was furious at the unexpected detour! But they hadn't done anything wrong, and as soon as the doctor removed the glass, maybe with a couple of stitches, they could get on with their lives! She looked around for him, and her eyes widened with horror! Brad was nowhere in sight! And her dad advanced toward her, tears streaming down his face!

Before she could utter a sound, he spoke, sobbing, filled with remorse and self-incrimination for failing her! Steeling herself, she met his anguish with her iciest stare!

"I'm fine! You got Mallory to the marriage altar unsullied! That was really all you cared about, anyway! I'm not sure what you're doing here! I'm an adult, and I know exactly what I'm doing!"

The overheard words sliced into Trent Morrison's heart on behalf of his friend, confirming his long-held opinion that Alexandra was a snot-nosed brat! No one deserved to be spoken to like that!

Pretending not to hear, he gave directions for cleaning out the craft's interior. Then, suddenly, he pulled his phone free to issue an order to Jim Bailey, his head man in the San Juan Forest Law Enforcement and Investigative Services:

"Go to this crime scene and go over it with a fine-toothed comb!" He supplied coordinates! "Check for the presence of broken glass, and whatever-else-you may see~" He felt a certain gratification in Maxwell's alarmed response!

Trent didn't know all the details of Daniel Faulkner's having agreed to accepting a 'Guardianship', of sorts, over seventeen year old Mallory O'Shaughnessy following her father's death several years earlier! But from Alexandra's remark, she seemed to deeply resent Mallory's interloping into their family!

Surprised that anyone could resent Mallory, he tried to drive the disturbing remark from his mind!

⚏ ⚏

Certain that Al's injuries were superficial, Daniel forced himself to deal with insurance issues and ER admission! Moodily, he wondered why Maxwell didn't step forward to assure him of his love for Al, and his commitment to her care and well-being! He scoffed to himself, certain it would be the best thing all round if the two young people called this a mistake and walked away from each other! Part of him had held out hope for the promising young Geology grad student; but that was before Alexandra had become so taken with him! Brad still wasn't saved, and though, earlier in the summer, Daniel thought he was honestly seeking for answers~now he seemed to have decided in favor of pleasing his ungodly grandfather who held the reins on the Maxwell family fortune! Forcing his emotions under control, he struggled with the pesky, business-part of receiving medical attention!

Trent stood, not certain whether to fade away into the woodwork or offer moral support! He couldn't imagine the other man's mortification~Amazing that Alexandra was, 'all grown up', but her dad was running financial interference for her with the insurance thing! 'Kids!' An anguished sigh escaped!

⚎ ⚎

Diana paused before her connecting flight to contact her brother, Gray, who oversaw some of the accounting and insurance issues for their various corporate entities. Blessedly, he simply responded with helpful answers and no questions of his own! Uneasily, Diana figured he was aware of the situation, or at least, it didn't surprise him!

Not usually one to get airsick, she dosed for it anyway! Turbulence was certain for the small, regional jet crossing the Continental Divide! On board, she spread her Bible on her lap; then gazed at it, unseeing!

⚎ ⚎

Alexandra's fear and frustration rose as minutes ticked by on the big wall clock! Megan Green stuck close, and Alexandra wondered if her presence was deterring Brad from being at her side! She forced tears back! More than likely he was scared of her dad! Which, she couldn't figure out why he was here instead of at home in Tulsa! She shook harder! If they needed X-rays, why didn't they come take them? And she needed to talk to Brad!

⚎ ⚎

"Can I get you something?" Trent approached Daniel, who was still trying to work out his daughter's insurance coverage. "Coffee? Have you eaten anything?"

7

"No, thanks, though! Did Alexandra have a purse or wallet with her? I need to get this taken care of and see how she's doing! Diana was worried about her having a back full of glass!"

Trent ran the scene through his memory! "Not that I saw! Maxwell has a backpack-maybe he has some of her stuff with him." Seeing his friend's horrified expression, he offered, "I'll look for him and find out!"

He wheeled away, not sure he could be any more civil to the kid than Daniel could! Walking out to meet blistering heat rising from the pavement, he circled the parking lot! Sweat beaded on his forehead and dampened the back of his freshly knife-pleated shirt! What a nightmare of a day! The only thing that could be worse, was if it were one of his four! A stinging memory threatened to undo his emotional control! Of the previous year, when he and Sonia had nearly lost Megan to a severe asthma attack! Well, actually, had lost her-on life support, but technically-

He squinted. There sat the object of his search on a park bench! As he regarded his quarry, he saw him take a covert swig from a paper bag! What a total piece of dirt! He couldn't do this! Clenching fists at his side, he forced himself forward!

"Okay, Lord, I'm a law officer! Help me not to do anything stupid to end my career! Or send myself to prison!"

Although he felt tempted to call the local police department to report the illegal drinking, he approached the youth, circling into his line of vision.

Brad's turbulent blue eyes blazed at him, and he spoke though clenched teeth, "It wasn't a crime scene! No 'crime' was committed! We're both legally-" he broke off, "What's Alexandra saying?"

Trent forced himself to deal with the immediate issue, resisting angrily contradicting the kid! Public lewdness was a legal violation, consensual, or not! And no matter the ages of the offenders! "Okay, take it easy! As a law officer I have certain parameters I'm required to follow-have you eaten anything? Listen, Mr. Faulkner's having a hard time with Alexandra's insurance coverage! Did she leave a purse or billfold with you?" Trent forced his tone to be both authoritative and controlled!

"Uh-no-I think she might have left it locked in her car-"

"Which is where?" Impatience tried to boil into full-fledged rage!

Brad couldn't exactly remember the name of the rural road leading to their rendezvous, and the slur in his speech further antagonized the Forestry Law Enforcement Investigative Division head!

"You asked me if I've eaten"?

"Yeah, come on! Let's get something!" He made a call to his team to locate the cars and their contents!

CHAPTER 2: PERIL

Gray Prescott put in a call to Joe Hamilton regarding Alexandra's medical insurance! It seemed as though she had dropped her own coverage from the group policy that covered her mine employees! Gray frowned in consternation! Even if her budget was tight, dropping her own coverage was unwise! She had been forced to use it just a few months previously due to a broken ankle! Life was simply too uncertain~

⇥ ⇤

"Mom, what are you doing here?" Alexandra's humiliation at being caught hidden behind thinly veiled rage!

"You're hurt, Alexandra! Why do you think I'm here?" Diana smiled sweetly at Megan as she approached, introducing herself!

"Hello. I'm Alexandra's mother, Diana Faulkner! Could I see, please?"

The trauma nurse hesitated before asserting, "Miss Faulkner's legally of age, so her privacy rights are protected."

As a nurse, Diana was well aware of patients' rights regarding dissemination of medical information. This time she was on the parental end, facing the distinct possibility that she and Daniel would pay the financial liability in the aftermath of Alexandra's escapade! But they weren't entitled to any information.

Impatient, Alexandra spoke through clenched teeth! "Let her look! I'm tired of sitting here~"

"Okay, calm down, Alexandra! No one is deliberately stalling your care!" Diana's soothing tone, more professional than concerned mother. "There are some issues to address!"

Still, she took advantage of Alexandra's permission to assess the wounds! Worse than the picture revealed! Not that the photo wasn't scary enough. She looked up, relieved to see an x-ray tech roll a portable machine into the space! She stepped out to find Daniel.

"Well, hopeful news," he greeted her, looking drawn and exhausted! "Gray and Joe checked out the timing of the group policy revision. They think her coverage is still in effect! Are they nearly finished with her?"

Her solemn expression halted him.

"What?" He fought a deep seated panic. "Can't they just pull out the piece of glass and sew her up?"

"I'm afraid it's not that easy! That is good news about the insurance! She's sliced up quite badly, and there may be glass broken off in the wounds! She's lost some blood, and she's subject to high risk of infection! She's shocky; there's a possibility, somewhat remote, that some of the fragments might cause spinal cord damage!"

Her words, spoken softly, pierced him like a knife, crushing his carefully nurtured optimism!

She continued, "The x-rays will take a while. Let's get something to eat!"

"I'm not hungry; wh~what do~you mean? Spinal cord damage? Are~are we talking a wheel chair? I mean, she did wrong, but surely God~" He broke off as tears welled up.

"I'm not hungry either! But in emotional times, we need to keep up our physical strength! A surgeon and anesthetist are coming in! She's being started on strong antibiotics." She paused to order the standard bowl of vegetable soup, and he opted for the same!

Finding a table in the nearly empty café, Daniel choked out a blessing and a prayer for their child!

⚞ ⚟

Neurosurgeon Timothy Frasier introduced himself to Alexandra and her parents before carefully examining the damage and consulting the x-ray images! Delicate! A knife-blade of glass angled from the girl's left Scapula, to terminate a scant few millimeters from her spinal column! His questions about the nature of the accident were met with stony silence!

"Alexandra, we're stepping out! You need to tell Dr. Frasier what happened! Whatever you tell him will be confidential!" Diana's professionalism yet in control!

Still, Alexandra hesitated! She knew the whole thing cast Brad in a bad light! But it wasn't his fault! It was hers! Plus she didn't know the medical terminology to phrase the course of events! Her involuntary trembling escalated.

"Okay, let's get her prepped! Caution is the order of the day! That thing can't get jarred any more deeply, or break up~" He issued further pre-op orders before stepping out to converse with her parents!

⚐   ⚐

Trent met his investigative team in a motel meeting room! He hesitated on impounding the two cars! He could suggest that Maxwell retrieve his vehicle and save himself some time and money! But he didn't want the kid to flee, in case he decided to arrest him! If the surgery went south, and Alexandra lost her life, he could charge him with involuntary manslaughter! And if she ended up spending the rest of her life on a respirator, Daniel and Diana could sue him for damages! A tête-à-tête in the woods was one thing! But how could a guy be so clueless, or worse yet, so uncaring~so~yes~cruel~ The entire thing defied logic! Issuing orders regarding the carefully gathered evidence, he returned to the medical center!

⚐   ⚐

The wait seemed like ten eternities! Daniel's concern skyrocketed when Diana began pacing with him! Her voice trembled as she pulled her wallet free! "I'm getting more coffee!" She halted mid-motion as the surgeon appeared! Exhaustion made it difficult to steel herself for the news!

Daniel watched, bewildered, as the surgeon spoke to Diana in Medicalese he didn't understand! And her expression remained frozen and stoic!

"Thank you, Doctor!" The first intelligible words, as she shook the man's hand with genuine gratitude!

With a curt nod at Daniel, he spun on a plastic foot protector and disappeared through swinging doors!

Not sure about the strange discourse, Daniel shoved hands into slacks pockets before demanding, "Was there a reason he couldn't talk to both of us? In English? What did he say? Is~is~she gonna~be okay?"

"Well, it was a little annoying that you couldn't just give her a kiss and reassurance when she faced such a risky procedure! But no, you had to send her off with your ominous, 'We need to have a talk'!"

⚔ ⚔

Trent sat at the wheel of the government issued vehicle, staring vacantly at the little chain hotel! He was exhausted, but nervous energy drove him! That and caffeine! Pocketing the key, he decided to take time to clean up before pursuing his investigation! Blood stains on his clothing seemed to have a strange effect on the general population! He was torn between throwing his shirt away, sending it out locally, or taking it home where Sonia could send it out! He paused at a hospitable-looking coffee station in the lobby, but the pots just spit coffee droplets and air at him! Why did they always seem to be empty when he needed coffee the most? Ignoring the elevator and the desk clerk who issued an apology for the coffee lapse, he loped toward the stairs! Charging up them two at a time, he couldn't outrun the specters that dragged at him!

Like the late Undersecretary Coakley! Why couldn't the man's evil have died with him? Why did the nightmare still continue to plague him? Day after day, week in and week out, month in-He paused on his floor landing, chest heaving; not from exertion, but from terror! The soft ring of his cell phone made him jump! Faulkner!

"Hey, Daniel, any news?" He waited, breathless, while something hammered in his head, obliterating the voice on the line! If there was one! "Is-is she gonne be-?"

His head cleared and the other dad's voice joyfully announced that his little girl could move her toes!

Entering his room, he sagged brokenly against the door! He should call Sonia! But he couldn't tell her about Alexandra's lapse of judgment; and he would never be able to fool her! That he was fine! Everything was fine! Hunky-dory! A pervasive evil suffocated him, filling him with hopeless dread-

Ephesians 6:12 For we wrestle not against flesh and blood, but against principalities, against powers, against the rulers of the darkness of this world, against spiritual wickedness in high places.

He sat sobbing helplessly! Why was he so powerless to stop it? Why, in spite of his efforts at law enforcement, his attempts to be a stalwart Christian, his tithing and giving of offerings, his love for his family, his criss-crossing the country, trying to be everywhere at once~ Futile! Why waste so much time and energy in the face of such overwhelming depravity? Society was so wicked, sin so pervasive~It was all so unfair! For some beast to take advantage of a beautiful, treasured child, like Alexandra! For medical personnel to be so crazy as to tell a parent that their child's medical condition is none of their business, but; 'Be sure to stop and pay at the window before you leave'! How could someone be as revolting as Stephen Maxwell? And his grandson who seemed no better? Why could wickedness pass down easily from generation to generation, while raising a righteous heritage was so fragile? Clasping his knees in his arms, he surrendered himself to defeat in the spiritual warfare! Struggling for breath, he gasped, "God, I can't do this! I think I pray for power! Sometimes I feel even optimistic! But, I'm fooling myself! My efforts, Erik's efforts, our pastors and church members! We're not a drop in the bucket~this country is~"

He started to say, 'Doomed', but caught himself! "Not as long as I have one breath left in my body!" Pushing himself upright, he softly quoted the next verse:

Ephesians 6: 13 Wherefore take unto you the whole armor of God, that ye may be able to stand in the evil day, and having done all to stand.

By memory he quoted the remainder of the passage about each piece of the armor of God!

"Lord, I guess it isn't Your fault, when You give us clear instructions on winning the war, and we don't pay enough heed! We **can** win, but we have to do it Your way! I didn't even bring my Bible with me! Guess I've gotten confident in my own abilities~"

Pulling up the Bible ap on his smart phone, he read until balm flowed across his spirit and faith once more lit her ember in his bosom!

⚰ ⚰

Trent crawled into the back seat of Faulkner's rent car, pretzeling knees beneath his chin! Faulkner laughed for the first time in twenty hours, "Comfy?"

"Yeah, great," the dry response!

"I offered to trade," Diana parried! "You preferred martyrdom to comfort!"

"Well, what can I say? Don't martyrs get special perks in Paradise?"

An infectious laugh from Daniel, "Better be careful or Sonia may dispatch you there early!"

"Yes," Diana added, "Only to learn that those fantasies aren't based in Scripture! Abuse of women ends at heaven's gates!"

Following the short period of comic relief, they rode in silence! Trent needed to talk to Faulkner, but not necessarily when Diana was along. In the historic downtown district, they entered an elegant turn-of-the-century hotel and strolled back to the Western-themed steak restaurant!

Seated with coffee steaming in china cups, they ordered prime cuts before conversing softly.

"Alexandra's still doing okay?"

"As well as can be expected! Her fever spiked, so they're fighting the fever! Infection is one of Dr. Frasier's main concerns now! It can still invade her spinal column~I know you're wondering why one of us isn't there with her~"

Daniel patted her hand before taking up the conversational thread! "Maxwell hasn't come to visit her, so she's extra-emotional! Certain that Diana and I are deterrents for him! What was your bead on him when you fed him? If he's got millions in trust, why were you buying, by the way?"

Trent considered before speaking slowly! "To be honest, I'm still mulling it over! His grandfather is dead set against his having a relationship with Alexandra! Well, Steven's not much into relationships! He doesn't want any frivolous women to get their hooks into the Maxwell family fortune! A wicked man! The FBI arrested him~well, at first they figured his DC links to the late Undersecretary Coakley made him complicit in the kidnapping and human trafficking ring! Turns out he was only one of the most avid customers! As for the family fortune; I guess Treasury attempted to seize it~but they can't find so much as a dollar! If he's managed to move a fortune off-shore~well, highly unlikely! It seems as though between paying for his expensive tastes, the estate has also been frittered away paying off blackmailers and extortionists! Pretty sure Brad doesn't know there's nothing there!"

"Hm-m-m, I can't figure out if that's good or bad!" Daniel admitted being stumped! "I hate to say so, but I think a huge part of his appeal to Al, is his money! She sees him as being a willing and loving partner to forward her mining goals! Geologists and miners together, with her operation boosted forward by the mining equipment he could provide! Does he control anything?"

Trent scoffed, "Were you listening to me? There's nothing left to control! Stephen denied Brad's recent requests for his normal allowance, and reprimanded him for looking his mother up! Erik Bransom thinks it best to hide the truth from him about the squandered fortune! Facing that upset could put Brad on the rampage and make Alexandra and her mine seem to him like a plum ripe for the picking! And here's something else! Norma Engels' medication was switched, inducing her fatal stroke! And at first, Erik thought Brad was behind it! He figured maybe Norma wised up to Brad and warned Alexandra to steer clear of him; so he killed her! But the evidence points to the elder Maxwell! He was more opposed to their tryst than the two of you!"

Seeing their injured expressions, he added quickly! "Just for less noble reasons!"

᛫   ᛣ

The phone on the nightstand rang endlessly, but Alexandra couldn't reach it! Her incisions were painful, and to her chagrin, the surgeons hadn't removed all of the glass! Just the most critical shards, before they started having difficulties keeping her stable! Brushing at tears, she fought guilt and frustration! The mine needed her oversight and she needed to resume her efforts to land Brad! Nevertheless, she had no choice but to build up her stamina to face another surgery!

A nurse rustled in softly when the phone began again, answering it. "It's Brad," her voice a whisper. "Do you want to talk to him?"

Amazed by her patient's brightened demeanor and affirmative answer, she tucked the receiver in and tiptoed out!

᛫   ᛣ

Brad struggled to mask his impatience at the woebegone little voice! "Yeah, I can't come tonight! By the time I could get there, your folks will be back! I don't particularly care to see them, since you've done a poor job convincing them I'm not the one at fault! I'm still furious you didn't correct that Morrison character when he called the area, 'a crime scene'!

"Well, the surgeon said it's a miracle I didn't die up there! So, I guess part of Mr. Morrison's job-but I've told people, Brad, that it was both of us! Believe me, I never dreamed of landing in the hospital with my parents here-and I have to have more surgery-I wish they'd release me in between times, so we could spend time together again-" She hesitated before declaring diffidently, "I love you, Brad!"

"Yeah, tell them I said they better take good care of you, or I'll be on their cases! I'll call you again tomorrow!"

Alexandra listened to the connection break, both elated and disappointed! He did call! And, he just had a hard time expressing his love!

᛭ ᛭

Brad studied his face in the rear-view mirror, pleased with the handsome features staring back! His feelings for Alexandra were ambivalent, at best! A mixture of forbidden fruit and trophy-lookin' gal! He winked at himself! Her adoration for him was good for his feelings of self-worth! Why couldn't he make Stephen see that he could keep the situation under control? 'But,' he assured himself softly, 'If I'm smart enough, I can play it both ways! And I'm smart enough!'

He bore down on the accelerator and the car shot smoothly past a semi!

᛭ ᛭

Trent studied the forensics report, shocked! No matter how much he knew as a law enforcement officer, new horrors he was unprepared for managed to present themselves! Reminding himself of his Spiritual armor and the urgency of his work, he lifted his extension and barked some orders! There was far more blood and DNA evidence on that ridge than that of the two most recent visitors! Curiously, he wondered who had selected the rendezvous site: Brad or Alexandra! He frowned! No point in asking, because they would both say it was her! She was pretty blind to who he really was! Sighing, he headed out to his vehicle! Time for him to get boots on the ground up there for himself!

Fifteen minutes into a chopper flight from the high country ranger station, weather blew in! Wind, downpour, heavy lightning! Frustrating, washing away evidence! Still, DNA wasn't easily eradicated! Anyway, nothing he could do about it but go back, to try again another day! Like the Hare in Aesop's Fable, 'Slow and steady wins the race'! And he would win! Exiting the craft, he returned to his agency vehicle, whistling a little chorus from childhood days in a little Sunday School class! *With Christ in my vessel, I can smile at the storm~*

Back in his hotel room, he connected forensic evidence retrieved from the ledge, to a case where a girl had 'fallen' to her death! Highly questionable when there was so much of her DNA on a ledge fifty feet above where her broken body was recovered! Didn't happen! He opened a murder investigation! Beginning, not surprisingly, with re-interviewing a boyfriend! He gazed sadly at the beautiful girl smiling from her senior picture! So alive one minute, and then so irrevocably-lost!

He shuddered, wondering~ 'What would Brad Maxwell have done had he been more frightened by Alexandra's injuries? If her spinal cord had severed and she could no longer breathe? Would he have performed CPR on her~with no help in sight? Or~?'

CHAPTER 3: WARNINGS

Daniel Faulkner braced himself as he stepped from *The Sullivan Building* elevator where *GeoHy's* corporate office suite was located! Concern creased his brow! Leaving his firstborn in Colorado to finish her recuperation tore at him! And according to his executive secretary and his father's forewarning, Brad had returned here to work, as if he considered himself to be in good graces! Brash, to say the least! Still, with pleas from both Diana and Alexandra, he was supposed to embrace the kid to his bosom! As a dad, he wanted vengeance~ A thought struck him and he loped to the staircase to descend one floor! He needed to ask Diana's father where he got his restraint not to kill him! Then, pausing at the bottom of the flight, he jogged back up! Everyone wasn't aware of Al's judgment lapse! And they didn't need to be! He figured his brother-in-law, Gray, and the insurance guy, Joe, guessed something was up about Al's hospitalization; but that was all!

After checking a calendar ap, Diana was sure there was no issue with a pregnancy~a huge relief~ he sagged on the top step, gasping!

After a few desperate pleas for strength, he composed himself and sailed into his office, head held high! To his consternation, Maxwell's cubicle was deserted, plants and all! Paling, Daniel made the sanctum of his executive office and dropped wearily into his chair! 'So, at least I don't have to fake being nice to him!' Even as he sensed relief at that, a deeper dread assailed his mind! Maxwell was undoubtedly en route to Colorado for another shot at Al! And there was nothing he could do about it! Alexandra was legally of age, and she had made her little declaration of independence! Defiant and determined, she wanted what she wanted! And that was Brad Maxwell! Well, not the real Brad Maxwell! Not the one who was heartless to her cries at being injured by broken glass! But a rosy, romanticized Brad, who simply did not exist! One she was exuberantly confident she could reform by the sheer force of her love! When he thought he had cried until the tears were spent, he found that there was a fresh fountain, welling up from his depths, and spilling over~

⊰ ⊱

Alexandra followed a realtor through a small house located in the historic district of Durango! It was dark-looking, and well-historic~ Accustomed to modern and up to the minute top of the line appliances and a spit and polished look, this might take some getting used to!

"New furnace; new roof-yada-yada," went the sales pitch.

Obviously, nothing else was new to brag about! But the asking price was good-this would be as good a place as any to crash when the drive up and down to the mine wasn't practical! And following the second surgery, she had been backed into the corner of promising her parents that she would do the prescribed PT on her ankle! Every inconvenience made her miss her elderly friend, Norma Engels! Obediently, she followed the agent to the carport and then the backyard! A little storage area at the front of the carport for a mower and yard stuff! Imagining Brad mowing the postage stamp yard was a stretch! Well, when they were married and stepped into his millions~

The realtor excused herself to take a call, and Al let her mind travel to some of the things Brad had filled her in on! Like his scoop on her mom and dad! She always assumed they were pretty well off, but according to Stephen Maxwell's research, her parents, were 'wage slaves', barely making it! Barely keeping up appearances with the, 'built on to', mansion! Though they were busy owning two corporations, things were barely afloat!' That was a jolt to her already troubled reasoning! She had to make it! She simply had to! No room for failure-and her parents couldn't keep making emergency trips to see her through crises!

Annoyed that the agent took her no more seriously than to take another call, she informed her she needed time to think! With the usual caution about, 'striking while the iron's hot', the agent left another business card and pointedly locked the box as Alexandra headed to her car!

Seated behind the wheel, she let her thoughts wander to Trent Morrison's advice prior to her release from the hospital: "Your dad didn't report you missing for no reason, you know! And the Forestry Department doesn't pay what it costs for a rescue without pretty good cause!" With that he had reminded her that the human trafficking ring had specifically stated that they wanted her and her younger sister, Cassandra, as well as his two daughters! Consequently, when she refused to answer her phone, both her dad and Mr. Morrison had feared the worst! That, and the recent broken ankle, not medically released; and her mother had envisioned her fallen and hurt out on some ledge!

"Just answer your phone! Have the nerve to say you can't talk! Or text the same thing! Just, maybe you can include a duress or lack of duress punctuation mark, or some sign, that a kidnapper wouldn't know to use~" Before taking his leave he had added the stinging admonition about 'public indecency'!

She shuddered! Sobering thought! Now as far as she could tell, Mr. Morrison was back in DC and her parents were back in Tulsa! Maybe Brad~

She phoned the realtor back with her decision to purchase! Pre-qualified, she was able to set up closing within the week!

☙ ❧

Brad fumed with anger! With no knowledge of Stephen's arrest and the tightening noose, nor of the dissipated and defunct Maxwell family fortune, recent orders made no sense! Why was Stephen so dead-set against Alexandra? Sure, some things about her needed to be smoothed out, but she loved him so much she could change to be the kind of trophy wife he needed! He couldn't see why Stephen couldn't see it! And though it was true that her family wasn't wealthy in the Maxwell sense of the word, they had a certain presence among the moneyed set in Tulsa! Of course, the East Coast big-wig, Stephen, had mocked Tulsa, Oklahoma as, 'that back-water village'! Even his grandfather's admiration of Faulkner's skill as a violinist no longer meant anything! Partly because of the inclusion of the 'religious' number, and one of the critics' opinion that Faulkner only seemed emotionally moved by that inconsequential piece! And not by the grandiose classics! So, his grandfather was anti-religious! So was he!

He forced the concern aside that tried to surface occasionally, about an unnerving incident the past spring~a Tulsa University Geology professor, Professor Stone, and a crazy coed, and the prof's ensuing taking of his own life! A crazy series of events, having nothing to do with God, or creationism, or evolution~who knew what demons tormented the man? Well, not literal demons~just~

He called the frat house and gave notification that he no longer resided there, and to sell or give away, or whatever was customary~his remaining possessions!

⌐ ⌐

Alexandra signed the final document, wrote a check for the down payment, and took possession of a set of keys! Purposefully, she began the process of moving in! And doing a deep cleaning! A fairly nice floor emerged, and she straightened, gratified! Some of her incisions were still tender, but they were improving! A new bed frame with mattress set seemed lonely in her bedroom! She unboxed an office unit which had warned, 'Some assembly required', and frowned! She wasn't sure which would be the most reasonable; paying someone to put it together for her, or buying the tools! Wearily, she sank into the new mattress! She needed to buy the tools! No telling what else they might come in handy for! She didn't want some handyman knowing she was a woman living alone~And she could be tough and resourceful!

⌐ ⌐

Diana met Daniel for lunch in the Bistro! Functioning without knowing what was going on with their first-born was a horror they had never contemplated! Aside from praying for her, they tried to leave her alone! Although Daniel had contacted his brother-in-law, Gray Prescott, as well as Jacob and Tim at their heavy equipment rental business south of Silverton, none of them mentioned Alexandra or knowing how she fared! They hoped that, 'No news was good news'! No word from Maxwell, either; not even to leave an address for his final *GeoHy* paycheck! With Brad's internship unfinished, Daniel contacted the University! He didn't like the news that Brad no longer resided at the fraternity house!

"Well, we just have to place her in God's hands! We taught her what she needs to know~" Diana's attempt to lift both of their spirits!

Daniel spoke softly in turn, quoting: *Psalm 127:*

Except the LORD build the house, they labour in vain, that build it: except the LORD keep the city, the watchman waketh but in vain.

It is vain for you to rise up early, to sit up late, to eat the bread of sorrows: for so he giveth his beloved sleep.

Lo, children are an heritage of the LORD: and the fruit of the womb is his reward.

As arrows in the hand of a mighty man; so are children of the youth.

Happy is the man that hath his quiver full of them: they shall not be ashamed, but they shall speak with the enemies in the gate.

"I love you so much, Diana! I'm grateful to the Lord, and to you, for our children! I'm grateful that He preserved Al's life up there-He-He's in control! Manoah and his wife couldn't understand why Samson did the things he did, and yet God used his escapades to help deliver Israel from the oppression of the Philistines-"

She nodded, "Yes, in spite of Samson's rebellion! Still, it leaves me wondering how much greater Samson might have been, in obedience! I-I guess Alexandra's flawed reasoning is my fault! I married you against my parents' wishes, and-"

He patted her hand! "Yes, but we've always been clear with the kids, that God is against premarital relations, as well as against believers even making close friendships with unbelievers! Not to mention marriages! I loved you, Diana! From the moment I came to, and saw those big blue eyes! I don't have a sense that Maxwell even cares about Al! She made herself available to him, so why not-but-marriage? Al wants that; I'm pretty sure he doesn't!"

Diana nodded! Daniel always said that, about falling in love with her! But then it had taken over a year, and another bout of the strange illness, to make him honor his marriage vows and earnestly seek to please the Lord! There were no guarantees of happy endings when Christians knowingly defied God! She spoke contemplatively, "I thought it was tough when Cassandra first went with Lilly-but this-" Tears welled up, and she blotted them with a paper napkin.

He considered, "Yeah, that we were kind of forewarned about–I mean knowing and agreeing in advance–still, it was kind of crazy–and sad–" He forced a smile! "At least Al's almost twenty! And she's been saved a long time, and fairly well grounded in the Word! Cass just got saved that morning–and she was just–five–" His resolve not to cry at the lunch nearly cracked.

"Yeah, the little pill; just asking the Lord to save her, so He could send the 'violin people,'–" Diana's eyes alight, triumphed over her earlier tears! "And yet, the Lord took her at her invitation and saved her and held her very closely to Himself! Why would He do less for Alexandra? We simply have to keep Alexandra in our prayers while we focus on the other children! And we need to keep praying for Brad! That's the right thing to do for any unsaved person!"

≒ ≓

Alexandra closed her Bible and placed her coffee mug in the sink! Trying to stay busy and take her mind off of the absent Brad, she had thrown herself into her new little property! A refrigerator, the bed, the office furniture, and a recliner were new! With costs mounting, she placed herself on a moratorium of further spending! Still, she had found a cute spinning wheel and most of a small loom at a weekend flea market! They looked cute in the living area, balancing her mom's love of textiles, with her dad's passion for rocks and Geology! To her amazement, she missed having a piano! Strange how not having one mattered! She laughed at herself for walking past the Steinway baby grand in the music room every day, almost without seeing it! It was either the duty of practicing or dusting it! Without a TV, playing the piano suddenly appealed! So, she focused on playing her violin! She could fairly well keep it tuned by ear! She was sure she lacked perfect pitch like her dad and sister possessed, but she wasn't tone-deaf either!

Her office was adequate! With new electronics linked to those at the mine, she could oversee quite a bit remotely! She felt a great frustration that her rock crusher, ordered in late spring after making a hefty down-payment and completing payments for six months, was still encountering difficulties in production and delivery! Her terse email, met with a terser one from the factory, that delivery would now be postponed until at least February! She kept praying about it, too! She pulled a throw over her feet as she settled back into the recliner with her prayer journal. Pensively, she wondered if the equipment delay was normal, or if God was mad at her and thwarting her efforts! She opened the dainty little notebook and poured out her hopes and dreams about Brad Maxwell!

⚔ ⚔

Tim Alvaredo grasped Jacob Prescott's arm in a hard, pincer grasp! "Look, there's your cousin! Let's go talk to her!"

"Ow, Dude!" Jacob pulled his arm free! "First of all, she's not really my cousin! She doesn't even refer to Brenna as her aunt, but as her, 'Uncle's wife'! She's a snob! I'm not from her kind of background! I just don't particularly enjoy her attitude reminding me of that every second! You go talk to her if you want! I'm hungry! Unless you have an update for her from Maxwell, betcha a buck she freezes you out!"

Tim grinned mischievously, "Good point! Guess I'll make something up! Should I tell her he's going out with his grandfather's pick, or that he's been in France visiting his father at the family winery?"

"Neither one! We need to eat so we can get back! There she goes anyway!"

⚔ ⚔

Alexandra brushed angrily at tears as she steered into the line of traffic on Silverton's main drag! Not much a 'main drag' but she liked it! She fought humiliation! It seemed like everyone was aware of, and laughing behind her back, for her indiscretion with Brad! Like there was no reason for Tim and Jacob to stand on the corner talking about her, and then not even wave! All the residents of the small community waved! Guiltily, she wondered, if Brad had bragged about his conquest to those two! Or at least, they knew something~

"Lord," she whispered, "I'm sorry! Please give me Brad! I went about things the wrong way, but~"

Back in Durango, she stopped at the grocery store! Her mainstays were cereal, toast, and TV dinners! As she exited, a big, handsome guy with sandy brown hair and warm brown eyes, stepped into her path! She frowned, wishing she had Brad and a wedding set to discourage passes!

"Name's Doug Hunter, and you are~?"

She passed huffily, eyes fixed on her car! Why dared he be so brazen? Did he know about her, too? Did it show that she was cheap? Durango wasn't as small as Silverton, but still, it was a cozy community-She drove home slowly, making certain he didn't follow her! Once home, she wrestled with the decision of phoning Brad! Still, she hesitated. There was no question he loved her! He must, or why would he have met her that day- She tried to conjure up a pleasant memory, but pain and embarrassment crowded everything else from her memory bank! She knew it for sure, though! Brad loved her! It was just that he was being forced into a balancing act to keep Stephen snowed and get his money-and being together with her!

Feeling restless, she opened a book, then pulled her violin from its case! Sighing, she put it back, and cleaned and oiled her pistol! Drifting off to sleep, she formulated a plan!

⊰ ⊱

Alexandra arrived at Mountain View Baptist Church one minute early! Finding a seat near the aisle half-way forward, she grabbed a hymnal and joined the singing!

> *What a wonderful change in my life has been wrought,*
> *Since Jesus came into my heart!*

Singing the marvelous lyrics without thought for their depth, she was probably pretty much in league with the other worshipers around her! Saved young, she couldn't really relate to Jesus' working any marvelous changes in her! Her Christianity mostly represented restraints and restrictions to her! Not that she planned on throwing it all overboard-after all, if she wanted God to see Brad her way, she should probably stay in church! Gazing through one unfrosted window pane, she tried to let the sermon bounce off! She was a good Christian! In the hospital, she had asked God to forgive her! A couple of months removed from the incident, she allowed herself to consider the implications of her life-threatening injuries! Just that fast-

With the final amen, she broke toward the rear doors! Freeing herself from matronly women offering dinner invitations, and compliments on her singing voice, she reached the parking lot! And there stood Doug Hunter, grinning at her!

"Welcome to *Mountain View*!" With outstretched hand, he advanced! "I mean, I'm new here, too! I just recently transferred in here with the US Forestry Department!"

Aggravated, but cornered, she responded limply to the handshake! "I usually attend a small church up in Silverton, but since I was down here~"

'Undeterred', seemed to be his trademark, and he continued blithely, "Yeah, actually, Silverton is more in the middle of my turf! I visited that church, but the 'Praise and Worship Team' isn't my preferred style! Uh~can I buy you some lunch?"

"Thanks, anyway, but I'm kinda seein' somebody! And my afternoon's crammed full!"

He continued grinning at her, his frame leaning casually against her car door.

"Excuse me!" Aggravated, she gritted the word out!

He straightened, "Yeah! 'Scuse me!" Shot down, he wheeled away toward his own vehicle! 'Cute? Definitely! A Christian? Maybe! But a real icicle of a gal! Who needs it?'

He shot gravel peeling out, then apologized to the Lord for his poor testimony~and as a law enforcement officer, too! Back at his room he heated a can of soup and made a bologna sandwich! He didn't really have money to spend on a girl right now, anyway! And Alexandra looked high-maintenance! With a sad sigh, he placed a worn picture beside his bowl!

꼭　꼬

Hardy Johnson slipped from deep cover of Blue Spruce into lengthening shadows! After a few months of unsettling developments, he was back! And loaded for bear! He grinned to himself! Not really! Knowing better than anyone, that he was in the thick of brown bear country, he didn't want to conjure one up! Usually, his crossbow was his weapon of choice; but against a bear, he would need a perfect shot! And rifle shots could call attention to his activities! So, on second thought, he wasn't loaded for bear; but anyone from the Forestry Department? They better keep their distance! This place belonged to the American people, of which he was one! And he planned to defend his rights!

CHAPTER 4: MÊLÉE

Alexandra sighed in relief as she closed her front door, kicked free of stylish boots, and brought the fireplace to life! Quite the emotional roller coaster of a day! Starting at the registrar's office at Ft. Lewis State College! She trembled at the harrowing memory! She wanted to begin on her Master's Degree, and for more reasons than she could count, she didn't plan to follow Mallory's route of individualized online courses via Mr. Tom Haynes! But, she had failed to consider the likely link between the local state college and Colorado State University! When the registrar proudly boasted of the ease with which she could transfer credits to the larger university, her failed earlier course popped into her mind! Already buried with an online CSU course, she had failed it completely after breaking her ankle and being hospitalized! Making as smooth and graceful of a retreat as possible, she gained her car and raced away! She did possess something of a lead foot!

Deciding to calm her nerves with some retail therapy, she had stopped at the downtown historic district, pausing to admire an oil painting in the first gallery! From the talented hand of family friend, Risa Perkins! It would look stellar in her office at the mine! Thoughts of Brad and his inheritance took her off into realms of fantasy! But without an immediate and unforeseen influx of cash, the painting wasn't destined to be hers! She moved on, enjoying the divine, early autumn afternoon!

⚜ ⚜

Trent Morrison focused his troubled gaze from his copy of *The Washington Post* to some point down the street! Page after page of garbage! He wasn't sure what the truth was in the various DC scandals, but he was pretty sure the news media didn't care! He considered his empty coffee cup, debating a refill, or returning to his office! His recent increased travels to personally oversee his Division Heads left him more restless than ever when he was in the Capital! Plus the never-ending swirls of accusations and lies and cover-ups got on his nerves! He preferred sitting on the vibrant street to being closed in, but he needed to go back and make some calls! Still, the pleasant weather tempted him to stay; he checked his cell phone! No search parties looking for him yet!

Which, he was surprised at! He kept expecting the axe to fall! Well, surely his active participation in not one, but two, search and rescues for Alexandra Faulkner-must have come to the attention of someone! Accusations had come before, that he was Faulkner's 'boy', using Federal resources to protect various private corporate entities! Not true! But he could see why his detractors enjoyed putting that spin on things! His thoughts turned to his beautiful wife and her 'mysterious' job as a 'representative', for Diana Faulkner and Mallory Anderson's *DiaMal, Corporation*! A dream job that seemed to demand nothing more than that she appear here and there in DC in the most gorgeous garments known to womankind! Which got him woebegone complaints among politicians and lobbyists that his wife was the best-dressed woman in the Capital! And the implications of how that shouldn't be so! At his government pay grade! Trent attributed it to The Lord, but others saw it as a way for the Faulkners to boost his income for 'favors granted' in return, and without his paying accompanying income taxes! And why would they do that, if he wasn't looking out for their interests? He jumped when someone interrupted his reverie!

"Mike Behr!" The announced name came as the startled Trent stared into mirrored sunglass lenses and noted a grimly drawn mouth! His nightmares were coming true? He rose to his feet, he hoped calmly!

"Trent Morrison! Pleased to meet you! I'm done with the paper-" he extended it slightly!

"Maybe the sports page, the funnies, and the puzzle, Trent! The rest of it isn't even good any more for starting my fireplace, since there's so much lead in the colored ink!"

Trent shoved it at his chest, trying to walk away. "Just take what you want and leave the rest!"

"Join me for lunch?"

Trent's puzzlement deepened as he grew slightly less alarmed! Still~Behr was known as the Treasury Department's 'Bear' in Washington circles! The fact that he knew Trent's name was cause for panic!

"It's early," Trent stalled. "I usually try to separate my coffee break from my lunch break with a small modicum of work!"

"The only guy left in DC with such a work ethic!"

Trent wasn't sure whether to laugh or run!

"Most people consider their coffee breaks, lunches, happy hours, and dinners as being their work! And expense out all the fun!"

"Yeah, golf games and attending sporting events! I can actually see some validity to that! It's possible to get some work done while bonding~" The Forestry Agent paused uneasily! Remembering the last time someone really big in the DC scene had tried to socialize with him~Undersecretary Theodore Coakley!

⌐ ⌐

Alexandra became aware of a group of young women staring at her! Shining clean faces and hair drawn back from center parts and pinned into netting, definitely set their little group apart! If her parents took Christianity to an extreme, they at least allowed cosmetics and cute clothes! And jewelry! These girls probably considered her to be a heathen hussy, even if they didn't know about~

"We're sorry we were staring at you! You're so pretty! I'm Charlotte!"

"I'm Alexandra, and thank you!"

One of them giggled, "She sounds beautiful, too!"

"That's Rebekah! You do sound like a southern belle! Where are you from?"

Alexandra laughed. No one had ever told her that before! "I'm from Tulsa! Not exactly the Deep South! I love it here, though! Are y'all from here?"

They laughed again at the 'y'all', before explaining they were freshmen at a small private college, *Grace College of the Rockies*! And they were from various states! Alexandra's guess was that they were Mennonites, although, beyond that, she was pretty unfamiliar with the sect!

"Girls, what are you doing still sitting here? The bus was supposed to depart for campus ten minutes ago!"

Alexandra's wide gray eyes took in the flustered staff member sympathetically, even as she wondered how girls without wrist watches were expected to keep track of time! None of the girls seemed to be in possession of the ubiquitous cell phone, either! She smiled diffidently, to meet a hard stare!

"None of you were talking to strangers, were you?"

"It's okay, Ma'am! We're not strangers!" Alexandra wasn't sure why she made that crazy defense! "We're friends! Charlotte and Rebekah introduced me to Dendra, Hannah, and Lisa! My name's Alexandra; what's yours?"

The suspicious countenance softened slightly! "Ann Gates! And no, I'm not related to Bill!"

She laughed at her own joke or Alexandra wouldn't have caught it!

"I guess time's gotten away from me, too!" Alexandra offered her hand as she rose! "Maybe we'll see one another around town again!"

Curious, she pretended to window shop as the clucking mother-hen, Ann, herded her charges aboard a run-of-the-mill, yellow school bus! Interesting; she wasn't sure why! She headed slowly toward home, but then, catching sight of the bus at the stoplight, she decided to follow it!

It labored, belching thick black smoke that threatened to foul the whole pristine mountain environment! She hung back slightly as it turned left across the highway onto County Road 202! Lowering her window, she inhaled the fragrant air! Well, the fragrance of pines; without the diesel exhaust! Pretty place for a small private college campus!

"Are you lost, or did you follow us?" Ann demanded as Alexandra pulled into a space beside the bus.

An hour and a half later, a thrilled Alexandra headed back to town! The college registrar had agreed to help her advance toward her Master's Degree, online, under their auspices! And after she auditioned to study piano and violin in the Music Department, she came away with a teaching position! She would be teaching part time in the Physical Science Department, as well as Strings and Piano!

⚔ ⚔

"Your wife works a real job for a real company, by the way!" Mike Behr's reassurance as they settled into a table at a busy spot! "I know because The Department has sent me twice to go through every fragment of business ever done by *DiaMo*, *GeoHy*, or *DiaMal*! I came away impressed both times!"

Trent nodded uneasily! That was good to know, but did anyone at Treasury think that he personally rendered any services to said companies, other than fulfilling the responsibilities of his job as head of the Forestry Law Enforcement and Investigative Services? Being on Behr's radar seemed to bode ill! He willed his phone to ring so he could scurry away, but it was silent!

When the other man recommended a menu item, he went with the choice.

"People talk about what a lucky guy you are! I find that lucky people are usually 'clever', more than actually, 'lucky'!"

"Or, that luck is directly in proportion to hard work!" The last thing Trent wanted the Treasury muckety-muck to think was, that he was, 'clever', as in being able to outsmart the government, the IRS, or anyone else!

"Right!" Behr frowned, "I'm not implying you don't work hard, but you did go straight from your break to lunch!" Still without a hint of a smile, "I'm kidding! People tell me you usually say, 'It's the God-thing'!"

"Ah, you mean giving God the glory when things work out in my life! That is the key, but it's a tight-rope walk what to say and when to say it in this town!"

"You attend *Henderson Park Baptist Church*; don't you?"

Behr leaned in intently once their plates were settled in front of them! "Why do you donate so much? And how do you know if you're giving enough to get you in?"

"Well, they let you in whether you give anything or not!"

"Right, into the church! What if I showed up some Sunday; would you sit by me and introduce me around?"

Trent was confounded, "Look, if you want to examine my church's books, just go into the church office on Monday morning and say so! You don't have to sneak in on Sunday!"

Behr patted his lips drolly on the fabric napkin. "We examine your church all the time! Compliments of the Patriot Act! It wouldn't be fair for us just to breathe down the necks of mosques and leave all the other religious institutions alone! You didn't answer my question about why you give as much as you do! And I'm asking personally, and not officially! And I know it's really none of my business~"

"I give what I give because God gave so much for me! He sacrificed His only Son to die for my sins! My sins being forgiven, that's what, 'Gets me in'! You were talking about getting into heaven earlier; I apologize for being dense! I give so the Gospel can be proliferated around the world!"

"Really? And that's the only reason?"

"Well, it doesn't hurt me on my tax return!"

⊨ ⊨

Infused with excitement at the teaching venture, Alexandra lost track of time! She studied *Beginning Music Theory*, surprised how much she had forgotten! Again, she missed the convenience of having a piano! After checking and cleaning her violin, she tackled the *Earth Science* course! This was going to be great! Well, the textbook lacked, filled with the usual evolutionary folderol! The challenge was separating out the truth-for lectures! And there was no place like the Rocky Mountains of Colorado for a Geology student to cut her teeth on for field work! She liked Dr. and Mrs. Allen, who were in charge of the school! She even had a little faculty sticker in her car window so she could park on campus! Like the security guard of the little faculty and staff wouldn't know the cars!

She rolled into bed, realizing how scornful Brad would be of the little fresh-faced Mennonite college freshmen! How scornful he would be of her and her new little wage-slave job! But the truth was, that another winter threatened to put the silver extraction on hold! The mine was okay, but she could use the money from teaching-and it was a diversion from waiting on him! And it was gratifying that the Allens said she was gifted on the violin! She wasn't! Her dad and sister were-

⊨ ⊨

Alexandra sat up suddenly, struggling to locate her buzzing phone! Two things registered through the haze of sleep! It was five-thirty in the morning, and her mining engineer was the caller!

"Hello, Jared; what's up?"

Moaning, she ran her hand through sleep-tousled hair! "Someone stole some of our dynamite? How could they-the explosives shed was locked; right?"

She listened, horrified as she pushed a coffee to start brewing, and shoved through clothing selections in her closet! "Okay, okay, stop everyone from tromping around in there! Whoever broke in probably left some kind of evidence! Have you called the sheriff or anyone yet?"

"Well, not yet! I told you I'm worried~"

"Yes, that you gave your key to your dad, and he's not sure he locked~we still need to notify authorities! I mean~okay, I'll call! I'm on my way up there as quick as I can~"

⚎ ⚎

By the time Alexandra reached her mine property, her hair had air dried into a haystack, and every stripe of law enforcement vehicle circled the mine office! Her personal spot was taken, so exasperated, she parked across the lot and tried to pick her way past muddy spots to gain the back door! She paused, shaken, as fifteen sets of eyes drilled into her! And one set belonged to the overly-friendly Doug Hunter! The irrelevant thought went through her mind that maybe she should have been nicer to him; she shrugged it off impatiently! She was a robbery victim, and justice shouldn't be conditional upon clever parlaying of passes!

She shrugged her way through the intimidating circle, extending her hand! "Al Faulkner! What have you found out?"

The San Juan County sheriff, Bill Cassidy, always seemed to have his chest puffed out! Alexandra guessed maybe he was afraid the citizenry might fail to notice the huge badge! He began blusteringly, that it was no secret to him that Jared's father often over imbibed!

Level gray eyes met his, and a soft but commanding voice spoke up, "Okay, enough irrelevant gossip! Are you working on finding out who trespassed on my property, broke into one of my buildings, and made off with a small fortune in dynamite and blasting caps?"

Doug sent up a silent cheer for her! He agreed that the mine foreman might have a drinking problem that should be addressed! But he felt like it had no bearing on the theft, and that Cassidy wanted to pin blame quickly and get back to the local coffee shop where he hung out! An elected official, more than a real lawman! And, Doug wasn't the only guy she shot down! Still, she should get a perception that having friends never hurt!

Not surprisingly Cassidy bowed up in response! "Now, listen here, Sister, you ain't one of the locals!"

"My name is either Miss Faulkner, or Al! And I beg to differ with you about being a local! Now if you mean, I'm not an 'old-timer', of course you are correct! But my name on the deed to this mine indicates I'm a local now! And because you haven't know me all my life is no reason for you to suspect me of wrongdoing! Jared's father has no reason to steal explosives! He's a Vietnam vet, and I'm sure he bleeds red, white, and blue! He's the last person you'd suspect of planning attacks against the US! Have you processed the shed for evidence? What about the security cameras?"

Cassidy frowned, hoping to garner support from the other represented agencies. "Okay, all in due time! County personnel stay log-jammed! We'll get it all sorted out, of that you may be certain, young lady!"

Alexandra resented the condescension, "Do you have a problem remembering names, Sheriff Cassidy? You may call me Al or Miss Faulkner!" Even as she repeated herself, she wished she were Mrs. Brad Maxwell! Doubtless, that would garner more respect!

Doug stepped out to call his superior, James Buford, the Rocky Mountain District head, headquartered northwest of Denver in Golden. Buford suggested Doug use caution! Without relating details of two rescue missions to save the mine owner, he simply stressed that the theft hadn't occurred in their jurisdiction: US Forests or Grasslands. His suggestion was to let the FBI handle it!"

"Well, that would be fine, but I don't guess they've received their invitations to the party!"

"Well, I'll personally issue them another one! But if you ask me, that gal over there is on the flaky side!"

Doug ignored the comment. New to the job, he wanted to distinguish himself! "Thank you, Sir, if you can contact the FBI that would be a good thing!"

He stepped back into the mine office where Cassidy shot him a dirty look! He didn't know why! He wasn't under the sheriff's jurisdiction, and the momentous nature of the crime wouldn't make a county guy like him the lead investigator any time soon! He was troubled at the careless attitude about immediately examining the crime scene! The FBI should probably hurry!

⊰ ⊱

Trent Morrison just happened to see a feeder line across the bottom of a Fox News report! Theft of dynamite and blasting caps from a Colorado silver mining operation! Annoyed, he phoned his division head!

"Hey, Jim, this is Trent! What's the scoop on that explosives theft? Why didn't you make me aware of it immediately?"

Buford responded testily, "What's your interest why you stay on top of the Faulkner woman? You seem to show up out here~"

Trent curbed his rising temper! Buford's inference was worse than that he worked at the behest of Daniel Faulkner and *GeoHy*! An insinuation of romantic interest? Alexandra was a kid to him, in the first place! No, in the second place! First place was his concern about explosives in the wrong hands!

"Who's leading the investigation? What have they found out? Any suspects?"

Buford supplied the scant information he was aware of; that the mining engineer's father, who happened to be the explosives expert, was a hard drinker! And that he was the last one to check out the key to the shed!

Trent was stunned, "That's it? Even assuming the man was so drunk that he left the key somewhere, that mine has state-of-the-art security! Access to that shed-key or no key-this is connected to Noë Keller, the anarchist leader, and the other two who got away! Don't forget that Alexandra Faulkner is the one who shot Keller to death! If his group's looking for payback, they might try to implicate her in the disappearance of the explosives! And then, who else might they be seeking vengeance against? The Forestry Service LEIS! We're the ones who rooted out their hide out and have kept a presence up there to discourage their regrouping!"

Buford wasn't sold! "Well, that new kid up there, Hunter's on it! And I made sure the FBI is in the loop! Why are you trying to divert attention from the girl? What is she to you?"

"She's a robbery victim! Of a substance that should never have fallen into the wrong hands! I have a feeling I'm right on target! I'm serious, Jim! Watch your six! And look after all our guys out there!"

CHAPTER 5: SOLUTIONS

Forestry LEI Chief, Trent Morrison, resented the resentment shown him by the Rocky Mountain District Head, James Buford! "Sorry, Jim, but you know I need the monthly reports right on time! I'm aware everyone has heavy caseloads, but if all the bad people stopped what they're doing, we'd all be out of our jobs! I know it isn't easy to delegate~"

He paused to listen to Buford's excuse for the tardiness of the paperwork! About ongoing drama with a determined female bear and her two troublesome cubs! With absolutely no respect for the US Government's claim to the headquarters building in Golden, she stayed territorially bonded there!

He laughed at Buford's story; because it struck him funny, and he hoped a laugh would ease the tension!

"Let me get this straight, they relocated the pesky bear family to Montana; and told Mama Bear to, 'Stay put!'? What did she say? She realized they're deputized by the US Federal Government; right? She'll be back! Unless of course, they provided her with coordinates for the Montana state boundaries!" Neither man laughed at the attempt at levity!

The entire scenario frustrated Trent more than his teasing words divulged! He figured the problem was as good as any excuse Buford could come up with; well bears posed genuine danger! Still, he feared the recently stolen explosives more, confident that they posed a direct threat to Alexandra's mine, and his employees!

The realization that everyone out there still considered Alexandra and her miners, likely suspects, aggravated him to no end! Was she snotty? Usually! Beautiful and privileged? Definitely! The type of person villainized by the media as the sole reason for wage caps on struggling working people-like they and their peers all were! The only thing she was guilty of was being better off financially than the average Joe! And though it had taken a long time for him to overcome his middleclass bias, he now believed firmly that wealth gendered wealth! And that if Alexandra Faulkner could get that mine up and producing, she would lift the entire county up a notch!

"Well, get my report done before the bear trio wanders back in!" He hated to say it, but the relocations of pesky animals cost the Forestry Service, who knew how much? Prudence would suggest occasionally shooting some of them with something more powerful than tranquilizers! Unpopular thought, so he refrained from stating the obvious! "Maybe I need to pray about it! I often beat my head against the wall of a recurring problem, and never think to pray!"

❧ ❧

Alexandra remained defiant toward those who suggested she had stolen her own explosives, or was covering up for those who had! The key had disappeared, and Jared and his dad, 'Pick', both felt awful! The key wasn't the issue! The only person who seemed to have any confidence in her was Doug Hunter, and that was because he didn't seem to get it, that she was Brad's!

She loved the teaching job at *Grace*, adoring Dr. and Mrs. Allen, even the thorny Ann, and of course the students! Just driving onto the small, neat property brought soothing to her troubled spirit! And the use of the small computer lab where she logged in for further study! She sensed a hope that God still loved her, and might in time, forgive her! She was still of the longing opinion that marrying Brad would undo the wrong! After all, she had done what she did because she loved him! And he loved her! It was just that Stephen-

❧ ❧

Doug rode thoughtfully along a Forestry service road in the San Juan National Forest! He loved the mountain grandeur, but now as autumn colors turned the ride positively vibrant, he was too immersed in worry to notice! The Feds seemed on the cusp of issuing a warrant for Alexandra's arrest, and he was powerless-Well, evidently, his big boss, at the top of the chain in DC- He was missing something! He reined in at the top of a rise and trained binoculars in! Taking in the tranquil campus, and taking note of her car parked in the little lot, he wheeled the big mount around and prodded him to a rapid trot! Returning to a ranger station where he was attached, he switched to a dirt bike and headed toward the mine!

"What had her words been during that first morning's interview?" Racking his brain for her exact words-Following the early summer flood, a huge army of her friends and associates were helping her rebuild everything-and one of them-David? One of them had told her she needed beefed up security surrounding the explosives shed! She had thought that was in the works, along with numerous other projects-and then they had all mysteriously decided to pull out-leaving her high and dry!

Leaning the bike against a tree, he made his way to the crime scene! The perimeter of yellow crime scene tape was gone, and a solid new padlock secured the door! That was okay; he didn't need to get in! Had anyone really begun work on extra security? Maybe he should ask for a number to contact David-He paced the area slowly, eyes trained on the security cameras-cameras disabled prior to the theft-another reason for suspecting an insider in the heist! What additional security might have been in the works? Stymied, he decided a call to David must be his next move!

Hating the helmet, he was nevertheless snapping it in place-and right there, slightly above where his bike leant, was a knot in the pine tree! Clever! And if he and all the agents scouring the crime scene had missed it, perhaps, so had the thieves! Hope fluttered in his leaden heart, even as he asked himself why he cared so much! He stood indecisively, suddenly certain that a foot away, rested the answers he sought! Pulling his smart phone free, he shot several photos! None of which showed up the tiny lens concealed so cleverly! Was it operational? He wanted to dig it free, but caution overrode eagerness!

Why the rush to blame the beautiful Alexandra? Because she was an outsider? As Cassidy seemed to be troubled by? Was there really any wealth to be gotten from the 'mine'? If so, why was the beautiful and enigmatic Alexandra teaching for a pittance for the Mennonites? Everything about her piqued his curiosity! And although several other guys in his division seemed down on her, and eager to fill him in, he refused to listen!

An intense loneliness settled around him! Like he was the only one who believed in Alexandra and the miners' innocence! And that he was in a dangerous position, going against the stream-like if he produced this new body of evidence-he might be accused of manufacturing it-

This was ultimately, absolutely, his dream job! Although it was lonely! Returning from Afghanistan, where he had distinguished himself as an MP, he pursued this coveted position with the US Department of Agriculture where he could continue his dream of being in law enforcement! Following FLETC, this was his first assignment! Although the realist in him knew that a beautiful and accomplished girl like Alexandra Faulkner would never tumble for him, he hated to see her framed! And for what reason? Although the flawed logic escaped him, it made him wary!

⚐ ⚑

Trent frowned! Why would this kid be calling him? He didn't even have the right to report to his division head; James was too far up his chain of command to contact! He stared at his buzzing device, trying to make sense-Was Hunter that much of a dunce? Trent didn't think so- After all, the kid had a stellar military career behind him! If anyone understood chain of command-people with military backgrounds did! The kid didn't leave a message! Against his better judgment he made a call back!

"Hunter, this better be good!"

⚐ ⚑

Buford braked in consternation! Arriving at headquarters early to finish his monthly report before everyone showed up for the day, he was stunned to see his nemesis nosing around dumpsters guaranteed bear-proof! Her two offspring rollicked beyond her, evidently leaving the foraging up to the parent! Kind of reminded Buford of his teenaged kids!

"So much for your prayers, Morrison! And Clay, your orders to her, to take up permanent residence in Montana, didn't make much of an impression with her!" He moaned! She was one huge and powerful animal! And Morrison would never believe-he pulled his phone free: maybe snapping a picture would validate his excuse!

A deafening roar split the silence of the morning air, and flames shot upward and outward, sending debris and glass flying! Dazed by the percussion, and ears ringing, Buford stared in shock at the hole where the Divisional Headquarters Building had stood scant seconds before!

40

≒ ≓

Trent took in the confused rescue scene and emergency response from a TV at a business down the street from the Sidney R. Yates building! Obviously, he needed to spring for a plasma to hang on his office wall! But Buford was busy leading the investigation and answering questions for other agencies as they responded! Agonized, and feeling like his hands were tied by distance, he phoned Hunter back!

"Just making sure that your station has evacuated!"

Doug's response was troubled, "Well, no Sir, we haven't received any orders! As you know, this is basically a Ranger Station, and they don't take orders from us~"

"But their chief has had them on alert~"

"I don't believe so! Everyone is still of the opinion that Alexandra Faulkner is guilty of some type of complicity! Whether intentionally, or not! They actually figure another mine might have run short on dynamite~and figured she'd be an easy target~to lift some from!"

Frustrated, Trent placed a call to his colleague who headed the Ranger Service! Learning that he was on the golf course with phone turned off, he placed an emergency call to the Undersecretary of Agriculture!

Cursing the red tape, the Undersecretary agreed to order the evacuation! What you had to go through to make a bunch of bull-headed guys save their own lives!

≒ ≓

Thoroughly shaken, James Buford finally sat down for a cup of coffee at a Red Cross station! One that fortunately, due to the early hour of the blast, had dealt with few casualties! What a total failure he was! He fought the shakes and an overwhelming urge to cry, as reporters bore down on him! Part of his job was dealing with media circuses, should the need ever arise! He had even pictured himself before, being in the limelight for some heroic reason! Now his only wish was that they would all go away! Rather than barking a 'No comment', he faced them squarely!

"We don't have too much definitive information for you at this time! Investigators have found a timing device; although it's so damaged they haven't determined what the timing of the blast was to have been! My assumption is that the detonation was to be later, when we were all well into our workday! Our troublesome mama bear apparently stepped on the device, causing~" He waved numbly at the blast crater! "It's only by the grace of God, that there isn't a body count near a hundred!"

"What can you tell us about the two victims?" The avidness of the reporter forced Buford to step backwards!

"A little space, please! The two victims are Amos~don't know the last name! A homeless guy; he crawls into the basement occasionally to sleep it off when the weather's brisk! The other victim, as you are aware, was one of the paramedics who attempted medical aid on the wounded bear cub! For crying out loud, why don't people have enough sense to know that these animals are dangerous? Wild and wounded animals have no sense of, or appreciation for, our kind intentions toward them!"

※ ※

Trent watched the interview numbly, even as he dreaded receiving reports of additional blasts! Sure enough, the San Juan National Forest Station blew! But all personnel had been evacked! He called Sonia to meet him at Dulles with his packed bag! There would be just enough time for him to have a late lunch with her before he caught a flight to Denver!

"I'm sorry, Sonn; what?" He smiled at her and kissed her hand! If her chatter was intended to cheer him up, he mostly tuned it out! She repeated herself and he mumbled an answer that seemed to suffice! She was beautiful, the mother of their four kids, and he adored her! Still, Doug Hunter's assessment of the suspicions regarding Alexandra Faulkner, almost brought a smile to his face! If the FBI could arrest Alexandra for being a ditzy blond, Sonia might be at risk, too; as well as ninety per cent of the female population in DC! Maybe he should send a memo to all the DC legislators to increase conjugal visit schedules at all the women's prison facilities, just in case!

"What's funny?" Sonia paused in her chatter to frown at him. "Did I say something funny?"

"No, you're just so cute! I hate leaving again! Tell the kids if they give you any problems, I'll put a knot on their heads when I get back! I love you! Try to stay out of prison! I'll call you tonight from the motel!"

She stood staring after him until he disappeared!

ᚼ ᚽ

Alexandra sought refuge in her cozy little house! She should have stopped for a few groceries, but her head pounded! Everyone at the school was worked into a frenzy because the entire world didn't just fall into line with their non-violence stance!

Dreamy as the idea sounded, the Bible was clear that 'Peace on Earth' would never happen until Jesus ruled from the throne during His Millennial reign! This was her first time feeling relieved to leave campus! Idealism could only accomplish so much!

She changed her bed and started a load of laundry, then dust-mopped her hardwood floor! Hungry and restless, she decided to splurge on fast food! Soft, indescribable hues stained wispy clouds as she drove toward Burger King! She braked, frowning! Who should pull in behind her but Doug Hunter? She was going through the drive-through anyway! When he mischievously blocked her, she figured he must have news in the ongoing investigation! Weary, she pulled into a space next to his!

"Let me spring for burgers! I have lots to tell you!"

Her headache's intensity increased, but the temptation of his buying prevailed!

"Your headquarters blew up! I'm glad everyone was out!"

He nodded! A huge monetary loss for the Government in both property and equipment! And everyone attached to the station had left personal items behind! In the rush, but also with a firm belief it was a false alarm!

Seated with a loaded tray of food before them, he prayed silently while she frowned at him.

"You said you have stuff to tell me," she prodded–not so gently!

Nodding, he placed a burger and small fries in front of her while keeping most of the stack for himself! She wasn't flattered that he seemed to think she was a light eater! After taking an eon squeezing twenty ketchup packets into a neat mountain, he looked up to meet her stormy gaze!

"I'm getting to it!" And then shoving a triple cheese whopper halfway into his mouth, he took the biggest mouthful of food she had ever witnessed!

She rose, "You have my phone number! Call me when you really know something!" She whirled toward the door! And there stood Brad!

CHAPTER 6: EXPLANATIONS

Alexandra stood imploringly, lips parted slightly! The right words refused to come, and she was positively abashed at how frightful she must look! Busy day teaching, then housework and laundry! With the drive-through in mind, she had failed to check makeup and hair! She hadn't applied lipstick all day because Dr. and Mrs. Allen didn't prefer it!

Brad reacted first with a string of profanity such as Alexandra had never heard! And then he launched into a tirade accusing the hapless Doug of things that definitely never happened!

The special agent finished chewing and swallowing the mouthful, and without a word to either Brad or Alexandra, requested a bag to take his food! At last, Alexandra found her voice!

"You can't believe how happy I am to see you!"

He wrenched away at her approach, his fury intensifying! "While the cat's away~"

A rosy flush shot up, and she attempted to make him lower his voice! "You're making a scene, Brad! I love you, and~Doug's a cop, and I thought he was going to give me an update about who stole dynamite from the mine! But then, he has the table manners of an orangutan! I look so awful because I was just going to grab something from the window and take it home! Please don't be mad! Calm down and tell me everything! How~how's Stephen?"

Suddenly aware of alarmed stares from the few diners, and the fact that the 'cop' sat in his car watching the scene unfold, Brad did pull his emotions under control! Still, he couldn't resist whispering a taunt against her ear! "I expected better of you than this!"

Clasping her arm none too gently, he led her to his car! She wasn't afraid of him; after all, he was under the Lord's control! And her prayer assault on heaven had to be changing his heart as surely as her father's had at her mother's earnest prayer!

⚔ ⚔

Special Agent Hunter sat in his car for long moments after the Charger peeled out onto the highway! Although the food he couldn't afford was growing cold, his hunger was gone! Shocked, he finally turned on the engine and turned left, following Brad's general direction! He wasn't sure what he expected! Well, he had begun to doubt that she even really had anyone on the string! That she simply claimed she did in an attempt to field his passes! He shuddered! The guy was a maniac! Swinging by one screw on one hinge!

What a day! Two major bombs detonated at Federal properties! Feeling profoundly sad, he wondered idly if Trent Morrison had gotten the chance to send agents to secure the hidden cameras and their contents! Now he wished, he had just dug them free himself, and checked for any images! Now doubtless, all of the Forestry LEI brass would be hunting down the bombers! He berated himself! Must be exhaustion, or being so shaken at Alexandra's crazy boyfriend! If there were images on the new, high-tech security cameras, they were doubtless of the terrorists behind the two bombings!

He spent a couple of hours cruising slowly around town, but Alexandra's car remained parked at BK and there were no lights on at her house! No sign of the Charger anywhere!

⚔ ⚔

Trent met Buford at the Rocky Mountain Division blast site! Assessing the damage quickly, he demanded why Buford hadn't already traveled to the Western Slope to rally his stunned troops at the second site!

"There's nothing you can do, here, Jim! The investigation will take weeks by the experts whose job it is to decipher everything! We're people; not buildings! You did already meet with the personnel here~"

Chagrined, he tried to mask his frustration. Feigning sympathy, he listened to Buford's excuse! The Division Head blamed himself for the demise of the paramedic! Because the media, in their usual role of judge, jury, and executioner, had implied Jim should have been aware of the unfolding scenario, and stopped it!

Trent shook his head emphatically! "I've found that you can save a lot of people from a lot of dangers! But, you can't save them from themselves! His actions as a grown man were fool-hardy! The media has you on video! · That once you realized what he was attempting~You had more on your mind than, 'What if someone tries to administer first aid to an injured bear?' I mean, instead of letting the press blame you, fight back, and blame them! They're the ones who don't cover stories when police officers and firemen put their lives on the line day after day, safeguarding the citizenry! But then let a police woman pull a puppy free from a storm drain, and it's on all the channels for days because that's what resonates with the American public! I can't for the life of me figure out why! I don't know why a paramedic should try a stunt like this to get accolades! When they deserve them every day they show up for work! The injured cub should have been shot immediately, to end its suffering! But not in front of news cameras! Which is crazy! A bear cub with no mother, and it's limbs blown off~but the whole of America would tune in to his progress, and demand the veterinarian hold news conferences to keep them updated! And no one cares a lick for military veterans fighting their way through rehab`via a corrupt VA medical system!"

Buford stared at him, stunned.

"Assemble everyone and brief them with what we know! Assure them how relieved we are that none of them lost their lives! Tell them that we'll find a temporary facility and be back open for business! Then put your assistant on top of locating temporary quarters, getting moved in with phone and internet in place~and get ready to fly out with me on the early flight!"

"Well, I hate to stick him with all the thorny details!

"I don't remember asking you what you hate! It's called delegating! Do it!"

⚔ ⚔

"Do you want to be married to me; or don't you?" Brad was still on a rampage! "You know, I risk Stephens' ire and my inheritance, to come for you! And what do I find? You! All cozy with some dumb cop! That's what

Stephen basically has against you! Well, he doesn't trust women! And I tell him you're different, and what do I find-you cheating on me!"

"Brad, he told me-"

"I'm talking! And it has to be a cop! Lucky for him he was carrying, or I wouldn't have backed off from him muscling in on my woman! See, that's my grandfather's beef with you and your family! Well, besides your poverty level! Is that you're always all so chummy with a bunch of cops!"

"Well, unless he's into something illegal, why would that bother him? And we're not all always chummy with them! They actually advise our family on security matters! They're just normal people! Nice people, Brad! Don't worry about it! Come on! Lighten up, Babe! I've missed you so much, I don't want to fight with you!"

She paused, longing to be in his arms with whispered assurances of his love! And as much as she yearned for him, she really wanted the rings and the marriage license this time! Still worked up, he didn't seem to be in an amorous mood, anyway!

And he was so scornful! Her cute little home, he dubbed a hovel, demanding to know why she wasted the money when she could live up at the mine! Then they were discussing the mine, and for the first time, she felt that they were on equal footing! Her mine and Brad were her two passions and she dreamed of seeing it soar with him at her side!

"Let's drive up there now!" Suddenly charming and cajoling!

"No, it's supposed to snow up there tonight! And, the feds might still be up there investigating! I'm sure it's the dynamite stolen from my shed that was used to blow up those two Forestry Department buildings! I'm trying to prove I haven't done anything criminal!"

He drove in stony silence before suddenly pulling onto the darkened BK parking lot! He jerked her close and forced his mouth over hers before he released her suddenly! "Meet me at the courthouse at ten and we'll apply for the license!"

Her limpid eyes met his pleadingly! He really wasn't a reasonable person! God would have to soften him down! "Could we please make it three? I have classes scheduled for the early part of the day!"

"Do you not want to marry me?"

She tried to ignore the demand in place of a tender and humble marriage proposal!

"I do, Brad! More than I can ever express! It's just-I haven't heard from you in months-and I have this schedule-"

"Three then; don't be late!"

Agreeing, she pulled her keys free, but rather than waiting to be sure she was safely in her car with it started, he roared away!

�␣ ␣⚐

Doug couldn't remember ever feeling quite so down! He berated himself for initially missing the significance of Alexandra's statement about added security for her explosives! If only he had found those cameras that first morning, before all the other guys had it so much in their heads, that she and her miners were the thieves, they might have found out who the thief actually was in time to foil the bomb plots! He tried to concentrate on anything but the unpleasantness in *Burger King*! He drove aimlessly through the darkened streets of town, out to *Grace College*, back past the hospital! Hmmm, her car was gone now, from the parking lot! Once more past her house! Car in the carport, lights shining dimly through curtains and blinds! He circled in ever widening blocks looking for the Charger!

Back at the old downtown, he parked to place a phone call he dreaded! Every month, when he thought he was about to get his head above water financially, something happened! He thought morosely of several verses that promised great things to Christians if they tithed! And he believed them! He kept thinking things would get better so he could have some extra to try it with! Two hours later on the East Coast! Maybe his grandmother would still be awake! Problem was, he didn't want to wake her up to break his bad news! She'd have plenty to say~without being like a bear with her hibernation interrupted!

He recognized several of the cars, aware that the guys he worked with were in one of the hotel bars, drinking away their shock at the blast intended to end their lives! If not for being so broke, he might have been tempted to join them! But no, not after already making them mad with his teetotaler stance! It wouldn't solve his problems anyway! It never had! And God wouldn't be pleased!

Reluctantly, he pulled his phone free, nervous when it rang up to nine! Due to her arthritis and inherent motor difficulties, she had it set to ten rings before it rolled over to voice mail!

"Hello," came her rasping voice! "Dougie! I've been so scared that you blew up~"

48

☙ ❧

Forced to a front row seat in one of the hotel meeting rooms, Doug slumped down, trying to be invisible! Feeling totally beaten, mentally, physically, and spiritually, he reminded himself that he was, 'More than a conqueror'! That it was a fact, despite what his feelings told him!

He studied the floral pattern of the carpet beneath his feet, wondering who on earth designed such, and then why any hotel chain put it in! Maybe it was a bargain! If not, it should have been!

"Hunter, what were you thinking?"

His head shot up, and he met the irate eyes of his immediate boss, Todd Bailey!

"That this is a hideous carpet design," he shot back!

Sadly, Bailey wasn't amused!

And then the big boss, the Chief from DC, stood there! Trent Morrison! Along with the Division Head, Buford!

Doug wished longingly that one of the huge, man-eating flowers in the carpet design would swallow him, but he couldn't be that lucky!

Morrison interrupted Bailey, introducing himself, and deflecting his attention from the hapless Doug!

"Coffee, juice, and pastry arriving out in the corridor about now," he announced.

A general buzz surrounded the lonely newest hire! Coffee sounded sublime; but no way was he attempting to socialize!

"Hunter, go get some coffee! We're about to start!"

Morrison's terse order galvanized him! Grabbing a cup of coffee and the last donut, he returned to the unwanted spotlight inherent with the front row seat!

"Okay, first order of business!" Morrison possessed a natural mantle of authority as his firm control brought both the rowdy and the hungover to order! "I want to speak on behalf of the Federal Government, and personally, how relieved I am that all of you are here present with us today! We have some hard intel on the culprits, and James Buford will share that with you later this morning!"

"Let me direct your attention first to Federal Form 9//00-839P/-11Q87654321/-!" He held up a handful of plain sheets of printer paper as he spoke, "Nine, slash, slash, zero, zero, dash, eight, three, nine, P, slash, dash-"

A few chuckles from behind Doug relaxed him slightly!

"Hunter, please pass these Federal Forms around! Okay, this Federal Form is for each of you to begin itemizing personal items you lost due to the blast! Whatever you left behind when you evacuated the building, I'll try to get replaced for you!"

Bailey noticed sadly when the new agent assigned to him, the one he didn't like, began printing in a small firm hand, his losses! That was the reason Morrison was at the top! Why instead of flying off the handle at a guy like Hunter coming unshaven and looking like he slept in his clothes, Morrison figured it out! The obvious! Hunter's razor, tooth brush, extra changes of clothes, incinerated in the blast! Temporarily barracked while locating an apartment in the area-his personal effects were vaporized!

Morrison noticed, when at the first break, Bailey sought Hunter out and apologized! He always noticed things like that! He grinned! And, 'Hideous,' didn't begin to describe the carpet!

⊱ ⊰

Trent rushed up to his guest room to give Sonia a quick call in private! Although, the real estate utilized by his Forestry LEI Division was beneath a different department (naturally) his position gave him authority to locate temporary quartering for the Rocky Mountain Division of Forestry LEI! Reestablishing in the San Juan was less cut and dried! The destroyed National Forest Ranger Station wasn't actually his problem to deal with! Although it left his local guys without a base of operations! He sighed, actually relieved when his wife didn't answer! Doug Hunter, the newest hire, being the hardest hit by the course of events! Buford was lobbying to have Hunter let go; and he didn't know yet about the probationer's serious violation of Chain-of-command! He smiled wanly at his reflection! If he could talk to Sonia before this next set of meetings, probably the only thing she'd say would be, 'Bee-Beep'! That feeling, like he was standing on a precipice, made him pause a moment to pray for wisdom and favor!

Filling three Styrofoam cups with lukewarm, complimentary coffee from the lobby, he made his away across the ugly flower patch of carpet and sat down in the empty meeting room to sort his swirling thoughts!

Surprised at clarity, he penciled a quick outline! He needed to stick to the main issues. Still, he chafed at the rationale of his agents regarding alcohol! Any agent who refused to join the camaraderie of going out together for drinks, found himself on the outside looking in! For himself, he didn't mind! If it was lonely at the top, he was still on the top! With the vista unclouded by peer pressure! He frowned! But according to the prevailing flawed thinking, Pick Harrelson was a bad drinker! Hence making him a prime suspect for the theft of the dynamite! Whereas, the homeless alcoholic, tolerated by Buford and housed against Federal Regulations in the basement of the LEI Headquarters Building, was just a sad victim! Buford and all the Rocky Mountain Division Agents were simply 'social drinkers'! With ten minutes before the meeting, he phoned his secretary and instructed her to put the process in motion to replace the personal property losses.

⚔ ⚔

Alexandra paused at home long enough to change and apply extra makeup! Butterflies gave her a queasy feeling, and she wondered why she didn't feel happier! Even Brad's tantrum in Burger King meant that since he was jealous over her, he loved her! And, she loved him! So, what was the problem? The loss of the big church wedding, swirling in a white design dreamed up especially for her by an adoring mother? Walking down the aisle on her father's arm, to have him bestow a tearful kiss, and quaveringly answer, 'Her mother and I do'? She had laid all that to rest with her fateful decision to meet Brad up in the mountains that day!

Besides, according to Brad, her parents couldn't afford her long-dreamed of event! This was better all the way around! Pulling her coat around her to ward off the chill of a cold front, she walked up the courthouse steps! Not surprisingly, there was no sign of her bridegroom! She was hardly surprised! With Brad, there always seemed to be a payback! If she couldn't meet here at ten this morning, who knew if he would appear on her timing at three?

Ignoring curious gazes of the few who passed her, she waited. Finally at three-fifty he put in his appearance! Ten minutes before closing, to apply for the license, but they made it!

⚔ ⚔

Trent made no attempt to cover for Doug Hunter's faux pas! Buford and Bailey, especially, but others in the meeting, were livid! Standing relaxed at the lectern, Trent allowed the grumbling!

"He should never have contacted you without going through me, first!" Buford's feelings not totally out of line as he shot Trent a wounded look! "To my way of thinking, if something was eating at him like that, he should have taken it to Todd! If he didn't get what he needed there, his next shot should have been me!"

"Grounds for dismissal," Todd Bailey muttered, "but better watch yourself; guess he has friends in high places!"

Trent took a calm sip of the cold brew! They needed to vent! First of all, they were all shell shocked at their close brush with death! Secondly, they were of the opinion that they were not highly regarded! As much as he had issues with them on a personal and philosophical basis, he needed each one of them!

"Do you know how dumb you made us look to the other regions? Bringing them in to take possession of evidence in our case?" Buford speaking! But they all used plenty of profanity!

The others held their breath~not sure how far the DC Chief could be pushed!

"Gentlemen, for that I apologize!"

A scornful raspberry from Buford brought a warning frown!

"My intention was not to embarrass anyone! And we all know, Hunter shouldn't have called me! He knew it! He has a commendable military record! And if anyone understands chain-of-command~"

"He should! I agree! But, he didn't!" Bailey's ragged emotions! "He didn't even try to come to me and give me a chance! My_____, he's such a high and mighty loner!"

Trent bit his tongue, determined not to make this more of an issue on drinking than was necessary! He began softly,

"For the record, Hunter isn't my friend! I admire him as a law enforcement officer! He was good at what he did as an MP! His training at FLETC, impeccable! I also admire and respect each one of you for also being at the top of your games in this investigative agency! Crime statistics nationwide continue to climb, and as law enforcement personnel, we need to overlook petty differences and see the fact that we are on the same crime-fighting side! We don't all have to be best buds to accomplish our objectives! But gentlemen, please put yourselves in my place! I'm responsible for enforcing the laws of the land within one hundred ninety-three million acres of National Forests and Grasslands! When I receive a call from a new agent two-thirds of the continent away, that he feels like he can't trust any of you, I admit, it rattles me!"

"What? He thinks we're all on the take?" The rumble erupted at the back of the room!

Fortuitously, motel staff arrived with hot coffee and cookies.

"Okay, gentlemen, if we can get back to the issues! Nothing has been implied about anyone's being, 'On the take', although I might pause here to add, that would have serious consequences! Hunter's reason for not trusting you, was that all of you who have been involved with the dynamite theft, came to an unwarranted and premature supposition-that you brooked no contradiction-regarding! When does an entire Federal Unit cave in to a shoddy local yokel's assessment, and consider a case closed? I have little patience with the 'herd' mentality! I thought I had some serious criminal investigators who could look at evidence and assess facts and come to some sensible conclusions!"

"Hunter's the one with blinders on! He has it bad for that girl!"

Although Trent hated that revelation for Hunter's sake, he didn't flinch! "If that's true, he still showed more objectivity than did any of the rest of you! He likes her! The rest of you don't! But when do you conduct a criminal investigation to frame someone because you don't like them? There was no evidence whatsoever, to implicate Alexandra Faulkner in the disappearance of her own dynamite! I'm not aware of much effort on anyone's part-to even think through the absurdity of the allegations! Hunter really was afraid that with the bias he was up against, that the contents of the extra security cameras would never see the light of day!"

"So, you're in favor of Miss Snooty taking over Western Colorado! Haven't you managed to be here personally, on two different occasions, to conduct search and rescues for her? Maybe Hunter isn't your friend! Maybe Alexandra Faulkner is!"

The heated accusation came as no surprise to the Chief who was prepared for this meeting! "I'm not sure who you mean by, Miss Snooty! Perhaps if we could refrain from name calling-I see both gender and class bias in the sloppy work you've served up to me! You may fire Hunter; he has no protection from me! But if you do, be assured that you're wronging a man with a bull dog tenacity at solving crimes-fairly and equitably! Women have rights; rich people have rights; I don't care if you like it, because that's just how it is! If you're incapable of fair objectivity, perhaps you should consider changing careers!"

"Hunter has a crush on her, and for all we can tell, you do, too!"

"Hunter and I could both tell that Alexandra Faulkner was a victim; and not a criminal! What we haven't ascertained yet, is, 'who the criminal is!' May I remind you that in an investigation, we try to find out whodunit? Hunter solved the mystery by reviewing the statements and the evidence! Bailey, could you hit that light switch?"

As the room went dim, images appeared on the wall! "Gentlemen, the evidence Hunter was determined to preserve! The image you're viewing is of a felon named Hardy Johnson, who is a known associate of the late Noah Keller! He's the one who's trying to 'run Western Colorado', and he's doing it practically unhindered! While you're fixated on humbling someone you consider high and mighty, this man has been plotting our deaths! He's still at large! And he has no more regard for us today than he did yesterday! That's it; I have a flight to catch! Email Agent Buford it you have anything further to add! Thank you for your good work! Next time, don't lose objectivity!"

En route to the airport, he phoned his friend, FBI Agent Erik Bransom! Sadly, he feared that San Juan County Sheriff, Bill Cassidy, had his own agenda for wanting to take Alexandra into custody! Erik was the man to instigate that investigation! And then he made a call to the US Marshall's Service to check on the status of Alexandra's reward in the shooting death of Keller! Maybe there was class and gender bias in play with that issue, too!

CHAPTER 7: LONGING

I'm fine! (

        Daniel Faulkner reviewed the curt text on his smart phone heart-brokenly! Evidently, Trent Morrison had instructed Alexandra to stay in touch to avoid any further unwarranted search and rescues on her behalf! So each morning at 7:00 AM MST, she sent a text with an extra mark-to prove the text wasn't sent under duress! So every morning when he received the text, he prayed for God's hand of protection over her-

He and Diana had covenanted to trust her to the Lord, and allow Him to make real to her, all of the truths she had been taught! But he could barely stand it! They refrained from flying in to check on her, and also discounted the idea of hiring a PI! She would know, and her ire and bitterness would understandably skyrocket!

And if Trent, or Gray, or Jacob, or anyone saw her and knew anything, they didn't mention it! The only thing keeping him from losing his mind with worry, was knowing that God could see her-

But that was no guarantee that she wouldn't suffer heartache!

With a sigh, he caught the elevator to the *GeoHy* office suite! A mess greeted him! Hardly able to cope with passing the two cubicles between the suite's entrance and his private office, he had made the decision to remodel! Timely! Actually, long overdue! Because he hated messes! He didn't understand why God would shake up his orderly life! And although the cubicle dividers were long gone in some dumpster, he still longed for his daughter in the one area, and loathed Maxwell, whose short stint in the other, had wreaked havoc on his heart!

Paula Rae Wallace

⚞ ⚟

Alexandra Maxwell shivered as she waited for the gas pump to turn off! The air was brisk, and at the mine's higher elevation, the cold would be brutal! She fought nausea as she hung the nozzle back in place, gas fumes assailing her senses! Yes, it was official; she and Brad had a child on the way! Not that Brad knew about it yet! She punched the button to close the transaction and headed onto Hwy 550! Thursday was her day off from teaching, so she handled matters at the mine!

So, with the arrival of the marriage license, she had again met Brad at the courthouse! Within thirty minutes of meeting him, she was Mrs. Bradley Faraday Maxwell! No rings yet, but she had the license! Their union now legal! A thrill still coursed through her at the thought! Because things would work out! She still read her Bible every day, and she just knew~

After purchasing a large coffee from a drive through, she pulled over to send her cryptic text to her dad! Back on the highway with her music playing softly, she resumed her musings:

So, Brad had kind of blind-sided her with a pre-nup agreement~in case Stephen found out about the marriage~ Which~no big deal~she had signed! It was only in the case of a divorce~and she was married to Brad~until death…

And then, some lady who worked in the JP's office had asked her if she wanted to back off and have her attorney draw up similar paperwork~to protect her assets! She figured the busybody knew the prominent local attorney, Ray Meeker, and the fact that he was a member of the mine consortium~but Brad had a fortune of his own~the last thing he cared about was the mine~And besides, they loved and trusted each other~ She hummed happily to romantic lyrics coming through the speakers!

⚞ ⚟

Trent Morrison sat, stunned, behind his large, scarred desk! The latest development from Colorado jolted him! There was no way he could save James Buford's job or his years toward his government pension! That was a foregone conclusion! The big issue, was, could he save him from going to prison?

56

Trent longed to escape the confines of the office and hit the streets; a brisk walk in the cold~might clear~no, too much to do!

So, he had returned to DC without mentioning to his Rocky Mountain Division Head, the violation of permitting the homeless man to take up residence in the headquarters building! There were shelters to provide warmth for the homeless~Golden, Colorado nights were too cold for sleeping on the streets, even in summer~ He accessed the file again! Amos Weldon~deceased in the blast!

Immediately upon his return to DC, Trent had begun the paperwork for Buford's official reprimand~It was a mess! Possibly rendering the Government liable if any relatives came out of the woodwork to file a lawsuit~or now, the possibility seemed grave, that Jim had opened himself up for the liability~

A bank statement from the deceased Weldon, taken into evidence, revealed payments made to Buford! Trent groaned! He had no choice! Rather than placing a call to warn him, he had to go in person, confiscate badge and weapon, and arrest him!

'On the take,' was the expression that had come up at that meeting! Trent stared at the small payments, totally nonplussed! What could Buford have been thinking?

⚐ ⚑

Brad's fury at a new butler boiled over! "What do you mean; he won't see me? He~he always sees me~"

This new development rattled him! First, his grandfather's appearance at every turn in his road~and now~he was hiding behind household staff? If the trust money was off limits until Brad turned twenty-five, that was bad! But there was always the allowance! One he once chafed at, but would now be delighted to see!

Back in his rental car, he watched the massive front doors of the palatial family estate as his alarm grew! Maybe he wasn't smart enough to have both worlds! Surely Stephen couldn't really disinherit him? The rift between Brad's father and his grandfather was too great, for Stephen to decide to leave the fortune to him! Trying to assuage his doubts, he pulled through the circular drive and headed toward the exit!

In the small enclave of an exclusive village, he parked in front of the bank! Rather than the accustomed figurative rolling out of the red carpet for him, no one even glanced up as he approached. Annoyed, he cleared his throat importantly!

"One moment, Sir!" A teller who seemed equally annoyed. After rattling papers and stalling interminably she met his stony look with a sweet smile, "How may I help you, Sir?"

"My name's Brad Maxwell!"

"And what do you need, Mr. Maxwell?"

"Alan Morgan ordinarily assists me! Would you announce me, please?"

"I'm sorry; Mr. Morgan is on an extended vacation at a safari park in Kenya!"

After an eternal run-around, Brad once again found the solace of his car! Stephen Maxwell's accounts were all closed! Brad still didn't believe it, but with bank security edging him toward the exit, yielding was his sole choice!

Where was all the money?

⊨ ⊨

Mike Behr issued an order, and Treasury Department personnel moved smoothly into action! He smirked, satisfied! Enough playing along with FBI Agent, Erik Bransom! A personal favor costing Behr nothing but a couple of months! Bransom's game, sadly failing to work!

Bransom's plan, to keep Brad Maxwell from realizing his grandfather, Stephen, was nailed on Federal charges he could never beat! And the minute there was a conviction, Treasury was poised to auction what little of the estate was left!

Bransom's concern, that a destitute and desperate Brad would make a move toward Alexandra Faulkner and her silver mine~thus his rationale for the rather elaborate masquerade~

Now the 'butler', a Treasury Department plant, ordered the crating and removal of accoutrements exhibiting the false appearance of wealth!

⊨ ⊨

FBI Special Agent, Caroline Hillman, repeated herself firmly as she smacked a script meaningfully! "We're bringing your cell phone! You're going to call Brad, and be convincing!"

Stephen scoffed, "Why should I do that?"

58

"Beat's me!" Hillman leaned back coolly! "It's been your line of advice; so just stick with it! Tell him you know about his 'secret' wedding, and that you're not pleased! If he ever hopes to inherit, he needs to steer clear of Colorado!"

Injured features, "You're asking me to deceive my grandson?"

"In a sense! Actually, I'm telling, and not asking! And I'm simply ordering you to keep up what you've done for a decade! Yes! Keep deceiving your grandson! Read the lines, although, you're just echoing again what has been your drumbeat! Pretty sure it's a memorized script!"

"Again, I ask; what's in it for me, if I do!"

"Let me ask the questions! You actually require several prescriptions, do you not? That help your vital systems to function properly? How would you like the prison system to keep your meds up?"

He crumbled and pulled off the call without a hitch! Hillman drove away from the facility smiling! The prison infirmary would never have agreed to withhold the meds! She hadn't stated that they would! All she said, was, 'How would you like the prison system to keep your meds up?'

⊰ ⊱

Alexandra ran through the various mining bank accounts! The balances continued their downward courses! Sufficient to make it, until hopefully, spring would bring mining activity with an influx of cash! Barring no unforeseen emergencies! Each month she was amazed that David and Mallory continued to pay for the utilities of her operation! A blessing, for sure~but if they stopped~David and Mallory had so much going on, that they might not be aware~

So far, her mining engineer hadn't put in an appearance! Although no actual mining was taking place at the moment, he was using the winter to plan and organize for when the blasting commenced! She frowned! Jared needed to patch up his relationship with his wife! Their estrangement gave him crazy ideas about having a workplace relationship with her! The last thing she needed was rumors flying about~especially with Brad's temper!

⊰ ⊱

Following a meeting with staff Geologists in the Sullivan Building Bistro~due to the noise level of the office remodel, Daniel returned to his

59

office! The thing about Al-he could never divert his thoughts from his firstborn for long-her accusing words continued to haunt him! Words so painful he couldn't bear to share them with Diana! Al's words were seared into his brain, 'Well, you got Mallory to the marriage altar unsullied! That's all you cared about!' If Al felt like Mallory was all he cared about, did his other kids feel the same way? He sat, holding his ears to soften hammer blows, remembering making a promise to Patrick Shay O'Shaughnessy in this very office-what-nine years ago? Where did the time-His promise that in the event of the Irishman's demise, he and Diana would do all they could to help his daughter Mallory stay on the right path of serving the Lord! Well, a momentous request-which only after prayer and deep soul-searching, had he and Diana together, committed to!

No, Al's cruel dig was more a result of her being caught red-handed, doing wrong! The best defense being a good offense! So, she had packed the initial blow-and he was still reeling from it! And Alexandra wasn't talking to him, anyway-suddenly concerned for neglecting his responsibility to Mallory, he picked up his extension. With a lull in the hammering, he placed a call to the *DiaMo, Corporation* office in Dallas! A crisp voice he didn't recognize came across the line, naming corporations he was unaware of! The kids kept moving on! His request to speak with David met a chilly refusal!

"I'm sorry! Mr. Anderson is unavailable at the moment! May I have him return your call at his earliest convenience?"

He didn't recognize the receptionist's voice, and evidently, she didn't recognize his name! After a brief attempt at pleasantries and friendliness, he disconnected! Whoever she was, she was good! No nonsense! It wasn't either Marge or Gina, and he envied Mallory's uncanny ability to find the good help she always mustered!

≒ ≓

Mallory faked a frown as David's phone rang! As usual, they were deep in family drama and trauma!

"It's Daniel," he mouthed as he accepted the call!

He pulled his overwrought firstborn onto his knee as he responded, "Hey, Daniel! David here! Long time-"

Daniel couldn't help smiling as sounds came through the receiver that would surely put the screams from, *Murder in the Rue Morgue*, to shame!

Then, to compound the confusion, the remodeling crew, with their break apparently over, resumed hammering!

Raising his voice above the din, "What's going on?"

Mallory's voice~ "Well, we're on *Tenerife*~"

The Canary Islands?" Not certain he heard correctly through the racket!

"Yes, Sir, but don't say *Canary*! We're at the *South Airport* ready to depart~well, I guess the girls all thought we were getting canaries~and now~they're like, hungry, exhausted, and heart-broken~they don't understand we can't take animal species from country to country~"

"Wow; how long have y'all been there?"

Rather than subsiding, the noise level intensified!

Mallory's face appeared in Face time as she answered. "Ten days! We're going to the *Sandwich Islands* next, and if they don't really have sandwiches, David's going to be the one crying!"

David good-naturedly snatched at his phone! "Actually, she lied; we're heading to Arkansas next!"

⚔ ⚔

Diana placed finishing touches on several designs for her approaching fashion line! Delectable colors made her sigh at the prospect of dressing in deep tones of autumn! Joining Jeremiah, Cassandra, and Xavier as they enjoyed a snack break from their afternoon schedule; she was uncertain if they felt glum or merely mirrored her feelings! She tried to brighten the mood! With the holidays pretty distant and no trips or breaks on the horizon, it was tough! There was simply a serious stretch of work and lessons that were mostly the stuff of life!

"Sometimes, life is simply digging in and doing what must be done! Life can't always be, 'fun and games'! And though you may not realize it, we all have it very good!"

"I think we all realize that! It's just~that some days we miss Alexandra more~" Jeremiah's admission with an energetic nod of agreement from Cassandra!

"Absolutely true, and I would feel that I failed as a mother if you hadn't learned to care deeply for one another! And when you do care; being separated is hard! But change is inevitable!" She laughed suddenly, remembering one of Mallory's one-liners: "Confucius say, 'Change is good'!"

Her sage observation was met with three hang-dog expressions! She added the punch line, "'But folding money better'!"

Xavier got it, and it cracked him up, which in turn made the older two laugh at his hilarity!

"Alexandra is fine! She's just trying her wings~"

Jeremiah nodded wisely, "We know, Mom!"

With the kids' return to the classroom, she went back to her studio! Pulling a crushed box from its hiding place, she prayed for Alexandra! The returned package sent daggers through her heart! Three lovely autumn ensembles~returned without having been opened! She couldn't bear the thought of her lovely daughter's preferring to dress sleazy~but it was such a prevalent attitude~even amidst the Christian community! What kind of places were luring her naïve child? Who were her friends?

Drying her eyes, she hid the package in its place! Daniel didn't know about its return!

⊰ ⊱

Dr. Harold Allen met his wife's troubled gaze! She moved to sit beside him in his small administrative office.

"The school isn't going to make it; is it?"

"I'm afraid, short of a miracle~"

She nodded understanding. Through their years together in ministry, they could attest to many miraculous happenings! Enough prayers answered to keep them praying and trusting in the goodness of God. But sometimes prayers were vetoed by a loving God Who knew a better way!

"Charitable giving is down overall through the entire denomination, I'm afraid! It's a sad thing! I mean, I know overall, God's children are good people who want to do the right thing! It just seems harder and harder for families to make ends meet! It takes great faith for a man to donate~when he sees his family~going without!"

Sally spoke up tartly! "Going without things they don't need, and have no business chasing about after, you mean~Such a worldly generation! They should read their Bibles more and spend less time tuned in to advertising!"

He nodded sadly, "Well, of course materialism is a problem! But some families are having a hard time with the basics of life!"

"Well, they lay up treasures for themselves in heaven; the Lord promises to bless those who give by faith~"

"We shan't give up without bringing it to the throne, my dear! In the meantime, we mustn't let on to anyone! Hopefully we can keep our enrollment, and with tuition kept paid up~if more students should enroll for spring semester~"

Sally concurred slowly, "Have things crossed the threshold? Where there's no going back?"

He pulled her near," Sometimes, it seems as if Satan is winning! And it seems like American Christians are lulled into a trance they refuse to emerge from! And yet, Jesus left us with the promise that He would build His church, and the gates of hell could not prevail against it! There's still a strong, vibrant body waging the warfare! A spiritual battle! God's will most certainly will be done, in earth, as it is in heaven! But we know the Bible warns that wickedness will increase before that dreadful and terrible day of the Lord! We must be faithful to stand for righteousness, and work, and pray and trust!"

⚜ ⚜

"Yeah, Honey, give Frances the rest of the week off with pay," Daniel's voice more vibrant than it had been in months! "I'm heading home now; how quick can we be ready to hit the road if I pitch in and help you?"

"Well, there's not really too much packing involved, with so much of our stuff duplicated at the cabin! What made you decide~"

Joyous laughter rang through the phone! "Well, I haven't checked in with David and Mallory for a while~"

"Yippee! They're going to be there, too? I haven't heard much from Mallory, and I haven't known if she knows about Alexandra~or if she thinks it's my fault~"

"Okay, Honey; I don't think they know! And it isn't your fault! I'm pretty sure Trent keeps things to himself! And they are coming~it's just that it will take them a couple of days! They're en route home from the *Canary Islands*! Like when I first hung up after talking to them, I felt some pangs of envy! That's a cool travel destination, and very interesting from a Geological perspective~ I considered putting a similar trip together, and for all of us, it would cost a small fortune~maybe even a medium-sized one~"

"But then you thought about going to the cabin~what a great getaway to break up the doldrums! I just gave the kids a little lecture on doldrums being a part of life~ But we can bring Frances along, and the kids can do some of their~"

"No, let's all take a break and enjoy~

❧ ❧

Mallory enjoyed the time with Diana, and the kids all played together, for the most part, without a cross word!

Forgoing the chow hall, they all caravanned to *McKenna's Steakhouse* in Hope for dinner!

"Okay, promise this can be our treat!" Diana's insistence as she mixed a bottle for Adam! "We've been living on your nickel for a week! It's been a great get-away, though, and much needed! We're still amazed, every time we pull in!"

"We really are," Daniel added! "Incidentally, what have you heard from *Rodriguez*? Any more drama since the intervention?"

"Not much," Mallory admitted, "except that they meet their orders! That's pretty major! Actually, I'm afraid David and I have dropped the ball about praying for them!

Silence fell as the foursome considered the crisis precipitated by Deborah Rodriguez' Aunt Rose! Deborah and her parents did an amazing job with her fashion business! But then Deborah's talented aunt, demanding more money for less work~maybe that should have been a sign~began a sister company! Which also enjoyed a good launch, showing great promise! Sadly, still too little and too slowly for the voracious Rose, whose gambling problem nearly sucked everyone under!

"I need to call Deborah! Probably since the fire, she's been extra-embarrassed! Which, it's not her fault! And it is all Rose's fault and she goes on her merry way, still blowing money she doesn't have on lottery tickets! Okay~enough about that! We're sorry we didn't get it put together for all of us to attend Fashion Week! With all the events of the summer~time got away! I don't think we're going to the Gem Show, either~but let's start planning now, to do both next year!"

"Absolutely," Daniel's agreement filled with enthusiasm! "Incidentally; who answered your phones last week?"

"Wendy Brenton; she's great!"

Daniels' face flushed with guilt!

"We've prayed for her," Diana spoke up, breaking the awkwardness of the moment!

Mallory nodded, "Yeah, we figured your attorney cautioned you not to contact her! Kerry gave us the same warning! But after praying about it, we decided we had to reach out! She amazes us with her faith and outlook!"

Daniel fought emotions! Chris Brenton, a good Christian family man and acquaintance! Gone! Due to a crazy situation! Leaving Wendy a widow with four kids still at home! And Daniel's attorney, Clint Hammond, had indeed counseled him to leave her alone and wait for her to file a 'Wrongful Death' lawsuit against him!

"Look, it wasn't your fault!" David's attempt at comfort! "You hired him because he was a driller, and because he was between jobs! He needed the money and he and Wendy agreed together that he should go! How could anyone have guessed that someone would fire a fifty cal at a research ship?"

"What was the bottom line on *The Rock Scientist's* repairs?" Daniel felt more guilt for not following up with the entire fiasco! But with his thoughts so absorbed by Al–

"We haven't heard!" Mallory's tone was matter-of-fact! "Our insurance company is suing that corporation's insurance company! But the other company is extremely nebulous–shell companies on top of shell companies–not surprisingly–" She laughed, although it wasn't that funny! "It was definitely an instance of being in the wrong place at the wrong time! Crazy–Brad Maxwell starting to drill right into *Richard's Deep,* in the *Atacama Trench*!"

She started to ask if they ever heard anything about Brad, but decided against it! Instead, "Why did you lease her? I tried to make that lease agreement so crazy you'd back off! We figured out that there's a reason why there's so little interest in exploring beneath the bounding main! But, then we figured the eastern coast of Central and South America would yield better results–if we ever decide to tackle it again– Moving her to the opposite side of the continent seems cost prohibitive! *Panama Canal* transit costs a fortune, but so would taking her around *Cape Horn* and the *Drake Passage*–"

Daniel frowned, not sure if the news was good, or not–

"Roger Sanders' boat broker is eager to take her off our hands, if she ever makes it through the suits and gets repaired!" David's matter of fact tone "But, if it turns out to be a total bust, we can use the loss on our taxes–"

CHAPTER 8: CHASTISEMENT

As weeks stretched into months with no word from Brad, Alexandra took Sally Allen more and more into her confidence!

"You shouldn't have been unequally yoked together with an unbeliever!" Sally's deep lively eyes were pinpoints beneath silvery brows!

"Well, he made a profession of faith-and so I hope-but how can you be sure you're not married to an unbeliever?" Alexandra enjoyed lively exchanges.

"Why, Harold was a strong Christian and studying for the ministry when I met him-"

"Well, so you think! I mean, since y'all believe you can lose your salvation-you're kinda in and out-married to a believer-unbeliever-believer-In a state of grace one minute, and then out-"

"Well, let's agree to disagree on that one! Baptists and their eternal security think they can live for the devil and shame the cross of Christ-"

Alexandra's complexion pinkened slightly! Maybe she should have left this debate alone!

"Well, when we sin, we don't stop being His children; He does chasten us!" She sighed, "And no chastening for the present seemeth to be joyous, but grievous…"

❧ ❧

Trent flew into Denver to testify against his former Division Head, James Collin Buford! A tight knot of the offender's family, friends, and supporters sat in the court room! Trent took them in casually! It was truly sad!

And it was sad that they blamed him! Buford was the one who had looked the other way from a habitual trespasser on Federal property, until finally deciding to 'make a little' to compensate for the risk he took allowing the situation to continue! Bailey had tried to insist that Trent was aware of it from the get-go! Looking the other way, himself, until the bomb literally blew the whole thing wide open! Rather ridiculous! Like he could be aware of local events like that from his DC office! The truth was, that unless it came to him as part of the paperwork filled out in triplicate, it was mostly off his radar! Even his increased personal visits to oversee things more closely-they let him see what they wanted him to see! That they were doing a bang-up job, and he could stay in DC!

In cross examination, the defense attorney suggested the ludicrous supposition that Trent knew and looked the other way!

Of course, the skilled attorney tried to control Trent's responses by asking 'yes' or 'no' questions!

At last, the judge intervened, "Special Agent Morrison is not the one who's on trial here! However, the court is interested in the truth! There can be a lot of pressure exerted on a boss to be a good guy and not blow the whistle! Special Agent, is there anything to these claims?"

"Absolutely not, your Honor! I'm shocked that Jim Buford allowed this to go on; because, for one thing, how could he be sure that Mr. Weldon, with unrestricted access to the entire building, simply slept it off in the basement? I mean, we're not the *Department of Defense*, but we do have confidential information-Even just payroll information, social security numbers, Direct Deposit information that includes personal checking account numbers and bank routing information-" Even as he spoke, he was aware of new changes he needed to implement!

"Thank you, Special Agent Morrison, you may step down!"

Trent exited the courtroom, pierced by accusing daggers from Buford's family and friends! But doing the right thing was important! More important than being in their good regard! There was the possibility that Weldon, with pretty much the run of the headquarters building, might have planted the bomb! Buford certainly granted the opportunity! One thing seemed certain in the months following the investigation; Mama Bear's having detonated it early, saved countless lives!

Now Jim's fate was in the hands of the judge! And he was known for being tough!

Psalm 57:1 & 2 Be merciful unto me, O God, be merciful unto me: for my soul trusteth in thee: yea, in the shadow of thy wings will I make my refuge until these calamities be overpast.

I will cry unto God most high; unto God that performeth all things for me.

Alexandra played and replayed in her mind, the short few days following her abbreviated wedding ceremony at the La Plata County Justice of the Peace! Brad had been a Jekyll and Hyde, leaving her first wounded, and then hopeful, and then wounded once more!

When she brewed coffee early that Sunday morning and started getting ready for church, he had patted the mattress beside him!

Her counter offer, "Get up and come with me! It'll just be a little over an hour!" She vacillated between trying to appease him and taking a stand! "You might find out you like it-"

"I won't like it! All of that, 'worshipped the creature more than the creator-' And Stephen won't stand for it! Everything you do wrecks our chances of making it! And why don't you focus on mining that little hill and quit teaching at that cult place?"

"I would love to do more at the mine, but I can't get delivery-"

Using a string of expletives, he told her he was tired of her whining!

Offering him a cup of coffee and curling up beside him, she again tried to share her dream of their managing the mine together! "If you could call the manufacturer about the delivery of the machinery, I know you'd get results!"

A deep pouting frown was his only response!

Blowing a kiss from the bedroom door, and telling she'd be back as soon as possible, she headed out!

When she returned an hour and a half later, his Charger was gone-and so was he-and his belongings-

Despite his grandmother's insistence that he come get his daughter, Doug sent another check! It was all he knew to do! Nothing was working out!

"Dear God, please help me! Daycares are so expensive-and they don't take kids if they're sick-and sometimes my hours are so irregular! And I don't have any buddies to help me out in pinches-"

His mind traveled to his fight with Jeanine when her pregnancy test showed positive! With the Marine Corps being her life, she planned to terminate! Newly saved, Doug pled against it! Putting her life and goals on hold for nine months, she despised him! She wasn't interested in hearing about his newfound faith! After giving birth and receiving her medical release, she was gone, attached to a forward unit in Afghanistan! Rather than re-upping in the Army, Doug had opted out! Hired by the Forestry Service LEI, he completed FLETC in Cheltenham, MD! That was when the news arrived that a convoy Jeanine was attached to sustained heavy casualties! She made it to Ramstein Air Base, but lost her fight there! The condolences from the Navy Chaplain and Marine Corps officer left him numb! Not much of a relationship, but a blow, nevertheless! Her family was as fractured as his! Consequently now, Leisel, his inifant daughter, was under the tutelage of his grandmother! The same grandmother who had never wanted to raise him!

Stationed in Southwestern Colorado, where he felt like he should have been all of his life, his plans for assuming the care of his child kept falling apart! And, no surprise, Jeanine's military life insurance paid out to her designated beneficiary, her brother!

⊰ ⊱

Alexandra tried to keep her worries at bay! Every day, she dreamed of a new and happy Brad appearing on her horizon with his charm and money, making her problems all go away! Day after day, no word! Glumly she conceded defeat to Stephen! Something crazy she had tried subjected her to further humiliation! Deciding to apply for a credit card using Brad's name, she was flatly turned down! Not sure if he and Stephen had blocked her, the thought occurred to her, that there might not even be a Maxwell family fortune! At any rate, she withdrew, humiliated, from the jewelry store, still devoid of wedding rings!

And then, a couple of weeks later, a modest set arrived by registered mail! Although she treasured the idea they might be from Brad, she doubted it! She considered Mallory, or even the Israeli Diamond executive Lilly-but hopefully they were neither one aware of her dilemma!

Experiencing strange things with her pregnancy made her wish she had a girlfriend to confide in and who could explain the ropes! As it was, she considered herself too broke to be under the care of an Obstetrician! Her plan when labor started was to appear at the ER, like the rest of the indigents! They couldn't turn her away; could they? She wasn't sure! Another item added to her long prayer list, which seemed to be mostly prayed over in vain! She hadn't seen Dr. and Mrs. Allen since classes ended in early June, and she was scraping to make her money last until her salary resumed in September! By then, her baby would be born.

⇥ ⇤

Erik Bransom commiserated with Trent Morrison! They were both of the opinion that James Buford, basically a good guy and ally in law enforcement, simply got caught, guilty of far less than others who never got caught! Heavy fines and probation! He would need to sell his house and start over! And he was subject to danger! An ex-law enforcement officer, who couldn't be around weapons, as part of his probationary status, was like a sitting duck for criminals who bore grudges! And they all bore grudges! None of them ever seemed to man up and admit doing time because of their own wrong choices! It was always, 'the cop's fault'!

Then, Bransom casually mentioned his suspicions regarding Norma Engel's death; the stroke and subsequent car accident! It was news to Trent that nearly bowled him over, that Erik thought it was a murder case, with Brad Maxwell his prime suspect!

⇥ ⇤

It was hot! Alexandra's little house was wide open, but not so much as a breath stirred! Summer afternoons did get hot, but rather than installing air conditioning, Colorado natives opened their houses up at night to allow the cold night air in; and then mid-morning, drew curtains and shut doors and windows to retain the cool air! Then by early evening, the air turned pleasantly cool again!

Totally miserable, she packed a bag and headed to the higher elevation of the mine! It frustrated her how little progress it was making; and with

Abby separated from Jared, she had to field his passes! She viewed the profile of her tummy! Maybe not this time! If she stayed for a week or two, it would be cooler in Durango by the time she returned! Dining in the chow hall would save her meager grocery budget, and once up there, she wouldn't burn any gas! Stopping at the post office to forward her mail, she decided there was no point in leaving Brad a note! He was probably never coming back! But if he did, he knew where the mine was!

The Frito pies tasted good! With nausea gone now, for the most part, she was left with chronic indigestion! Sleeping sitting up was a given, so she indulged in seconds! Followed by two small bowls of chocolate pudding! She was eating for two, and without having to ration grocery money, she fed both of them more liberally!

She was formulating a plan to patch things up between Jared and Abby; even as she wondered sadly who would do that for her and Brad! Pausing in the cool dusk to watch stars pop through darkening purples, she prayed for the jillionth time to hear from him!

⫧ ⫨

Doug Hunter sat hunched in his Forestry Service SUV! Word was that Hardy Johnson might have returned to his favorite haunt in the San Juan National Forest! There were other rumors floating, too! Although trying to avoid running into Alexandra since the fateful scene in the Burger King, and her subsequent marriage to the deranged nutcase, Doug was aware of her recent presence at the mine! It made Bailey, Doug's superior, nervous that Johnson might be back, and that Alexandra Faulkner was still one of his prime revenge targets! Both Alexandra, and the Forestry Service LEI personnel! Although the mine wasn't actually in the National Forest, it was in the Forestry Service's best interests to tighten security around it! No sense in handing Johnson more dynamite to use against them!

Biting his tongue to keep from swearing, Hunter stared after a reckless vehicle which missed hitting him by mere inches! The Charger! Maxwell on another rampage? Although Johnson was the quarry, Doug debated with himself! Alexandra Faulkner and her safety were of prime importance! And Maxwell might have her-against her will-At any rate, Maxwell needed to slow it down on the mountain road! He shifted and roared into action to overtake the speeder!

Paula Rae Wallace

Alexandra grasped her side with one hand as she bit back a scream! Panic made her straighten out the curves and pain made her want to curl up and die! With the spasm easing off, she once again bore down on the accelerator! She was losing her baby! Brad~ Tears streamed down her face, and as lights appeared behind her, she threw what little caution remained, to the wind~

⋈ ⋈

Doug's jaw tightened! Maxwell was a fool! He better not~Grabbing his radio, he enlisted help in the high speed chase! And then, the object of his chase pulled to the narrow shoulder, and stopped! With his service revolver ready, he eased forward, pausing and sinking lower as the driver's door opened!

The beautiful Alexandra, haloed by the interior light, held a revolver warningly! "Stop right there, Brad! Don't make me shoot you~"

Doug hesitated as her lovely features contorted with pain!

"Forestry Service Law Enforcement; Special Agent Doug Hunter!" Although his voice carried clearly in the crisp night air, she retained her grip on the weapon.

"Alexandra, put the weapon down!"

"No, Doug, you need to get out of here~uh~" pain cut off her warning, turning it into a horrible moan~

"I'm not afraid of Maxwell! Are you hurt? I'm coming over to help you! Don't shoot me!"

⋈ ⋈

The dazed Forestry agent followed the soothing instructions of a 911 operator~and angry screams pierced the night air! To Doug's immense relief, a Careflight chopper settled on the road, and someone rushed to set flares! Not much traffic, but still! Suddenly weak, he relinquished his charges to a competent Medevac nurse!

Still no sign of the pursuing Maxwell!

His eyes met terrified gray ones! "Okay, see you down at the hospital!"

⋈ ⋈

72

"Wow, she's a mad little girl!" An observation made by the flight nurse!

Alexandra brushed at tears! "Yeah-um-he-tasered us- He-he-was mad-he-didn't want-her to be-born-"

The astonished nurse made a good recovery of her professional poise, "Okay, Honey, who tasered you? Oh, my goodness, no wonder she's such a mad little girl!"

Her snuggling and sympathetic cooing did nothing to calm the frantic newborn!

At the medical center in Durango, the chopper discharged Alexandra! With a quick consultation, the staff opted to transport the baby to the NICU at St. Mary's in Grand Junction!

Alexandra was inconsolable, "She's going to die! He's getting his way! He-he's always gotten-When do I tell you what her name is?"

The ER charge nurse intervened smoothly! "She's just slightly underdeveloped, and the larger hospital has more to offer-and they can assess if the electrical-" her voice trailed off, and she patted Alexandra's hand sympathetically. "Oh, your hand's hurt, too." She indicated the additional injury to assembling staff. "Okay, Dear, what's your daughter's name?"

"Um-it's Angelique-Angelique Farrah Maxwell!"

⊰ ⊱

Suddenly trembling with reaction, Doug Hunter stomped out what remained of the smoldering flares! Nothing at FLETC ever covered delivering babies-on the side of the road-in the dead of night-with an enraged and jealous husband somewhere in the wings! His intention was to lie in wait for Maxwell-Alexandra seemed to think he was in hot pursuit-Doug tried to figure out where he might have gone-and when he would appear- His instincts told him the guy was a threat!

Longing to be with her and protect her, he scolded himself! After all, she was married! And whatever she was fleeing from, county law enforcement had jurisdiction! His concern deepened! If Brad was guilty of domestic violence up at the San Juan County mine, Alexandra had been lifted to Durango in La Plata County!

He wasn't sure why he just sat there! He wasn't certain that delivering her baby granted him visiting rights! The last thing she needed was for Maxwell to have reason for his craziness! As he lingered, the deserted road suddenly sprang to life with emergency response vehicles charging up past him! Tuning to the police band, he turned around to follow the new action!

⚑ ⚑

Gray Prescott frowned as his vibrating phone roused him enough to turn one eye toward the device! Brenna slept deeply beside him! Whatever the issue was, he needed to address it before anyone else in his household awakened!

Grasping it, he moved to his office, rummaging for his glasses! Two hospitals were simultaneously checking the status of his niece's hospitalization insurance!

Actually, Joe Hamilton usually dealt with the insurance nuts and bolts! He assumed Alexandra's logic for giving his contact information, was that she expected his discretion! So, Alexandra Marie Maxwell was being admitted to a hospital in Durango, while St. Mary's NICU requested confirmation of coverage for a newborn, Angelique Farrah Maxwell!

"Oh Dear," Gray mumbled! Even as he waited for his computer to open, he prayed that there was hospitalization he was unaware of, and for the safety of the new little baby! Gray hoped against hope that Alexandra, or Daniel, or someone, had the right policy in effect! Although not totally in the know about the Maxwell Estate, he doubted that it would provide much help! A huge sigh of relief escaped as the information he sought appeared! It looked as if Alexandra had taken care of business, reinstating her own health coverage in the mine's group policy! And, the coverage included the newborn! Even as he breathed a prayer of thanks, he wondered curiously why Brad didn't insure his wife and child! Obviously derelict! After forwarding the policy information to both facilities, he called to make certain that both admissions went smoothly!

When he returned to bed, sleep refused to come!

⚑ ⚑

Doug didn't realize he was smeared with blood until his appearance brought sympathetic grins from the hospital staff! The abstract thought went through his mind that it must have come from his mid-wifely duties! He was pretty sure he hadn't touched anything at the crime scene at the mine! He had gotten a quick glance before the sheriff's department

74

muscled him out of their territory! Brad Maxwell was dead! Self-inflicted gunshot wound, as far as they could tell! The county coroner was en route!

Consequently, it wasn't his duty to break the news to Alexandra! He had just promised that he'd come down to check on her and the baby! In spite of whatever had transpired between her and Brad earlier, he was certain the news would be a tremendous blow to her! Chalk it up to exhaustion, but he didn't figure Maxwell to be the suicidal type! Hopefully county would actually investigate this one and get to the bottom of it! Finding a vending machine, he spent a dollar on a thimble full of weak coffee!

Someone in scrubs took pity on him and led him to a full, freshly brewed pot! He nodded exhausted gratitude; then finding a restroom, he cleaned up to the best of his ability!

He was pacing nervously when a deputy accompanied by a county chaplain hurried past him! His heart hurt for Alexandra! Not just Brad's death! But the death of a dream! He flashed back to the afternoon when he had received word of Jeanine's critical injuries, and then the finality of her death a couple of days later! Had theirs been a tortured relationship? It wasn't ever a marriage made in heaven-but still, he had cherished that hope! That they could make it, be a family, rear their daughter to be someone-

CHAPTER 9: COPING

Alexandra's tormented memories replayed, although the floor nurse had given her a seative! Her jolt of joy at Brad's appearance, relishing his embrace-and then his rage at her pregnancy! At first furiously accusing her of infidelity-then admitting the possibility of his paternity-But it didn't matter! He didn't want a child! He didn't want Alexandra to have a child!

Abhorred at his insistence on her getting an illegal, late-term abortion, she tried the disastrous tactic of reasoning with him!

In a frenzy of wrath, he screamed how the complication of a baby-and Stephen-

At which point, Alexandra mistakenly mentioned how tired she was of hearing about Stephen with every breath! Especially since no money seemed to be forthcoming, regardless of Brad's tightrope walk!

Pistol to the nape of her neck, he informed her that both she and the baby had become liabilities he was tired of! And that if he rid himself of the problems she presented, he could simply take over the mine and function until-

⚜ ⚜

Doug drove in silence to his one room apartment over an old storefront in Silverton! With the destruction of the San Juan Ranger Station, renting this was his only option! He couldn't make sense of the past few hours! Not that things usually made sense! He said a quick prayer that the Lord would help him trust- Such a beautiful woman as Alexandra, and so smitten with Maxwell-

He wrote himself a note! Not that he forgot things that were this important! But his mind seemed to have quit functioning normally! Certain the Sheriff's Department wouldn't divulge any information to him on the domestic violence that culminated in Alexandra's fleeing, and Maxwell's taking his own life; the thought occurred to him that Jared Harrelson, the mining engineer, might!

Aside from Alexandra's admission that Brad had tasered her in his wild attempt to make her lose the baby, she hadn't given any further statement! The deputy and the chaplain's attempts to convince her, simply resulted in the medical personnel suggesting another time would be better!

So, back to Alexandra's radiant and fragile beauty–'How could–?' He tapped his pencil eraser thoughtfully against the page–the only way–if Maxwell was hopped up on a substance! If the coroner's report indicated the presence of CPC's, that would make the pieces fall into place! It would explain such lack of rationale in the face of Alexandra's steadfast devotion, making him violent toward her, and then, ultimately, suicidal–

He frowned, aware of a couple of jeering remarks from a deputy at the scene of the suicide before they pushed him out! About the foolhardiness of Maxwell's tasering his wife while he was in bodily contact! Doug didn't consider any of it humorous! Maxwell, as a scientist, would be aware of the folly of jolting Alexandra as he pinned her down–except for raging drugs and the total loss of all reason!

So, he must have sent a jolt through both of them, rendering them both, unconscious, or temporarily incapacitated! When Maxwell came to, the contact burns must have sent him screaming for cold water–or some type of relief–evidently presenting Alexandra a window of opportunity to escape in his Charger! The faster of their two automobiles, and possibly just parked closer!

꒰ ꒱

Dr. Heath Barrows entered the NICU to find his small patient still distressed and exhausting herself! He listened to the most recent report gravely! IV fluids were going in, but little Angelique wouldn't suckle! All she wanted to do was scream!

He rubbed the fuzzy head gently, and the screams lulled. "That's better–" although his voice was barely above a whisper, the little body tensed with fresh distress! He frowned. Was it his masculine voice? Did he somehow remind the newborn of her father's violence and assault? Motioning the NICU nurse to follow him from the unit, he suggested,

"Let's try phoning the mother-maybe her voice will sooth the baby! If so, we need to transport her up here! Have you tried playing music?"

※ ※

Jared frowned as Doug appeared at his mine office. "Look, Hunter, I know county messed it up with the explosives theft! But this is different! Straightforward, he threatened her, she got away, he killed himself-but not before inflicting pain and agony on himself! This isn't the National Forest, and I told the deputy every word I heard! Get it from them! If they think you need to know, they can fill you in!"

Doug dug in. "Was your wife here? Did she hear what happened? Did you two feel like you were in immediate danger? Is there a reason why you waited to call 911?"

Jared's face contorted, "My wife is visiting her father on the east coast! If it's any of your business! And if you knew Al like I do, you'd realize it would have made her mad for me to call the law! She figured she could handle him! When his car raced off, and then I heard the shot-"

Doug squinted narrowly, quite certain the engineer was staking a claim to the beautiful mine owner! And warning him to keep his distance!

Jared muttered, "Like I asked you; who invited you into the middle of this?"

"You know," Doug considered his response sagely, "the entire county rumor mill wants to know! Exactly what is the value of the mineral deposits up here? The stories range from zip to zillions! Evidently, Brad Maxwell thought it was beneath him to run a mine in partnership with Alexandra! But you-that would be your dream come true! You have a small percentage in the mine, but-"

"Get out!"

※ ※

Grief-stricken and frustrated, Alexandra pushed herself to a sitting position! She guessed she had slept, but then someone from the nursing staff, and the lights and beeps of monitors, left her wide awake with plenty on her mind! Her pretty mental construct, about how she thought God should work on her behalf to straighten Brad out, was shattered beyond repair! She didn't mourn Brad so much as she mourned the loss of the dream! Cold reality struck her! She had sinned against God, and against her parents, and against what she knew to be right! There was no rationalizing-explaining! Sin brought suffering! And raw, searing suffering, she was experiencing!

Brad was gone! And with him, the hope of a money influx! Suddenly, it dawned on her that she and Angelique might be in grave danger from Stephen! Would he be heart-broken at his loss of Brad? And blame her? With Angelique Brad's heir, would Stephen consider her a threat? Why would he? He had a firm grip on his money-until he died-at which point-what difference would it make? Maybe, as she had earlier surmised, there wasn't any money-Maybe he would make a move toward kidnapping Brad's offspring-

≒ ⊨

The light switch flipped and her private anguish went on hold.

"Sorry to disturb your rest, Alexandra! The NICU in GJ called and they want you to say or read something! They think if your baby can hear your voice, it might soothe her!"

Alexandra blinked back tears! "Well, the only problem with that is that she's never heard my voice!"

"I'm Becky, by the way! And although you never heard her voice until last evening, she's been listening to you for several months! It's a good idea! Here, just talk to her-"

Alexandra's shocked gray eyes widened as Becky placed her phone on 'conference' and Angelique's screams pierced the air.

"Hey, Baby, what's wrong? Mommy's right here! I've been praying and asking Jesus to help you! It's okay; the doctors and nurses are helping you! Mommy's coming to be with you just as quick-"

The screeches paused, and the NICU nurse smiled at the intense concentration on the newborn's features as she paused her angry wails to listen to the new stimulus!

"Keep talking until they can find a means to record you," Becky encouraged.

"Uh-maybe she'll like violin or piano music, too." Alexandra, suddenly bashful to mention it! But she had spent a good deal of her time honing her skills in order to be a better teacher!

≒ ⊨

Doug shot extra antiperspirant, wishing he could afford the luxury of cologne! At one time, his modus operandi before a date was to stop by a drugstore and use their samples! Now he was a Christian, and although it wasn't a huge deal, it was theft! But, Alexandra had left everything behind when she fled from her husband, and now a sweet sounding phone call had him dancing like a puppet on a string! It was Saturday, and actually his day off! Going up to the mine to retrieve her list of items was out of his way, but–His hope was that it was also Harrelson's day off, and that he wouldn't hassle him about gathering Alexandra's things!

Not to be! Harrelson awaited him at the padlocked gate, handing him the requested articles in a grocery bag!

Doug had a hard time keeping it cordial as he gritted a thanks and maneuvered his pickup around! Harrelson obviously resented the thought of Doug's rummaging through Alexandra's personal belongings; and Doug had a real problem with Harrelson's having done it! Alexandra was a prize to be fought for, in and of herself! But Doug couldn't shrug off the suspicion that the mining engineer was positioning, not just for Alexandra, but for an increased share of the mineral wealth!

⚎ ⚏

Alexandra bolted from the car and into a dead run before Doug could get his truck in park! The Durango hospital had been reluctant to release her, which worried him to no end! He loped after her and caught up in time to see her scrubbing to enter NICU! He watched until she disappeared behind hissing double doors! Maybe he could scrounge around and con a free cup of coffee!

Idly, he wondered if she had any family to help her! Usually a mom came to help with the first kid; at least, that was his understanding! He paced as he raged inwardly at his powerlessness to help her as he wished he could! But, his entry level government job was far from high-paying; now he owed rent and utilities each month, as well as truck payment and insurance! And whatever he could send his ailing grandmother to help out with Leisel's expense–

"Lord, I can't even take care of my own kid! I feel like I'm trying really hard to be a good Christian! Law enforcement has never been a lucrative field! I want to tithe, but I need oil and a filter–it's just always something–and as much as I want Alexandra, and to protect her–You know

I didn't have gas money to bring her up here, today-But, thank You, that she asked me, and not Harrelson! Well, I'm pretty sure he's still married-

☙ ❧

Alexandra sobbed and shuddered, overcome with a gamut of emotions she could never have explained! Surprisingly, the NICU staff seemed to understand! She hugged Angelique so closely that the aide came to her rescue! Other babies in the unit were so sick, or so tiny, or both, that she felt profound gratitude!

"When can we go home?"

"Not for a while! She needs to gain weight! We weighed her in at six pounds and two ounces at admission! Seventeen and half inches! She's lost down to five-thirteen!"

"So, what are you thinking, time wise?" Alexandra fought panic!

"Time wise? I wouldn't render a guess! I'm sorry! But babies are all as different as snowflakes! We've just now gotten her settled down and stabilized! I'm sure Dr. Barrows mentioned a CAT scan to try to determine if the taser did any organ damage!"

"A-a CAT scan? How-how much will that cost? Is there any chance they can do it today? Staying up here isn't really convenient for me; but neither is the drive back and forth-"

"Hon, I'm afraid that's par for the course! Other people figure out a way! None of these parents have money to burn-as for doing the scan today? That won't happen! Monday at the earliest, if it's been ordered by then! Watch this, though, she does like violin music!" She pushed a button, and tenderly sweet music played softly.

Alexandra fled!

☙ ❧

Trent frowned as he laid a letter aside! It was so wrath-filled he was surprised the edges weren't singed! He leaned back in his office chair, closing his eyes! Evidently Henry Eldridge didn't believe in the old adage of getting more with honey than with vinegar! This was his first contact since Buford's forfeiture of the top position in the Rocky Mountain District! Having been assistant head didn't mean Henry automatically stepped up a notch! Both Buford and Eldridge had always resented Trent's shooting to the top,

81

still figuring he was a green 'kid', and they were better qualified for his position! Not that it mattered. Trent credited the Lord with having given him favor, and if his men didn't resent his comparative youth, it would be something else! Trent had serious doubts about Eldridge, but the man made some good points, that since he was acting District Head, why didn't he get the promotion with the accompanying pay grade?

Trent sighed. So, the buck had stopped with Buford about permitting a hobo to take up residence in the government buildings~but Henry had to have been aware of it! And yeah, snitching on his boss would have been delicate~

It was just troublesome to Trent that so many of the agents bonded together and covered for one another! But then loyalty and cohesiveness were important, too! But when did they cloud judgment to too great of an extent? He wearily admitted to himself that he didn't know! He lifted the pages and reread the PS. Nonsense about Doug Hunter's being Trent's 'pet', and what a stretch it would be to name him as the next District Head!

He chortled aloud! It would be more than a stretch! It wasn't happening! Hunter didn't figure into the short list of top candidates for the coveted position! Trent reread the letter for the fifth time! It seemed that Eldridge's top concern was the pay increase! The poorly conceived epistle didn't mention the added mantle of responsibility and why the assistant felt ready to take it on!

"Lord, I don't have a good option! I don't like Henry for it, but moving someone else in from any of the other divisions will cause resentment! Not that I haven't been resented before and often! I'm talking counter-productive to the entire District, though!"

And it wasn't like Trent had a beacon of excellence anywhere else! Just guys along the spectrum from acceptable to questionable!

That was one of the reasons he liked Doug Hunter! Hunter could swim uphill against the flow! Problem was, he needed to learn a little more finesse~and get a whole lot more years on him! He was definitely out of the question, for even the next promotion in the process! He did know ugly carpet when he saw it, though!

⚐ ⚑

The moment Alexandra fled from NICU, she regretted it! She finally had her baby in her arms! Not just hers, but Brad's baby~but then, the recording of her father's playing his violin had stampeded her! Probably everyone thought she was crazy! Of all the violinists in the world~But it was true~her daddy was exceptional~

What would he think? Learning he was a grandpa? And his granddaughter was already a member of his fan club? She sighed, wondering how much in the know they were! Obviously her Uncle Gray now knew some information she wished he didn't! She hoped against hope he would keep his suppositions to himself, and not even confide in Brenna!

Finding her way out to manicured lawns, she drank in tranquil Indian summer beauty! She had to face it! She was a single mom! Brad was gone! As sad as the thought made her, she was glad to be alive! What a monster! How could she have been so deceived? And there was no money! Somehow she would have to stave off the medical bills that were accumulating! In spite of an insurance policy that cushioned from total disaster, her costs would accumulate! She needed to get squared away and with Angelique on a schedule in time for fall semester! Maybe she could convince the Allens to let her teach more classes to increase her pay! And she could increase the silver output~even without the long overdue equipment! Jared was just mad not to have it yet~and yet he left the confrontations with the company to her! His job was designing the mine and managing the miners~

⚔ ⚔

Doug returned to his dinky apartment alone! As usual, Alexandra had paid his pleas no heed! Well, he could hardly fault her for staying with her newborn! It was just~that she didn't have a real plan~A sigh escaped, and earnest eyes returned his troubled frown in the rear view mirror!

So, in response to his question about whether she had a mother to come help her and the baby~

"There was an accident!" After which she hadn't elaborated, leaving him with the assumption that her family was dead! Poor kid!

Sitting at his small table under a dim bulb, he refigured his budget! Getting the same dismal and discouraging results! Maybe he could still reenlist! Chow and barracks provided! If you didn't mind being the prime target for deadly enemies! He grinned to himself! Enlistment was never his choice to begin with! Raised by his lone grandmother, who got the responsibility by default; when he had gotten into trouble with the law, she had railroaded him into the Army! Probably really the best thing that could have happened to him!

Thinking about his grandmother brought on fresh pangs of guilt about Leisel! Somehow, he needed to start being a dad! But he needed far more than the paltry amounts of money he was able to squeeze out!

Escaping the confines of the apartment, he hit the highway that served as the main drag of the high altitude hamlet! Two miles later he slowed to a trot, chest heaving! Perhaps he had managed to escape the confines of the one room apartment, but in every other aspect, he was still hemmed in!

※ ※

Immersed in the amazing experience of being a mother, Alexandra lost all track of time! "I can't just stay here with her?" Her eyes pled as she forced desperation from her tone!

"I'm afraid that's impossible! Visiting hours are strictly adhered to! You can come back at nine in the morning! She's doing better!"

Alexandra nodded understanding! Other parents were leaving, whose babies were really touch and go! Would this be the last tenderly blown kiss to their living infants? Aware of the seriousness of her predicament, but profoundly grateful at the same time, she headed toward the elevator with other reluctantly straggling parents!

"Your baby's sure pretty!" A compliment from a mother of preemie twins!

"Thanks," Alexandra agreed with the compliment! Nearly full term, Angelique was beautiful! A miniature Brad with dark hair and blue eyes fringed with luxurious dark lashes! "Your twins are so tiny; but they'll be handsome as can be, once they get filled out some!"

A barely perceptible shy nod was the response! "We're not a family of pretty people! If they just make it~"

"Yeah, that's the main thing," Alexandra agreed! "Nelson and Wesley; right? I'll be praying for them!"

"Would you really? Barry and me, we've never been much church people! We've been trying to pray, but then~we figure we don't wanna make Him mad!"

Alexandra's laughter rippled. "Make Who mad?"

The other woman pointed heavenward as she whispered, "You know; the Man upstairs!"

Alexandra bit back the urge to quip, "What man upstairs? Are you talking about the hospital administrator?" They were passing the administrator's office anyway, on the ground floor, as they approached the front entrance!

CHAPTER 10: CHANGE

Bob Porter sat facing his wife, Terri, across a table in a crowded coffee shop.

"Have you called Trent Morrison?" Terry's cute features showed a haggardness that tore at Bob's core!

"No, Babe! It isn't like I can just call him for a chat! We just need to keep praying!"

"No! We need to do something!"

"Shhh," he cautioned! Although no one was around that they knew in the cross town establishment, people glanced up when she raised her voice. "When we pray, we are doing something! We're placing our problem into the hands of the LORD of Sabaoth! The Lord of Hosts, with an innumerable company of angels at His disposal, sends whatever is necessary when we cry out to Him!"

"Then why isn't anything happening?"

"Well, maybe things are! Just because we can't see it doesn't mean it isn't happening! I accessed John Anderson's sermon from this past Sunday on the *Faith Baptist* web site!"

A frustrated puff, and she dabbed at her eyes with a napkin. "We go to our church every time the doors open-"

"I know, and I wouldn't preach you an extra sermon, but Pastor Anderson's sermon title was, *God's At Work under the Dirt!* He talked about planting a garden when he was a kid! And how, every morning, he begged his grandfather to let him dig the seeds up to see how they were doing!"

The absurdity of the childish thinking elicited, first a smile from her, and then a chuckle!

"Trust with me; that God is working in ways we can't imagine! I mean~maybe it's time for me to leave the Forestry Service!"

Sheer panic drove away the worried expression! "You can't do that! Your seniority! Your retirement! The insurance!"

His turn to chuckle, "Ah, so maybe we have more than you realize! Well, I guess I'm the one who really lost sight of it! That's what made me a party to trying to burn Trent that time!" He paused remembering the scenario! "It's thanks to his being such a man of integrity, that he didn't force me out following that incident!"

⚔ ⚔

With seemingly no better options, Alexandra accompanied Barry and Penny Hightower to their small apartment! Like they said, they didn't have much, but they were willing to share what they had!

Muttering something about spending all of her time at the hospital so she couldn't clean, Penny swept the litter of clothing and newspapers onto the floor, indicating that the recently unearthed sofa was Alexandra's bunk for the night!

⚔ ⚔

Doug struggled through the sermon! He believed in tithing! It was something the Bible said Christians should do! Helping to further the Gospel was what he wanted more than anything! With the rise of criminal activity in the US, he gave assent to the fact that the populace needed the regenerating power of salvation! He avidly followed stories of hardened criminals who met the Lord in prison! Some returned to their lives of crime upon release, but some kicked free to live victoriously, making a difference!

Between worry about Alexandra, and guilt at the sermon topic, he squirmed uneasily! When the plate went by, he surrendered his last five bucks! He should probably fast instead of buying lunch, anyway! With the final amen, he bolted for the back, to be stopped by one of the deacon's wives!

⚔ ⚔

"Why don't you fly to Atlanta and test the water with Bob?" Sonia was ready for Trent to appoint someone to the vacant Rocky Mountain position! His anguish over it was telling on him, and making her frustrated that it was the only thing on his mind!

"I don't know! It's just a lateral move for him! He and Terri are entrenched in the Atlanta area! The last thing I want to do is yank his chain! I have no perks to offer him for uprooting his family to Golden! He could earn double his income in the private sector! And he's the best guy I have out there, bar none! If you think I'm preoccupied now, think how I'd be if I had two Heads to replace!

⚔ ⚔

Alexandra didn't wait for an offer of breakfast! Skittering sounds in the kitchen during the night made her sure she didn't want a meal with the Hightowers! Welcoming the cool morning air, she set off at a brisk trot toward the hospital! Grand Junction was laid out in a way that made sense! Five blocks up from the apartment on Second Street, to St. Mary's on Seventh! The problem was how far north it was, once she reached Seventh~

Not exactly wearing walking shoes, she slowed, then paused on a low wall to rest! After a few minutes, she proceeded, eager to reach her newborn, but pacing herself to conserve energy! Mentally, she combed through the various mine bank accounts! There was just nothing for her to drain off right now! And the viability of her mine was paramount! Well, Angelique~and then the mine! And there was no one she could turn to for help! Brad's revelation of her parents' financial plight worried her to no end, making her more determined than ever to be successful with the mine; to at least make her own way~for herself and her daughter! Maybe she could eventually~well, at least order clothing from *DiaMal*! She was forced to admit that she was spoiled and hooked on the elegant and adorable clothing her mother designed!

The previous year, before she and Brad were married, she had returned an unopened package to her mother! Now, she felt like kicking herself! But Brad had told her how broke they were~and her guilt for her actions was through the roof~Now a year after the fact, she wondered how many outfits she had sent back; the colors, the themes! Her reason for not having opened it! She could never have resisted!

She stopped to rest again! Amazed how little stamina she had! Like Brad's vicious attack and the trauma of childbirth were just now catching up and overtaking her! And Brad's death, and where was his body? And was Stephen going to arrange burial? Because she sure couldn't! And would Stephen have it in for her now? More than ever? And for Angelique? With that specter growing in her mind, she forced herself onward!

At last, the hospital came into view ahead of her! Atop a hill, of course! With the warming air and her exertion, she perspired, even in the low humidity! No place to shower, nothing to eat, no money~

"Lord, what am I going to do?"

⚜ ⚜

Doug didn't remember when pot roast with roasted potatoes and carrots ever tasted better! The only drawback with the Sunday dinner invitation was that Boyd and Lisa Chambers had a plain-looking daughter they were trying to fix him up with! A senior in high school, but evidently they were worried another single man might never appear! (And he was afraid, at twenty-seven, he might be too old for Alexandra!) Apparently, able to tell he wasn't sold on their daughter's charm, they encouraged her to entertain him; first with a piano solo, then one on the flute, and lastly by reading him an essay that had won her a writing award in seventh grade! He escaped; at least the food was good! And the praise and worship style up at the Silverton church suddenly didn't seem so bad, after all!

⚜ ⚜

Daniel reread an email! Hmmmm! Strange! He guessed maybe so! Definitely a new dynamic! But maybe it could help him and Diana move forward better! Which they both worked valiantly at every day! He picked up his extension and called her!

Caught off-guard, she carefully measured her response! Their family's musical routine was shot full of holes, and a week's notice seemed about fifty-one weeks too short! "Well, maybe you and Jeremiah and I can work out some trios, and Xavier's good enough to pass on his violin, and little enough to be cute!"

"Well, yeah, and it's just a little country church!" Daniel tried to mask his aggravation at her valid points!"

89

Diana's laughter effervesced! "Right; small country church gone viral! But let's see what we can put together!"

⚒ ⚒

Alexandra ignored a beep as she closed in on her goal! First thing, though, she needed to find a ladies' room and clean up a bit! A louder toot, and then someone saying her name-probably the Hightowers offended by her early and sudden departure! She nearly went limp with relief as she looked toward the sound, to see that it was Dr. and Mrs. Allen! She paused as the car pulled toward the curb!

"What a great surprise! What brings y'all to Grand Junction?"

"Well, we heard from Mr. Hunter that you were here! Well, we hardly know what to say! Congratulations on the birth of your daughter! And we're so sorry to hear about Brad! Please, get in!" Sally's voice was infused with tenderness, and Alexandra slid gratefully into the cool space of the back seat!

"Yeah," she broke into sobs! "Crazy week!"

⚒ ⚒

"Oh, what a little beauty!" Sally's sincere coos over Angelique through the NICU window, made Alexandra beam with pride! "She looks fabulous! We were afraid something was the matter with her! Why they flighted her so far from you!"

Alexandra nodded numbly! There was no sense going over the drama with Brad for these sweet anti-violence Christians! "They want to do a CAT scan on her, just to be sure!"

Dr. Allen frowned. "Well, don't let them take advantage of you in your widowhood, to order tests and run up expenses! I've read that sometimes the doctors own the labs, and they line their pockets by ordering unnecessary tests!"

With her mother being a nurse and having great respect for doctors, Alexandra had never heard of scams associated with medical care. She was naïve, and wanted what was best for her daughter! But how could she know? Well, the CAT scan must seem frivolous to her friends because they weren't aware of the taser attack!

90

"I'll be careful, and we have pretty good insurance at the mine! I was wondering about the possibility of teaching another class or two in September!" Her hopeful visage traveled from Sally to Harold, and back.

"Well, that's one of the reasons we hoped to find you! Well, to make sure you're okay, first of all! But we're afraid the school isn't going to see its second year! You have been such a valuable addition to the faculty-the Lord just sent you when He did-we are heading northeast toward Omaha; and perhaps we can raise some funds! Although, denomination-wise, giving has been down across the spectrum! God can do great miracles, and we're praying to that end!"

Alexandra nodded blankly, trying to mask the devastation of their inadvertent sucker punch! "Well, thank you for looking me up! Drop me an email occasionally?"

"Absolutely, Dear! Take good care of your little one! We will have to return in four to six weeks, regardless of whether we find funding or not! Hopefully, to gear up for another academic year! But if not, then to get everything in order to list on the market!"

With a squeeze from Sally and a lingering handshake from the distinguished administrator, Alexandra buzzed for entry to the NICU!

⊰ ⊱

Doug dropped a thank you note in the mail box outside the post office! Nice of the Chambers to feed him; now hopefully, he'd never see them again! Nor MariBelle! Ding-dong! A little bit of an odd afternoon, but had God really fed him when he placed his meager lunch allotment in the offering plate? It seemed like! And better than he could have purchased for fifteen or twenty dollars! Exceeding abundantly?

⊰ ⊱

At the new temporary headquarters, he grabbed a cup of coffee and bumbled his way to the front, to the sole remaining seat, without a second to spare before briefing! Bailey's hard stare knifed through him, but he simply sat attentively until Bailey's gaze faltered and dropped to his notes!

The usual report! Some tourists left their RV wide open while they fished for several hours, and then were amazed that some of their stuff got stolen! Doug agreed with the general rumble and frustrated sneers! 'Duh!' A little help from the general population to look after their own stuff-

A few other new reports of crimes within the San Juan National Forest boundaries! Followed by the usual admonition for them to keep their eyes open, at which some of the jokers of the bunch started playing blind! Doug fought a grin, thinking that 'their keeping their eyes open,' was a given, without the daily reminders! But then, he was all attention as Bailey addressed the latest on Hardy Johnson and his ferocious band! Although no one had seen him in the area in several weeks, there were plenty of places for him to hide! There was no hard intel that he was still in the area!

≒ ⊨

Under the careful tutelage of Deanna, Alexandra bathed Angelique. Nervous about touching the umbilical; generally nervous about the entire process, she fought overwhelming hopelessness! How could she have so many younger siblings, to have learned so little? Her mom just took everything so much in stride, making everything seem so easy! Mixing up a tiny bit of formula, she eased down into the rocking chair with her tightly swaddled baby!

Instead of attaching to the nipple, the newborn bowed backwards and let out a howl! Not expecting the sudden movement, Alexandra nearly dropped her, feeling less competent than ever! The squalling intensified, and she tried to pass the distressed baby back to the NICU nurse!

"You're doing great!" came the cheery encouragement!

Alexandra practically laughed, despite her general mood of despair! She was pretty sure she wasn't even performing acceptably; certainly not, 'Great!'

"Okay, don't force it with the bottle! Try to get her to make eye contact with you! Talk to her, or sing! Here, cuddle her up a little more!"

≒ ⊨

Before heading out for his shift, Doug paused to don a vest! He wished he could get an assignment to charge into the high elevations on ATV or horseback, and track down the notorious Hardy Johnson! As it was, he made his way to one of the department SUVs! As the probationary and junior agent of the outfit, he got the dull assignment of patrolling the roads!

92

Not for traffic violations! The sheriff's department, the local PDs in the hamlets, and an occasional Highway Patrolman covered those duties! He watched for anything related to criminal activities in the National Forests! Not the National Parks! The National Forests! Like most Americans, he had been oblivious to the difference between Parks and Forestry! Actually overseen by two separate Cabinet Secretaries! Parks was under the Secretary of the Interior, while The National Forests and Grasslands were under the auspices of the Secretary of Agriculture!

He pulled out and headed upwards toward Lizard Head Pass! It was a devil of a road, not greatly improved, popular with bikers! Consequently, other traffic was minimal, especially on weekdays, and for the brave-hearted! The morning shimmered and he lowered the windows to breathe in pine forests and listen to the symphony of songbirds! This was the job! So perfect! He turned off the little tape recorder that ran and reran the grumbling among the other agents! His assumption was that Mr. Morrison would appoint someone to take Buford's forfeited position when he was ready! It was a plum of a position, to be certain, and Doug was certain that Bailey entertained hopes! He shrugged. He couldn't see it happening! Well, not within the next twenty-five years! Personally, he wasn't that ambitious! Playing politics bored him! He wanted to make a difference with reducing crime and seeing that felons were punished! Still, he needed to advance to a higher pay grade! Getting Liesel seemed more impossible with each passing day!

⊰ ⊱

"Does this sound as pathetic as I think it does?" Diana turned from the piano to Daniel!

Seeing the wounded expression on Xavier's face, he tried to put a better spin on it! "No, we just need to run through the selections a couple more times! I think it's coming together!"

"Face it, I'm not Cassandra! And it isn't coming together!"

Brown eyes shadowed with self-contempt signaled a seasoned father to proceed with caution. "Zave, Buddy; you're young, and you really haven't been studying very long! You have a lot of natural ability, and I wouldn't tell you that if it wasn't the truth! But, I don't want us to push you before you're ready–And, no, you're not Cassandra! You don't need to be your sister!"

"Well, maybe she can come home and help us out!"

Daniel smiled, "You know, this is just Sunday night at *Faith Baptist~*"

"Well, yeah, but we're doing it for the Lord! Where are David and Mallory?"

"We don't know! They stay busy! And Pastor Anderson asked us!" Diana's upbeat voice trying to save the day! "Look, Cassandra is for the most part out of the picture, and so is Alexandra! Families change!"

Jeremiah rose, stuffing his fists into his pockets, "Yeah, they do, and right now, we're not a cute musical family like we used to be! You talk about us not adjusting to change, but y'all are the ones not giving it up!"

Daniel studied his oldest son for several moments, not certain if a reprimand was in order! Cassandra had been back and forth between home and Israel for several years! The new situation with Alexandra was the hard thing for them all to deal with; and the kids were less in the loop than he and Diana! Although, for the moment, Al's only communication was the terse morning assurance every day~with the, 'no-duress', code!

⚔ ⚔

Doug tromped down on the brakes! Some of his pre-salvation language nearly escaped, and he apologized to the Lord as he warily surveyed the sketchy scene blocking the narrow road! Uneasily, he reached for field glasses on the seat beside him and scanned boulders and forest cover above him! He eased his weapon from the holster! Something was definitely off!

⚔ ⚔

"Why don't you break for lunch?" Deanna reached for Angelique as she spoke!

Alexandra started to argue, but then gave in and moved toward the door. No use arousing anyone's suspicions that she was broke and not eating! A blast of heat hit her as automatic doors banged apart! Driven by desperation, she found a solitary spot on the grounds, and sank onto a bench! It was past noon and no word about the scan or about discharging her baby! Fear clutched at her, tying her empty belly into tighter knots! She was pretty sure Deanna still wasn't pleased with Angelique's feeding process! The IV was still hooked up; and the baby still tended to cry~make that~scream~at every upset~

94

"Lord, please let her be okay," she pled for the hundredth time! "Please help me! Let them either do the test, or forget about it-and discharge her-" Even as she prayed, she was in hopes she could con Doug into giving them a ride home-once they obtained the release!

⚑ ⚐

Trent hastened from his arrival gate to the main area of the Denver International Airport! He was growing more familiar with it, than with Reagan and Dulles! He scanned the crowd, many business executive types-he heard his name called before he spotted Porter!

Trent extended his hand congenially, even as he slapped the other man on the shoulder! "This is so clever, I'll bet you can't see through it!" His laugh almost self-conscious!

"Well, it raises my interest and my hopes," Porter parleyed.

"Oh, yeah?" Trent frowned thoughtfully. Even with an opening from the other man, he needed to proceed with caution! If Porter was open to switching districts, he undoubtedly hoped for extra remuneration for doing so! There were salary caps in place that weren't negotiable, and Porter was at the top of the pay grade! "Let's get a rent car and find a quieter place that offers better food!" He led the way without saying anything further!

"I'm surprised you're renting a car," Bob's observation as Trent slung his carryon bag into the trunk!

Behind the wheel, he responded. "Not exactly announcing my presence here by requesting a forestry car!"

Porter nodded, "Yeah, bad feelings if they think you're not promoting Eldridge into Buford's vacated spot! They're still miffed at you for blowing the whistle on Buford, anyway!"

"Well, I didn't, 'blow the whistle', on him! He got caught! And the sad thing was that he was squeezing money out of his homeless tenant! But it certainly wasn't enough-I mean-why risk losing what he had, for a couple hundred bucks a month-he'd only been getting it for two months! Four hundred dollars-"

"Well, at least he got probation!"

"Yeah," was Trent's only response!

⚑ ⚐

Doug sat frozen, knowing he was in trouble, but drawing a blank for getting out of it! Going forward wasn't an option; but turning around and heading back didn't seem too fortuitous, either! No movement, but he knew he was in their sites! No way were they going to allow him to see what he had, and just let him go! He sweat under the vest, figuring it wasn't even going to do any good!

Then, to his amazement, with a grinding of gears and the sound of a straining engine a tour bus hove into view! Maybe there was hope! Thanking the Lord, he hopped down and walked back to speak to the driver! To his relief, the coach was full; well thirty or forty people! Hopefully too many for the militia to try to make disappear! And too many witnesses to his disappearance! Taking on a mantle of authority, he moved forward to ask the driver of the weird, blockading vehicle to move it so that he and the coach could pass~ It worked, and once both vehicles cleared the bottleneck, he sped around the coach and disappeared as fast as the grades allowed!

CHAPTER 11: TRAPPED

Daniel stared thoughtfully at a small, neat frame home in Durango! Lowering the windows of the rent car, he pushed the driver's seat all the way back and raised the steering wheel! After a fitful few hours the previous night, trying to sleep, and feeling an intense burden unlike any experienced about his eldest to this point, he had scrawled an unintelligible and vague note to Diana and caught an expensive last-minute flight to Colorado! It was now mid-morning of a beautiful day! A deep sigh escaped as he struggled with a jumble of emotions!

Rather than opening her door with a shriek of delight at his appearance, Alexandra had peeked through the blinds, and that was it! After a second ring, and her refusal to answer, he had retreated, not sure but what she might call the police! After reading his Bible for several minutes and draining his coffee, he made a run for gas, more coffee, and some snacks! His siege might last for a while! Surely she couldn't hide in there forever! Maybe she was embarrassed at being caught without her makeup! That was his hope! Worry tore at him! What was going on with her?

⚐ ⚑

Alexandra crouched in the bedroom, trying to keep the girls quiet! Angelique wasn't too much of a problem, but Liesel~ She moaned in anguish, not sure what to do! After an hour, she peered cautiously through the blind! He was still out there, and tears freed themselves! Of all the times~

⚐ ⚑

Bob Porter answered his cell; his big boss! "Morning, Trent! How're things in DC?

"Hot and muggy! How are things in Golden?"

"Literally, Golden! It's gorgeous here! The fall colors are incredible! The temperature's about fifty-five right now; the high's supposed to be about seventy! So much for the pleasantries~what's on your mind?"

"Just checking on how things have been going with your relocation! Are Terri and the kids happy?"

"Yeah, they're thrilled!" He didn't go into details with Trent about Terri's indiscretion with a neighbor, facilitating her desire to relocate! "We found a great church and everyone's been really friendly! Can't say I've gotten a welcoming committee from the Agents! The real fly in the ointment is Hunter!"

Trent frowned; he liked Doug Hunter better than he did any of the rest of them! "Oh yeah, what's the problem with him?" Trent didn't want to know particularly~he had bigger issues to deal with than one probationary agent in Colorado!

"Well, he claims he had this run-in with Hardy Johnson's men! He's the only one convinced the guy hasn't flown the coop! We've hunted for them again; they're not out there! But he's like so honed in on Hardy he hardly wants to do the humdrum daily duties! Maybe he's bucking for the reward! Did you know he married Alexandra Faulkner? And that they both have a kid each? He came in and changed his W-4 to claim the other dependents!"

Trent was surprised at the news! Aware of Hunter's infatuation with Alexandra, but surprised that she reciprocated any of the feelings! And he thought Alexandra was married to Brad Maxwell! And he didn't really want to be in the loop on any of it! It reminded him of overhearing conversations between his daughters about who liked whom; who was dying of a broken heart this week; blah, blah!

He switched the subject back to the felon in question, "Well, he's the prime suspect in the two bombings of our facilities, and he's like a shadow! You're aware of the underground lair, right? I wanted to destroy it! I think it continues to give refuge to the bad guys and poses a serious threat to our people, as well as civilians who enjoy the forests! When I had an explosives crew ready to cave it all in, I got a direct order from Defense to leave it alone! I mean, our government is obsessed with underground bunkers and surviving to run the country another day!"

Porter snickered. "Maybe this will be a new *Cheyenne Mountain*!"

"Yeah, maybe," Trent hesitated, unsure how much to share. "I guess I'm paranoid, but no one here in DC has appointed me a rabbit hole to run down in the event of a national emergency! Sometimes I feel like I'm the token Christian that they tolerate-to demonstrate their tolerance-but I'm not a good enough Christian that they consider me a threat!"

Bob laughed, "Relax, maybe this hole, is the one where they're setting up your underground office! In the meantime, we're keeping our eyes opened! Hunter's story is kinda strange! The vehicle he claims to have encountered-had his run in with-well déjà vu-"

Dread settled around Trent like a dank mist! Disconnecting, he wondered how Porter could be so casual in his revelation! Punching Maureen's extension, he asked her to make his travel arrangements to the area-again!

⚐ ⚑

Restless, Daniel made his way to Alexandra's car parked beneath the carport! Unlocked, so he took it in interestedly! Actually, the same used car that he had purchased when she and Cassandra first came to take possession of the mine! His car, so he decided he could go through it! Plates and inspection were current, along with proof of insurance! He should probably take 'collision' off of the policy and just carry liability! It was an older model sedan! The keys were in it, and he scoffed. Maybe she was hoping to get it stolen. Trying to process, he took in the two car seats! A toddler seat, much the worse for wear! Like disgusting! And the other, the base to snap in an infant carrier! Frowning, he reminded himself not to jump to conclusions! Things probably weren't what they seemed! Maybe she just babysat, or helped a neighbor-

With a quick, guilty look at the shut up house, he slid behind the wheel and started it up! Not surprisingly, it was alarmingly low on gas! What could she do? Report it stolen? It was his car! After filling it up and checking the oil, he found a car wash! Before relinquishing it to the attendant, he grasped scattered bits of mail, and threw out petrified French fries and other fast-food remnants! Waiting in the car wash, he turned his attention to the handful of letters!

⚐ ⚑

Alexandra sat forlornly in the darkened bedroom! How horrible to be so trapped! It was hard keeping the girls quiet; they were hungry, and both in need of diaper changes! She was mad at Doug! Well, mad at herself for believing him! Dumb! Dumb! Dumb, Alexandra!

Well, when Angelique was released from St. Mary's she was faced with little choice but calling Doug again, and asking him to come to Grand Junction and pick them up! Then, somehow he had convinced her that they needed each other, and that he could take care of her and the baby~and something about getting his little girl from his grandmother~And so here she was~with two babies; no money, no food, not even diapers in either size!

Before leaving for work, Doug had told her there was no choice but for her to pawn her violin and the wedding rings she guessed had been sent to her from Brad's mother! Although they didn't have a lot of sentimental value, she questioned whether they had any value at all~to pawn! And she was conflicted about her violin! Prior to Brad's having tried to force the rings from her swollen fingers in his rage, injuring her ring finger, she had found tremendous joy in playing!

Kind of cavalier, Doug just reminded her that they couldn't handle the cost of the elective surgery to repair the damaged finger, so she might as well get something for the violin! Get some gas and diapers and a minimum of groceries to get by until his payday! All of that was overwhelming enough, but then having her dad appear at her door! Her plan was to pull herself together and make a success of the mine, and only then could she reunite with her family! As a success, rather than such a total loser!

And Liesel! Alexandra was aware of her existence and the fact that Doug planned to get her from his grandmother! She just didn't know, he meant, immediately! Or that the child seemed to have never been corrected in her life! She was cute enough looking except that she acted like an animal! Feeling hopeless and despairing, she tried again to pray!

≒ ⊨ *

Daniel's eyes traveled uncomprehendingly across the addresses of the correspondence in his hand! Surely Al's mail was none of his business! He had grasped it out of habit, to eliminate the security risk of the carwash people getting personal information from papers left carelessly! Alexandra Faulkner~Alexandra Maxwell~Alexandra Hunter~he shoved it all into his attaché! Scarlet O'Hara attack! He'd think about it tomorrow! When he could stand it! Maybe he could even locate a plantation named Tara! Diana would definitely need it when she found out!

He took his time returning the vehicle to its spot! Maybe he could aggravate Alexandra enough to bring her from hiding! The house was still closed up, though, and he knew she was in there! Resisting the temptation to take her rejection personally, he walked slowly back to his rental car! With dread, he pulled the purloined letters free and pulled a letter from the top envelope! Maybe since it was already opened, he wasn't breaking any laws! Tears filled his eyes! A threatening collection letter from St. Mary's Hospital for neonatal care of Angelique Farrah Maxwell! Well, this was news to him! Not particularly good news, either! Maybe he could find Maxwell and hand him his bills for his kid! Evidently the Maxwells had so much money! Maybe Erik could get the bill to Stephen in jail! Might be worth a try!

Resolutely, he admitted those actions wouldn't solve anything! Pulling out his iPad, he photographed the letter and forwarded it to his attorney! Clint could buy some time and get the exorbitant charges reduced to a more manageable amount! Even more alarming was a bank notice informing Alexandra that they had paid a large overdraft in her mine payroll account, but she needed to make a deposit to cover the overdraft and all of the accrued charges! His mind reeled! He thought she was at least taking care of the mine! Maybe she had taken care of it-he phoned the bank to make sure!

That conversation left him wondering if he had nibbled from the wrong side of a mushroom! Surreal! According to the banker, Alexandra always held plenty of reserve in the payroll account, but then her husband had come in and drafted out a large sum of cash! Then he had shot himself, and Alexandra had transferred money from another account to keep the payroll drafts covered! But now, according to her, someone kept transferring her money away! The possibility of its being Stephen occurred to him! Not that the man could do it personally from lockup! Maxwell had shot himself? He had married Al, produced a daughter, and left her a widow? Then who was Doug Hunter? Evidently she moved along! Well, this settled it! He wasn't leaving town without seeing her!

᚜ ᚛

Doug slowed to take careful notice of a couple of cars pulled over; the occupants seemed engrossed in photographing the splendid colorful vistas! Still, he remembered the plate numbers until he could round a curve and access information! Sometimes things weren't what they seemed! In this, case, though, nothing aroused suspicion! He drove on, lost in thought! His thoughts turned to Alexandra and the strange situation he found himself in! Beautiful as she was, she didn't seem able to have a hot meal on the table for him when he got home! And he was gone for long hours! Moving into her home from his small Silverton apartment created long commutes-and that was without any snow-And saving the rent on the apartment wasn't noticeably easing an overstrained budget!

And his little girl-not quite what he had imagined-well, all he really considered was the financial obligation of fatherhood, and getting his grandmother off his back-no wonder Alexandra felt overwhelmed at caring for her in addition to Angelique! Still, if he could coax Alexandra to stay, things would smooth out, surely-She was beautiful and he knew the other agents envied him!

His thoughts turned to the new district head, Bob Porter! Most of the other guys grumbled about him, and his getting the post because of being Morrison's friend! Doug scoffed! They accused him of being Morrison's pet, too, which was ludicrous because the head honcho was probably totally unaware of his existence! Rumors could come from no basis in fact! So, then, the scuttlebutt continued that Rob Addington was moving to fill Porter's vacated Southeastern post! From what Doug could discern about Addington, all of the moves were brilliant on Agent Morrison's part! Addington had fallen from his perch of heading the Southwestern Division because he discovered gold nuggets and was more concerned about gathering them up, than following orders! Now after more than a year as a lackey to Morrison in DC, Addington was getting another chance!

⚔ ⚔

Daniel opened an email from Clint Hammond and read it in amazement! Before the attorney got a chance to negotiate with the hospital business office, Sophia Cox Vincent had somehow been made aware of the costs! Daniel tried to shove aside feelings of embarrassment that their friends and associates were more in the know about Alexandra's actions than he would wish! At any rate, in this instance, the Cox's being in the loop seemed strictly beneficial! Sophie was paying the entire bill, asking that it not be renegotiated! Her thoughts were that doctors invested great amounts of time and energy to train, and the socialization of medicine–and everything else, wasn't fair! That it made them susceptible to participating in questionable to illegal medical activities! Daniel shrugged, figuring she principally referred to Dr. Darius Warrington, the cosmetic surgeon responsible for botched eye surgeries which had left her totally blinded!

Daniel didn't totally agree with the rationale! Doctors, like everyone else, needed to determine to do the right thing–even when others did wrong and seemed to prosper in it! Still, as the truth dawned on him, he drew a deep breath of relief! This should be great news for his daughter–and whoever Doug was–

✠ ✠

At her wit's end, Alexandra placed the last saltines and Cheerios in front of Liesel and mixed the last of the formula for her daughter–She was on pins and needles! Why couldn't her dad get the message and leave? The last thing she needed was him still sitting out there when Doug got home! And Doug would be grumpy that she hadn't done his errands! Now she wished she had left first thing–so she could have taken care of it before her dad started his stakeout!

She looked out again and his car was gone! Maybe– Still, she was afraid to hope! Each time he left, he came right back! Maybe she should stalk right out there, inform him she was fine, and tell him to go home! Big gray eyes returned her hunted look in the mirror! "God please send him away," she begged, "before Doug gets here! And before the pawn shop closes!"

As usual, the Lord didn't answer her prayer! At least not in the way she wanted!

CHAPTER 12: FREED

Doug sat, trying to readjust his mind to new evidence! He was sure Alexandra had told him her family had been killed in an accident! He scoured his memory bank for her exact words! At any rate, her father sat across the table from him at a fine steakhouse, shoving bits of bread and French fries at Liesel! Very much alive; bon vivant! Incredibly handsome with an amazing élan! Doug had known a couple of army officers, and Trent Morrison~as men he admired and emulated! Mr. Faulkner seemed echelons above them!

"Brad told me you guys were broke," Alexandra's sniffles as she explained to her father, enduring such a tough time without reaching out!

Doug felt a certain sense of relief that at least Mr. Faulkner was as confused as he was by Alexandra's behavior! When he finally addressed his new wife, he spoke slowly, "That explains a lot! You were born with a silver spoon in your mouth!"

Faulkner laughed easily, "Well, according to Brad, she was only born with a silver-plated spoon in her mouth! We can't afford the real thing, but we try to keep up appearances!"

Doug smiled, bemused. At least that explained why Alexandra worried about getting her 'nails done' when they didn't even have gas and grocery money! And a steak dinner? That was an 'exceeding abundantly' answer to his prayer! Well, actually, his prayer had been that she pawned the rings and violin for enough to get diapers and still have something left to provide a decent meal~So, if the Lord wasn't capable of turning her into a decent cook, He provided a steak dinner at a fine establishment instead~

"I was afraid something was wrong with mom or one of the kids," Alexandra's musical voice penetrated Doug's thoughts as she spoke softly.

Daniel hesitated before responding! If his appearance had really alarmed her, she could have answered the door at his first ring! And she should have figured that if anything was very wrong, he wouldn't waste his time camped in front of her house! He considered carefully before asking, "So, can Mom come? She'll be upset that you didn't ask her to come before the baby~"

"Noooo!" A soft wail! "I didn't even want you to be here! I~I wanted to get it together~promise me you won't tell her anything~"

❧ ❧

"Is daddy seeing Alexandra?" Diana glanced up from her sketch book to see Xavier standing hesitantly at her studio door!

"I suppose!" She tried for a brighter tone than she felt! "His note said he was just going to go check on the mine! He'll probably be back tomorrow or the next day! I know; I really miss him, too! But he wouldn't have gone if he hadn't been sure it was necessary!"

A heavy sigh as her son turned away.

"Come back! Come here!" She rose when he didn't respond immediately. "Is there something on your mind I can help with?"

His handsome features twisted with anguish! "Is he gonna see Alexandra? I'm the reason she left! As soon as I get a little bigger~to make it on~my own~I'm moving away~so she can come back! I know~everyone~feels sad~"

"What? Xavier, that's not true~" Diana was nonplussed! "We all do miss her, but the Lord worked it out for her to purchase the mine~Baby, why would you think~" She paused, taking in obstinate little features that showed he wasn't buying into her reassurances! "We'll be just as sad when you get big enough to leave! But don't rush~it'll be a while!"

He burst into tears!

❧ ❧

Doug pushed a cart dazedly through a super center, following two other brimming carts, pushed by Alexandra and her father! Diapers, formula, jars and jars of baby food, snacks, groceries, household goods, over the counter meds, paper goods, cleaning supplies, TV dinners, oil and filter, coffee and soda~ He reeled, imagining what it was all going to total!

105

His father-in-law had already made one trip, buying cribs for both girls, as well as pack-n-plays and myriads of toys! Now he sought a tool set for assembling the cribs! Then, wheeling around for a second run, he told Alexandra to pick whatever she needed personally~ All manner of cosmetics and skin products, bath stuff, new pajamas~ The total stunned Doug, but a credit card swiped, and~

"Wow, I haven't shopped here in years~" Daniel's good-natured memory-sharing with Alexandra! "I was a nervous wreck, and they called me back that day, too, to answer a security question! Your mother's, mother's maiden name!"

She nodded mutely, still profoundly embarrassed!

With everything stashed in all three of their vehicles, Faulkner paused to help double the girls' diapers and put them in new sets of pajamas! "With any luck the ride home will put them both to sleep," he explained!

To Doug and Alexandra's astonishement, the plan worked, and the snoozing babies were deposited onto the queen sized bed!

⚎ ⚎

Morrison and Porter rode in silence except for the sighing breezes and their horse hooves' soft clopping along the trail! Both men kept their eyes trained for signs of danger! Tripwires, or ninja-type warriors in the treetops!

"I tried to order a suit of their body armor," Bob confided, "but, I guess whoever takes orders recognized me as law enforcement, as well as a Federal agent! The order was canceled and I was blocked!" He sighed. "Not before they got my credit card information, though!"

Trent shot a troubled sideways glance! "Hope you canceled the card and requested a new one!"

"Yeah; I'm still nervous about it! I guess Hunter's wife~she's had a run-in, and she concluded that the suits are tough, unless you're really point blank! Otherwise, there's a small facial opening! She figures they literally have an *Achilles' Heels*, though, so to speak!"

Trent listened without responding!

"The armor ends at the ankles, and they wear work socks and boots! Hunter's take is that if we hope to bring them down~"

"Mmmm; blow their feet off," Trent finished! "Not taking a lethal shot gives them time to return lethal fire on us!"

Porter nodded thoughtfully! "Yeah, but they're armed with bows for the most part! I assume knives for close combat!"

"Well; don't take any chances or make any assumptions! They're a grave threat! I'm not positive all of them brings knives to gun fights! That was a great idea; trying to get your hands on their protective gear! It might be more effective than what we have! Maybe we can cut their supply of the materials, if we find out the details!" He didn't tell Porter that Hunter's wife was Alexandra; he'd find out for himself, soon enough! Curious, he wondered if the Government had ever paid her the bounty on Keller!

⊰ ⊱

Alexandra started laundry while the two men unwrapped toys and assembled cribs! Having laundry detergent was a boost, but she planned to let Doug know that he could do his own laundry; and Liesel's! As things were, her adorable, cozy little home was littered with Doug's junk and gear, moved hastily to prevent further rent on his apartment! Everything's being so topsy-turvey doubled her anguish at her dad's catching her in such disarray!

"Here, wash these crib sheets next!" Daniel unwrapped cute pink print sheets as he spoke! "Mom always washes 'em before she uses 'em!"

With the final screw tightened, Doug tied matching crib-bumpers in place!

Alexandra's adorable antique spinning wheel and loom were shoved together into the living room to make room for the cribs, and they stacked Doug's stuff in the corner of the bedroom! She suddenly hated her cute little real estate purchase! Adequate for one didn't get it for a sudden family of four!

⊰ ⊱

Nervous, Alexandra regarded Doug covertly from the passenger seat of his pickup!

"You're quiet," he shot her a wink as he reached for her hand.

"Yeah, I still feel so stupid!"

He laughed, "You're not that! I am curious why you would have told me your family's dead when they're not!"

"I didn't! All I said was, 'There was an accident'! But-uh-I guess 'mistake' would have been more accurate than 'accident'! You assumed they were dead!"

She had purposely misled him into assuming that, but he let it ride! With both sleeping babies nestled into new cribs, her father had sent them to Ouray for a couple of days of honeymoon!

⚕ ⚕

Daniel figured it would probably be smart to sleep while his granddaughters did, but he still felt keyed up! Of course, he hadn't slept the previous night either!

Finally, with a few moments to think, he was overwhelmed! So-granddaughters-it sounded strange for a man unprepared for the next season of life! One grandbaby, much less, two! And even worse, Diana didn't know she was a grandmother! And she wouldn't know, either, until Al changed her mind about his telling her! He didn't know what to make of Alexandra's marriage to Brad, Brad's subsequent suicide, and her quick turn-around to marry Hunter!

Doug Hunter! He might have kind of liked him; had he simply met him as a Forestry Department Agent, working way down the ladder under Trent Morrison! As a mate for Alexandra, Daniel figured he would take some getting used to!

Not able to sleep anyway, he brewed a pot of coffee and spread his Bible on the little kitchen table! Hmmm; He should have bought a high chair! Angelique was too small for one, but for Liesel-

At a total loss for knowing what to think! Maybe leaving her alone and giving her space had been a mistake! Strangely, the things they had worried might be going on, weren't! No signs that their daughter was turning into a party girl! Drinking, sleeping around, experimenting with drugs! Her closet showed sparse belongings; Diana's designs, becoming well-worn, but nothing skimpy, as they had feared!

If it weren't two in the morning, he might be tempted to phone Erik Bransom for an official report on Maxwell's suicide! Maybe Doug knew more about it than Al did! And more than he had divulged! Trying to create order from tumultuous thoughts, he began jotting down tasks to complete while the honeymooners were away! Tasks that might be easy to perform, except that he had oversight of an infant and a tyrannical almost-two-year-old! One thing, he was certain of, his child-tending was giving him a fresh appreciation of Diana!

⊨ ⊨

"Erik Bransom!" Erik was awake anyway, and he grabbed his phone, hoping not to disturb Suzanne! "What's up, Dawson?"

"Just as we warned them, Stephen Maxwell died in custody!"

Erik sank heavily at the kitchen table, sad at the feared development!

"Has Brad been notified? Is he still up in Canada at that lodge?"

"Uh-actually-no! Seems like he got wise that something was up–I'm sorry for keeping you out of the loop; well actually, I guess we've dropped the ball on this! Well, let's blame the Canadian Mounties–"

"Sounds good to me," Erik interrupted the stalling confession! "What are you trying to tell me?"

With the call ended, Erik sat regarding the wallpaper opposite him! Quite the revelation! Stephen and Brad–both dead! Now he faced the conundrum of what to do with the information! At the moment his biggest struggle was with the Treasury Department's confiscating Maxwell's little bits and dabs of fortune that remained! The only reason they didn't have their hooks into the Canadian property was the international ramifications, and that if there was anything up for grabs, the Canadians had their hands out, too!

"What's up? Do you have to head out?"

Suzanne's concern preceded her presence! "Need me to make coffee?"

"Actually, I don't have to go anywhere at the moment! That was Jed, telling me some news! Coffee sounds good, but I can make it! Try to go back to sleep!"

Suzanne frowned. "At nearly four in the morning? It wasn't something that could wait?"

He smiled at her patiently! "It could've, but he knew I'd want to know!"

⊨ ⊨

Doug and Alexandra walked happily hand in hand into a fast food place! Hungry early, Alexandra had wanted to order room service, while the prudent Doug opted for using the wad of cash more sparingly!

"The room's on his credit card; he won't care if we charge a meal to it~"

Still, she acquiesced to his argument!

Placing a tray down between them, he blessed the food and sipped cautiously at hot coffee! "You're very beautiful, you know! Your dad is~uh~"

She nodded, fighting sudden tears in spite of a growing sense of relief and happiness! "Yeah~uh~he's the greatest~and my mom~she's even~cooler~" She dabbed at perfect, fresh makeup with the corner of a napkin! "I thought Brad knew what he was talking about when he told me they're nearly bankrupt! I've been worried about them! I've wanted to be successful and make the mine successful, so I could help them out!"

He nodded understanding, suddenly amazed! Brad Maxwell was a sadistic loser, and Doug had no use for him whatsoever! And yet, his telling Alexandra that~about her dad and mom's financial situation~if she hadn't believed that so firmly~she would never have felt desperate enough to marry him~

"The Lord helped me out, there! I love you, and I know I took advantage of your confusion! Yesterday, I was so worried all day, that I'd come home and find out you'd flown the coop~"

She flushed guiltily! "Well, first of all, it occurred to me! But hawking the rings and my violin wouldn't have gotten me and Angelique across the street! I mean, the wedding set wouldn't be worth too much, but then getting them cut off really mangled them!"

"Well, they're still gold, and even small diamonds are valuable!" He laughed, "And why should you leave, when it's your house! Your dad's showing up out there really hemmed you in!"

"Yeah," her voice was suddenly small and lost. "I defied them! And everything they taught me~for Brad! And, I've known I need to make things right~"

Comprehension dawned. "So that was the mistake, aka 'accident,' you referenced?"

She nodded miserably, "I should have told you about it before we got married!"

"It doesn't matter, Alexandra! I think you're incredible! You do realize, though, that I'll never be in an earnings bracket with your father?"

She rubbed his fingers gently before meeting his worried expression, "Never's a long time, Doug!"

⊨ ⊭

Daniel was making headway with his tasks! Angelique was easy to care for! Feed her bottles and keep her changed, with an occasional violin performance if she fussed! Liesel was unlike any child he had ever dealt with! Evidently Doug's grandmother had been correct that she wasn't 'up to' dealing with a baby! She had kept the little one alive, but that was about it! He added another task to his 'to do' list! To check on the elderly woman's circumstances!

He jumped up! First things first, though! Getting the trash out! An accumulation of diapers added to the urgency of the task! He made it to the curb with several bags and the discarded toddler's car seat!

Before he made it back inside, a car pulled over and a woman jumped out to grab the discard! Shocked that anyone who saw how worn and filthy~ Guilt overtook him! It was easy to forget how much poverty there was!

※ ※

Powerful muscles put aging exercise equipment to the test in the historic hotel! Following breakfast, Doug worked out while Alexandra went in search of hair and nail salon! He worried! She was already gorgeous beyond him! As well as spoiled and high-maintenance! Now he knew why! Still, a calm settled around him, almost unnerving in its palpability! A lighthearted chuckle escaped! Toweling off, he headed to the suite to shower! Under the steamy stream, he allowed tears to flow freely!

"Wow, Lord, I picked Jeanine, and it was a fiasco! Of course, I wasn't saved then! I'm overwhelmed that you've given me someone as beautiful and perfect as Alexandra! I've never had money, and never really expected to! But when I told her that~it's like she sees~something in me~Lord, forgive me for not being more serious about getting Liesel and training her for You~I'm not~sure~is it too late?"

※ ※

"Okay, I'm hurrying!" Daniel fumbled wet wipes, trying to control the extent of mess as he changed the thrashing toddler's diaper! Finishing, he delivered quick hug and kiss and put her back down in the Pack 'n Play! He was amazed at instant calm! He was figuring out some important tidbits! Evidently, she had spent her life to this point, confined! Either

111

to crib or playpen, or a combination! And that was her comfort zone! Taking her out caused her to scream in genuine terror! *Agoraphobia*? If he remembered his phobia lingo correctly! The fear of open spaces! He wasn't sure it was all bad! Like his kids had spent their babyhoods trying to escape confinement, Liesel only wanted to climb in! Welcoming the boundaries with obvious relief! And she screamed in terror if he tried to place a toy into her space-When she was awake, she sat playing with her fingers, then would stand and pace around and around the perimeter! No speech! Evidently Grandma didn't talk to her much!

"Do you want some Cheerios?" He reached for the box and she stretched her hands out! "Cheerios! Say, 'Cheerios'! Can you tell Grandpa, 'Please'?"

She stamped a foot and screamed, and he regarded her narrowly as he handed her some of the treats! She seemed seriously underweight, and he offered her a Sippy cup of chocolate milk! He wondered if she had been taken for infant checkups and inoculations but figured probably not! Something that would definitely need to be done soon; hopefully, though, they could eradicate some of the obvious signs of neglect first!

He gave Diana a call and she updated him how things were going on her front! She was responding wonderfully with his not sharing information in return! She seemed relieved that he was there, and that he was in the loop about Al, even if he couldn't explain things to her at the present! He was mystified by Alexandra's insistence, but she had always been hard for him to understand!

Instead of taking a short Sunday afternoon nap, something he rarely did, anyway, he brewed coffee to fight off exhaustion, and checked and double-checked both diaper bags! Like he figured! A new appreciation for Diana and her superb handling of the family logistics!

He loaded Angelique in, who gazed at him contentedly, before grasping Liesel! And she had a dirty diaper again! Trying to change the struggling little one on the car seat so he could keep an eye on Angelique was his most challenging mission to date! Good thing he had started out plenty early! Folding the diaper into itself, he noted glumly that the leg of her outfit was soiled! Scrubbing at it with a wipe helped! With a defeated sigh he headed toward the church!

᠊᠊ ᠊᠊

"Look; that's your dad's rent car!" Surprise registered in Doug's voice!

"Yeah, I should have guessed he'd be here! Let's go help him in with them!" Alexandra hopped out and picked her way carefully across the gravel of the parking lot! She looked back at her hesitant mate! "I'll check Liesel in! You get Angelique!" She wasn't surprised he was embarrassed, but good grief, he needed to step up!

"Why does she have her blanket on her head?" Alexandra's question accused her father as she freed her stepdaughter from the seat and the blanket!

"She actually likes it that way," he defended! "I think I figured something out! That she's spent her life in a crib or playpen in the little apartment! Being out terrifies her! If she feels hemmed in-"

"Really?" She planted a kiss on his cheek! "Sorry for my tone! Thank you for watching them! We had a great time!"

He nodded, relieved! She and Doug both looked relaxed and happy! He reached for his Bible as the couple took the kids-and,

"Oh-oh!"

Al turned back, "What?"

Red-faced, "Uh-I came off without my Bible! I'll be right back!"

CHAPTER 13: PROGRESS

"Are you going home today?"

Daniel placed a Belgian waffle topped with strawberries and real whipped cream in front of his daughter, unsure if she was as eager to be rid of him as she sounded! He poured her a glass of milk and refilled Liesel's Sippy cup!"

Don't pound with your cup," he admonished gently! "Say, 'May I please have more milk'?"

Alexandra spoke up, "She can't talk! She's like retarded, or something! Daddy, what am I going to do?"

He refilled his coffee and sat down across the little kitchen table from her. "She can talk! Talk to her and encourage her to respond! She's behind, because Doug's grandma really wasn't up to the task! She'll catch up with nurturing and training!"

She prayed silently before taking a bite of the delectable presentation! "Oh, those are good! I've forgotten how yummy!! I know what you said about her is true~but~uh~I'm not you~and~uh~I'm sure not Mom! I can't do it! I don't think Doug's fair to expect me to! He doesn't know what to do with her~" she broke off with an aggravated hand motion toward the high chair!

"Shhh; because she doesn't talk doesn't mean she can't understand! Where she is, isn't her fault! Don't show disgust for her! You don't have to be me, and you don't have to be Mom! Like it or not, the Lord seems to have chosen you for this job! If you depend on Him, He'll give you the wisdom and the grace you need!"

Her expression turned stony! "God doesn't exactly listen to me anymore and do me any favors!"

"He does! You just don't have your senses exercised to discern them! He daily loadeth us with benefits! I haven't had a chance to tell you, but the Cox's paid your St. Mary's bill in full!"

"Why would they have done that? Oh good grief! Does everybody know about me?"

"Nobody knows anything because of Mom and me! We haven't known anything! And we don't share our drama with anyone! But you missed the point of what I said!"

"The-the bill's really paid? In full? I-I'm not being sued?"

"It really is; but I was shocked that they turned it over so fast-for non-payment! Is Angelique even two months old? Why wasn't there a bill for you and your care?"

"There is! At the hospital here! And they charged me a lot! And I got this bill from an obstetrical doctor!"

He shrugged, "Probably! They don't deliver babies for free!"

"Well, Doug delivered Angelique! In the car-"

He choked on hot coffee, struggling to keep from spewing it! It spewed in spite of his efforts!

"I know! My life's weird!"

⚎ ⚏

Doug grinned bashfully as his bosses assembled in the small regional headquarters building! He blushed when Morrison shot a pointed look at the clock!

"Hurry and get some coffee and get in the conference room!"

He scurried to comply! Of all the mornings for Morrison to be here! No use explaining about the slow traffic on 550 and a highway system antiquated for the twenty-first century! Traffic was worse in both DC and Golden, and he assumed the other two men never ran late! He paused, baffled, when only Morrison, Porter, and Bailey, with one guy he didn't recognize, were in the room! Hot acid rose in his throat! This was it! His dream career, tanked! Alexandra would leave him now, for sure! Forcing a calm he was far from feeling, he extended a beefy hand at the introduction!

'FBI?' That didn't compute in his tired brain! 'Like, if Morrison wanted to get rid of him, he wouldn't feel obligated to try to shift him to another government agency! And he wouldn't come personally!'

Porter broke the uneasy silence with a laugh! "I hear your gears turning, Hunter! When do government agencies ever cooperate?"

"It's because Erik's a good guy!" Trent interjected the comment, not ready for Hunter to know he was off the hook for his tardiness! Porter needed to learn when to relieve the gravity of a situation with humor, and when to let things soak in! Thankfully, Hunter was smart!

Erik sat glaring! Formidable-looking was Doug's assessment! He had made a bad first impression!

"Go brew another pot of coffee, Agent Hunter, and bring it and a warmer in here!"

Doug sprang up, aware that the gracious head usually brewed coffee for his ranks and gave few such orders in front of others! Still, if this was the worst that transpired-

⚰ ⚱

"What about the mine, Al?" Daniel's puzzlement growing over the past several days finally begged the question!

"What about it?"

He turned his sternest look on her for using his usual dodge on him! "Why aren't you mining it? And don't give me that about your equipment-"

"Well, that's the reason! Jared says we need it, first and foremost-" She fought humiliated tears! This was it! His trust that she could do this-down the drain!

With a strange sound between a groan and a sigh, he rose for a coffee refill! "What aren't you telling me?"

She shrugged, and his sympathy for her turned to ire!

"Can we please have a conversation, for once? I asked you a question, and shrugging your shoulders is not an answer! This doesn't make any sense! The four of you living down here in this cracker box; Doug having an hour and a half commute each way, every day! If you're worried about Keller's gang, I am too! But the mine has better security than this does! Maybe you feel safer down here because there's a city police force, and you're a little further removed from their cover in the National Forest!"

She started to shrug once more, from habit! Remembering, she paused and met his gaze guiltily! Her lovely features contorted as she struggled to speak, and his sympathy and concern returned, surpassing his frustration!

"It's~um~uh~a little of~all of those~" She rubbed her injured ring finger absently, "but~mostly~it's where~Brad~died~"

"What happened to your finger?"

"What? This one?"

"Yeah, that one! Has anyone looked at it? Like an orthopedic surgeon?"

"No, Sir; you've seen our pile of bills! I want to get it fixed~so I can play the piano! Plus everything I try to do hurts it! Changing diapers~we'll~um~you know~"

"How did you hurt it?

"Brad did it!" The accusation erupted from a pent-up place she didn't know was there! "I thought~that God~would change him for me~like he did for Mom with you! But, I was so mixed up, praying for him! Well, about everything! God used that fever to get your attention! I asked God to get Brad's attention, but not by a fever! Because Mom was a nurse and she nursed you through! But, then, I didn't want to be a nurse~"

"Whoa~" He held up a hand to halt the torrent! He wanted to hear her story, but he needed to clear some things up~

"Okay, don't worry about not studying nursing! And God knew ways to get Brad's attention! I think He had it!"

She nodded slowly, the tears drying suddenly! "That's what I left out of my equation! The fact that you did exercise your free moral agency, to do a turn-around, and serve the Lord! At every opportunity God gave Brad, Stephen was there, dangling a fortune that was smoke and mirrors! I can't be too hard on Brad for being seduced by money; because I wanted it, too! I tacitly encouraged him to appease~" She sighed with relief, amazed that the locked away details wanted to expose themselves! "The only thing Brad could do to wake me up, was his move on the mine! I was happy here!" She looked around her little home with satisfaction! "I loved my teaching job, and I just had this naïve hope that Brad would come around, be glad for our child~" She shuddered involuntarily! "So, I left him alone! I thought he was off having loving thoughts of me, as I did for him, while satisfying Stephen's demands! And then, he raided the mine payroll account! It made me so mad! My first realization that he was broke! But he wasn't interested in being my husband and partner, and owning the mine together! I knew he was in the area because he drew the money out in person!"

Daniel's tone, hushed, as barely controlled rage showed in the set of his jaw! "So, you called him and he showed up~"

"Yes, Sir! I was still so happy to see him! The minute he walked in, I didn't care about the money~I wanted to get him~uh~" Her skin flushed delicately, and he nodded understanding!

She continued, "But when he saw that~uh~I~was~pregnant~well, he accused~but Angelique's his~"

Daniel nodded calmly! "But it didn't matter! Am I right?"

She nodded. "Yes, Sir! You're right! Fatherhood wasn't in his plans! He went off the charts mad! Doug said the coroner's report showed high levels of PCP's; which the investigators assumed~uh~all along~And he~uh~Brad started insisting we leave immediately~to terminate~Then his honing in on my rings was weird! He was screaming about they belonged to him, so he was going to sell them~and that his mother bought them for me! And she'd never bought him anything! She'd never done anything for him~and he started screaming about women~being evil~And he couldn't get the rings off, because my fingers were swollen toward the end of term~He said he was going to cut it off~"

"The ring?" Daniel's attempt at clarity!

"No, my finger! But he said he was having a hard time deciding whether to cut it off before he killed me, or afterwards~" The story tripped over itself to be told in her soft hypnotic voice! "I remember trying to reason with him~and then, things blanked out! I remember trying to get away from him in his car~and Angelique screaming~and the chopper~"

᙭ ᙭

Erik didn't like Hunter's briefing! Well, nothing wrong with the briefing! He didn't like what it meant!

"Okay, anything more you can add?"

Although feeling at a disadvantage with the other three men, Doug tried to keep his tone from sounding aggrieved! For one thing, the way he felt, being examined and cross-examined, reminded him of people he questioned in his investigations! Details, even the smallest, could make all the difference in the outcome of a criminal investigation, but they still got frustrated with repeated and refined questions! No point in getting all miffed~but~he couldn't figure out why Forestry couldn't deal with the culprits~His personal opinion was that most of his colleagues were a bunch of clowns, not taking this seriously~and thinking, hoping, maybe even praying, that Johnson had moved along~If they'd all take the menace more seriously, the FBI wouldn't need to be brought on board!

"The reason I've called Erik in on this one," Trent paused, not sure how much he owed the green kid in the way of explaining himself, "is that he has been personally involved for years, with a black-market-organ, and human trafficking ring! Based in Eastern Europe, they have a leaning toward the type of vehicle that you described your run-in with! Lucky for you that a lost tour bus bumbled into the area!"

"Yeah, hate to alarm you further," The FBI guy! "But Alexandra has a double target on her back now! First, because of the run in with Keller, and her subsequently eliminating him; but she's also been a target for the kidnapping ring!"

Fresh alarm filled Doug! Not that he hadn't sensed the danger to his wife, already! And, his having seen what he saw~up on the pass~marked him~well all of the Forestry LEI guys~since before the stolen explosives and subsequent bombings!

"So Alexandra's been a kidnapping target for a long time? For ransom, you think?" His voice sounded more squeaky than manly!

Erik shook his head sadly, "No, not for ransom! Because she's indescribably beautiful! And also a personal vendetta against a bunch of us for interfering in their business! I guess the thing that has amazed Agent Morrison since your reported sighting of that military-style transport vehicle~was that we've thought Keller and Hardy with their militia bunch, were a separate entity!"

"And they may be," Trent added. "Maybe they all shop the same military surplus sites and see the same possibilities the armored vehicles present for their illicit activities! Or, maybe Johnson figures he can rid himself of the threat Alexandra poses him, and get cash in his coffers from this other group, by nabbing her and turning her over! Why kill her~"

Doug blanched, and then the meeting adjourned!

Daniel lagged behind Alexandra as he struggled to get the double stroller through the doorway and over the threshold of the mine headquarters building! Astonishment nearly left him speechless as he heard Jared's enraged bellow:

"You married that Forest-gnome, dufus, Hunter? Just because you needed rides back and forth from Grand Junction?"

Forsaking the struggle with the stroller, Daniel popped his head into the mining engineer's office, "What business is that of yours?"

Shocked, Jared's face reddened and he stammered. "None, I guess! But if she needed rides, all she had to do was ask~"

"She did; she asked Doug! Where's Abby?"

"Not sure," came the belligerent response! "We didn't work!"

Daniel stood glowering! Was this another reason for Alexandra to give this place a wide berth, and hang out down in Durango? Tired of fielding unwelcome advances from her employee? Especially in light of Brad Maxwell's rage and jealousy?

"Well, call her up, get her back here, and make it work! If you hope to keep this job~" Daniel's exhaustion getting the better of caution!

"Where's she going to get another mining engineer?" He smirked!

"Same place she got you! By placing a call to your alma mater! You haven't exactly done a stellar job getting this operation up and running!"

"We can't get delivery~"

"I'm tired of hearing that! Your advice for her to order it wasn't sound! The order of the day here, seems to be starting small! If you can't handle that, walk away!"

The engineer shot Alexandra a hangdog look to intercede on his behalf, but she scoffed!

⊰ ⊱

Alexandra pushed the stroller in circles on the makeshift sidewalks, the plan to pave pathways with asphalt never having happened! Still, she felt a flicker of hope! Her daddy was getting a scaled-down mining operation started up! Today! The weather was definitely brisk, but amazingly, no snow yet! Actually, the ski resorts were worrying~but for Alexandra, it was fortuitous! Every shovel lode of ore she could get out would put money in her pockets! Now she wished she had stood up better to Jared rather than hiding from him! Maybe she wasn't competent to do anything but entertain a couple of babies! She felt like a loser! From her vantage point above her village, she noticed the scaled down crew still in residence heading to the chow hall! Why not? She called Doug on a whim, to see if he was nearby to join her and the girls for lunch! He was on the spot so fast she couldn't believe it!

"My dad insisted on coming up here! I mean, his ideas are all good-except-for going into my modular-and I still miss my friend, Norma, when I come up here! How's your morning been?"

He took a bite of Frito pie before responding! "I was late! Which-Bailey always takes note of-but this morning the head guy from DC and the head of this division were both here! With an FBI guy! Because of something I ran into several days ago!" Pausing the conversation, he attacked the fare lustily! He wasn't sure whether to alarm her further about her safety! He planned to redouble his efforts-he hoped the head guys were planning to do something! He glanced up to catch her frowning at him. "What?"

"Do you have to eat that way?"

He wiped his mouth guiltily! Something the DI's rode him about in Basic Training! He guessed he had improved during his military stint; but now, feeling pressed for time, being hungry, and wanting seconds of the hot and tasty lunch-

"Sorry," he mumbled.

Alexandra still cringed at the mention of Trent Morrison's name! A witness to her misguided rendezvous with Brad! And his ensuing hospital visit with her-filled her with fresh shame!

She was relieved when newcomers entered and interrupted her thoughts! "Looks like my dad is getting fast results!" She waved and motioned the three men to th table! Embarrassed, she made introductions! She wasn't sure what these guys had heard about her scrapes, but her marriage to Doug was sudden-and two babies sitting impatiently in the stroller-

"Hey, Jacob, Tim, and Warren, meet my husband, Doug! Doug, Jacob's my uncle's adopted son, and Warren's his real dad; Tim and Jacob are business partners!"

Doug nodded, trying to make sense of the convoluted introduction. "Uh-if he's your uncle's son, doesn't that make him your cousin?"

Jacob laughed! "Thanks for trying, Man! But Miss Snooty here, is kind of aloof from accepting low-lifes into her family! We own some heavy equipment, and Mr. Faulkner called us to get some earth moved in preparation for blasting! I mean, my Uncle Daniel!"

☙ ❧

"Okay," Daniel rolled his window down to better enjoy the cool mountain air! "I'm not sure that house will ever be livable again! It's being pulled out! A hydraulic drill is coming on-site tomorrow so they can dynamite! The miners are relieved to no end, to get going! Late snow with the almanac forecasting a moderate winter-that's a miracle-for you, Al!"

She acquiesced, her expression still clouded.

"What's wrong?"

"I know they're miracles, but I wanted God to help me-so I could do it without you! It's humiliating that you have to be here, bailing me out, getting results, when I couldn't! I-I've confessed my sin, but I still can't get Him to help me!"

"Well, what is it, do you think, that made me so I couldn't sleep and impressed upon me that I needed to come, after more than a year of Mom's and my determination to leave you alone?"

She started to cry! "That's not the kind of help I wanted!"

Handsome features crinkled good-naturedly. "You're like the guy who was trapped in his home in a flood-ravaged area! He prayed for God to save him, and felt like he had an assurance from God, that He would! So, pretty soon, a rescue team showed up in a rowboat to get him to safety. But he said, 'No; God told me He'll rescue me!' So the rowboat went on, and the guy moved up to his second floor balcony! A motor boat from the fire department threw him a line, but he wouldn't catch it, and he told them, 'No, the Lord told me He'll save me!' So the firemen went on, and the guy climbed onto his roof as the water continued to rise! Lastly, a National Guard helicopter flew over and lowered a basket! He cupped his hands to yell above the rotors! 'Thanks, but God told me He's gonna save me!'

So, then the guy was swept away and drowned, and God met him at the pearly gates and told him, 'You're not supposed to be here!' And he said, 'You promised You'd save me!' And the Lord said, 'I sent two boats and a chopper!'"

She actually laughed, before sighing! "You just don't understand!"

"Trust me; I really do! I once heard a preacher say that, 'God never uses the supernatural to answer our prayers, when the natural will do!' Sometimes we pray for something, and we end up working and earning what we asked for! It doesn't get dropped from the sky! We're you're parents, Alexandra; we love you! We wanted you and all your brothers and sisters! We'll love you and help you as long as we have breath in our bodies! It was Satan telling you that you cut yourself off from us-and Satan making Brad convince you~that we didn't have the wherewithal to help you, even if we wanted to! His trick made you jump on Doug's marriage proposal~"

"Maybe you're right~but if so, he still only fulfilled God's purpose! I think Doug is who God wanted me to have before I married Brad~"

Daniel tried not to show his total amazement! He more than anything wanted her to be happy~without hitting a hundred dead-ends first! "So, why were you teaching school?"

She lit up as she shared about and the Allens and *Grace College of the Rockies*!

"Mennonite?" His response was both shocked and pleased at the revelation! Here, he and Diana had been terrified that she was running wild, partying it up, and going against every decent thing they had attempted to ingrain~and she had fallen in with a group of Mennonites? Talk about God doing the supernatural in response to their earnest and urgent prayers!

"So, is that why you quit wearing cosmetics?"

She made a droll face! "Are you kidding me? No! I've just been out of everything!"

"Oh, I thought you got some the other night~at the store~ah~you prefer department store brands!"

She laughed. "Trust me; I've learned to make do with less! And, I'm saving it for special~"

"Well, let's go back to the store! They're both asleep! I'll stay out in the car with them while you get whatever you need~and want~"

She turned earnest expression and pleading gray eyes toward him! "Okay, but do you mind stopping for a few minutes at the school? I think Dr. and Mrs. Allen are there, closing everything up~"

"Why? Isn't it time for classes to be in session?"

She explained the financial problems the institution was experiencing.

"Well, of course I want to meet your friends who've been so kind to you! But just so you know~bailing you out is one thing! Mom and I don't have resources to assist an ailing college!"

123

CHAPTER 14: SUPERNATURAL

Alexandra felt a profound sense of both embarrassment and loss at the Allen's chilly response to her stopping by and introducing her father! Yeah, she could get it; their sorrow at closing the doors after one school year, but Angelique was so adorable that Sally could have at least emitted one squeal of delight! Maybe they were just being judgmental of her relationships: first with Brad, and then a quick turnaround to grab the life saver represented in Doug! At least it was good news that ore was moving up at the mine! Maybe teaching had been too much of a distraction! Even as she combed through the past year, she knew that the school had been a refuge and the diversion necessary to keep her from going crazy!

"Well, they seemed nice enough!" Daniel's comment as he closed her car door for her. "A little distracted! I think we caught them at a bad time! Maybe if we'd made an appointment-"

Before Alexandra could respond, her phone signaled an email! From Clint Hammond, long-time *GeoHy* corporate attorney, and by default, her legal counsel!

'What now?' She opened it surreptitiously. Maybe St. Mary's was still suing her! A gasp escaped!

"What?" Daniel reminded himself not to panic, but she had gotten herself into a couple of jams!

"It's from Mr. Hammond! Someone's agent approached him about leasing part of the mine acreage to graze Alpaca!"

"Wow! No kiddin'! How much per acre; or per head; or however they figure it?"

She leveled serious gray eyes at him, "You're pretending to be surprised! You-uh-told David and Mallory-about me-being in such a-pinch-" Her tone, injured and accusing!

"I did no such thing! How much, Al? Would you quit looking every gift-horse in the mouth? We hardly see David and Mallory; but I doubt they'd bother going through an agent!"

"Well, who else knows about my cattle being swept away in the flood water? And who else is in the Alpaca business?"

"I don't know, Al! Shay and Emma! But I question that they'd use an agent! Unless they know how much distance you try to put between yourself and everyone!"

"Well, I'm not trying to put distance-it's-just-the distance-is there-now-"

"Okay, whoa! I get that you're eaten with guilt! Alexandra Marie Faulkner, God forgave you the first time you confessed and asked Him to! Now, you need to forgive yourself! But you've always been stand-offish with people-even before you moved out here! Maybe we need to talk about Mallory!"

Color shot to her cheeks and she looked horrified! "I shouldn't have said that to you that day! I knew it was wrong when I said it-Mr. Morrison heard me, too; didn't he?"

"I don't know, Al! I hope he didn't, for all of our sakes! You know, when Mom and I first agreed with Patrick about Mallory, we prayed about it!"

"Yes, Sir; I know!" Her gaze focused ahead of her! "Do we have to-"

"Yes, I think so! Listen, we never intended to be so up-close and personal in-our family- All Patrick asked was that-well, legally, there were never any teeth in any of it! But our instructions were basically to supervise from afar!"

"Right! So, you got her out of Murfreesboro, and into her *Dallas Palace*-but she didn't stay put! I was young but I remember it all like it was yesterday!"

He laughed! To ease the tension, and he had never thought of the Dallas mansion as a *Dallas Palace*!

"Look, I like Mallory! Doesn't everyone? And even though you all devoted a lot of time to her, and she became Mom's closest friend-I don't know! Like I said, I should have never made that comment to you-that I did- You and Mom raised me better; I made a mistake; and I got caught! I lashed out-but I've never doubted that you guys loved me; loved all of us!"

"Okay, then, answer the email and ask for details! Explain how much security you have in place! How lush the acreage is! This is supernatural, Alexandra, if it is David and Mallory! And it isn't precipitated by me! I could never have thought of this as a solution in a thousand years! I thought you were right about not replacing the cattle operation~But the Alpaca will belong to someone else and ultimately be their responsibility!"

She nodded, hope taking hold in her heart! She drafted a response of being definitely interested and asking for details!

"Will you call Mallory and ask if it's them?"

"Why, Al? What difference does it make?"

One look at her pleading expression and he pulled his phone out!

They were entering the outskirts of Durango when he disconnected! "Satisfied?" he demanded jovially!

Wonder infused her beautiful countenance. "Yeah! Turn around! Head back up to the college!"

He complied before curiosity and good sense kicked in!

Mallory's words on speaker replayed in Alexandra's ears like music, even after the connection was broken! The crux of the conversation: 'Mallory wished that she and David <u>were</u> the ones making the offer! Instead, they had been mentoring Alex and Kayla Hamilton in starting a herd! So, although they really wanted to move some of their prize animals to the colder climate, they had suggested the opportunity to those they were helping along! So typical of them!

She paused in her thought process to assess the details of the offer in a new email! The numbers were staggering!

"Call Mallory back, and ask if they're serious about moving some of their stock out here!"

"Why? The Hamiltons already contracted for all of your available grazing land!"

She nodded, happily dazed by the vista opening to her!

Shining eyes turned toward Daniel! "Because if David and Mallory really want grazing land, too, there're lots of nice meadows~"

"At the college~" he finished, "Al, that's genius!"

She nodded, "Well, it'll require a sales job for both parties! David won't move Alpaca any place without good security and armed personnel! The Allens are death on guns! Wait! That didn't come out making any sense!"

They both laughed giddily the entire seven miles to the campus! And then they got extra tickled when Liesel broke into peals of laughter in the back seat!

"That's the first time I've ever heard her laugh!" Alexandra regarded the toddler who was doubled over in her car seat, laughing! She really was pretty cute!

⚔ ⚔

"Aren't you the two little beauties?" Kayla Hamilton, the hard-nosed, back-East attorney, donned a different persona in the mountains of Colorado! She was charmed by both Leisel and Angelique! "We apologize for already being on your doorstep before Clint even sent you the first email! But we wanted to be able to move, if you agreed; and to move along in the search of other landholders if you didn't! I guess all the locals are surprised that snow hasn't flown yet! We hope to, 'Make hay while the sun shines', to use a cliché!"

Alexandra nodded agreement! "Yeah, we're attempting to do the same with the mine! I've wasted another entire summer waiting on delivery of a specialized piece of mining equipment! Today, Daddy tore up there and told Jared he can get some production, even if he can't have a state-of-the-arts mine!"

Alex passed over the comment, but Kayla laid a manicured hand on his arm!

Alexandra cringed. If they got started, they could fight like a couple of wildcats!

"I'm sorry," the attorney apologized. "I nearly glossed that over, too! We're so excited about our new venture~but, what's the deal with your delayed delivery? Do you need an attorney to send a letter on your behalf?"

"Well, maybe so; I'm not sure! They just keep putting me off that they're having labor problems, and trouble with machining and getting parts delivered~every problem that could come up, has~"

"What kind of money are we talking?"

Her brows flew up in response to the dollar amount! "You didn't pay in full?~You should always hold back a portion~whether it's for labor, contractors~Business people are more motivated to finish a job or make delivery~if their money's still on the line~"

127

Alexandra blushed and Daniel shuffled uneasily! Things he knew full well! That he guessed he assumed his daughter had absorbed through his gene pool-or osmosis-or something! And still, he hadn't contacted Clint Hammond on her behalf! Just sloughed off her problem as a lame excuse! And he was still annoyed at Harrelson for holding out for high dollar machinery, rather than mining more primitively to bring in capital to put back into equipment-

Kayla rocked Angelique gently as she considered! "Well, on second thought, I think I need to see correspondence about what they've stated the problems are! I can hire a private detective to verify-"

Alexandra flushed. "Well, it's not really correspondence; mostly phone calls-"

"I'm not surprised; they probably want as little in writing as possible, especially if their business practices are suspect! I can get copies of your phone records, to verify how often you called, trying to get the matter resolved! Even though the calls weren't recorded-"

"I haven't even called that much-" Alexandra felt like a fool as she made each admission! "They kept asking me for patience, and I kept trying to-"

"Be nice!" the attorney finished crisply! "You do have records, though, for the order and payment?" Her features registered a mixture of worry and hope!

"Yes, Ma'am!"

"Great, if you can get copies to me-I'll see what I can shake loose!" She paused thoughtfully, shooting troubled glances from Alexandra to Doug and back. "Could I ask you a question? About the estate of your late husband?"

A gasp from Alexandra, caught off guard by the topic shift! "Uh-I guess so-Um, I'm not sure there-was an-estate! But if Brad did end up with anything-it doesn't matter! I signed a pre-nup- I know, call me Dumb! And then this lady from Raymond Meeker's law office overheard us, me signing-and she evidently thought I should protect the mine from Brad and Stephen-uh, I blew it off-"

Kayla held Angelique up to look into big blue eyes fringed with long black lashes! "What about you, Cutie? You weren't dumb enough to sign anything, were you?"

Daniel laughed, "I love the way you think!"

⚐ ⚑

Ned McAlister slammed the door of a rental car with attitude! He had never like Jared Harrelson for Abigail to begin with! Now, he really didn't! "Are you sure this is the address? It looks like a dump!"

"Well, this is the street and the number-guess if the key fits-"

It did, and she pushed the front door open! The space was clean, but crowded! She moved inside to allow her father access, figuring he would blast everything-again!

"Well, I guess it'll have to do!" He was at a loss! His only daughter had married the mining engineer against his wishes! He guessed the couple was happy enough-to begin with-Hey, he was no marital counselor, himself, having never excelled at the interpersonal relationships' game! Of three stabs at matrimony, his marriage to Abigail's mother had lasted the longest! For the sake of his daughter, he guessed! Hadn't delivered the heaven on earth he had hoped for!

So, Abigail had separated from Jared and come home to him! Where she moped and worried him to no end! When he could give her anything she wanted, why did she hang onto something dead and buried? Still, her happiness was paramount, and though he doubted a second attempt would grant it, nothing else intrigued her!

She turned and met his gaze! "I'm good! I can sleep on the couch if you want to spend the night and-"

He shook his head! "That's quite all right! I'll bring your suitcase in and return home this evening! Uh-you're quite certain?"

"Yes, positive! I'll purchase a piano this week and get it delivered! And I'll place ads where I think I might be able to attract voice students! And, there's no snow yet!"

"You could be in Borneo where there's never any snow-"

"Yes, Sir; I know! Love you! If you're sure-about not staying-I'm pretty tired-"

He agreed! "Yeah, it's midnight at home and we were up early! Call if you need-"

She laughed. "I hope I don't need anything, but I'll call anyway and keep you in the loop!"

"Jared should have met us-"

"I didn't want him to! Good night, Daddy! I love you!"

He stiffened, "Just keep your phone handy so you can call the cops if you hear anything! Get deadbolt locks put in! The whole town looks trashy to me~"

"Okay, well, it's Alexandra's house, but the deadbolts sound like a good idea! I'll run it by her! Thank you, for everything!"

※　※

Alexandra puffed with exertion! The altitude at the mine was a factor, but so was bundling two babies up! Just to push the stroller the short distance between the mine office and the chow hall! Windy and bitterly cold, but bright cerulean met the mountainous horizon like brilliantly glazed inverted bowl! A few minor skiffs of snow over the past ten days, but nothing to close down operations! So, here she was! The mine was producing on a small scale, the new modular home was nearly ready for her and Doug to occupy, and the Hamiltons' Alpaca were on site! The next phase underway would be a smaller pre-built for Janni Anderson, who planned to arrive within the week to assist with Leisel and Angelique! Then, it would be time to visit a surgeon about her finger! Her pledge to her dad to get it cared for! In spite of passing time, praying, and trying to baby it; it wasn't any better!

Warmth greeted her, along with the aroma of pizza and pasta! Now, the chore of removing coats, mittens, and hats!

"Can I help?"

"Abby! Hey, welcome back! Thanks, but I think I've got it! When did you get here?"

"Well, Tuesday night into Durango! I just got up here a few minutes ago for the weekend!"

"That's great! Have~uh~you seen Jared~yet?"

"Not yet! I'm nervous! Wow, the girls are beautiful! I'm eager to meet Doug! Your house down in town is adorable!"

"Thanks; did you find a piano yet?"

"I did! I mean, it's a little on the 'bright' side! It wasn't like anyone in these parts carries a huge inventory! I'm eager to get started! I've had eight responses and I've already given lessons to four of them! Your father suggested contacting the local college, but~"

"Yeah~a little over a year ago, I dropped in there! They encourage their student body to study privately with their faculty! Not surprising, I guess! But the rest of my dad's suggestions are stellar!"

"For sure! My dad can't help liking your dad! And he thinks a lot of David and Mallory! That gives me hope for his ever being reached with the Gospel! He won't listen to me! I've wanted to come back since the day I left~but~he's been kind of~against it~"

"Let's get some pizza; I'm starved!"

⚞ ⚟

Doug nudged his mount upward through a narrow and steep place! Since the briefing with the bigwigs, numerous resulting searches had turned up~nothing! Shivering, he pulled down his hood, and pulled on a knit cap before pulling the hood back into place! His zeal had earned a nickname among fellow agents, *Sir Galahad*! Mocking on their part! He smiled! Amazingly, though, Alexandra liked it, and affectionately took up the sobriquet! He liked being her knight in shining armor! Still, not to be swept away into realms of fiction, he addressed the reality! The other guys could laugh all they wanted to! Their wives weren't specifically targets; although, truth be told, Johnson and his guys had actually declared their war on all Forestry personnel, with no regard for their family members! They should all get more serious!

Reaching a flat spot, he reined in and trained field glasses around, scanning from treetops, then down and around! He surveyed his GPS! Close to the narrow road over Lizard Head Pass, approaching circuitously through heavy forest! Not wanting to be fool-hardy, nor cowardly, he proceeded cautiously! His thoughts returned to his earlier run-in with the criminals, and the amazing coincidence of a coach full of camera-wielding Japanese tourists~He wanted to trust God for protection as he served in law enforcement, but he didn't want to tempt God by acting foolishly! After all, he had a wife and daughters who needed him! So, they needed him to be around! But, they also needed him to eliminate a very real threat! A sudden gust of wind drove a cloud over the sun and pierced through him! This place gave him the creeps! Wheeling the large mount around, he disappeared back up the trail!

⚞ ⚟

"You are incredibly beautiful and absolutely the most perfect wife God could have ever~"

Diana's eyes sparkled mischievously, "You're just saying that so I won't ask any questions!"

He shrugged! She was right! "Even if you asked, I'm sworn to secrecy! But thanks for not~How's your steak?"

"Superb! This is my favorite place as you well know! Thanks for thinking of bringing me here for dinner when it's cold enough that I can wear my coat!"

He laughed, proud of having bought her the lush Sable! "Yeah, wish you'd remind me! I just get so happy and eager to come home in the afternoons~" He broke off as troubled shadows crossed her features. Wow, he was going to be tiptoeing through a minefield from now until Alexandra gave the decree to lift the silence!

"I'm not sure I should bring this up~" She broke off and waited for his prodding!

Whatever it was, he didn't know if she should either!

"Xavier feels like it's his fault that Alexandra left home! He's eager to get big enough to leave home so she can come back!"

He filled his mouth with steak! The best he could determine, Diana, nor any of the kids had an inkling of either of Al's marriages, or the two girls! Her coming home now would be more convoluted! When he could speak,

"Well, kids get off-the-wall ideas into their heads! I'll talk to him and tell him he can stay a couple more years!"

She sniffed indignantly, not appreciating his attempt at humor! "Well, on a different tack, have you been in my studio?"

This time, a mouthful of burning hot baked potato was his dodge! Swallowing desperately, he gulped at iced tea! "Well, maybe! Uh~I'm not sure! I mean, it's my studio, too! It's in my house~uh~our house~maybe! I'm not sure; why?"

She laughed, "Never mind! Forget it!"

"Okay!"

"No! Uh~did you see~uh~remove~a package?"

"Package? What kind of package?" His mouth was seared and she had him nailed! No wonder Al answered his questions with questions? He guessed he did it oftener than he realized. "Are you missing a package? Who was it to? You look incredibly beautiful, by the way~"

"You're talking in circles, and this is where I came in~" She made a move toward pulling her coat on! She did that a lot when he aggravated her~

"Oh, the one hidden down in the cabinet, wrapped in brown~"

"Daniel Jeremiah!"

"Yeah, I saw it! Why'd you try to hide it?"

"Why did you sneak it out? If you knew about it, why didn't you say something?"

He laughed, "Wow, do you realize that we're both gifted at asking questions? But we neither one give straight answers so good~er~well~

"DANIEL!"

"Shhh-hh, don't get us thrown out of here! Okay, guilty! I re-sent it last week when I got home! I'm sorry she returned it to you to start with! I know it had to hurt you~deeply ~why you never told me~Honey, I can't stand for you to be hurt! If I'm hurting you now~"

Tears filled her eyes! "It's not you: I just don't understand~what I did~to her~"

"Di, you didn't do anything~It's~well~you~know how she can~be~"

⚑ ⚐

"I really want to," Alexandra felt torn as she turned down Dr. Allen's offer! "But it's already late in the semester, and I'm still facing this surgery! I could teach the science classes, but I can't play either piano or violin right now~and they're not sure that the surgery can restore more than fifty percent~ If y'all could pray about it~"

"Definitely we can do that! Thanks again for intervening on our behalf to help keep our doors open! Keep in touch! I know that with two little girls and the mine finally under way~but you're our favorite teacher! Very gifted! As a musician, a teacher, and also a scientist!"

⚑ ⚐

Doug berated his cowardice! When he might finally be closing in, a stiff breeze had sent him into retreat? How could he be so down on the other guys; when he was sorrier than they were? Running from shadows; mirages? So close! And now he had basically wasted a day with nothing to show for it but a freezing horseback ride through the woods!

133

A clearing opened before him, and he reined in quickly in response! Not a natural clearing! Well, they hadn't felled timbers to create it! Natural of sorts, but trampled down with signs of recent heavy activity! Aware of his heart thudding in double-time behind the vest, he eased back several feet for better cover, and once more drew out the powerful glasses!

He frowned. So his discovering their site up on the pass must have rattled them! Making them retreat-to here- He accessed his sat map of the San Juan National Forest and frowned, deeply puzzled! His recon showed evidence of the heavy, armored vehicle, the distinctive tire tread still visible in the clearing! But there was absolutely no road access! Heavy forest surrounded the site! He considered possibilities! Air-drop? Not likely! The only other alternative that presented itself was the possibility of underground cave and tunnel systems! He shuddered!

The wind sighed eerily, rustling branches and delivering a new chill! Steeling himself, he dismounted! Weapon drawn, he moved stealthily to a littered edge of the clearing, where he removed random pieces of trash! Trash that might possibly reveal some tidbit of information! Seeing a larger paper fluttering in the breeze, he moved toward it, scrambling across a small pile of boulders to retrieve it! Then, at a dead run, he made it back to his mount and urged her full-trot back to headquarters!

CHAPTER 15: RECUPERATION

Alexandra moaned! Naturally, everything medical turned into an ordeal for her! After consulting with an orthopedist in Durango, who sent her to a specialist in Grand Junction, who in turn referred her to the most skilled surgeon in the state, in Denver-

Brad's jerking and ripping at the rings and her finger had inflicted serious damage, and the lag in corrective surgery now compounded the problem!

Pain, like unendurable, kept her punching the morphine pump! She thrashed restlessly, and vomited again! Fever and nausea puzzled the floor nurse, who had a call in to the physician! Probably indicative of infection-

⊨ ⊨

Doug finished a report and shoved it into his superior's box! Hoping it would make its way up the ranks where someone might recognize its import, he fought pessimism! Anyway, Friday afternoon, and having the weekend off, he needed to get on the road to Denver, post haste! Before he could make the parking lot, Agent Bill Abbott, one rung above him in the hierarchy, blocked his way!

"Just got a report of a robbery over at the Lizard Pass Campground! Head on over there and take the report!"

"I'd rather not! I was on call last week end!" He hadn't mentioned Alexandra's surgery to any of his colleagues, but she had toughed it out since Thursday morning without his being there! The plan was for him to head out for the weekend the first moment he could! His curiosity made him wonder briefly at the nature of the theft and whether the culprits he sought might be involved! Probably not! Definitely not their MO! "I'm headed for Denver, and it's a seven hour drive! If the Million Dollar Highway's plowed!"

"Well, everyone else's gone! Here's what I got over the phone-kinda scrambled up!"

"You're still here! You take care of it! Alexandra had surgery in Denver, and she's having a tough time! I gotta go!" He walked away!

⇥ ⇤

"Great game, Dad? Hunh?"

Jeremiah popped his head past his younger brother to meet Daniel's gaze! "Looks like the Mav's are gonna pull it out!"

"Yeah; they kind of came alive after half-time! Zave, Buddy, what do you think?" Daniel included his younger son in the conversation, feeling guilt at not really being into the father-son activity! Absently, he shelled out money for more concessions, hoping his sons wouldn't get sick on the drive back to Tulsa! He lapsed back into his musings about Alexandra-and the situation he had left behind the month before! He continued to receive the daily cryptic texts-Now the concern was not only for his child-but grandchildren-? Such a strange new concept to adjust to!

⇥ ⇤

Jim Bailey's ire erupted as Agent Abbott related the story to him about Hunter's defiance of the direct order! Phone calls being declined by the probationary agent didn't improve his frame of mind!

So Hunter had a wife now! They all had wives! Wouldn't have taken him but a couple of hours to go over there and take the report! Aggravated, he called the new District Head, Bob Porter!

Caught off guard, Porter couldn't believe they were pulling him into their fray! Bailey needed to handle things among his guys! "Yeah, I get it that Hunter's low man on the totem pole! I get it that he's usually all gung ho and willing to be anyplace and everyplace at once! But, if he was on call last weekend, and has plans in Denver, why couldn't Abbott go take the incident report? This job's all about give and take! It sounds like Abbott's a little over-eager to impose his tenuous seniority! Why were you already gone, by the way? We have someone who's been robbed at a National

Forest campground and none of you guys have responded? Go yourself, Bailey, if you can't get your men to do their jobs! What's to discourage the perpetrator from hitting more victims while you lollygag around?"

᚛ ᚜

Doug was shocked at Alexandra's appearance! "Hey, hey; what's going on? Still really a tremendous amount of pain? Is that what's making you so you can't keep anything down? What are they telling you?"

"I keep telling them it feels like it's on fire! It's what I told them in Durango when I broke my ankle! They didn't believe me, and then my skin was burned black! If they'd just unwrap it, and check-"

Doug regarded the swathed left hand where hardware protruded through the bandaging! It was hard to look at! No wonder the pain was so great! That was what they kept saying! This type of surgery just was painful! The hand had lots of nerves in it, and they were all screaming!

Not sure what else to do, he dampened a washcloth and sponged her gently! "So, when was the last time the doctor was in to check on you? I've been praying for you! I'll go out and try to find someone-"

Tears filled her eyes! "No, just-just stay-with me-I'm starting to feel better-just because-Did-um-you see Janni around-"

"No, have the girls been doing okay?"

A weak laugh! "Well, she hasn't complained-I think she feels sorry for me- They're-a-lot-"

"Shhh, it's okay! I'm here now! I should have just asked for time off from the beginning-"

᚛ ᚜

Diana watched the front of the house for days, tormented! She wasn't sure why! Although trying to trust the Lord and be patient, being in the dark about Alexandra was taxing her resolve! She felt she couldn't bear the rejection if the box of lovely ensembles came back to her again! Still miffed that Daniel had been aware of it for months without mentioning it-and that then he had returned from his mysterious mission, to send the package again-She sighed! Why did it matter so much?

᚛ ᚜

Bob Porter pulled into his space at the temporary headquarters in Golden! Time to get the big report all tied up with a pretty ribbon and forwarded to Morrison in DC! Too bad the mama bear that had been Buford's excuse for habitual tardiness with the paperwork, had blown herself to kingdom come! Still, the humorous thought caused him to pause and consider! According to the grapevine, Morrison had warned Buford about the stolen explosives and to watch out for all his agents~and he had also prayed about the problem with the bear and her cubs~And amazingly, the bear triggered the explosives earlier than intended by the bombers, saving the lives of the personnel who would have been in the building later! And taking care of herself in the process!

≒ ≒

Janni pushed the stroller through the broad corridor! She was rested and the girls seemed to be calmer, sensing relief about Alexandra! Not sure if God had answered her prayers, or those of others, she was still profoundly relieved! It had seemed to her that Doug would never get there, and that Alexandra was going downhill in double time! She would have called her parents or the Faulkners, except that Alexandra had forced her to promise~She hesitated in the doorway, but Leisel squawked her unintelligible protest!

"Come on in!" Doug made his way toward his daughters through an assemblage of visitors! "I'll take this one~" he swung Leisel up into his arms, "and you get the baby! We can leave the stroller out in the hall!"

"Good idea, it takes up quite a bit of space!" Alexandra's voice, though not strong, sounded brighter. "My dad was the pro, though, choosing that one rather than the side-by-side model!"

"What difference does it make?" Jared liked to argue!

"Side by side lets the kids pick at each other," Janni supplied!

Jared met Abby's gaze and he shrugged. "Something to keep in mind, I suppose!"

"Yes," she came back! "One never knows when such snippets of information might come in handy!"

Alexandra felt profound relief! One of the problems in Jared and Abby's relationship had been that she wanted a baby and he felt they weren't ready! His comments sounded more open to the prospect!

"Wow; what's all this? A package from your mom?"

138

Janni approached the contents spilling from a box onto the foot of the bed!

Alexandra swiped at tears with her good hand! "Yeah, isn't it the cutest one ever? It got delivered along with another insured package to my Durango house while Abby was giving her voice lessons! I can't believe they drove all the way here~"

"Well, we got kinda worried about you! For some reason we felt like we weren't getting the true picture when we called to check!" Jared's features registered relief! "For your information, Janni Anderson, you're a most unconvincing liar!"

"Okay, don't call her a liar! She's the most honest person ever! I told her to tell everyone I was doing fine!"

"Hey, you're wearing yourself out," Doug warned gently! "But thanks, guys, for coming to check on her and delivering the stuff! It has her feeling worlds better!"

"Well, I guess it should! Look at these, from my dad!" Alexandra caressed silky, black, fourteen millimeter, Tahitian pearls fastened with a white gold and diamond floral clasp! "And they're so perfect with the adorable things from my mother!"

Janni was awed! Not only by Diana Faulkner's talent as a designer, but also with Alexandra's personal sense of style! She liked to go with a practically neutral palette that flattered her gray eyes and flaxen hair!

A fine-denier silk sweater with jewel neckline featured the loveliest *Chinese*-influenced screen print! Typical craggy gray peaks, featuring the famous silhouette of Mount Huangshan, shrouded in monochromatic gray mists, brought the eye forward to the focal point of a Giant Panda; the Panda, executed in soft white with deep charcoal contrast! Soft, flaxen bamboo shoots sprouted a few leaves of gray into muted gray-green! Two knee length wool flannel skirts, one in charcoal, and the other the flaxen color, could be paired with a three quarter length charcoal wool coat, lined with matching *Chinese* motif printed silk! Shoes and handbag included, of course!

"And that isn't all! Doug brought me this letter from David and Mallory, telling me how thrilled they are with the deal with *Grace* for pasturing their Alpaca! They sent me a finder's fee! I forgot that they usually do that~"

⛧ ⛧

Bob Porter straightened in surprise! Then scanned over the information again! Although, since his conversion to Christ, he tried to watch his language- 'Crimenently', he amended to the office, empty except for himself!

No wonder Morrison stayed frustrated with this bunch! Unless Bailey was totally brain-dead, he should have acted on the intel in Porter's report, immediately! A stack of fake, Hollywood-prop-type rocks? And vehicle tracks commencing from and terminating at the spot? Enlarging the scraps of news-print on the wall monitor added additional unnerving information! A portion of a delusional article posted by the late Rudy Sunquist- Deciding to give Jim a chance by updating him on the investigation, he placed a call!

⊣ ⊢

Alexandra wrapped her coat more tightly and pulled the car door shut! Cold, but still amazingly little snow! Her dad's insistence that they move to the mine was a good one; except that with the Silverton Forestry Station's seasonal shut down the end of September, Doug worked out of Dolores! Hiring Janni was proving fortuitous, and Leisel seemed to be making developmental strides under her tutelage!

Exiting the acreage, she would have been annoyed at being stuck behind a slow ore-hauler! Except that it was her ore! The mine was in production! Not big-time production-but underway! Still, when she got a chance, she zipped around and bore down on the accelerator! Her final post-surgical PT session! And she was hoping for a chance-Abby's lessons for the week would be completed, and she could stop by her little house and play the baby grand for a few minutes before she had to return home!

She smiled at her reflection in the mirror! A trip back to the surgeon in Denver next week to be released-and the Brad Maxwell calamity would finally be behind her! Well, she had a sweet baby girl out of the deal-

And she had ended up paying for Brad's burial-much to Doug's chagrin!

She turned on a Gospel CD and sang along, eager to give God the glory for giving Doug to her and caring for them in such astonishing ways! The Hamilton's paid their grazing fee right on time the first day of every month! The mine, at last, provided a positive cash flow! The more-than-generous finder's fee! Doug still balked at tithing; she wasn't sure why!

She prayed for his safety! Being aware that Hardy Johnson and his band of thugs had it in for them kept her worried~

※ ※

Trent Morrison listened to Porter's update, surprised, but then, not! It seemed that he had a bunch of guys drawing their breath and a paycheck, and doing little else! And as they realized he liked Doug Hunter for his work ethic and investigative prowess, they resented him, rather than emulating him!

"What did Bailey say when you asked him about it?"

"Just hemmed and hawed around! They think everything Hunter does is because of being so smitten by Alexandra~"

"It isn't! He was a go-getter in Iraq and Afghanistan! And at FLETC! Even about the stolen explosives~he might have liked her~but it was obvious to anyone with any objectivity~that she didn't steal her own dynamite, nor make it easily available to any criminal elements! It isn't Doug's imagination that they're after her! Keller and two others spent hours in pursuit of her a couple of years ago; and the fact that she's alive and Keller's dead, is no thanks to anyone but her! And her reward money for that seems to be hung in limbo~I guess because she's rich and cute!

"But I digress! Sunquist? Really? Was there a reward on him? Because Mallory was responsible for taking him out! Where are my cops? Maybe I need to fire some of these guys and replace them with fashion-model-looking girls!"

※ ※

Alexandra forced through the discomfort! She needed her finger back, one hundred percent! Well, fifty percent would have been worth the surgical ordeal, but any number beyond that was worth striving for! Still, the key action on the new piano was stiff! After fifteen minutes, she drew out her violin and attempted to play it! It might take a lot of time and pain~but she was going to get there!

She looked at her watch~maybe she could squeeze out time to stop and visit the Allens!

※ ※

Porter and eleven guys from Roosevelt National Forest unloaded themselves and their gear from the fifteen passenger van! He introduced them to the San Juan guys who seemed resentful of outsider reinforcements! Porter attempted to keep his disposition in check! Bailey and his guys seemed kinda chicken to conduct the manhunt, themselves; but they resented reinforcements? When did guys act like such a bunch of babies? Maybe Morrison was onto something with the girl thing! They at least acted like they needed to prove themselves! These guys were just a bunch of apathetic, sit around on their haunches, and watch the world go by, kind of mind-set men! Evidently, Buford had let things ride! Now as the new head, had he been afraid to stir the pot? If everything really rose and fell on leadership-what kind of leader was he? It's just, that since Terri-

᪥ ᪥

Alexandra entered the chow hall alone! Even with lingering in town and at the college campus, she was back ahead of Doug! Her finger throbbed! Between the grueling final therapy session and the piano and violin, she might have overdone it! She nodded at Jared and Abby, who seemed to at least be keeping things civil, and made her way to Janni and the girls!

"Well, how have they been?" Suddenly overtaken with guilt at extending her afternoon in town, she felt relief at Janni's upbeat response!

"You're amazing! I don't know how you do it!"

Janni beamed at the praise and hopped up to get Alexandra's food.

"Whoa; I can get it! For once, I don't have a broken ankle, or finger, or anything! I can wait on myself! Thanks, though!"

She was in line behind three of the miners when the door swung open-

᪥ ᪥

Profoundly discouraged, Doug returned to his pickup! The clearing was still there, in sync with GPS coordinates! And he was right! It wasn't a natural clearing! But the fake rocks were gone, as were all tire tracks and any signs that the ground there had been disturbed within the past five years! Of course *Sir Galahad* was the laughing stock-again! Well, with darkness, Porter had sent everyone home, to resume the search again at daylight! They were all mad at that-first light didn't seem to be a time they preferred! But he was inclined to agree with them that there was no

142

use! Maybe he was nuts~He didn't mind reassembling at 0500~actually a couple of hours before the winter dawn~if they could get any closer to Johnson and his band! Clever, they were making a mockery of him, and all the law enforcement guys!

﹄ ﹃

Disappointed with the search results, Trent phoned Sonia and told her he was staying downtown! Something he rarely did! Since he worked hard from the moment he arrived until time to leave, he usually called a halt at five! Not today, though! He gave several last minute orders to his receptionist and she delivered sat maps to his desk in time to depart at her normal time!

"Do you need anything else?"

"Do you mind starting me another pot of coffee? Then, there's no use in your hanging around!"

﹄ ﹃

"Do you mind being invaded by a bunch of hungry people? If we'll make you run short~"

"No," Alexandra gasped in surprise! "Come on in! It isn't fancy, but there's plenty!"

To the newcomers' amazement, she hugged each of them warmly! "It's pretty user friendly! Trays, napkins, flatware~then join Janni and me and the girls at our table!"

When they all assembled with plates brimming, Alexandra made introductions! "My cousins, Jacob and Summer Prescott; Jacob's dad, Warren Weston, the heavy equipment mechanic; Tim Alvaredo, another Geologist and friend from *Honey Grove Baptist*; and Alex and Kayla Hamilton! Meet Janni, my right hand woman!"

"How's your finger?" Kayla's concerned inquiry as they settled in.

"Wonderful! Well, tender, following my last PT session and attempts at piano playing~I want to work through the pain, without setting myself back to square one! Are you guys staying in your modular? I'm not sure~"

"It doesn't seem to be suffering too much from neglect! Summer's going to give it a once over cleaning for us! She's amazing!" Kayla's response! "The guys are here because the Forestry Service hired their excavators! And I

143

hope you don't mind, but we wanted to check on our Alpaca, and we just love it out here!"

Alexandra laughed! "Why would I mind? I would expect you'd want to make sure everything's in order!"

After eating in silence for several minutes, Alexandra's curiosity got the better of her! "How come the forestry department wants to rent your excavators?"

"Well, because our equipment's the closest available on short notice!" Jacob answered, gratified that Alexandra had introduced him as her cousin! "The top guy in the state called about it! They're looking for those militia guys, I guess! But, they might be joining with another gang- Anyway, well, Doug saw that big camper deal, but now they think there are underground roads! We'll see what we can dig up!"

Alexandra nodded vaguely! It all made her nervous! She was glad Doug was on his way home, even though he had to do a quick turn-around to be back out early in the morning! Maybe with the excavation equipment, and the extra man-power, it would all come down tomorrow! She hoped so, without any casualties among the good guys!

⚔ ⚔

Trent studied the maps until his eyes burned and he decided he couldn't glean any additional intel! He emptied what little remained in the coffee pot and called Sonia to inform her he was on the way home! He strode jauntily toward his SUV parked in its reserved space! A presence startled him as he approached his car in the gloomy structure!

"I wondered if you were going to put in an all-nighter!"

Alarm turned to perplexity as he recognized Mike Behr! "Why? Are you still checking out my work ethic? I guess tonight makes up for the day I went straight to lunch from my morning coffee break! What on earth are you doing out here waylaying people?"

"Well, I know it's late, but I've just spent several hours sparring with a she-wolf attorney! When I got rid of her, I called your house, and your wife told me you were still down here! But you were heading home! Glad I caught you!"

Tired, Trent couldn't say he echoed the sentiment! "Is this anything that can wait until next week?" For the life of him, he couldn't figure out what the Treasury guy needed him for in the middle of the night! And, when he had this incident in Colorado ongoing!

"Well, you might find this interesting now! Meet me at the Denny's in McLean! Kayla Hamilton has been suing the Maxwell estate on behalf of Alexandra Hunter's daughter!"

Trent glanced over sharply! Why Alexandra's name kept popping up on his radar, he didn't know! Aware of the erroneous gossip, that his interest might be romantic, he wasn't sure what the best response was!

"Just meet me! The quicker we stop arguing here, the quicker I can tell you what you need to know! I already told your wife I needed to meet with you and not to wait up!"

꙳ ꙳

"Doug, why don't you treat her like she's your daughter?" Alexandra understood Doug's exhaustion, coupled with frustration at their quarry's continuing to elude him! But he showed little interest in either girl! Like he had done his fathering part by sending money to his grandmother! And now Leisel's physical needs were being met-food, clothing, shelter-

He bridled, "I'm sorry, and how is that? I guess I missed out on the window of opportunity when you bond-"

"Well, maybe it isn't too late! You could at least try!"

"She lives in her own world! She's autistic or something! Maybe when we get a little more money ahead, we can have her tested! I'm really worn out-"

She nodded! She got that he had put in a long day! She had put in a long one without him! "Speaking of money ahead-the bank showed that your paycheck was direct deposited, and you withdrew it as cash-"

"Yeah, that's right!"

She stared at him when he made no attempt at an explanation! What were his plans? To let her support them while he held onto, 'his' salary? Although the mining operation covered a lot of their day to day living expenses with the housing, auto, and chow hall, they needed groceries for their personal needs: diapers, snacks, and other essentials, not provided in the chow hall!

꙳ ꙳

Trent ordered more coffee! There wasn't going to be enough night left for sleep, anyway! He leaned back into the booth, aggravated! The last thing he was going to do was bring up Alexandra Faulkner's name!

Behr grinned annoyingly, and Trent guessed that that was how the Treasury agent unnerved his tax evaders! He could play the game, too! He pulled his phone free, making a pretext of checking emails, messages, whatever people who fiddled endlessly with their phones, did!

"So, are you going back to Colorado for this one?" Behr eyed the Forestry head shrewdly!

"I'm sorry? If you think I keep taking Colorado vacations at the taxpayers' expense, I don't care! And I do my job, not subject to your supervision! I haven't decided! I know those guys are out there! And I know they aren't planning anything good! I'd like for my guys to take some initiative-well, they do-sometimes things seem endless and discouraging! Too few victories to level out the defeats!"

"You ever been to Canada?"

"Yeah, to Niagara Falls, with the family when I was a kid! I didn't use taxpayers' money then, either!" Trent was so exhausted and frustrated he was tempted to get up and leave! Steeling himself, he resisted and settled back. 'Let Behr beat around the bush until the sun came up; he'd get to his point! There must be one, or he'd probably go home and go to bed, himself!'

⊰ ⊱

"Mmm-mmm! Mommy loves you!" Alexandra savored the quiet moment of bonding with her baby! During the days, she did try with Leisel, but at this moment she could dedicate herself and lose herself in Angelique! A wide smile was followed by a definite burp and spit-up, and she dabbed gently! "Ew!"

Alexandra's thoughts wandered as she finished the feeding. Instead of being aggravated at Doug, this was an opportunity to count her blessings! In the time since Brad's return and subsequent suicide, she had focused on the passage of Scripture that had tormented him! The words with significance to her were from:

> *Romans 1:21 Because that, when they knew God, they glorified him not as God, neither were thankful; but they became vain in their imaginations, and their foolish heart was darkened.*

Neither were thankful! Looking back, she knew that was how Satan had tripped her up! Because she hadn't been thankful to God for her Christian heritage, for knowing Him as her Savior, for everything provided for her by loving and successful parents~Her ingratitude and hardness of heart had set her up for going after Brad, against their wishes, and in the worst manner! In spite of the light shining brightly all around her, she had allowed her foolish heart~to be darkened!

She smiled at the beautiful, drowsy little countenance with a love she had never known was possible! And God loved her more than she did her child! In spite of her willful disobedience~She blinked tears back! It was definitely time for Alexandra Marie Faulkner Hunter to be grateful! On purpose!

"Lord, I don't understand why Doug took his pay back out~but thank You for him! Please help him on his job! He really is my *Sir Galahad*! He rushed to my needs when I was on the bottom~Help him want to tithe! Help them to catch these criminals and don't let him be hurt! Thank you my finger's better, and I have a piano! I mean, it isn't mine, but it's in my house~Thank you for helping the Allens and the school! And thank you that the mine's finally~" she laughed softly in the silence of the hour! "Okay, Uncle! I surrender! Thank you for sending Daddy! I was so horrified! And mad! At You~for putting Your insistent voice in his heart! I really wanted You to help me any way but that! But, of course, You knew best! I know~I know~You're right! I have to meet~with Mom~I know I have to~but how~can I~face her? And the little kids? I was such~a~bad example~ I guess~You have forgiven me! And You've brought me out into a wide place~please help me~find my way~back ~home!"

⚜ ⚜

"Kayla Hamilton! I'm seizing the Maxwell assets, what few I can locate~and she lands in the big fat middle~claiming everything she can research out~for Maxwell's infant daughter! You're aware of the baby, right?"

Trent frowned. "You know, since my job is often confused with that of 'Game Warden', maybe I can cite your offense for you, 'Fishing without a license'!" He sighed, "I get confiscating and auctioning the possessions of felons! They cost the system, and consequently, the taxpayer, a lot of money! I think that money illegally earned and not reported to the IRS should especially be open to confiscation! But, also, one of our rights under the US Bill of Rights is freedom from unlawful search and seizure! My opinion, which I don't know why I'm sharing with you in the middle of the night, is that any fortunes or parts thereof, earned in honest endeavors should go to heirs and family members who are not involved in criminal enterprises! I know the Federal deficit is in the trillions! I feel like that's because our nation has become spiritually bankrupt! Spiritual bankruptcy has always preceded material ruin! God's promise to the nation of Israel was that if they honored Him and His Word on a national, as well as on personal levels, that prosperity would naturally follow! They would be lenders, and not borrowers; again, at the national and individual level! We've lost our work ethic, much of our Yankee ingenuity-but even worse, our moral compass! Although Israel was God's model to the world, He deals with all nations and people in the same manner! If you're under pressure to get the US economy flowing with black ink, I pity you!"

Behr swirled coffee grounds in the bottom of the mug. "What about Alexandra and her baby?"

Trent frowned. "What about them? Yeah, I know she has a baby! I liked Hunter, wanted him in the ranks of Forestry Law Enforcement! I was aware of his concern for getting his little girl with him! I thought his getting married would be a-I didn't mean to Alexandra Faulkner, necessarily! What's your issue, Behr? Would you be less eager to confiscate Maxwell's goods, if Alexandra wasn't what we refer to as, 'upper class'? If it was for some poor single mom without a penny to her name or a family to fall back on? I think that's what I'm running into with the reward money for her having gotten rid of Keller! Like the 'good ole boy' club would have already seen to it that funds were issued to any bounty hunter out there! But since it's a girl, and one with financial means-"

"She's got that better-than-thou air about her-"

Trent laughed. "I get that! But justice and doing right isn't based in personality and who we like-There're a few tatters of an estate earned legally-and you're trying to decide how hard to fight this civil suit-what little money there is will go to a baby that hasn't committed any crimes, and whose father will never be around to support her-what's the dilemma? The amount won't be a drop in the bucket in the US Treasury! America's wealth is her people! Care for them, and the Treasury will take care of itself! But hobble and handcuff them-and ya get what we've got!"

"Is it true that Daniel Faulkner has been putting personal pressure on you to see to it that the Forestry Service Law Enforcement Division safeguards his daughter?"

"Unequivocally not! Any more than I demand that FBI Agent, Erik Bransom, safeguard my daughters! Our jobs in law enforcement are about stopping criminal activity! When we accomplish that, our children will be safe! Sadly, crime is growing at a faster rate than we can keep up with! Faulkner wants Johnson and his cohorts behind bars! Alexandra won't be safe until they are! To every last tentacle!"

"Well, why does he leave her hanging out there?"

Trent considered his answer carefully! The last thing he wanted was to allow his exhaustion to make him respond unadvisedly!

"What are you asking me, exactly, Mike? Are you asking why he doesn't keep her inside his mansion walls? A luxurious prison, to be sure, but a prison, nonetheless! Would she be safer, probably~I'm sorry, but that's the mindset of Middle Eastern men! To keep their women locked away~and yes, protected~but~"

"Yeah, no personal freedom~"

"Exactly! The only pressure he brings to bear is for me to do my job!"

Behr laughed suddenly! "Yeah, and it's hard to find good help these days!"

⚔ ⚔

Alexandra's joy knew no bounds! Released! From both her ankle and finger injuries! Bounding to her car parked at the Durango-La Plata County airport, she headed toward the historic district of town! Dropping into one of the art galleries periodically, she kept an eye on a painting by the renowned artist, Risa Perkins! Gone! Struggling to overcome disappointment, she headed up 550 toward her mine!

'They became unthankful and their foolish heart was darkened,' she repeated softly! 'Lord, You know I can't afford the painting anyway! Thank You that it sold and that'll help Phil and Risa! Thank You for the medical release~and letting my finger work so well again~'

CHAPTER 16: RESTORATION

"What are you doing?" Alexandra paused, amazed to see Doug directing the ballroom setup for the annual Forestry Department LEI banquet!

"Unh, I asked Mr. Morrison's assistant what I can do to help! Of course, hotel staff should have things set up, but between a language barrier, and the fact that they're swamped, with every ballroom reserved~"

"I'll turn the girls over to Janni and be right back~"

⊹ ⊱

Harold Allen finished preaching a chapel session and joined Sally in the dining room to greet the couple who leased pasture land on the foothills of the campus!

Stiff with reserve, he extended right hand, first to the young man, and then to his wife! "Pleased to make your acquaintance, at last! I see you have met my wife and better half!"

David Anderson, nodded, smiling and relaxed! "Yes, Sir, we have, and she has allowed us to sample homemade bread and strawberry preserves!"

Dr. Stevens nodded, maintaining his defenses against liking, even granting approval to, the well-to-do couple! Convinced that the Bible required strict adherence to simple attire and sparse utilization of adornments, he felt that these kids were over-the top!

Sally Allen spoke up softly, but firmly! "Dr. Allen, I have invited Mr. and Mrs. Anderson to join us and the student body in partaking of the noon meal!"

He smiled benignly! Usually, she sought his approval before doing such! Knowing him as she did, she knew his ploy would have been to escort the couple to the acreage, let them see the setup for their Alpaca in person, and send them on their way!

"Mr. and Mrs. Anderson, please," He swept a hand gesture and they moved to the prepared place settings!

After saying grace, a few students stepped forward to serve! Mallory flashed a smile more dazzling than her brooch, to the young woman who placed her coffee beside her plate as she thanked her and asked for her name!

❧ ☙

Trent hung up, aggravated! So the banquet room wasn't ready! His guys were used to camping out, anyway! Amazing how you could spell out exactly what you want, to three different people~and get none of it! He stalked through the lobby to the designated rooms and paused at the threshold in wonder! Tables set with spotless white linen and blooming with fresh and colorful flowers, filled the expansive space! Everything looked amazing! Why had they told him it was a disaster? Evidently someone was too picky, not to approve of this!

Piano music filled the space, and as he stepped in, he noticed Alexandra Hunter, with her two little girls and a scattering of toys at her feet, lost in the music!

She flushed and rose hastily as soon as she saw him, trying to gather the girls and their possessions and escape gracefully!

He frowned as he noticed a hotel staffer block her exit!

❧ ☙

Dr. Allen felt a sad hopelessness at the excited response of the students to the lunch visitors! It was so false!

He roused from his gloomy thoughts to realize that David and Mallory were both chatting amiably about some new courses he was offering! After having seen Alexandra's spinning wheel and loom, and growing more familiar with the Alpaca and their silken fleece, the little college was adding hands-on textiles and clothing classes! Like really textiles: from shearing, to combing and carding, to dying, to spinning, weaving, and creating garments!

151

David laughed; "That hits a chord with Mallory! Well, first and foremost, rocks do! And then after that 'Textiles and Clothing'! Those are our main ventures! Geology and Mining, and a clothing design and manufacturing business!"

Mallory nodded animatedly! "And David's an architect and mechanical engineer, contractor, builder! He designed a skyscraper in Dallas that's finally about to open! It has a good occupancy rate, too, in advance! He had a good eye for the location, even before he designed the building!"

"And Alexandra told us that you have children?" Sally's softly asked question! Having never had a child, the subject was painful for her!

"We do! We have four!" David answered proudly, producing a family portrait on his iPad! "Amelia Erin's four and a half, Avery Estee is three, Alexis Elle is two, and Adam Essex is six months–give or take– They–uh–keep us busy and–challenged! What about y'all?"

Dr. Allen gestured around to the tables where the students ate quietly! "The children that God has granted us–"

Mallory nodded politely, knowing that the students would be encouraged to return to their homes and closed communities–but she wanted to hire every last one–

"Thank you for your time!" David rose and shook hands with the couple once more! "We stay in touch with our caretaker, so we have no need to go out there! We just wanted to meet you and thank you for making the concessions to us that you–"

Dr. Allen's eyes met his! "Life is so full of decisions and contradictions! We are against war, fighting, and weapons! And yet we enjoy our wonderful nation–because–at the expense–of–and –sacrifice– And we proudly boast of how we keep no weapons–and yet at the first hint of a threat to my wife or these precious children, I would call the county sheriff's office so that they could respond with their weapons drawn–" He broke off with a perplexed sigh!

⁌ ⁍

"What seems to be the problem?" Trent Morrison's voice behind Alexandra made her jump, and yet she was relieved for his presence!

Before she could explain, the hotel employee broke in angrily! That no one could play the hotel's instruments without membership in the musicians' union!

"I was trying to tell him I won't do it anymore! I didn't know it would create a problem! It's just, that I finished with the tables, and Doug wasn't back for us~"

Trent shrugged meaningfully at the guy, muscling between him and the object of his ire! "Okay, the lady told you she's sorry, she didn't know, she won't touch your dumb piano again! End of story; okay?"

Trent stepped another step nearer as the idiot persisted by restating his issue in a rapid-flowing, hard to understand accent, of one type or another! Maybe he didn't understand~

"Okay! She no play! No more! Finish! The end!" Trent spoke slowly and deliberately, which seemed to irritate his adversary further and make him dig his heels in deeper with his grievance.

"What's going on?"

Alexandra burst into tears at the sight of Doug! Not sure why horrifying and humiliating things had to happen in her life! Especially around Trent Morrison!

"I mean~I used to be a member~we all were~but I have no idea if~my dues~are still~" She mumbled brokenly to Doug as Trent stood there creating a physical barrier between the infuriated employee and the hapless Alexandra!

⚓ ⚓

"You look incredible, Sonia! More beautiful with every passing day!" Trent carefully knotted his tie as he addressed his wife in the gleaming mirror of the hotel bathroom!

She smiled, unconvinced! "Thanks, Babe, that's a nice thing to say!"

He had a lot on his mind, with the banquet program and awards ahead of him! But as important to him as his career~

"I'm not just trying to say nice things to you, Sonn! I'm saying what I feel! We have a son who's about ready to get married~and he hasn't been in a rush~until the last three months~we're maybe at a new stage of life~but I love where we are, and who we are! It's true what the Bible says in:

Proverbs 31:30 Favour is deceitful, and beauty is vain but a woman that feareth the LORD, she shall be praised.

"You're still incredibly lovely, but your devotion to the Lord makes you truly special! Beautiful within and without!"

He paused to frown at himself, the combination of charcoal suit and rust/charcoal striped tie! "Is it just me or do these colors make my freckles stand out worse?"

She laughed, "It's just you! You're incredibly good-looking! And it was all those adorable freckles that made me agree to our first date! I'm not just trying to say nice things to you, Trent; I mean them!"

"You haven't changed your mind? Even though Maddie's cursed with them now, too?"

"Trent Morrison! Madeleine's gorgeous! Her freckles add to her charm and style! You're hopeless!"

"Well, she never says anything to me about them, but I know she has to hate them, and hate me, too, for the gene pool!"

"I don't think she does, Trent! She opts for a sheer foundation, when she could get heavy coverage! I think she's great with how she looks! You know, when you look at her, I wish you could see more than freckles!"

"Well, I do! I'm just glad the other three aren't saddled with them!"

Laughing she propelled him toward the door of the suite! "Go to your banquet, Trent! I'll be down closer to start time!"

"Did you think we fell on our faces with Dr. and Mrs. Allen?" David regarded Mallory seriously from his place in their shared office space!

"Well, they're so reserved; they didn't know what to make of us! I wouldn't say, 'we fell on our faces', but we didn't blow them away, either!"

"He had some baseball paraphernalia; why didn't you talk baseball with him?"

"Why didn't you?" she dug back! "If I had warmed him up with my incredible baseball trivia encyclopedia of knowledge, I'm not sure Mrs. Allen would have appreciated it! She wanted to talk bread-baking and jelly-making-my mom would be a hit with her-"

"Well, you never get a second chance to make a good first impression!"

She laughed, "Would you quit worrying? They need the revenue from us more than we need their pasture! If necessary, we can buy acreage, graze our Alpaca, and give me a Geological paradise to explore!"

Seeing his alarm, she laughed! "Not any time soon! You know, truth be told, Dr. and Mrs. Allen and their student body belong to Alexandra's sphere of influence! She found them, and she adores them, and vice versa!"

⚔ ⚔

Trent checked and double-checked the sound system and the awards! The program looked short and sweet; anemic actually! No speaker lined up, because he didn't like to bore his guys with some altruistic pie-in-the-sky banquet speaker, and Federal guidelines forbade him from having preaching!

One of the workers approached him with the bill, and he read over it! "Why am I paying two hundred dollars for a piano?"

"Yes, Piano! You request!"

"No! I no request! What I request, I no get! My guy fix table cloths and flowers!"

"Yes! Yes, piano! You request! Mr. Trent Morrison! Forestry Department! Request piano! But lady-she have to have-union! Union! She have!"

"Could I speak with the manager, please? I didn't ask for a piano for this evening's event! And Mrs. Hunter wasn't practicing-with the intention of-performing! She was waiting for her husband to return to help her with her daughters, after they set the room up, themselves! So she ran her fingers-She and Mr. Hunter set all the tables! Which the hotel staff was supposed to have done! Let me guess; you are the manager!"

⚔ ⚔

Alexandra sighed hopelessly! Her bangs were too long, and her nails looked atrocious! They were barely squeezing by, and Doug had spirited another paycheck away! They were here on a shoestring, having made the grueling drive from Colorado to DC, spelling off driving between the three of them! Janni was incredible! Now, with little rest, the plan was to head straight back, another fifty hours! Over two thousand miles! Her idea! Thinking it would forward Doug's career!

"You about ready?" Doug's voice at the doorway startled her!

"Yeah, I guess as ready as I'm gonna get!" She tried not to notice how worn his suit was, and how poorly-fitting; relieved for the new ensemble

155

from her mom and the exquisite pearls from her daddy! The room phone jangled, and Doug grabbed it!

"Yeah, Doug Hunter, here!" His voice, casual and annoyed, snapped to attention! "Oh, Mr. Morrison! Yes, Sir! She's right here!" He looked puzzled as he handed the receiver off!

She cringed inwardly, "This is Alexandra!"

She listened, surprised. Mr. Morrison always brought up guilty and shameful feelings, and it wore on her that Doug's future lay in his hands! She brightened visibly as she listened to the mix-up! Forestry Service was out two hundred dollars for having the piano in the room, and the planned program was bare-bones! He was inviting her to provide pop and light-classical music for the evening!

He finished by explaining that her union dues were current, if she could present any documents showing her maiden name!

Amazingly she had the bill of sale for her rock-crusher that Kayla was suing for delivery on!

⚜ ⚜

Trent relaxed! He wasn't sure why! Must be the music! Like when the shepherd boy David's harp-playing calmed the agitated king Saul! The banquet was actually launched, the food better than average banquet fare, and Alexandra was gifted! Worried that she didn't have any music with her, she was doing a masterful job! He knew Sonia was dying to ask-who Doug was, and where Alexandra had found him! They seemed like the mismatch of the age! As far as he knew, Sonia wasn't aware of the two little girls~ And, he had managed to track the musician's union dues from the union~without needing to contact Daniel or Diana!

His mind wandered! Several of the award recipients weren't present! Strange, because the honorees were aware of their respective awards! Bob Porter was especially conspicuous by his absence! Trent knew the said agents were in DC, and none of them had contacted him with any regrets or excuses!

His gaze traveled to Hunter who sat with a few guys he must know from FLETC! Trent liked him, and figured with some seasoning, he could distinguish himself! He had worried about the low entrance-grade pay when he learned about Leisel! Now, Hunter had a wife, too, and another child! And Alexandra Faulkner seemed like a high-maintenance brat who would be the absolute worst pick as a cop's wife! He wished he had an opening for the guy to move up the ladder! Sadly, that wouldn't happen any time soon! He wondered idly if the Faulkners and Hunter had met!

His mind returned to the event with a start, suddenly aware that Sonia had asked him something! Asking her to repeat herself wasn't always the wisest, so he pushed replay, hoping he could pluck it from the air-yeah, something about Megan, their youngest daughter-

"Yeah, I think she can get it!" The topic came up as music flowed from the piano! "Maybe we should have started her earlier-I never knew she wanted to play-she might never be this good-"

Sonia eyed him narrowly, "Good save! I didn't think you were listening! For as much as she claims to want it, I can hardly get her to practice!"

He laughed, "I'll discuss it with her again!"

⚓ ⚓

Trent smiled at Sonia! He liked this song; he was enjoying all of the selections! But it was nearly time to pull the plug on the enjoyable selections and start the ceremony, absentees, or no! And he needed to be certain Alexandra got a chance to eat her meal! Her fingers rippled gracefully through an introduction; she made eye contact with Doug, and began singing in rich, trained tones:

> *Only you can make this world seem right,*
> *Only you, can make the darkness bright…*

The moment was electric as she held his gaze and sang the entire selection, finishing,

> *You're my dream come true,*
> *My one and only you-*

Everyone burst into extra-exuberant applause before the inevitable teasing began! Trent rose smoothly!

"Thank you, Alexandra! We've all greatly enjoyed the music! I think the staff has a hot plate ready for you! Did you all enjoy the concert?"

They responded with enthusiastic nods and another round of applause, and Alexandra made her way to Doug's side as her plate appeared!

157

⚔ ⚔

Agent Erik Bransom mocked himself as he entered the warmth of the downtown DC hotel lobby! Well, his evening was free! It was just that spying on people was what he did for a living, so he wouldn't have minded watching college football in his hotel room instead of doing Suzanne's bidding!

So, Alexandra, whom no one was hearing much from, had called Suzanne out of the blue early afternoon, to ask if she had a flower connection in DC! At which Suzanne readily supplied a floral wholesaler's contact information! Then, curiosity piqued at Alexandra's presence at, and arranging tables for, a Forestry Department Law Enforcement Agency Banquet, she had decided it was beyond coincidence, but serendipitous, that Erik was right there in DC where he could check it out for her!

He sighed, wondering what he was doing! He adored Suzanne, but she did have a huge propensity for gossip! If anything shocking came to light, he was pretty sure she didn't need to know~

Ah his lucky night! Or blessed, or whatever! A big screen TV in the bar was easily viewable from an oversized leather chair in the lobby!

⚔ ⚔

Alexandra disassembled the floral arrangements so the wholesaler could retrieve the blooms! Hardy species that could be reused, the woman had allowed her the use of them in exchange for leaving business cards!

Janni appeared with the girls, and Alexandra gave her the key to the vehicle so she could start loading them up! "I'll find Doug, and we'll be ready to hit the road! I don't know if Mr. Morrison realized we drove, but he told Doug not to keep being late to work! We're really gonna have to hit it! Hope we don't hit any horrible weather!"

Janni nodded anxious agreement and headed toward the parking garage!

⚔ ⚔

Trent scrawled his signature on a department check prepared by his administrative assistant! Giving her a quick thanks he sprinted off in search of Alexandra! Her piano music had rescued the weird night! Porter never had appeared and a few of the others had straggled in like they were in town to party, and dropping in at the banquet was an afterthought!

⚔ ⚔

Alexandra stood in the lobby, perplexed at what could have happened to Doug! Seeing Mr. Morrison rushing toward her, she worried! If he held Doug over for some meeting-well, they needed to get on the road!

Instead of making a dreaded announcement, he presented an envelope from his inside breast pocket! "Great job! Everything turned out great! I know several people caught you to tell you how enjoyable it was; people have been raving to me! Have a safe flight home!"

Holding the envelope, she stared after him! Okay, so he didn't know they drove! As she scanned the lobby again for Doug, a woman scurried toward her!

"Can you help me, please?"

Alexandra tried not to gape at the strangely clad and made up woman! "I'm sorry; did you say something to me? Help you with what? Are you sick?" Alarmed, she sought a tactful escape! The woman must have seen her get the check!

"Could you get a message to my parents?" She looked over her shoulder nervously!

"Unh-what kind of message? Where do they live?"

"Ontario, California; Nick and Heather Babcock! I gotta go!" She spun and dashed away!

⚔ ⚔

Doug stood tapping his foot impatiently! They needed to head home! ASAP! But Alexandra had disappeared! He tried to disguise his impatience as Mr. Morrison and his wife passed him! Morrison paused, "Are you looking for your wife! She was across the lobby on the Fifteenth street side; looked like she was waiting for you!"

Doug laughed! That was Alexandra! Beautiful, obviously a talented musician, a Geologist! But she was geographically challenged! The Fourteenth Street side was where they had come in-hours ago-and nearest the parking garage-

159

CHAPTER 17: DURESS

Daniel Faulkner sat morosely in his home office! Another thing the Bible was right on: you can't serve two masters! Or split your loyalty between two women you love! He brought up the morning text from his daughter:

Fine! &

The & sign, and tomorrow it would be an @! Symbols she cycled through to indicate she was really 'fine' as her terse texts reassured! Although Diana seemed okay with his forced silence, he knew she yearned to be included in the loop! Wearily he tried to tamp down his own annoyance! He had spent a lot of time, energy, and money-of course, Al hadn't asked him to-was basically horrified when he had appeared! He relived the time with her and Doug-and two granddaughters! Granddaughters Diana didn't know anything about! Did she suspect? You really couldn't put much over on her! But now, his concern wasn't for his daughter alone, but for another generation! Was the money coming in better? Or were they doing without basics like diapers, formula, and baby food?

Also weighing heavily was his conviction that Hardy Johnson remained in southwestern Colorado, and that his plans for Alexandra-were too awful to think about! He was so frustrated with the Forestry Law Enforcement Division's failure to apprehend Johnson, that he was considering a plan of his own! One he knew would make both Trent Morrison, and Erik Bransom, mad! Friendships aside, if law enforcement couldn't get the job done- Desperate times call for desperate measures-a good-sounding rallying cry-Maybe he just wasn't trusting God enough-

Well, no point in sitting and brooding! Why make Diana come looking for him and pique her curiosity afresh? Finding her, he kissed her passionately!

Giving his tie her usual final straightening, she tipped her head back, studying his features with longing!

He was seized with inspiration, "Why don't y'all come into the city around four? We can try this new diner that's just opened, and all go bowling~"

"Bowling?" Her expression was more of puzzlement than disdain, "Yeah, why not? Might be fun to break out of the routine~"

⇥ ⇤

Arriving home from the enjoyable outing, Daniel hurried to his office while Diana oversaw the bedtime routine! No important emails; plenty of spam! He began the annoying task of reporting it and deleting, but was interrupted when his phone signaled a text:

#&'@&'^<>*=+

Duress? Was Al in trouble? As if in desperation she had run her finger across her keys and hit, 'send'?

⇥ ⇤

Alexandra ran for the ladies' room! Not that she would be safe there! She repeated the woman's strange message to fix the names in her memory as she punched crazily at her phone keys and pressed, 'send'! She had one lucid second to feel awful for failing to keep in contact with her dad and then sending him an SOS when she was in trouble! It was all she could think of!

Not surprisingly, the softly mirrored restroom seemed devoid of weapons! Taking a deep breath, she peered into the mirror and dabbed with her powder puff! To her surprise, it was a DC police officer who entered the space! She surveyed his reflection as he paused, looking around to make sure no one was around! A badge! But not a good guy to the rescue!

"Excuse me," she began indignantly! "This is the ladies' room! Even if you can't read, there's a picture!"

He shrugged, regarding her narrowly! "My bad!" He lunged at her and she brought her knee up! Moaning in fury, he grasped at her again, to get the palm of her hand shoved into his nose! With a forceful elbow to the side of his head, she gained the lobby! To her relief, she spied Mr. Morrison at the desk! She sprinted toward him as her bleeding adversary plunged after her!

⚔ ⚔

Bob Porter vomited, physically ill at his failure! Blaming Terri, in this instance, simply didn't assuage his guilt! What had he done? Although it had happened fast, he had been willing enough! He had sons that he warned against this kind of thing!

> *Proverbs 7:25&26 Let not thine heart decline to her ways, go not astray in her paths.*
>
> *For she hath cast down many wounded: yea, many strong men have been slain by her.*

⚔ ⚔

Ward Atcheson spoke calmly to the distraught Daniel! "She isn't here! The mining engineer said she and her husband and the au pair drove to DC for a big Forestry shindig! If she's in trouble, we're too far away to offer any help! I still know a few Washington-types~I can make some inquiries~"

The former army lieutenant disconnected, confused by the latest revelation that didn't sync with his carefully gathered intel! Of course, it wasn't unreasonable to assume that Johnson and his anti-government cronies would have boots on the ground in the nation's capital, too! That way, they could be in the immediate loop of pending legislation to oppose and use as their rallying cry!

⚔ ⚔

Trent mentally berated himself for not assessing Alexandra's peril quicker than he did! As it was, the DC policeman, with weapon drawn, got the drop on him!

Each man eyed the other with disdained recognition! "Back away, Sir!" Officer Kittrick growled at him warningly! "This woman is under arrest!" Dabbing gingerly at his nose as he spoke, he caught Alexandra by the elbow, playing to a gathering crowd! "Kind of a wildcat! Resisting arrest~" He shook handcuffs gleefully!

"You have no idea~" Alexandra gritted out the words! Then, more loudly, "Why did you storm the ladies' room? I was just fixing my makeup! When did that become grounds for arrest? What crime have I committed? I've been attending a banquet, it's over, and I'm ready to go home! Except you didn't like that woman talking to me! The one who got scared and ran away~I haven't done anything~" Her appeal directly to the growing knot of curious onlookers!

Her fear heightened as she caught sight of Doug! She needed his help, but she didn't want him hurt! She was relieved when he blended with the crowd!

⊰ ⊱

Erik sat tight, awaiting FBI reinforcements he had requested a few a moments prior to the developing situation! Amazing, how private sleuthing at the behest of his wife, was providing new insights into his ongoing investigation! From his vantage point, he had managed to see a great deal more than college football! 'Professional Girls' brought into the busy hotel, obviously under the control of three definite crime syndicate members, and abetted by a 'cop' on the take and a couple of hotel employees! He watched, unflinching, as the dirty cop held Trent Morrison at bay with a service revolver, while threatening Alexandra Faulkner with a pair of cuffs! Noticing Doug Hunter in the crowd of onlookers, easing forward casually to rescue Alexandra, he decided he'd better move; backup in position, or not!

⊰ ⊱

Daniel pushed Bransom and Morrison's speed dial buttons alternately, aggravated when neither man responded! No telling where Erik Bransom was, but Trent, doubtless was at the same big DC Forestry function where Al reportedly was! He couldn't imagine the nature of the problem in DC, and had no way of knowing if Alexandra was alone under duress, or if Angelique and Leisel were in danger as well!

And this skyrocketing alarm when he wasn't at liberty to share his concerns with Diana! If Al made it-through-whatever this current crisis was-he needed to tell her keeping stuff from Mom was too stressful for him to stand! He berated himself for being a baby and called the Washington DC police department!

Cracking his office door slightly, he listened and peered around the darkened hallway! No lights or sounds, at all! Could it be? That they were all in the media room, engrossed in a movie! Seemed that his disciplined wife might have deferred bedtime to keep the fun evening from ending! That would explain the silence, and give him a chance once again, to slip this past Diana-As long as-there was-a good outcome!

"Lord, this is so frustrating! Knowing something is seriously wrong, but in the dark about what exactly! And if it's getting worse-or improving-Father, You know! You can see all! Please give wisdom to Alexandra and Doug-and confuse the thinking-"

Breaking off, he called Atcheson back to ask for the name of the DC hotel!

⚐ ⚑

Trent steeled himself as his adversary backed cautiously, forcing Alexandra toward the exit! Carson Kittrick! Trent recognized both the man and his name tag from an unpleasant ordeal more than a year previously! Obviously Kittrick remembered, too! Trent was determined not to let him take Alexandra into 'police custody'! That was a joke! Whatever his plan was-that wasn't it! Nothing that noble and above-board! He considered the possibility of also trying to play to the tense on-lookers, but abandoned the idea! Even people who were 'Civics Majors' had never heard of his law enforcement position! No one would take his side above a uniformed, city police officer; the last thing he wanted was to start a turkey shoot in the crowded lobby!

⚐ ⚑

Bob exited his room, making sure the lock clicked! Hungry, his hope was that the banquet would be over and that the lobby would be empty of guys he knew! His plan was to call Trent in the morning, and tell him he'd been hit with a sudden stomach bug! For that reason, he didn't want a room service meal charged to his room! He needed to cover his bases and make his story convincing! No one needed to know about his weak succumbing to temptation!

⚰ ⚱

Schemes for extricating herself from Kittrick's pinchers paraded in orderly fashion through Alexandra's mind, to be discarded as foolhardy, endangering herself, Doug, or Mr. Morrison! But time was running out, and if he succeeded in getting her out onto the darkened city street-She couldn't let that happen!

⚰ ⚱

Kittrick licked his lips nervously! Time was of the essence, and the shocked bystanders wouldn't stand idly by forever! Time to make a bold move while keeping the crowd on his side!

"This woman is wanted on several kidnapping charges! Her real name is Brandi Wainscot, and I'm taking her in!"

"You should call for backup!" A jeer from the crowd, "As desperate a criminal as she is, and as many licks as she's gotten in on you already, you're taking a big chance trying to take her in alone! She probably has a couple of accomplices!"

Doug's tactic was a stall for time, and he was pretty sure Kittrick wouldn't dare try to muster backup from DC cops not on the take!

"Thanks for the suggestion, Buddy!" Kittricks' visage, enraged! "But I got this! Come on, let's go-" He jerked on Alexandra with his left hand, pistol still trained on Morrison!

"What? You're not going to read me my rights?" Alexandra made sure her objection carried! A legitimate arrest would include a suspect's being read their Miranda rights! Surely this group of stunned people would wake up-

⚰ ⚱

Erik Bransom's gaze scanned carefully around his position! On the third floor overlooking the drama in the lobby, he had a shot! It was just that he preferred not to take it if he could avoid it! A pistol shot from this range

165

was doable~just not totally advisable! He straightened and smiled at a couple passing by from their room to the atrium elevator before receiving a comm! 'Everyone was in place~'

Erik spoke softly, "Okay, before we're a go; Morrison's kids have been located and they're en route to a safe house; And Janni Anderson with the Hunter's two babies?"

"Yeah, and some arrests made already, in the grab!" Jed Dawson's reassuring voice! He spoke into the headset, issuing the order~

CHAPTER 18: STRUGGLE

Doug stared after Alexandra as FBI agents hustled her toward a bureau SUV for transport to a safe house! No invitation for him to accompany her! Gathering his wits, he made eye contact with Morrison!

It didn't take Trent long to spring into action, relieved to learn that the FBI had already secured his kids and were escorting Sonia to join them! With the safety of his family relatively secure, he moved into action!

"Hunter, you're on me!"

Doug fell in a couple of paces behind Trent, who demanded entrance to the ball room where Kittrick and several other suspects were being assembled for transport to FBI headquarters!

"Morrison, we got this one!" Dawson's voice held an edge that didn't suggest inter-agency cooperation!

Kittrick mocked from his place! "Special Agent Morrison, I guess we recognized each other from that evening at the Chelsea Club! It's always been amazing to me, how you were the last person to see Undersecretary Coakley alive, after which you and your family hurriedly fled the country, and yet you've never been questioned in regards to his demise!"

Trent shrugged, grinning! "I guess his suicide was pretty cut and dried! Although, had anyone questioned me, I would have told them he didn't seem depressed! I guess I missed some signs, someplace! I wouldn't make a good mental health clinician, I guess! I mean, I took the required psych classes, but-He seemed fine to me! Filled with evil intentions that didn't seem to include taking his own life! Well, I guess life's full of surprises~"

Surprisingly, Dawson stepped aside! If Morrison's presence could gig his bad guys into talking, why exclude him? He regarded the dishonest law officer with fresh contempt, suddenly interested in the incident he had brought up! It was Officer Kittrick whom Morrison considered a threat to his daughters! Dawson considered: evidently Kittrick's duties for the syndicate went beyond working 'hotel security' when the women were in play! Evidently, he also fulfilled duties in the kidnapping arena~targeting Madeleine and Megan Morrison! No wonder Trent wasn't willing to head back up to his forests just yet!

Erik Bransom shoved his way into the space, propelling another suspect forward! Although there would be plenty of hotel security footage to support the arrests, his observation post had provided him with plenty of intel! He still gloated inwardly about the professional results from his personal snooping mission! He owed Suzanne! Big time!

César Cantelli blew a kissing gesture toward Trent, "You should thank me, Special Agent Morrison~" some kind of accent that struck a phony note~ "That I provide for your agents coming from the backwoods~"

"My agents have families, for the most part; and they're not so far removed from civilization~" Trent paused, biting off his words in fury as reality struck him with brutal force!

᛬ ᛭

Alexandra complied with instructions issued by FBI Special Agent Caroline Hillman! She surrendered her phone and pistol, wishing Doug had been allowed to accompany her! Leisel screamed at the top of her lungs, and Janni looked ready to drop!

"Why did they have to take our phones?" Janni's frustrated whisper. "I want to talk to my dad!"

"Yeah, but I guess they figure our phones can be tracked! They know what's best, and they notified our families that we're okay! Look, you've wrangled the girls for hours! Why don't you get some rest? Things'll look brighter in the morning!"

"Doug looked like he wanted to come! Why didn't they let him?"

Alexandra laughed softly. "He looked guilty, like he should want to come! I'm pretty sure he's where he'd rather be! Solving crimes and getting to the bottom of all of this! He doesn't know what to do with Leisel, either! I've got it! Go! Shower! And go to bed!"

᛬ ᛭

Daniel turned off the lamp in his study, nearly limp with relief at Erik's assurances! Alexandra and her children were secured in a safe house with FBI agents, for the time being! Forcing aside the panic of the past couple of hours, he plastered on his highest-wattage smile for his family emerging from the media room!

"Well, how was the movie? Let's make ice cream sundaes and you can tell me all about it!"

※ ※

Trent Morrison involved himself with a criminal roundup of his own!

"Quite frankly, our morals are none of your business!" Bailey, filled with wrath at the inquisition! "We're grown men, and personally, I weary of your constant piety!"

Another guy nodded agreement with Bailey, although most of the others sat dejectedly, heads down, studying the op-art circle pattern on the carpet!

"Surely you don't feel like it's your business to inform our wives~You-you've lost perspective!"

Trent didn't respond, allowing the guys to vent! Let 'em stew a bit~and spew a bit! Something of interest would doubtless come to light as they incriminated themselves further!

※ ※

Bob Porter signed the meal to his room and left the steak, practically untouched! Maybe he really was coming down with a stomach bug! His phone buzzed, and he stared at simultaneous callers! Terri, and his boss!

He answered his wife's call first, "Hey, Babe! Trent's calling! Get back to you!"

"Hey, Trent! How'd the banquet go? Sorry for my absence! I shoulda called, but~"

※ ※

Agent Hillman paced! She'd worked scads of safe-house details before! But this one was on her last nerve! That kid's screaming could surely be heard from three counties away! An army could be advancing on their position, and she wouldn't hear it! She was pretty sure the agency manual didn't cover operations with this dynamic! Sometimes she worried about her biological clock ticking, and if her FBI career could ultimately satisfy her! At the moment, she felt like it could! 'Heaven have mercy!'

※ ※

"We're in the Lincoln Ballroom! We're waiting on you! What I have to say isn't going to make you feel any better!"

Bob disconnected, following signs for the indicated ball room! He couldn't figure out why Trent acted so ticked about his missing the banquet! It wasn't like he called in sick very often! And for a banquet-was really no big deal-

※ ※

Alexandra felt genuine empathy for her unhappy child! The toddler seemed finally to be adjusting to her new life, and the new reality-to be uprooted and endure the endless drive from Colorado to DC! And then-the craziest day of her life-ever-Alexandra could think of a few things that might bring relief! A pack-n-play! Leisel was happier when she felt caged in and secure! Chocolate milk! Her favorite, thanks to Grandpa! Even violin music! She controlled frustrated tears! You didn't exactly hand a bunch of FBI agents a shopping list! Especially one that would pinpoint who they were safeguarding! She recalled a long-forgotten afternoon in a panic room in David and Mallory's Arkansas ranch house! Also not equipped for babies-Not sure where that memory sprang from, but it suddenly made her miss her mother!

Tears flooded her cheeks! How she wished she could be the kind of mom her mother was-she might as well face it; she was Leisel's mom now, as well as Angelique's! She loved Doug, and they needed to be a family!

"Come here, and let Mommy hold you! I know you miss Daddy! So do I; but-uh-he still had some work-"

※ ※

The muscles in Trent Morrison's jaw rippled as he regarded eight of his agents with genuine regret! Bob Porter, he felt the most profound sorrow for-

"Okay, if you ask me, you're really overplaying this one!" Another unsought opinion in the uneasy silence!

Trent figured his silence would elicit reaction! He was seasoned at his job! He stood, leaning casually across a lectern, one hand thrust into trouser pockets!

At last, he moved, ever so slightly! "Hunter, close the door, please!"

Sullen faces; curious, angry, nervous, looked up, searching the boss's features!

"Just tell us you aren't going to tell our wives!" An agent named Johnson spoke softly from the back of the group!

"He better not! That's not his job!" Another gritted!

Porter wished they'd all shut up! They didn't know how Trent could be as well as he did! His stomach did cartwheels, and he fought down a mouthful of bitter stuff!

Hunter's pacing the back of the ballroom like a bailiff was unsettling, too! Of course, he wasn't on the hot seat! His wife had come with him!

"Gentlemen!" The address spoken in a barely audible and controlled voice! "You're in this meeting because allegedly, you have broken a District of Columbia ordinance!"

Bob felt himself blanch! The morality of his actions had eaten him since he had succumbed! But the legality had never entered his mind! Trent had them! Every man-sworn to uphold the law-was guilty of willfully violating one-

"Shouldn't be a crime! Most places in Nevada, it isn't!" A guy named Cloyce Blanchard, more brazen than smart, represented the Southwestern Division which included Nevada! "If it's a crime, it's victimless!"

Trent struggled for control! These agents hadn't just witnessed his being held at gunpoint while thugs tried to isolate Alexandra-had no clue about his constant mental anguish, knowing his lovely daughters were on their wicked radar- Victimless? Surely these guys couldn't be clueless enough to think the women enjoyed their lewd companionship -that they did what they did-willingly and eagerly, because the money coming in was theirs to spend-

Bob eyed his friend and superior warily! Smoldering brown eyes and the ripple of jaw muscles indicated barely suppressed fury! Porter couldn't really say, in fairness, that the guys' general response was making the situation worse! But it wasn't helping anything! This was just bad!

Trent spoke softly: "This isn't Nevada; this is the District of Columbia, and you're suspected of having committed a misdemeanor! Hotel cameras don't lie; I'm asking for resignations! Criminal proceedings will be determined by the DA for the District, and whatever actions the Forestry Service legal department decides upon! Surrender shields and weapons to Special Agent Hunter!"

"Okay, this is out of hand!" Bailey's desperate voice rose sharply! "Can't you just give us a warning? A week without pay; or something less drastic? You're trying to force your belief system down our throats!"

"A warning?" Trent's tone still soft and controlled! "What are you? A bunch of school kids? I need agents who are grown men! This has nothing to do with my belief system being foisted off on you! Have you, or have you not, taken an oath to uphold the law? You may try to blame me for your lapse in judgment! But the blame remains with each of you!"

"Man, what are our wives gonna say?"

"Probably-a lot! Maybe you should hope you get locked up for the ninety days! Protective custody! You guys may be a lot safer that way! And, I hate to seem callus, but you guys are the ones who risked your marital relationships-"

He broke off as Dawson entered with a contingency of FBI agents!

☈ ☊

Daniel hit the swinging doors into the kitchen, jumping in alarm when Diana let out a startled screech!

"Sorry, Honey! I didn't know you were-" He broke off! "What are you doing in here in the dark, anyway?"

"It isn't dark," she parlayed, backing away from him!

"It almost is, and you'd have the lights turned on if you weren't being sneaky!" He advanced, eyes alight, enjoying her plight! "What were you eating?"

Cornered, she thrust a small tin at him-a small, empty tin!

"Caviar! Quite the coping mechanism you've devised!" He laughed, "Good thing I caught you before your addiction got out of control!"

"I can handle it-"

"Di, that's what all the addicts say! Come on; show me where you keep your stash!"

Catching her, he pulled her against him. "Come on; share and I'll help you hide your guilty secret! Whoa, this is the good stuff! You don't mess around, do you?"

"Well, this catalog came, and-"

"Mmmm-hmmmm, and they promised delivery in plain brown paper?" His lips crushed hers and his eyes sparkled with mischief!

"Know what?" he asked.

"What?"

"You're the most gorgeous Caviar addict I've ever been married to!" He released her and sank down on a bar stool. "Come on; crack out another one! You know you want more, too!"

⊰ ⊱

Alexandra studied her reflection somberly! Adorable new outfit-ruined-by blood stains from her assault on Officer Kittrick! And she really liked it! Her first new outfit in more than a year! Plus, possibly the most adorable things her mom had ever designed for her! She tried not to worry about a parting jibe from the corrupt policeman! That he was HIV positive! She couldn't be certain in the melee, that his blood hadn't touched injuries she had sustained! And maybe it wasn't true, and he just wanted her spooked! With both babies asleep, she was tempted to shower! No telling if one them would awaken the moment she started! She should wait for Janni to appear!

"Good morning, Agent Hillman," she greeted meekly in response to a tap on the doorframe!

"Sorry, when they've barely gotten to sleep, but we just got orders to move-"

Alexandra nodded as she moved toward Angelique and the few possessions she had with her! Loading her first would be-she smiled at Janni, who appeared none too happy-

"Okay, you load her and this stuff! I'll get Leisel! Usually when she's so exhausted, she stays asleep-"

Four hours later the convoy split up, and the SUV carrying Alexandra, Janni, the babies, and Caroline Hillman pulled into a garage on a suburban street! The ignition turned off as the door descended!

"Okay, all of the blinds and curtains are closed," The Agent's voice intoned mechanically! "Leave them as they are and stay away from doors and windows!"

With that, she unlocked the door to the house, stepping into the kitchen with pistol drawn~

"With the all clear, Alexandra and Janni unfastened car seats and carried the babies into the new location! A silent inward cheer, as Alexandra took note of a high chair, and beyond, to cribs and pack n play with toys similar to those Leisel liked!

"Thank you for doing this!" Alexandra fought tears of relief as she addressed Hillman.

"No need to thank me! This is my job! I like it!"

Alexandra nodded meekly, but persisted, "Well, thank you for doing your job! I'm thankful for good people in law enforcement! I feel like I'm such a pain, and I've cost the tax payers a lot of money recently!"

Hillman paused to consider! "It's the criminals that cost taxpayers money! Look at all the costs nationally of all the different law enforcement agencies at all the levels, the industries and labs, the legal system, the penal system! All the fraud, theft, what have you, gets passed along to consumers and tax payers! This safe house detail isn't of your asking! You're more inconvenienced by it than anyone!" She paused as Janni brewed a cup of coffee! "I'll have that one! Then make one for your boss! Don't try to contact anyone!"

Alexandra made sympathetic eye contact with her friend, "Just be patient, Janni! Anything we do that's uncooperative will simply draw this out longer~"

⚖

Trent's gaze traveled to hazy gray clouds that threatened to drop a foot of snow! Nearly four o'clock, and he had spent the day dealing with legal issues regarding releasing the agents and doing the groundwork for prosecution! He rubbed his forehead! A roller coaster twenty-four hours! His cell phone buzzed again, and once more, he declined the call! He had nothing further to say to Bob Porter! Never one to knock off early, he made an exception! He had worked through the night!

The house looked quiet and empty and he wondered idly how long the Feds would prevent contact with his family! Thankfully, following an unnerving experience with officer Kittrick the previous year, Trent had alerted Erik to the DC cop's questionable actions!

His mind traveled to the baking Egyptian shoreline along the Red Sea-where he and Sonia had fled with their kids after his upsetting encounter with Undersecretary Ted Coakley! Not that he and Sonia could have afforded to flee across the street! He smiled to himself, then sobered quickly, as he recalled Coakley's threat in the Chelsea Club, followed by a meaningful nod to the policeman working the club's security! And then, as he and Sonia had raced to get their family gathered together, the diving trip to the Red Sea had come together for them as miraculously as the waters had parted there, centuries before!

The lovely home was eerie in its silence! Moving to his study, he deposited his brief case on his desk before removing his top coat and slinging it across a chair! He should be relieved to be home ahead of the storm-but now the evening stretched, lonely and gloomy before him! He considered turning on the fireplace, instead turning on ESPN! No one around to fight him for the remote! Hmmm! Might not be all bad! He decided to phone Donovan Cline, too! Memories of the diving trip left him suddenly curious about Cline's continuing exploration!

First, he needed to check on something! Mounting the stairs, he fought off the feeling of uneasiness that assailed him! In the bathroom shared by his girls, he began rummaging around, suddenly curious if Maddie really did use a sheer foundation because she wanted her freckles to show! He wasn't sure why, but his assumption had always been that she hated hers as much as he did his!

Mystified, he considered giving up! 'Foundation'! Was that the term Sonia had used? What in the world did they use all this stuff for? Intent on his mission, he forgot his strange sensations of dread!

"Caught you! Reach for the sky!"

⚔ ⚔

Doug dropped his gear into the living room of Alexandra's little Durango home! Every inch of the space attested to her charm and grace! He turned on the TV and fireplace and pulled burger and fries from a bag! Trying to shove aside troubling thoughts of his failure to rescue her, he surfed channels! What a relief that the FBI just happened to be on site with their ongoing investigation! He punched the power button off! Strange coincidences! And of all the people in the lobby who seemed like they might be sympathetic and helpful-why had the woman cherry picked Alexandra? He frowned contemplatively! Not a random choice, obviously! And although the FBI sought the woman, she had yet to be apprehended!

Pulling out a notebook he kept handy, he scrawled a couple of names! Hardy Johnson, of course, was after her! And after him too, for that matter! And the anti-government group very possibly could sprawl all the way to Washington DC! Remembering the grueling miles he and Alexandra had covered to reach the nation's capital, he had serious questions! Possible! But the most likely?

He turned his attention to the other name: Stephen Delane Maxwell! Incidents clanged into place in his mind! Maxwell was the monster behind it! After fighting Alexandra desperately for total control of his grandson, he had lost! Well, in his own mind, anyway! Alexandra had come away far from being a clear winner! But for her even to dare to rival him for Brad's attention and affection~insufferable~Although now also deceased, could he have set things in motion~

Idly, he doodled around the names, then sat up straighter as a thought occurred to him! In his absent mindedness, he had circled both names together! Was there a link between the two felons? Did his subconscious mind think so? That there was a link between the two organizations? Cooperation, anyway, to accomplish a mutual objective?

Maxwell had to have been madder than a hornet, that Alexandra had not only survived Brad's attack on her, but had borne Angelique! And now, thanks to Kayla Hamilton's efforts on Angelique's behalf~to sue for what remained of the estate~his ire must have known no bounds!

⚏ ⚏

Trent recoiled instinctively from the sudden jab and puzzled voice, "What are you doing, Daddy?"

Caught, he stammered, searching desperately for a plausible excuse!

"Well, I left the city early because of the forecast, and I decided to come up and see what you might be running low on~to take you shopping"!

Her screech of delight made him jump again! Evidently, his nerves weren't as steeled as they used to be!

"Oh, thank you, Daddy! You're the greatest daddy ever!"

Freeing himself from her exuberant embrace, he studied her carefully! Gorgeous beyond words, freckles and all! And 'they' wanted her!

"The FBI thought you'd be okay, now~"

"Yeah, I guess; can we go to the mall before it starts snowing any harder?"

"Well, let's put that one on hold! I have a better idea!"

CHAPTER 19: REFLECTIONS

Alexandra put pen to paper! She couldn't avoid the inevitable meeting with, and apology to, her family members, forever! She needed to make a plan for rapprochement! Doug's new fascination with her dad made him eager for her to make her move! She jotted some thoughts:

1. After the holidays! Too much to do before!
2. Increased production from the mine!
3. Her hand to be totally healed! Overdoing the piano and then the fisticuffs with Officer Kittrick had set her progress back!
4. Leisel's behavior to improve!

She glanced up to listen to an agent's announcement!

"Time to return home!"

The news was so unexpected that she reeled mentally! Did that mean that everyone was dead or arrested who had sought her harm? Or fading media interest and budget constraints decreased her importance? She went in search of Janni!

"Anderson is being escorted to her home," Hillman's abrupt announcement! "We're taking you and your two children; everything else will be sanitized! Hurry! Flight leaves in forty minutes!"

⚞ ⚟

Trent relaxed on the deck of Donovan Cline's dive boat as it rocked gently in the Gulf of Agaba! GPS coordinates assured that they were in Egyptian waters! Trent considered bemusedly, remembering David and Mallory

Andersons' seizure by Saudi dissidents, from a nearby spot! Of course, there were no guarantees that dissidents regarded the accepted boundary line! And, there was always the possibility of equally demented Egyptians! Amazing!

He rose courteously as Sonia joined him, carrying two glasses of tepid tea! The local beverage of choice!

"Did you finish your emails?" He planted a peck on her lips as he reached for the glass!

"I did, but then, when I checked, I have a whole slew of new ones~"

"Well, don't worry about me! I'm doing some mental exercises~" he laughed! "A lot on my mind about my former agents and their recent escapades! Please, carry on your business as usual! I love what you bring to my table!"

She paused, doing a double-take!

He laughed, "Yeah, call me dumb, and slow to figure things out; or admit them~when I figure them out~I mean, even when Mike Behr, of all people, told me you're legit~Sonia, I apologize!"

Tears sparkled suddenly on mascaraed lashes, making her more enchantingly beautiful than ever in the soft, marine twilight-scape!

⊰ ⊱

Disconnecting from another call with Doug, Trent took mental notes of the past several days! He recalled feeling helpless to promote the promising, but impoverished, Agent Hunter the previous week! Although he was solid and talented, there was no way in the world to advance the kid through a system fraught with seniority and other impediments! He whistled softly as stars brightened, reflected in limpid ripples!

Softly, he whistled a song that always brought him encouragement, *God Can Make A Way*!

⊰ ⊱

Erik Bransom listened to briefings, thinking it a wonder that Alexandra and her babies, and Morrison's family, had survived in spite of the protective details, more than because of them! Due to some confused communications, Trent's family got dropped back on their doorstep in less than twenty-four hours! Blessedly, he was home when they showed up, and with the wisdom to once more take them and leave the country!

Alexandra-he sighed! Kittrick's gloating about being HIV Positive was true! Part of his motivation for going to the dark side, was that they funded his expensive meds! And yet, not aware of the danger, Hillman had transported her charges from one safe-house to another, not cognizant that danger lay in the bloody clothing Alexandra was stuck wearing throughout the entire ordeal!

He was still mystified that clothing hadn't been provided for her! The answer from Hillman was that she hated to stick the elegant young woman is some plain-jane looking thing from a discount store! Hardly a good excuse, but the haughty Alexandra could be intimidating! Although, Hillman had expressed to him her relief at the grateful response and cooperation Alexandra had exhibited! He jotted a memo, 'Agents needed to take the upper hand, intimidated by their charges, or not!'

⚔ ⚔

Up early, Doug caught a regional jet from Durango to Golden! With Agent Porter's, 'resignation', following so closely on the heels of Buford's, the division was in chaos! Not that the remaining agents appreciated Doug's efforts!

He drove slowly past the blast site en route to the new temporary headquarters, reminded that dynamite pilfered from Alexandra's silver mine had caused the damage! Sad, but a smile played at the corner of his lips as he considered the fate of the problematic bear and her two offspring! Trent Morrison was a man he respected, both as a leader, and a Christian man! A man, obviously, of prayer! He paused in the parking lot to ask for God's wisdom and favor!

Interrupted by his phone, he frowned as Bob Addington's number popped up on his caller ID! Barely acquainted with the Southeastern Division Head, he answered with some trepidation!

"Good morning, Agent Addington; what can I do for you?"

A pleasant laugh from the Atlanta office preceded the answer! "Well, I'm hoping it's what I can do for you! Crazy week; hunh? Trent's on a mission, too! So, I won't be surprised if more heads roll! I guess that's a heads-up to hire anyone mobile who walks through your door! I kinda feel for these guys; especially since I was among the most moronic of the bunch, at one time! I've been spending an amazing morning, considering the way

God got my attention! Man, Morrison made me so mad! Before I caved-Well, I digress! Don't wanna keep you when you have such a plateful-but seriously, anything I can do to help-"

Doug disconnected, comforted by the fact that the entire Law Enforcement Division didn't resent him! Curious as to the details of Addington's story, he made a mental note to find out, once things calmed down!

⚏ ⚎

Trent sat on a café terrace on the Marbat Waterfront Promenade in Dahab, Egypt, overlooking the Red Sea! The shopkeeper, in broken English, asked how he liked the coffee!

"Like the end of the day, in my office!" He smiled at the puzzled local, "Very good! Delicious!" Downing the thick and bitter brew, he signaled a refill!

Not sure how exorbitant overseas charges might bill to his electronics, he forewent using his Bible ap and pulled out a New Testament! He located a verse in *Luke 19* that utilized an expression that had run through his mind since the night of the banquet and throughout the intervening days:

V22b ...out of thine own mouth will I judge thee...

Caught in the traps of their own actions, the guys had voiced nearly identical excuses to the arresting agents: to the effect that, a banquet hosted by Trent would restrict their alcohol consumption! Consequently, they had felt the need to hit the watering hole early! Then their imbibing caused their judgment to lapse when they got hustled! He scoffed at how it boiled down to, 'everything was all his fault'!

They were right! Alcohol abuse among them was rampant! And with that in mind, he had begun some investigating! It didn't take an advanced degree in snooping, as they seemed to enjoy putting nooses around their own necks, via Facebook!

Federal law for his agents mirrored that of most law enforcement agencies; that officers couldn't drink within eight hours of reporting for their shifts!

A birthday party video where a wife warned her husband not to open another beer because it was midnight, showed him mockingly toasting Trent at 12:05 AM!

He sighed! Not only did they drink too much, but evidently they were morons, as well!

But in an attempt to justify their legal violation with the call girls, they pinpointed the heart of the problem! *Out of thine own mouth will I judge thee*! They drank too much!

The whole nation seemed to be falling under the definition of a drunkard nation! Absenteeism, mistakes, hangovers! It had to be a contributing factor as to why America was losing her prominence in world markets! People everywhere! Less sharp than they could be, than they should be! Personal excellence was foreign to the majority! The reason they laughed at him; criticized newcomer, Doug Hunter-It wasn't just a Christian oddity! It made sense, in a competitive world, not to go around half-snockered!

His mind traveled back to his one experience with juvenile drinking! He smiled, remembering sneaking in late-to be met by his infuriated father! He could still remember his backside being 'lit up' for days! But that wasn't the extent of it! He lost driving privileges for six weeks and researched and wrote a twenty-five page paper on the evils of alcohol! He turned himself in at the small town police station for underage drinking, which opened the investigation of who bought, who possessed fake ID's, and other things that had forever burned his relationships with his 'buddies'! Then, he had gone forward and asked the church to forgive him, and picked up every scrap of litter in Johnson County for an entire summer! 'Yep! His dad was big on 'overkill'!

Amazing how your gratitude for your parents grew as you got older!

His heart swelled with pride as Sonia and his kids joined him, laden with packages! Did he have money for an overseas vacation for six; and shopping, too? Not with pen and paper, and yet, somehow-

He forced his worries away, "So, show me what treasures you found!"

Michael's eyes twinkled with mischief! "No salt and pepper shakers that look like 'Elk'!

"Watch your language, Son," he intoned warningly!

"I said, 'Elk'!

"Not what it sounded like to me-"

They all laughed at the family memory, bringing typical stares from locals! 'Loud Americans!'

Alexandra had known happier days! Delivered home to her mine, she assumed she was to stay within its perimeters, due to its security measures! And she wasn't certain but that she might have lost Janni, who seemed to have struggled with the ordeal of being shuttled from safe house to safe house by FBI Agents! Maybe Pastor Anderson wouldn't let her come back!

And the mine! Jared must be a total imbecile! Hauling ore (with the reprieve of little snowfall to date) that was totally devoid of silver! Well, hauling rocks! That he assumed contained silver! Doing a slow count, she reminded herself that his field was mining; hers, the Geology! Now, she needed to figure out why the vein had played out! Where others were, and if a fault and slippage might be the problem! None of which she could accomplish, with two little girls to tend to! Doug was in Golden for some reason he seemed to enjoy the mystery of not sharing with her–until Friday afternoon! Still, she had penciled in a deadline for meeting with her family!

Mixing a bottle for Angelique, she buckled both girls into the stroller for the little jaunt down to the chow hall! At some point, she needed to get to a lab and be tested for HIV! Nearly overwhelming to think about, but think about it she must!

And, she assumed she was still being pursued by criminal elements! Both those associated with Stephen Maxwell, and by association, the late Undersecretary Coakley! And close to home here, Hardy Johnson! Aside from that, life was great!

"Welcome home, Miss Alexandra!" Maxine scurried from the kitchen to greet her and fix a plate for Leisel!

"Thank you! It's great to be home! How have all the miners been treating you?"

"Well, since the way to men's hearts is through their stomachs, they all love me and treat me great! Long as there's plenty and it's hot!"

To Alexandra's amazement, Leisel folded her hands and bowed her head expectantly! Maybe she was learning! Maybe the familiarity of being back– She prayed, rewarding her with a glowing smile!

"Good girl, Leisel, to wait until we pray! Daddy'll be happy about that–"

At the word, 'Daddy', the toddler whirled toward the entrance expectantly, further astounding Alexandra! "I'm sorry, Baby! Daddy isn't here! But, when he comes, he'll be really happy that you obey–"

She nodded and mumbled a bunch of unintelligible stuff!

⚔ ⚔

Trent floated easily along next to Sonia, on the heels of Michael and Matt! The Red Sea was a premiere dive site! Michael employed a metal detector, certain he could find an elusive artifact in the few short days they would be here! Still, no harm in joyous hope and anticipation! And the beauty of colorful fish and coral was bound to soften disappointment if he failed to make a discovery!

Keeping an eye on time and air supply, he was ready to give the signal to surface, when apparently the metal detector beeped and Matt veered aside! Signaling Sonia and Michael to ascend, he joined his second born, who decreased visibility in the pristine water with his swishing of sediment! Still, handsome features behind the mask exhibited pure joy as he grasped the object of his quest! With a brisk wave of whatever it was, he headed to the surface with Trent on his heels!

⚜ ⚜

With orders from Trent, Doug skipped scheduling second interviews! Hire now, and winnow them out later! After a lengthy discussion, they had agreed that the predominant thinking of HR departments, in both public and private sectors, seemed to favor fun above function! Like if someone was a partier, fun to be around; that was more important than ability to do a good job! A lot of emphasis on bonding among employee groups, everyone's being part of a whole without causing ripples, was the dominant school of thought! Not that Trent wanted a boat load of troublemakers! He did however, want guys who could think for themselves and walk a lonely road if need be!

In the meantime, he continued to formulate a list of men to give warnings to, suspend without pay, or release permanently!

He mentally replayed a previous incident when he had flown into Arizona to head up a search for felon, Rudy Sunquist, brought to his attention by a private investigator! Based on information from the PI, the quarry posed a threat to users of the National Forest! With that in mind, he had rallied his troops to conduct the search! To be met with amazing opposition! They had no use for a lead from a PI; rattle snakes were active! The main thing, though, as Trent looked back, was that at least three of them were hung over! Making them balk at the thought of a mounted horseback search through rugged terrain! Who wanted a jarring horseback ride when their heads felt like they were exploding? With their resentment toward him building all day, they had been guilty of dereliction of duty! Refusing to follow his orders~

And because of their stalling, they had nearly cost David Anderson his life!

⚔ ⚔

Alexandra dropped, exhausted, into a recliner by the fireplace! Getting both girls down was a struggle~but they were finally both asleep~ So far, she had refrained from calling Janni! Maybe a little decompression time~and she might be willing to return!

Handling Leisel was just plain work, and then in the grueling marathon drive~and Alexandra had planned to watch the girls after arriving in DC so Janni could get a break~but then, Doug was stuck decorating for the banquet! Of all people! Of all tasks! So, Janni had been stuck~She stopped her mind from running and rerunning through the scenario!

Anyway, that reminded her~She hopped up, suddenly energized! Trent had presented her a check for five hundred dollars! Hoping it was still in her handbag, and not something that had gotten bloody, to eventually be burned~

"Voila!" Her eyes sparkled and color rushed to her cheeks! She still couldn't come to grips with Doug hanging onto his salary~but the Lord had provided her with some extra~

Not to go toward the mining operation! She kept funds earmarked for that, to Doug's frustration, who seemed to think every dollar needed to be spent immediately! She could use a little of the money for needs for the girls~

She sighed! "Okay, push reset! Tithe first, and then just deposit the rest in their joint account! There was no need for her to respond to him in kind!"

She jumped when her phone jangled!

Tears started at the sound of his voice!

"The girls misbehaving?" By that, he basically meant his daughter! Alexandra's baby was perfect! It was Leisel who kept things stirred up!

Alexandra laughed through tears! "Both sound asleep! They're fine! I'm fine, really! Even though I don't sound like it! So, are you where you have a better chance to talk?"

"Yeah; alone in a motel room! After I knocked off after six, I went and had a big steak! Hadn't taken time to eat all day!"

She didn't know whether to be jealous or happy for him! What was he doing? Living large with the money he didn't seem inclined to share?

"Well, there's a big shake up going down in the Law Enforcement Division! We can't disqualify agents for drinking-as long as they do a good job without referencing drinking with every breath they take! We're taking a hard look at everyone, and interviewing broadly with the purpose of hiring immediately and sending new hires for FLETC training to get them into the field! I'll be really busy between now and Friday afternoon when I fly home! I really miss you-"

"I miss you, too! But, I guess I should warn you that I might be HIV positive following my scuffle with Officer Kittrick! I need to go down into town and be tested! Are you sure they really keep your information as confidential as they're supposed to? It's kind of a small town! And small towns are notorious for everyone's knowing everyone else's business!"

"Hmmm, maybe instead of me flying home Friday afternoon, you should fly to Denver! We can spend the weekend; we can find a big lab where no one knows us!"

She considered- "Mmmm, I don't know, Doug! I'm not sure if I'm supposed to stay within the mine's perimeters, or if I'm generally safe now! I'm not sure if I can handle both girls on that flight, especially if it makes us all sick! I-um-I'm pretty sure we lost Janni!" In addition to those concerns, she questioned the expense of a Denver hotel for two nights! Even her cash reserves for the mine were based on ore reaching market-and she needed to locate another vein, pronto!

As if reading her thoughts, "With all the positions opening up, I'm actually moving up two grades! I'm acting as regional head, in Porter's absence, but Mr. Morrison doesn't plan to shoot me up there permanently! Temporarily, I'm earning extra! Then I'll revert down to my new grade, which will be up from where we have been!"

"That's good!" She bit her tongue to keep from asking if he had any plans for melding their funds! "In all the craziness, I didn't get a chance to tell you that Mr. Morrison paid me five hundred dollars for playing the piano during the banquet!"

He emitted a whistle of surprise, then laughed. "Well, you're really good! How's your finger healing?"

"Uh-trying to take it easy on it- Between playing before and then throughout the banquet, I might have overdone it! And then, I kind of wrenched it during-you know-" Emotional again, her voice wouldn't come!

"Okay, maybe I'm tired, but things are slow to sink in! I'm praying about the HIV thing, and your finger! And-what happened with Janni?"

Almost afraid to ask, he figured it was the difficulty with handling his undisciplined little girl!

"I'm-I'm not sure! It was just-scary-and the FBI confiscated our phones! I knew why, why we couldn't contact anyone! She just-wanted to talk to her-dad-and they wouldn't let her! And it was just-every time we started to settle in someplace-they yanked us up and moved us again- I mean I'm grateful that the FBI was there to intervene for me! They kept Trent Morrison from being shot, and I appreciated the security detail-I hope I don't have to do it again-any time soon-"

"Yeah, I hope not, too! Maybe I'll call Pastor Anderson, though! Is it okay if I ask him to pray with us about the HIV thing, and your finger? I really want you to come meet me in Denver! If Janni agrees to come back, you two could drive together-"

"Uh-I'm not sure-I think they all think I'm pretty much horrible-"

"Okay, no problem! You're not horrible: I'll be glad when you've made peace with your mother, though-"

⊰ ⊱

Trent sat studying a handful of gineih, quirsh, and malleem!

Sonia startled him coming up behind him, her eyes sparkling with laughter! "Are any of those rare and valuable enough to fund this jaunt?"

"I have to admit that I honestly don't know! Probably not! Donovan's flying in tomorrow, but he told me we're welcome to stay on-"

"Really; did you tell him about Matt's find?"

"No; pretty sure it isn't that earth-shattering-"

"Well, it's an old metal spear tip-"

"The best we can tell, with our boatload of expertise on the subject! And Cline's looking for multitudes of spear tips, to prove that the entire Egyptian army drowned right here! And Matt's bringing whatever it is out of the water, it might decompose into a pile of rust!"

"Well, maybe that's why you should mention it to Mr. Cline, to start preserving it; in case it's something!"

"Let's just take Matt's picture with it, and call it good!"

⚞ ⚟

"Hello, Kayla; I hope I'm not calling too late!" Alexandra's voice brisk and purposeful!

"No, we're usually up until after the nightly news! You probably know I don't have any information about the suits yet, so-what's on your mind?"

Alexandra quickly went through the high points of the episode at the DC banquet! "I can see why Trent Morrison let them go," she added, "-for breaking laws when they're sworn to uphold them-and I know it's criminal! Criminals keep trying to kidnap me and a bunch of my friends to feed into their money-making ring! I know the whole industry is awful-"

"But?" Kayla's probing question!

"Do you think the DA will decide to bring criminal charges against the agents, and will they be convicted?"

"Uh, no telling- Why are you asking?"

"Because I need to hire some of them to provide more security for my ranch, my girls, and myself! One of the guys, I know, doesn't make a habit of this-Robert Porter-I think he really got caught in a perfect storm-well, the devil knows how and when to set Christians up-"

The attorney was at a loss for words, not accustomed to clients' talking about the devil and his MO!

At last, "Let me think about it! The laws are on the books, and the responsibility of the DA's office is to prosecute offenders! However, the courts are backed up, and funding is always a consideration! In a perfect world-"

"In a perfect world, there will be absolute justice," Alexandra cut in! "I look forward to that day; but until then-"

Kayla was still puzzled by the girl's words: 'The devil'? And, 'a day was coming'? Oh yeah, it sounded like what Gray and Brenna Prescott believed!

"Well, it's none of my business, but you'll literally be putting your life, and the mine, and your children in their hands! Are you sure you trust them that much?"

"Well, more than I trust Hardy Johnson! I know he's up here, and he has both Doug and me in his sights! Since I'm surrounded by forests these former forestry department law enforcement guys probably have the necessary skills-and there's a reward for him! "I'll run it past Doug! You're probably an expensive person to use as a sounding board! I'm hoping charges will never even be brought-because if they get indicted, the best they can get is probation; right? And then they can't have weapons?"

"Or they could be acquitted, but that's not likely! Hotel security footage has them nailed, as I understand it!"

CHAPTER 20: INCIDENT

Donovan Cline grimaced angrily-stabbed in the back-by Morrison-whom he thought he treated pretty well! Figured! And the guy's lack of thought for anyone but himself had Cline's carefully-built relationship with the Egyptians on the verge of collapse! He felt like telling the customs agent to go ahead and clap the whole family in jail! And it wouldn't be a nice jail!

He sighed wearily! Maybe he should give Morrison a chance to explain himself, because the Egyptians wouldn't! Having been one of the most oft looted nations in history of their ancient artifacts, they had clamped down! Sad Morrison was pincered in it! Maybe he should have warned him! His assumption was that Morrison would report any finds they made to him, as their host! Well, his assumption: they wouldn't bring up anything of interest!

He sent an email to a friend higher up in the customs department, an Oxford graduate, who spoke impeccable English, explaining that there was a mix-up, but that he didn't yet know all of the details!

⚔ ⚔

Bob Porter sat dejectedly in the den of their new Golden home! Terri had gone to visit her parents, and the kids were at friends'! Idly, he surfed channels before clicking the TV off! Maybe taking a walk! De Leon probably needed to get out, anyway!

The Golden Lab was at his side the moment he made a move toward the leash! He patted him affectionately! "Guess you're the only one in the whole world not mad at me! Yeah, let's take a walk! Come on! Come on!"

He even managed a chuckle at the dog's excited bounding! "Okay, don't knock me flat! I'm coming!" Pulling on his jacket, he headed out into softly falling snow!

He liked snow! Loved the new Colorado relocation! Different after so many years working out of Atlanta! Terri-didn't seem-to like anything-Not that his retaliation-or whatever- He tried to keep his thoughts from going back there! He had failed! Failed so miserably! And the job and pay grade he had taken so for granted-even despised-gone! And he still faced charges!

The wind increased, driving snow into his skin and snatching air from his lungs! He liked it! It suited his mood! He pressed forward, stopping to wait for a traffic light! 'Yeah, Porter, don't walk against the light! That's breaking the law!' He scoffed, because there was no car traffic from any direction! Still, his failure was not a trifle! Maybe in the eyes of some segments of society-but not in the eyes of the perfect, has it together, Special Agent in charge, Trent Morrison-

He felt his phone buzz and pulled it free, shocked when the caller ID showed Alexandra Hunter! Declining the call, he thrust his device into a deeper pocket and broke into a run! Reaching a deserted and softly blanketed park, winded, he undid the leash, allowing De Leon his freedom!

He had overloaded his lip with Trent, in front of all the guys in the fated DC ballroom meeting! Accusing him of being a 'Crusading do-gooder'! Especially when Alexandra Faulkner was in trouble! The others had taken up the gauntlet, echoing the same suspicions! Now the phone call from Alexandra must mean she had heard the accusations- Maybe she was threatening to sue him! Good for her! Let her try! 'Can't get blood out of a turnip'!

He sank down on a snowy bench, heedless of the cold wetness that quickly soaked through his jeans, watching the dog frolic in unending white freedom!

He shouldn't have said that! A cheap shot, because he was guilty! And caught! Tears started! He could swear it was because of the cold!

彐 㐅

Trent fought panic! At least he seemed to be the primary target of the official's wrath! If they would just let Sonia and the kids go, he could-not that it would be a picnic! He castigated himself for his thoughtlessness! He presided over law enforcement in America's National Forests and

Grasslands, and they enforced every rule! Forest users couldn't legally pick a flower or carry out a pebble! Why it had never occurred to him that Matt couldn't simply keep his hunk of junk-His stomach roiled, and he tensed more!

"This isn't Donovan Cline's fault! He didn't offer us hospitality so we could steal things! We didn't mean to steal-can-uh-we pay a fine?"

The officer scoffed, "You bribe me?"

Trent wasn't sure whether to deny it or try it!

᠄ ᠄

Alexandra redoubled her attention to her daughters as Jacob and Summer Prescott and Tim Alvaredo entered the chow hall and began serving themselves! Why did they assume she was made of money; to feed the whole county? Pushing bites at Leisel, she forced a laugh as she did a slow count to ten-

Getting a measure of control on her exasperation, she sailed toward the uninvited threesome with forced cheerfulness, "Hey, what brings you guys up here?"

"Is it okay if we join you?" Jacob seemed uncertain.

"Yeah, please do! Doug's out of town, so I'm wrestling the girls single-handedly! I guess that's a warning to join me at your own risk! You may leave, wearing more than you eat!" Even as she pronounced the solemn warning, she knew it was Leisel she wrestled with! Angelique was an adorable baby- An involuntary sigh escaped!

"So, you haven't answered my question about what brings you up here-" She stirred whipped cream and an ice cube into hot chocolate for the demanding toddler!

"Okay, Leisel! It's hot! Mommy's trying-"

An enraged shriek cut her short! Leisel seemed fiendishly smart at times, while at others, impossibly slow! Sly, she knew how to take advantage of a situation, sure that Alexandra wouldn't bring her behavior to a head in front of the guests.

"So, you don't need Janni's help anymore?" Summer's question, not coming out as innocently as she hoped, brought a sharp glare from stony, gray eyes!

"Well, you might as well get straight to the point; but for your information, I can do more than anyone gives me credit for! I'm not sure what the deal is with her! I know the FBI never liked it when Mallory and Jennifer Moa'a'loa were in close proximity! Since they were both targets for kidnappers, Erik Bransom never wanted to~my point being~maybe the FBI sent Janni home to Arkansas and brought me here, and maybe they want us to maintain a distance~"

That was one scenario her mind had devised during a sleepless night! Why was it their business? Why were they here? Spying? To make a report to her Uncle Gray?

"So, you're saying the FBI thinks Janni is still in danger?" Jacob's features weren't handsome~he was just okay looking! His tone of voice was troubled!

Alexandra's puzzled frown gave way to dazzling smile! "You like her! I guess she's still in danger! The whole world's crazy, evidently! So~" She broke off, still trying to make sense of their mission! "So, I guess if you like her, you want her to come back here! That makes sense! Does she like you, too? Does Pastor Anderson know?"

The threesome sat across from her looking guilty!

"I'm getting coffee!" she rose abruptly! "Anyone else?"

"I'll get it!" Tim hopped up eagerly! "Everyone in?"

꼭 跬

Trent tried not to mind the smells! And this was still just the customs offices~the seamier ones, removed from the glitzy façade most tourists encountered! Longing to access his Bible app. for strength and comfort, he refrained! If he pulled his phone out, they might confiscate it! As it was, he should save what was left of his battery charge! Keeping it charged by means of converters and adaptors was a challenge in the Dahab Hilton! Probably nothing~from in their dungeons! Cheery thought! He scoffed to himself!

"You try and bribe me?"

The agent was back, and Trent frowned at his repetition of the question! "American Embassy!" was his only response!

꼭 跬

Daniel scrolled through emails, deleting some and reporting others as spam! Wearily, he wondered whether that accomplished anything! Nothing from Alexandra but the cryptic morning texts! Not certain whether she was still in FBI protection, he paused again-to pray for her-and for Doug-and the two little granddaughters!

He admired Diana's forbearance, not knowing even what he knew, and not demanding to know! He smiled at her most recent coping mechanism! Caviar! Not a bad idea! Rising, he strode purposefully to the kitchen!

⚔ ⚑

When Leisel was finally full, and they had all finished several cups of coffee, Alexandra leaned back with an air of total satisfaction!

"Well, that worked out well all the way around! I hated to call Janni, because I figured we had taxed her patience beyond endurance-"

"And she was afraid to call you and apologize for falling apart and not being more help," Jacob's finishing off the thought! "And, you were right! Uh-I did need to talk to her dad! It's amazing how FEAR really is False Evidence Appearing Real! You were afraid to call Janni when she wanted a call; she was equally scared to call you! I was petrified at the thought of calling Pastor Anderson, but then he was really nice-"

⚔ ⚑

Dannia Peters pushed back from a scarred desk, rising part way to reach a document lazing its way through an ancient printer!

"Okay, Mr. Morrison!" Her voice held a clipped, Eastern US accent! "This artifact is the only one you retrieved during your dives?"

"Yes, Ma'am! Again, thanks for coming!"

She frowned, "So now, all we have to clear up is your attempted bribery-People always make their issues worse-"

"I didn't attempt bribery! What I asked was, if it's possible to just pay a fine-he misunderstood my-meaning-"

Her face twisted laconically! "I understand! You must understand, Mr. Morrison, that I've heard it all before! And so have they! Americans tend to treat the rest of the world like they're a bunch of buffoons! They have a due process, and offering to 'pay a fine' seems like an attempt to operate outside their system! Or, like 'bribery'!"

Trent squirmed! "Maybe that was what I was trying to do! I don't know!" He ran both hands through his hair before clasping his temples!

194

"I was scared! I thought they were going to throw all of us in jail-I know nothing about the legal system here! I wasn't sure if they release people on bond-or if we might all just disappear-forever-"

⚐ ⚑

Alexandra moved quietly through the house! Both girls were asleep; she was caffeine-wired! She laughed at her beautiful reflection! It was late! Past time for Doug to call! Still, she felt a happy peacefulness! Janni-flying in tomorrow-And Janni and her cousin, Jacob, were an item!

"That's right! Jacob and Summer are my cousins; I will never again refer to them as my Uncle Gray's adopted children! Doug was right! I do tend to hold people at arm's length! (Uh-I'm a snob!) And Brenna! I shouldn't refer to her anymore as my Uncle's wife-although-she's way cool to be called my aunt-And Tim likes Summer-and vice versa-"

Pulling a suitcase free, she began packing for the weekend trip to Denver! Time to be nicer to Janni, too! After a brief talk with Doug, who had put in another long day, and was exhausted, she fell into bed herself! Before sleep overtook her, she replayed her cousin's words about False Evidence Appearing Real! First thing in the morning, she needed to put her fears aside and call Robert Porter again, and-Trent Morrison!

⚐ ⚑

Diana disconnected following a lengthy visit with Mallory! If Mallory knew anything about Alexandra, she didn't mention it! It was a great visit, giving friends an opportunity to catch up! Humming softly, she climbed the winding staircase to check on Frances and the children, before sequestering herself in her design studio!

After trying to concentrate on developing a new theme, she gave in and revisited the famed Chinese scene of Mount Huangshan, with the Panda and bamboo! Not sure Alexandra liked it, she shrugged! At least it hadn't been returned unopened again! Putting finishing touches on a large canvas satchel, she emailed the design to the Riveras, a family in Spain that manufactured her exclusive handbags! Although they had been even slower than she at branching out into materials beyond leather, they now admitted that the coated canvas allowed for fun design options!

⇇ ⇉

Trent watched as the plane banked above the Mediterranean and surged northward toward the coast of France! Still berating himself for his mental lapse, he realized the recent events were a warning from the Lord, that although doing right, and doing it vigorously, were important, his actions might have been too harsh with his men! One mistake, one lapse~His eyes drifted closed, then popped open in alarm! The passenger liner was changing course! A lump formed in his throat as the Nile Delta reappeared and the plane sank lower toward the landing strip of the Cairo International Airport!

"They haven't brought back an entire airliner full of passengers just so they could apprehend you," Sonia comforted.

Still, surprisingly, there was no explanation, but simply calm orders for everyone to gather all belongings and deplane!

Complying and bringing up the rear behind his family, he prayed desperately! "Lord, I got the message! I was already starting to reevaluate~"

⇇ ⇉

Aggravated, Porter answered his phone! Ignoring it wasn't working!

"Robert Porter, what can I do for you?"

"Good morning, Mr. Porter! This is Alexandra Hunter! Hunter's my married name! I'm Daniel Faulkner's daughter! I'm sorry to keep calling but~well, no one knows for sure what the fallout is going to ultimately be! If you find yourself no longer employed by the Forestry Department, and don't end up on probation so you can't be around weapons, I'm really interested in hiring you! My mine is actually producing, and I need security both for the mine, the ore hauls, and personally!"

He listened! What she described was a tall order! Of course he was aware of Johnson's still being at large and out to get her! And what was to stop the felon from funding his activities by hijacking a load of ore? He had stolen the dynamite! And used it, too! Porter was intrigued, but as good as he was, he couldn't be everywhere, watching everything, at once!

With the silence, she continued! Time for her highest powered pitch! "I have a really comfortable double wide available for your use while you're here! You could keep your home there in Golden, and go home on weekends! Of course, this is all pending the outcome~and hopefully some of the other agents will emerge~whom you could also hire~Our chow hall offers three squares a day, I offer good hospitalization; your take home pay might be~uh~a little~less~but utilities are paid up here! I'll provide some vehicles for security's use! If you sign on, you can help me figure out which would be the best vehicles to obtain initially~" she trailed off.

"Well, I have to admit I'm interested! Pretty sure I'm going to get the book thrown at me~and hey~I deserve it~"

She cut in, "You made a mistake! I made one, too, and I've really regretted it~but ~uh~the Lord~I've been trying to call Mr. Morrison, but he doesn't answer my calls, either~I don't blame him for not liking me! Mr. Porter, I promise that if this all works out and you become an employee, you won't be working for a spoiled brat! I'll treat you right, and as the operation grows, so will the security needs~ There's opportunity here; if it does entail a reduction~initially~"

"Okay," He chuckled for the first time in weeks! "If I get off, you have yourself a head of security!"

⌐ ¬

Chatter among the passengers was that someone smelled smoke, or that something in the avionics seemed off! Still, the official announcements from the airline simply stated that there would be a two to three hour delay!

Trent felt like he was staggering and that his knees were going to drop him on the spot! He didn't laugh when Sonia turned to him with her standard *'Bee-beep!'* With a disgusted shake of his head, he veered toward a men's room! *Coyote* and *Road Runner* were both going to blow sky high this time! And it wasn't a laughing matter! Here he was, on a trip he couldn't afford to be on, spending money he didn't have, to escape a bogey man back home, and face a worse one here! His phone buzzed, making him jump like a scaredy-cat; it was Alexandra again!

Aggravated, he declined the call! For one thing, charges were exorbitant for overseas calls, and his agents were fighting him with accusations, or implications, at any rate, that he had something going on with the girl! He didn't! He didn't even like her! She was only Maddie's age! He knew Sonia was aware of the gab, and so far, seemed to trust him~Glaring at brown freckles against a colorless face, he forced himself to rejoin his family!

⌐ ¬

Putting Ponce de Leon on his leash once more, Porter trotted behind the dog like he was the one who was leash-trained! Figured! He wasn't in control of any aspect of his life! Even the Lab thought he was boss!

'Give the reins to Me!'

No audible voice, but the soul-whisper brought tears springing to the defeated agent's eyes!

He scoffed inwardly, 'Why do You even want them?'

'Because I love you, and I can straighten things out for you! Trust me! How well are you doing on your own?'

Two miles later, he paused at a coffee shop, tethering the dog while he went inside to order! With the cold, the entire outdoor seating area was his, and he sank down in the solitude! Well, there was plenty of traffic and exhaust from the busy thoroughfare, but solitude from intrusions by people!

Upon first disconnecting from the job offer, his defeated attitude nearly shrugged it off! The offer, obviously, was dependent upon his ability to carry! Which, he figured, might be a privilege he had forfeited forever, with one stupid moment's decision! What had Alexandra said, 'He made a mistake! So had she~how long did you have to pay for it~That there was forgiveness with God~that He could turn things around~

"God, can You really turn things around? What I did~was so bad~I guess I haven't asked You to forgive me, because~well, I'm not sure~ I didn't just want to say words~to~impress Trent and keep my job~Or even just say words to Terri~ I don't blame my kids for hating me! I hate myself so bad~My life is in shambles~but if You want it~it's Yours!

☙ ❧

When Trent didn't think terror could strengthen its grip upon him, it did! A circle of uniformed Egyptian authorities surrounded his family! Maybe if he surrendered himself~

CHAPTER 21: HUMILITY

Trent leaned back, starting to relax once more, then pulled a check for ten thousand dollars free to stare at in amazement for the tenth time! From Cline! Not for the artifact, which was firmly in the control of *The Egyptian Antiquities Department*, but for having found it just as Cline was considering abandoning his search! With fresh zeal and subsequent dives, Cline had brought more and more artifacts to the surface! Which supported the hypothesis that the ancient Israelites, fleeing Pharaoh and his army, had crossed the Red Sea at the Strait of Tiran on the Gulf of Aqaba! Supported the hypothesis! Wouldn't prove unequivocally! Just like the discovery of Noah's Ark, atop Mount Ararat, should it ever happen, would support the Biblical account of the great flood! But it wouldn't prove the truth of the Bible to those who refused it! God's plan was that people should receive Him by faith, and then continue walking by faith throughout their entire lives! An intelligent faith! A faith according to the knowledge available through God's Word! To him, Cline's dearly-held theory made sense! And Mt. Sinai and the site of the wilderness wanderings must surely have taken place in what was now Jordan and Saudi Arabia

Not that most of the Egyptian authorities favored the theory! Tourism dollars from pilgrims visiting the St Catharine's Monastery in the Sinai Peninsula helped feed the national economy! They were reluctant to let Cline mess with that! Discovering the truth was therefore, a moot point with many of them! Trent shrugged, not sure how they could consider themselves scholars and historians if they ignored compelling evidence! Well, not his place to stick around and argue with them! He was just eager to return home!

He studied the check in awe! Deliverance and enlargement! One of God's too-good-to-be-true, and yet, true, promises! Granting both deliverance from trials and testings, with enlargement on the other side! His frantic prayers, of course, were for deliverance, only! Deliverance for his family and himself from the clutches of Egyptian mid-level government employees eager to make an example of an American!

"Well, once we give our Uncle Sam his share of this and pay for the trip, we might break even!" His joking words to Sonia, whose response was a withering stare!

"Oh-oh, what'd I do? Oh, I know! I didn't laugh at your, '*Bee-beep*', just before the uniformed guys closed in on us again! Sorry, but at the moment, it didn't strike me funny! Am I the only one who always feels like I'm standing there staring at the bomb in my hand as it blows up in my face?"

She flopped back disgustedly, letting him know that that wasn't the issue! Meaning, one was eliminated!

"Uh-Dad, I think she has an issue with Alexandra's having called your cell phone a thousand times!" Michael's voice from across the aisle!

"You're kidding; right Sonn? If you notice, I haven't taken or returned her calls! I figured if it's anything very major concerning her safety, I'll hear from Daniel! I didn't accept the calls for a number of reasons! The main one's being that it costs a fortune overseas! Look, I know my agents have made some innuendos-but the reason I've spent so much time in Colorado is that I'm sure Hardy Johnson runs an illegal organization that's gathering steam, from the San Juan Forest! I can't tell you how desperately I wish I could have gone through with my original plan to blow up that entire underground lair!"

෧ ෨

Bob Porter, coffee in hand, sank at an outside table where Ponce was tethered! In the chilling cold, they had the area to themselves! Sipping slowly, he allowed the terms of Alexandra Hunter's offer to sink in! A double wide on the grounds, utilities provided! Hmmm! He was pretty sure Terri didn't plan to return home until he moved out! Separated! But, with his being fired, now was a poor time financially to set up another household! He sighed! Sad, how he had chosen a course of action with no thought about the never-ending ramifications that would follow! And follow, and follow- So a double-wide would provide him a place to live, and the position would also provide a vehicle, insurance, and other perks he desperately needed! All hinging now, upon the legal woes hanging over his head~

"God, I need Your mercy~not to get the bad things I deserve! And Your grace to give me the good things I don't deserve! I keep asking You to forgive me, and I guess You have! You promise that You do! Help me forgive myself! I'm pretty sure Terri and the kids never will! Coffee finished, he sat, lost in thought, until the dog nudged him from his reverie!

⚔ ⚔

Sitting at the kitchen counter, Trent settled Sonia next to him! "Okay, I'm placing this on conference, and you can listen to the messages! I hated to say too much to you on the flight, because our kids don't know all of Alexandra's story! And they don't need to!

Hello, Mr. Morrison,

This is Alexandra Hunter! I apologize for bothering you, especially on your cell phone, but your secretary told me you're out of the office for a few days~Okay, so, I hardly know where to start~except, I need to hire more good men for security for my mine, and also personally! I'm really thinking about Robert Porter! I know what he did was wrong; and I understand your feelings about it, I think! He made a mistake, but having made an awful one myself, I've come to realize that you can start to hold your head up again, and move on! I'm not sure how much Mr. Porter's future is still in your hands~but if he gets conviceted~even if he makes probation~well, you know the problems about not being able to be around firearms! I'm not even sure why I'm calling you, but if you could in any way help him get leniency~

Thanks for your time!

Trent's eyes met Sonia's as they finished listening to a dozen more messages, saying basically the same thing!

"I overreacted to the whole thing, and let guys go~"

Sonia drew up!

"I'm not saying what they did was okay, Sonia! But to pay forever for one lapse in judgment! I mean, it's such a relief for me to be here, and not in prison in Cairo!"

"Well, it's not the same, Trent!"

He frowned! "In a way, no; but then in another way~ You have to realize that in the Egyptian context, someone attempting to plunder their historical artifacts! I mean, they're tired of it! And rightfully so! From the standpoint of their society and our society, my crime was worse than the men hiring companionship! I know it's a sad commentary on the morals of our national fiber, but those guys~ In their minds, their actions were nearly as inconsequential as I thought ours were in letting Matt keep that thing~"

Her features twisted as she considered his argument! She was cute!

"I'm not condoning them, but~I owe an apology! I've gotten~arrogant~about being Mr. Super Christian! Now I hope I can help Porter! He is basically a good guy!"

He laughed at her stubborn expression!

⚼ ⚼

Doug jabbed in his ATM card, and once again withdrew the total amount of his payroll direct deposit! The 'Rule of thumb' regarding purchasing a diamond engagement ring was, three months wages! This was six weeks, half of what was recommended, and he felt that he must be pushing Alexandra's tolerance! The first time, he received an off-handed comment! The second time, silence! If it was resentful silence, he couldn't tell for sure! Alexandra had money; she just refused to use what was earmarked for her mining operation for diapers and baby food! 'But she could, 'rob Peter to pay Paul,' if she needed to; couldn't she?' Saving money was a new concept to him, and already, some of what he was trying to accumulate to purchase rings, had slipped through his fingers!

Closing down his computer, he headed toward the mall! Grab a bite to eat and begin the shopping process! The thought of stepping through the entrance of a jewelry store made his stomach churn!

⚼ ⚼

Alexandra fought raw emotion! Feeling like she was trying to put her fate into God's hands, she realized she still held tightly to what she wanted!

202

Living as Doug's wife, and raising her little girls without the complications of HIV! Comforting her wailing girls as they got Disney themed band aids, a case of the shakes suddenly overwhelmed her!

"It's okay," Janni's voice amazingly soothing!

"I know! I'm not sure what's wrong with me!"

"I wish you would have allowed me to put it on the Faith Baptist website prayer requests!"

Al strove for patience! "And then my parents, and David and Mallory, and everybody and his uncle would know!"

"My point! All those you just mentioned are amazing prayer warriors! I mean~I'm not sure about all the uncles~but everybody else you listed! If I faced something like this, I'd want them all bombarding heaven with pleas! It isn't like you're facing this because of using drugs or being immoral~"

"I know; let's hurry! Maybe we can beat rush hour getting to the hotel! Why don't you drive?"

Janni laughed, "Gladly! You must be shaken up!"

Alexandra's response was a mildly disapproving frown! She was a good driver, not sure why others took umbrage with it! In the passenger seat, she accessed one of the bank accounts!

'Yep, Doug took his money out again!' She chewed her lip thoughtfully, trying to figure out his actions! One of his reasons that she should agree to marry him was that they could help one another! Now, he lived rent-free at either the mine or the Durango house! Chow hall meals were available, when he wasn't traveling with his job! She took the main oversight of both girls! It seemed as though she was giving, and he was taking~and it was a one-way street! She stared at the balances again! Hmmm! The extra income Mr. Morrison pledged for Doug's temporary advanced position and extra workload reflected in the deposit! Doug must not have thought about the extra when he made his withdrawal! Temptation welled up, to transfer it into another account!

She refrained! Maybe he wasn't perfect, but then, neither was she! Marriage was a constant refusal to dwell on the other's faults. She loved Doug! Had committed to him before God and men! She reminded herself to focus on his solid good points!

Philippians 4:8 Finally, brethren, whatsoever things are true, whatsoever things are honest, whatsoever things are just, whatsoever things are pure, whatsoever things are lovely, whatsoever things are of good report; if there be any virtue, and if there be any praise, think on these things.

᚛ ᚜

Donovan Cline's ecstasy boundless, he ordered photographs taken of bits and pieces of history as they emerged from encrustation and assumed recognizable forms! It was fascinating to him, something he needed, if the rest of the world remained unconvinced forever! Hands trembling with excitement that had once trembled from Delirium Tremors, he sent the best shots to his daughter, Callie!

> *Hey Baby, your old dad's still at it! Morrison and his family showed up and managed to stumble onto an amazing cache of artifacts~ After some snafus with the antiquities department, they have returned to the US! Hope all is well with you!*
> *Can't describe how happy you and this new life have made me! Hug Parker for me and cover Victoria over with kisses from Grandpa! Hope to see you soon!*

᚛ ᚜

Trent emerged from a conference call, mentally exhausted, but pleased and relieved! His guys had granted him more mercy and grace than he had extended to them! Over all! Some were disgusted with his Christian values and planned to make career moves, barely grateful for the fact that Trent no longer planned to push the prosecutions! Well, it was another opportunity, so hopefully they would learn a lesson! As he gulped big breaths and reconsidered the call, he realized that the cleansing was for the best!

The sad loss to him was Robert Porter, overall a good guy, just sucked into a vortex~ Porter planned to accept Alexandra Hunter's offer to head security for her operations! And it did seem as though the perks she offered were tailor-made for Porter's present situation! An ideal opportunity to separate from his wife while they worked on their relationship!

There still remained the very real possibility that a zealous DA might pursue criminal charges for some of them, but Trent figured the odds were

204

minimal without his pushing it! His new lesson in humility and mercy made him ready to put the situation behind and move forward!

As he approached McLean, he placed a call to Madeleine! Her response on the first ring was a relief!

"Hey, whatcha doin'? I'm on the way home; can you meet me at the mall? I think I promised to buy you whatever cosmetic items you're running low on?"

A wail from her, and he laughed! "Okay, I see why you gave up on me! I'll reimburse whatever you spent! How much we talkin'?"

He laughed to cover his involuntary gasp at the amount! "All right! I'll settle up, then, when I get home!" Disconnecting, he considered the bright side! At least he didn't have to go to the mall! And he and Bransom had once more foiled a criminal attempt to grab her and Meggy! He could buy their stuff for them! How many fathers in the world had been robbed of the privilege?

⊰ ⊱

Alexandra tried to talk to Doug about a number of matters that she felt they needed to deal with jointly! Besides being distracted with his extra job demands, he was feeling romantic!

"Doug, I don't know what these test results will show! Quit saying you love me so much you don't care! Your health is important, your ability to work your job! If we can keep from both having bouts in the hospital and expensive prescriptions-"

"I guess it gets under my skin that I failed to look after you following the banquet!"

She shrugged, "Like you could foresee what was about to come down! And Kittrick was hoping for a reason to shoot Mr. Morrison, due to their previous run-in! Anything you would have tried-let's just pray for negative test results!" She began crying, "I wanted to change out of the disgusting clothes! Well, they were adorable to begin with-I didn't know that hugging the girls placed them at high risk!"

His lack of response concerned her because he didn't seem to have a real attachment to either girl! She made an attempt about the money, telling him that there was extra in the account he hadn't withdrawn! Which to her chagrin, caused him to turn his laptop back on!

She sighed, new at the wife thing, establishing communications, and being on the same page!

¤ ¤

Alice McKay gazed from her reflection to Niqui Whitmore, and back again to the image in the mirror! She was amazed at the transformation! Suspicious! But amazed!

"Who are you again, and why are you doing this?"

Niqui grinned! "You didn't tell me what you think? What do you think?"

"I think I look like a new woman! Like the professional woman I used to be! Before I got old, and retired, and lost my teeth!"

She studied herself again! Yeah, she didn't look twenty again, or even sixty-but the work on her teeth, the cosmetics, hair style-she felt better, and yeah, younger, just looking better!

Settled in at a luncheon spot, Niqui tested, "You really know who I am; don't you?"

A machine gun like chortle preceded the answer! "I remember what you've told me! I haven't completely lost my marbles yet! Your name's Niqui Whitmore, and you know my grandson, and you're doing all this nice stuff for me for taking care of Leisel when it was beyond me-If this is an attempt to get me to-"

"Let's check the menu so we can order! I have a plane to catch later this afternoon!"

With orders placed, Niqui divulged more information to Doug's apprehensive grandmother!

¤ ¤

Alexandra's mouth went dry as she stared at the number lighting up her phone screen! Her startled eyes met Doug's before she pressed the accept button.

"Hello, this is Alexandra Hunter!"

Bracing herself with the windowsill, she nodded, turning partially from her concerned spouse!

"You-you got the results back fast! The tech said-are you sure-it isn't too soon to-say-"

206

She listened to the voice at the lab, not sure how Erik Bransom knew she was in Denver, to phone the lab and put pressure on them to rush the tests~

"And~um~my girls? You said they~came back~negative, too? Yeah, thanks! Yes, Sir, it's a huge relief alright! Okay, have a nice evening!"

Doug swept her into his embrace, covering her with kisses, and she laughed as she struggled free!

He released her, perplexed! Maybe concern for the HIV thing wasn't the only issue coming between them!

"I need to let Janni know! She's been concerned about us, too! Then we can work on a plan for dinner! I'm hungry now, with the stress~Oh wow! Praise the Lord! Isn't it amazing how we never thank and praise Him with the same measure we beg and worry? Thank You, Lord Jesus! Thank You! Thank You! Okay, now we can focus on Christmas, and then the thing~with my family~"

Sensing his hurt, she moved nearer as tears flowed freely. "I'm sorry, Babe! I love being in your arms, and I've missed you like everything! Crazy times!"

He clasped her against him as a case of the shakes hit her! She laughed through tears! "What am I falling apart for now?"

"Like you said, 'Crazy times!' I've been gone; you've had both girls as well as your mining responsibility! You were under FBI protection, and you've had the specter of the HIV thing hanging over your head! Hardy Johnson is out to get you~ And, you're terrified of your mother!"

She sniffled, "Well, I'm not terrified of my mother! It's just that what I did~was so~"

"But it's forgiven by God! Is your mother that unforgiving?"

"No, it isn't that! It's hard to explain~but now~I've just allowed the situation to~drag~on~"

⇃ ⇂

Emails pinged alerts to hundreds of devotees, then were quickly expunged!

A wicked laugh! "Maybe this will bring this situation to a close!"

An assistant made the mistake of shrugging and voicing an opinion!

"Problem, Helms?"

"Well, we make ourselves out so idealistic and blast greed and commercialism! To my thinking, if we need the girl taken out, we should appeal to the way she's hurting our causes! Offering a monetary reward is lowering ourselves to their standards!"

🀫 🀪

"Check this out!" An encrypted text from Michael Cowan to Ward Atcheson, to get an encrypted response!

Cowan frowned! 'Yeah! True! Daniel Faulkner had tried to hire them to clean out the San Juan National Forest of Hardy Johnson and his band of camo goons! Concerned about the welfare of his firstborn! And true! Trent Morrison, catching wind of it, had ordered them to steer clear of his forests! He didn't have any use for mercenaries!'

Cowan didn't make it a habit of backing down from threats, or going by the rules of others! But, since they had refused the job and Faulkner's money, they weren't mercenaries! And this email where Johnson was offering a reward for Alexandra's destruction? He scoffed, 'I thought they had a problem with big-business and political greed! Well, when Michael Cowan was finished, that would be the least of their worries!'

🀫 🀪

Alexandra took in the expensive décor of a fine steakhouse, still shocked that Doug wanted to celebrate the good outcome of the HIV tests! Just the relief was enough! The fact that restaurant staff seemed to be overlooking them made her acutely aware of their inappropriate dress! Not that other patrons seemed resplendent in suits and ties, but the labels of their casual attire, coupled with expensive wrist watches and electronic devices bespoke the fact that they were worthy of a table! It made her miss her dad! A persona who was hard to overlook! Doug, on the other hand, seemed to be trying to fade into the high-priced woodwork!

"Step up there to the hostess and ask for a table for two," she encouraged!

"Well, she must be blind not to see us~" Still when another party stepped in front of him, to be escorted away immediately, he summoned his courage! 'Crazy that he hoped for another run-in with Johnson and his band of hooligans, and was cowed by a restaurant hostess!' He frowned when he and Alexandra were led to a table practically in the kitchen, wondering since the hour was early and the establishment not crowded, why they didn't get a table by the long bank of windows!

208

The Captain seemed further put off by them when they refused choices from the bar!

"Still with their iced tea delivered and a silver tray of bread between them, Doug took her hand and prayed! With a smile, she pointed out her entrée choice: "You order for the lady, and then tell him what you want! I'd like mine medium rare!

He frowned, having never ordered for a lady in a fine restaurant, and also at the, 'medium rare'!

"Are you sure? Christians aren't supposed to eat blood!"

She laughed, "One of the, 'forbiddens,' of the Christian life that has NEVER been a problem for me! I won't be eating blood! As soon as steers are slaughtered, they're immediately bled out; and the sides are hung and aged! I was the short-term owner of a cattle operation, if you recall! My mom and dad are both gourmet chefs, and it isn't necessary to ruin a juicy cut of meat by cooking it to death! My dad knew a guy in college whose family slaughtered their own meat, and one of the things they loved was saving the blood to make 'blood pudding'! That's eating blood, which New Testament Christians are commanded to steer clear of! Also, in Scotland they make blood sausage, and I actually saw on TV one of those weird food shows, where they were eating blood soup! I turned it off–couldn't stand the idea–"

"You're just a better Christian than I am," she laughed when he finished ordering!

※ ※

Trent read the forwarded email and deleted it! Aggravated! He thought he had made it clear to Atcheson and company to steer clear of San Juan! The ex-army guy was gonna get people killed, and not necessarily the bad guys! Still the news was alarming that Johnson had placed a bounty on Alexandra! And when Forestry Law Enforcement was in the middle of an in-house shakeup!

Low on available man-power, he placed a call to Porter!

※ ※

Over coffees, Doug once more reached for his wife's hands, kissing the surgical scars, still red, on her ring finger!

"I hoped to surprise you, but I'm sure you've figured it out!" He snapped a little box open and sparkles shot from black velvet!

She spoke softly, genuinely amazed! "I never had a clue!"

He laughed, "Well, you had to notice I was drawing my pay back out!"

She shrugged, "Yeah~but I never~wow!" Tears started as he slid the set into place!

"I hope you like them! I put all three take home amounts towards them, and the balance is still financed!"

She nodded through tears, surely even with making payments, some of his salary could now be applied to their living expenses!

"I love them! Uh~did you take~"

"Your other set? Yeah, didn't get offered much for them~but if you want, you could get like maybe a hundred and a half~"

"I want to keep them!" She laughed when he looked stunned! "Not because of any affectionate memories of Brad! Of that you need never doubt! I want to hang onto them at least until I see if Brad's mother makes contact! I'm pretty sure she was a Maxwell Men's victim, too! If she wants to be in Angelique's life, I would like it! As long as she isn't a threat~I don't know much about her!"

He grinned his engaging boyish grin and took a sip of coffee!

"Unh, I just found out that I have to go back to Golden; just for a few more days! I feel torn all the time! Because I really love you so much, but I love my job a lot, too! And I want to help with Leisel; I didn't know what problems~she~"

"I feel the same! I love you, and I love my life! And your relationship with Leisel will come! It's slow, but I think we're making progress with her! Janni is a huge blessing! And I think she's romantically inclined toward my cousin, Jacob! The best I can tell, he plans to stay in the Silverton area, so, if something develops, and they get married, maybe I can keep her on my staff!"

"You do realize that you just admitted that Jacob Weston is your cousin!"

She flushed! "Jacob Prescott, you mean! Of course he's my cousin!"

⚐ ⚑

Doing fine ^

Daniel sighed raggedly as the text binged his phone, right on the minute! In view of the circumstances, knowing Al was safe should be enough! With Diana's being such a trooper not to cajole and whine about the situation, he wasn't sure if their daughter's stalling was wearing on her as much as it was on him! He assumed so, then grinned about the Caviar expense that was hopefully, still helping her cope! He nearly dropped his phone when a second text came through:

Will you be free to talk if I call you later this morning? Say, about 10:00?

He responded eagerly:

Yes, anytime!

CHAPTER 22: CHRISTMAS

Ellis Vaughn poured on a little more steam and her mountain bike passed the city limit sign for Silverton! Usually combining skiing and hiking into her winter vacation, she refused to be deterred by the unseasonably warm weather and lack of snow! That's the way things went now and then! 'Why fight it or get all down in the mouth over things you have no control over?' She grinned to herself as she chained her bike in front of a café! After all, as owner of her own business, there were plenty of things within her control! Climate and its vagaries fell outside that parameter!

Still panting slightly and cheeks rosy with exertion, she entered the eatery! Careless about her attractive looks, she didn't give an ornate, turn-of-the-twentieth-century mirror, a glance! Glossy brown hair, controlled ever so slightly into a long French braid, escaped into wispy tendrils at face and nape of her neck! Aware of both admiring and disapproving stares, her big brown eyes met the gazes of the locals with open friendliness and good humor!

"Seat yourself! Be with you in a minute!" A disembodied voice spoke from the cavernous back area!

Undeterred, Ellis complied! 'Rude! She better never catch any of her employees acting so disinterested in her customers'! Still, she smiled brightly when 'Margaret' made her limping appearance carrying a glass of iced water!

"Good morning, Margaret! I'm Ellis! I see you're limping! If you don't mind I can get my own coffee! I'll go around and give everyone refills, too, and save you some steps!" Without waiting for permission or refusal, she sprang up! "Do you have chicken fried steak? Big ones?"

"Well, we're still serving breakfast–"

"Fantastic! Throw three over medium eggs on with it! And hash browns; and biscuits and gravy?"

⊰ ⊱

I came downtown to see if you're interested in breakfast!

Daniel stared in consternation at the text! Nothing like Diana's being downtown before she sent the text! Which, usually, he was thrilled to have her come! Only thirty minutes until his scheduled appointment to talk to Al! No way that he could get served, eat, and visit with Diana in that timeframe! The practical thing would be to tell Diana to give him ten, and call his daughter! She had told him ten o'clock! And he assumed she would make the call! Strange to be so on eggshells with her!

'Okay, Lord, please give me favor,' he pled silently as he punched his speed dial!

Placing his phone on conference, he sent a response to Diana to order him his usual and he'd be down in a few minutes!

"Hi, Daddy!" Al's voice sounded breathless and flustered! "I'm glad you called! Right after I set the call for ten, the morning started going to pieces! This is actually better! I'm wondering if you guys can come right after the first of the year–"

"Well, unless you guys can make it here for Christmas–" His tone was hopeful! He didn't want Diana to have to endure another Holiday season without knowing anything definitive about her! Silence on the other end let him know Al wasn't pleased with the suggestion!

He laughed stiffly, "Or we could all come there right after the first of the year! Are you all doing okay? I mean, I get texts that let me know you're alive and not under duress!"

"Just fine! I had the surgery on my hand, and it's nearly healed! Well, except the scars are still dark! I can play the piano again–although I have to go down to Durango to play Abby's when she isn't down there giving lessons! And I can play my violin again! That makes me want to teach! I miss it, and the Allens, and the students! I'm so busy though! Between the mine and the girls, I keep hopping! Well, Doug's gone more than ever! Which is both good and bad! He's making more money and getting promoted three grades at once–because of some internal things with the

213

department! But we really miss him! At least Janni's on the payroll! She's a tremendous blessing-and she and Jacob have this romance budding! I hope it's the Lord's will for them-" She laughed, "For my own totally selfish reasons! Well, I need to go! How about Tuesday the sixth! Meet us at the ski lodge at about ten-thirty? Hopefully we'll have some snow by then! What am I saying? The warmth and drought are making mining conditions ideal! Thanks for calling me! I really have to run-"

He laughed jubilantly as his screen went dark! "So did he!"

⚌ ⚍

Tim and Jacob laughed as the newcomer refilled their mugs! Kind of a gorgeous go-getter to invade the little hamlet and take over waitress duties! They exchanged significant glances, as though to remind each other that they both had romantic interests already!

"I'm Ellis! Are you guys from around here?"

"We are now," Jacob's answer, noncommittal!

"I'm Tim; my partner's name is Jacob-"

The beautiful woman stood with coffee pot poised, "Partners? As-in business-partner?"

"Uh-yeah! We own the heavy equipment company here in town," Jacob clarified! "We usually brown-bag our lunches, but today we decided to splurge!"

"Ooooh! Heavy equipment! I'm impressed! You'll have to fill me in more, later!"

With that, she moved to other tables, supplying coffee with the same open friendliness!

⚌ ⚍

Alexandra flung the door open to Shannon O'Shaughnessy and a biting wind! In her robe and not expecting an early morning visitor, she admitted him!

"What blew you in? Besides a biting north wind?" She was nonplussed! "Why don't you go-" she pointed beyond him to a larger building with log facade where smoke curled from the chimney-"to the chow hall? Help yourself to coffee and some breakfast! I'll join you as soon as I can pull myself together!"

214

"Sounds good! Can my crew get chow, too? If so, we can just eat and get to work! You won't need to rush!"

"Your crew?" Although she was sincerely trying to cut her superior-sounding sarcasm, it came in handy when she was at a total loss!

A hurt expression crossed his handsome face, "Uh-your dad didn't tell you? Well, maybe it's supposed to be a surprise-like for Christmas-it's kinda hard to install another building on your property, stealth, though!"

"Well, yeah, you can all go ahead and eat! I'll be out later to see what you're up to!"

⊰ ⊱

"Hey, what's up?" Janni's sleepy voice! "I thought you didn't need me till noon!"

"Something's come up! How late were y'all out?"

"That's your business because?"

"Well, because I care about you! And there isn't that much late-running entertainment up here! I'm sorry, though! Don't mean to overstep! Shannon O'Shaughnessy just showed up and banged on the door! Miraculously, the girls are still asleep! He's here with a 'crew' that's invading the chow hall, and then setting up another modular building-at my dad's bidding!"

"Shannon, you said? Isn't he kind of a sloppy builder? What's wrong with your dad having David send a crew?"

"Just come on over; bring your makeup! I won't be gone any longer than necessary! Then maybe I can answer your questions better! When I figure out what's going on, myself!"

"All right! I'll be over in a jiffy! Sorry for being so defensive! Jacob and I were out late talking to Andy and Shelley McGuire!"

⊰ ⊱

Daniel slid into the passenger seat and sent a sideways grin at Jeremiah! "Okay, once we get on the freeway, set the cruise for four miles over! And put your phone down! Don't want you driving and messing with it!" He checked his side view mirror to make certain the other SUV was behind them!

Jeremiah complied and at his younger sister, Nadia's, request started a movie playing for her! Awesome feature that she could listen through the headsets and he and his dad could listen to music!

> *O glorious love of Christ my Lord, divine*
> *Who came to save a soul like mine!*

"Whoa, who's that?" With a discerning ear for music, Daniel Faulkner wasn't easily impressed by vocalists!

Jeremiah laughed, "You really don't know? Take a guess!"

Daniel forced a laugh! It seemed his whole family used his dodge of answering questions with questions rather than giving straight answers! He considered,

"Rhonna Abbot! Wow, she was good, but~she's really worked~"

Jeremiah smiled, pleased at dazzling his father in the musical realm!

"So, is Alexandra~" he broke off, nervous at bringing up a subject that seemed nearly taboo!

Daniel sighed, trying to feign a jolly Christmas spirit when his heart felt like lead!

"No, she isn't," He kept his voice level, "But the Morrisons are! Easy!" He jammed an imaginary brake pedal as the vehicle veered sharply! "Keep it on the road!"

Figuring Jeremiah still held strong feelings for Megan Morrison, he shared the information! Managing to change the subject from Alexandra, he wasn't ready for Jeremiah's response to be so intense!

☙ ❧

"I didn't know we were going to have a buzzard attack!" Maxine's defense when Alexandra reached the chow hall to find, no chow!

"Well, I didn't know either, or you would have gotten a heads up! Is there any cereal?"

"Well, yeah, but they done drank all the milk!"

"Okay, well can you at least brew more coffee? I need at least one cup and time to count to ten thousand before I go out and find out what they're up to! Besides eating everything in sight!"

☙ ❧

Checked into the Westin at the Dallas Galleria, a one-time tradition that had fallen by the wayside, the Faulkners headed out for some last-minute shopping! Most of their gifts, ticked off, person by person throughout the year, consisted of their various products! Jewelry from Herb, clothing and leather goods from *DiaMal*! Linens from Delia O'Shaughnessy! Diana's eyes glowed with anticipation as Mallory had assisted her in acquiring a rare and beautiful mineral sample on matrix for Daniel! Still, they needed stocking stuffers, hostess gifts, and miscellaneous last minute ideas! With plenty of chatter and laughter, they hit the stores before crowding onto the ice rink!

Waiting for a chance to sit down together in a crowded coffee shop, Zave isolated Diana, "Remember what we talked about?"

Looking into somber eyes and tense features, she nodded tenderly, "I remember, Xavier! But-Alexandra has-grown up! Her growing up and buying the mine have nothing to do with thoughtless words she spoke to you years ago! Honey, Alexandra loves you! We all do! Christmases will continue to change! You were just a newborn when we made it through our first Christmas with Cassandra off in Israel! I guess God used that situation to show me how important it is to enjoy each moment! They may not be as perfect as we would wish! Sometimes perfectionist tendencies destroy moments that may not be perfect, but which are still very, very good!"

He nodded in relieved comprehension as tears clouded the vision of his eavesdropping father!

⊐ ⊏

Alexandra struggled with emotion as she sent the golf cart purring toward the knot of men assembled around Shannon! Tears stung her eyes! From the cold, of course! She didn't care anything about Brad Maxwell or his memory-it was just that she avoided this area of the camp! Following her father's visit, the crime-scene modular where Brad had ended his life, had been removed, leaving an unsightly wound of eroding earth! She couldn't imagine why her dad was sending Shannon of all people, to replace it with another building! Hopefully none of them were planning on moving in!

The worry tugged at the edge of her mind every month, too, that David and Mallory would stop providing utilities! There was no practical reason why they bore the expense month in and month out! She figured it was one of those things paid automatically, that they weren't totally cognizant of! But that, if they hired Heather's services again, to go through and find expenses to cut-she was just worried about putting another house back on-it might be the straw-to break-the camel's-back!

The thought occurred to her that that might be the logic behind her daddy's hiring Shannon and his crew, instead of David! So David and Mallory wouldn't realize they were paying for an extra household! But then, that seemed unlike her dad! Like something she would do-slightly underhanded-but not like her parents! She breathed a shamed prayer: "Lord, help me be like them! Make me be like you! Even Doug-well, you know, and his mentality-of robbing Peter to pay Paul-I mean he's a Christian! More than I could say about Brad! But, he-he can't see tithing-"

She frowned as she braked! "What are you guys doing? Moving in the Taj Mahal?"

Shannon chortled, "Yeah, the Indians were selling it and we got a steal! Now millions of tourists will flock here every year!"

She laughed, and the worried thoughts fled!

⊨ ⊨

"This is a treat!" Mallory hugged Diana as the kids broke their shy silence! "We were planning on hot dogs! The maid has the place shining and we hated to destroy the kitchen before mom and Erik come to start Christmas dinner!"

"In that case, I'm doubly glad we invited you!" Daniel shook David's hand amiably! "We've been eating food court food since we got here! As opposed to letting the kids order room service for every hunger pang! So, now we've opted for a steak dinner! Surprised you could all make it on such short notice, but really glad you could!!"

⊨ ⊨

Alexandra wrapped the few packages she had managed to purchase! Doug kept telling her there was no money! Except the grazing fees for the Hamilton's alpaca! And the generous finder's fee from the Andersons! Which, yes she had it earmarked for the mining operation, and no, she didn't want to just start frittering it away-she struggled- Crazy how she could be so determined their income would go farther if they tithed on his pay, but she didn't want to break up her nice round numbers for a

218

tithe! 'Once I withdraw some, it'll just all start getting away,' she spoke, practically aloud! In her bedroom in the small modular home, Christmas music played softly,

O, come let us adore Him,
O, come let us adore Him,
O, come let us adore Him,
Christ, the Lord!

She stared at the dismal array of gifts! And she had nothing yet for her parents and siblings! Uncharacteristically cranky, she shoved the girls into winter gear and got them strapped into their spots in the backseat! Bearing down on the accelerator, she tried to ignore the equipment working on repairing and enlarging the pad site!

⚞ ⚟

Knowing she couldn't withdraw the cash through the drive-up window, she parked and moved her kids into the stroller! What a blessing her dad's foresight was about getting it! Now if the girls would just halfway act decent while she conducted her business~

To her amazement, Doug pulled up behind her. Her heart lurched when he loomed over her, and she straightened to meet his lips with hers!

"What's up? Didn't know you were coming to town!" His tone a worried reproof!

She swiped at sudden tears! "Well, I was wrapping gifts, and it's such a pitiful stack~so I came to get some cash out!"

He surveyed her silently, worried that she was outside the relative safety of the mine, knowing that all the intel of his office indicated Johnson and cohorts were nearby! The only thing making her more of a target would be having a large cash withdrawal on her!

"What are you going to shop for? You're headed down to Durango?"

"Uh~good question! I'm not withdrawing to shop~"

He frowned, "I thought that was what you said~"

"No~sorry! Guess that's what it sounded like! I'm transferring cash to our checking account and then taking the tithes from both the grazing and finder's fee to the church! Then, I'm going home! Will you be home~Can you watch the girls while I run into the bank? I can put them back in their car seats, and they'll be adorable if you just drive around-"

"I'm working!"

She bit her lip! He was always working! With the hours he was putting in, he couldn't circle the block with their daughters for thirty minutes? Where was the mutual help they were going to provide for each other?

"So, are you having a blond moment? How is taking money to the church going to supplement the meager gifts under our tree?"

She scoffed softly, "I know you're right! It doesn't make sense that you get by giving; it's something you have to see through the eyes of faith!"

"Well, while you're withdrawing, your car can use a brake job!"

She wanted to argue! That was what she meant, by 'once you start withdrawing, where do you stop?' But still, bad brakes on the mountain roads, with the additional precious cargo of the kids-

"Okay, how much are we talking?"

Tears stung her eyes at the amount, and she was suddenly tempted to forsake the entire mission! And he was right! How exactly was her plan going to translate into more gifts? Maybe it was a 'blond moment'!

※ ※

Ellis checked into a bed and breakfast, rich with history, dating back to 1898. Carrying her bike through the common area, she stashed it in her lovely space! The last thing she wanted was to have her bicycle stolen! Back on the main drag, she wandered, driven by relentless interest and curiosity! Dropping into one of the few businesses not closed for the winter, she perused several books that outlined the vibrant history of the mining boomtown in its heyday! Unable to choose, she presented her platinum card and opted for all, cognizant of the fact that they would add weight to her backpack for the morrow's ride! Grinning to herself, she drew comfort from the fact that it would be mainly downhill! Back on the street, she jogged to the end of the row of businesses and crossed over to return up the other side of the street! *Weston-Prescott & Alvaredo Equipment Sales and Rental* announced the heavy equipment company, and was the only new sign in evidence in town! Pulling her collar up against the cold, she turned left at the corner, jogging easily in spite of the nine thousand plus feet in altitude! Onto a residential street, adorable with turn of the twentieth century gingerbread houses! She could see why it was preserved as a historic district! Most of the houses sparkled with festive Christmas decorations, and she began to whistle softly as mountain shadows brought early dusk to the little hamlet!

> *Silent night, holy night,*
> *All is calm, all is bright.*

A block farther and an empty house, sagging from neglect and the onslaught of time, captured her attention!

'It needs me!' The revelation startled her, but there was no escaping the insistence! She picked up speed and ran past it, but then, irrevocably, was drawn back! Hard to believe the fierceness of the inner argument between rational Ellis and the one who wanted ownership of the property against all reason!

⚮ ⚮

Shannon O'Shaughnessy saw his workers off toward Durango, where they had reservations for a late night flight connecting into Little Rock! They had done an amazing job of repairing and enlarging the site and getting the building ready for a very special delivery! For some reason he couldn't put his finger on, he had no desire to return to Arkansas in time for Christmas! No family there, to speak of, since his Aunt Suzanne and her husband Erik were going to Dallas to spend Christmas with David and Mallory! As were his grandmother and his brother and his family! Maybe he just needed some solitude and think time! Not certain why, he left the mine property and headed his rent car toward Silverton

⚮ ⚮

"It's so strange that they never say a word about Alexandra!" Mallory's concern erupted as they headed home from the steak restaurant! "I wonder if they're kind of upset with us for pulling out like we did, and leaving her high and dry~"

"Hope not! We did lots to improve that property! And we're still providing utilities with every month that rolls around! And have been for better than a year! Whatever it is, probably still has to do with Maxwell~and their family dynamic! Don't worry about it!"

221

She nodded, her lovely features illuminated by city lights, "Well, I'm not worried about it! I'm just going to call Alexandra and invite her to come spend Christmas, too! All she can do is tell me, 'No Thanks!'"

David cringed as she punched a button on her phone, figuring it was a bad idea! Then he listened as Mallory pled and cajoled, to disconnect, defeated!

⚐ ⚑

Alexandra fought exhausted tears! Aside from a stiff-lipped, "Thank you," from the pastor for the sizeable check, there seemed to be little financial breakthrough! Maybe the girls only reflected her emotional struggle, because they were extra-fussy and tough to get to sleep! Long day, and except for her unexpected contact with Doug on the street, there was no word from him! A little odd! At loose ends, she considered playing her violin; then chucked the idea for fear it might wake the kids! Then, a phone call from Mallory insisting she come to Dallas for Christmas added more to her turmoil! Janni was off, as she was most evenings, with Jacob!

⚐ ⚑

Doug's memory of the unexpected encounter with his gorgeous wife dissipated quickly in the face of an infuriated call from Trent Morrison! He understood Morrison's frustration, while understanding his father-in-law's worry about Alexandra!

"Well, if they're in town and not actually within the forest, I can't arrest them! Even if they're in the forest, they have a right to be! It'll be hard to prove they're mercenaries, unless they actually succeed in taking down the bad guys! And then, I don't totally get how exactly, they differ from bounty hunters!"

"Bounty hunters work for themselves! I keep telling these guys they're just muddying our waters and they risk precipitating a three-way gun battle!"

"I get that! But the only way I know to stop Atcheson and Cowan is to bring down Johnson and company ourselves! Which is what we've been trying to do!" Doug was exhausted, and having Morrison on his case for things so far beyond his control, was unnerving!

"Yeah, and it isn't just Atcheson and Cowan;" Trent's update, "there's a girl in the mix now, too!"

"Oh, yeah, the good-looking bicyclist? She owns all the infra-red and ground penetrating radar equipment! And she's really sociable and chatty! Well, not chatting me up, but her refilling coffee for restaurant patrons to 'help Margaret' has locals eating out of her hand!"

CHAPTER 23: SURPRISE

Ellis sat in a circle of light in front of the historic hotel! Trying to dismiss thoughts of the adorable house in need of TLC, she concentrated on her book purchases from earlier in the afternoon! She straightened with a start, thoughts of the deserted house literally zapped from her consciousness with the revelation before her! Her breath caught! Both from the cold night air and the import of her discovery! Pulling out her sat phone, she started to punch her speed dial! A shadow flitted in front of her, and a knife flashed!

"Well, ain't you the Little miss smarty pants? Now you've shot yourself in the foot real good! Them there maps and diagrams make all yer fancy stuff unnecessary! Why don't you just stand up nice and easy and let's take us a casual stroll?"

⚔ ⚔

Shannon froze, not sure he was seeing straight! He eased back into shadows to be on the safe side, watching in dread as a lovely woman closed her book and rose to accompany a scuzzy looking guy across the quiet street to a beater of a pickup! The entire scenario screamed coercion! Shaking off shock and indecision, he opted for placing a call to Erik Bransom!

"Yeah, Shannon, thanks for your call! I believe I'll talk to Trent! That's his neck of the woods, and he has doubts about the local sheriff! Look, you don't try anything heroic! He'll get response up there, ASAP!"

Shannon watched his screen go dark! ASAP might not be soon enough!

⚔ ⚔

The pickup truck reeked, making Ellis struggle to keep down her stomach contents! She swallowed hard, wishing she could adjust to the smell enough to concentrate on formulating a plan! Hardy Johnson was right, about her not needing her tech equipment! Not only because of the diagram of local abandoned mine tunnels in her book, but because she had evidently found him! No tech necessary! She fought panic!

⚔ ⚔

Shannon followed a group of locals making their way into a small church, evidently for a Christmas Eve service! He was torn between entering with them to pray for the situation he had just witnessed, or to pray as he pursued a more constructive plan!

"God, what can I do? Erik ordered me not to do anything foolish–I don't want to compound the problem~or increase her danger~"

He wanted to run to his rental car, but something whispered caution! Maybe there were accomplices still watching! Forcing calm he made it to his car and fastened his seat belt slowly! Grocery store! If he decided to search personally, he would need supplies! A car behind him, older model, with one dim headlight! Following him? Or just headed to the only grocery store in town? People would doubtless be picking up last-minute items for Christmas dinners! Still, as he headed toward the doors, whoever was in the vehicle didn't get out!

⚔ ⚔

Trent was nonplussed! Trying to do a turn-around in his thinking, he realized he had no choice but to combine forces with Atcheson and Cowan! His workforce was still seriously depleted, and it was Christmas! He still thought he was right! That a bunch of good guys who didn't know one another, running around in the forest, made 'friendly fire' a real concern! Glumly, he placed a call to Doug! It was strange to him, but Alexandra, whom he would have thought was too much of a diva to be a cop's wife, was proving amazingly understanding of the crazy life-style!

He quickly explained Shannon's call to Erik, who in turn had phoned him, "I'm working on a search warrant so you and Bailey can get into the girl's room and see what–In the meantime, Daniel Faulkner's getting word to Atcheson and Cowan! She seems to be working in tandem with them! We're not sure they're aware that she's been grabbed!"

"Maybe she hasn't been," Doug's voice of reason! "Maybe your so-called witness has an over-active imagination!"

Trent sighed! Not a bad point! He would like to hope that! "No, I've known Shannon for a long time! His facts are straight! His description sounds like Johnson in the flesh! He watched the pickup turn left on 10th Street, but didn't attempt to tail him! He assumes that since 10th runs into County Rd 33, he might have gone~

"Yeah, that would make sense," Doug agreed! "If it is Johnson personally who did the snatch~"

Emotion made it hard for him to continue!

"Yeah, bad news for anyone; but especially a girl!"

⚜ ⚜

Shannon strolled through the store, wondering if the sedan was still in the parking lot! Even though they weren't in a rush to come in and shop, it didn't prove they had an interest in him! Could be meeting up with someone else in the well-lighted lot, or waiting for an employee to get off!

The store didn't seem to offer a great deal in the way of survival gear! Maybe he should focus on granola bars and durable food items! He had a backpack with him! Then, he watched in amazement as an employee rolled a rack of new arrivals from the back! Very nice, heavy-duty, quilted jackets! He joined the melee and came away with a scratch by his eye, and a black jacket in his size!

A silvery-haired dowager smiled at him sympathetically! "You're not local, are you?"

"No, Ma'am! A Bostonian! Am I that easy to peg?"

She laughed, "Oh, yes, Dear! But I know everyone in six counties! You're not planning on eating granola bars for Christmas dinner, are you? You must come to our place for Christmas dinner at Six O'clock tomorrow evening!" She laughed at her own meager basket! "I already have most of my groceries bought! My name's Hallie Pritchard! You'll have no difficulty finding us! We're in the loveliest Victorian at the top of the street!"

He smiled, "Thank you very much! I'm Shannon! Merry Christmas!"

⚜ ⚜

Doug picked up a complaining Bailey and headed toward Silverton, sharing his plan as he drove, "I'm betting a search warrant's gonna be slow, what with its being Christmas! Let's head out the County Road!"

"What, just the two of us? Listen, Sir Galahad, I've said you're nuts already, so you don't have to prove it! If Morrison said to comb through stuff in the woman's room, that's where our focus needs to be!"

"Well, if and when the warrant comes through, we won't be that far out-" He turned earnest features toward the older agent! "You have a daughter, don't you? How would you like Johnson and his goons-they're-they're reprehensible-to have her in their grasp?"

⇥ ⇤

The pickup jerked to a stop! If Johnson wanted to drive a standard tranny, he should take it easier on the clutch! Ellis' fleeting thought, before another man opened the passenger door and shoved her over, forcing his huge girth into the tight space! A heavy hood slid over her face, and she panicked! Pinned by the weight of the newcomer and struggling to breathe through the heavy fabric, she lost consciousness!

⇥ ⇤

Shannon slid into the driver's seat, chortling under his breath! "Thank You, Lord, please keep helping me! Well, not me, so much as Ellis!" He caressed her name, having gotten it from Trent Morrison! "Thank You for making me run into Hallie! Which, somehow jogged my memory about the silver-haired warriors under the command of Steb Hanson! He already has it across his wire!"

Reaching the parking lot, he couldn't help smiling as a couple of serious local ranchers turned the occupant of the suspicious car over to the sheriff's department! One of the men leaned in to assure good-naturedly! "We don't totally trust the sheriff in some issues, either! We keep an eye out! Good eye, you noticing you were followed!"

⇥ ⇤

Ellis moaned weakly as she came to! The pickup moved forward slowly down a steep incline! Her dread sky-rocketed! They were doubtless on a steep ramp, descending into the earth! Doug Hunter's experience, related to her by Ward Atcheson, confirmed, again without benefit of her earth-penetrating radar devices! The criminal entity operated from an underground lair!

And she was helpless, bound tightly, obviously, while she was unconscious

⚔ ⚔

Christmas morning, and Doug hadn't come home! Or called! Alexandra fought tears! Not worried about him so much as annoyed! Since he was basically a bulldog for tenacity, she didn't doubt he was working! And she didn't mind that so much, as the fact that he was reluctant to request time off for the upcoming meeting with her family! Getting her Bible and tuning the radio to non-stop Christmas music, she tried to settle at the kitchen counter with her Bible! Blessedly the girls were still asleep, and they were too small to know their Christmas was going to be a bust!

Another frenzied banging on her door brought her to her feet with a start! Pretty sure Shannon and his crew were finished and gone, she clasped her robe about her and tried to sneak a peek! No security alert~who could have gained access~?

⚔ ⚔

Daniel watched Diana covertly as she helped Suzanne and Eric with last minute dinner preparations! If she was concerned about Al, it was hard to tell! He remembered her assurances to Zave~whatever had precipitated that~he was unsure of! But she was right! Change was inevitable, and there was no point missing present joyous moment with regrets of what was, but is no more! Alexandra was a survivor, and in just a few more days~

⚔ ⚔

"Here, better let me try a bite of that~you know~just to be sure it~okay~"

Suzanne laughingly complied, spooning a sample of her orange/cranberry relish! After a long night with no sleep, Erik was suddenly light-hearted and more jovial than she had seen him in months!

228

Trent Morrison dozed in front of the Anderson's big-screen, oblivious to football action! He too, was relieved at another successful rescue! But since he and Bransom were the only two of Mallory's guests aware of the Colorado drama, they were keeping it quiet! Well, for one thing, Trent didn't want Faulkner to make the mistake of thinking he was on-board with his methods!

⚐ ⚑

A screech split the frigid morning air! Followed by a second, that brought Jared from the mining office in his stocking feet!

"What in the world~" He stared, frowning, into the newly installed modular building!

"This is why my dad sent Shannon and the building!" Tears coursed down her cheeks as she swept a gesture toward the just-delivered gift!

"Hmmm, all that work and expense, just for a piano?"

Alexandra shook her head in wonder at the ignorant observation of her mining engineer! It wasn't 'just a piano'! It was a brand new Steinway Baby Grand! The deliveryman's comments hardly registered, except that once the instrument acclimated to the move and the climate difference, one of the company experts would come tune it! She watched dazed as other, brightly wrapped gifts were brought in and stacked in the spacious area!

And the building was extremely nice, with impressive finish-work! Not just a piano, but a music room/play area for the girls, in spite of the small size of her house! Leave it to her daddy to figure out a way, and spare no expense! She sighed! For some reason, she still tended to worry about her parents' finances!

⚐ ⚑

Shannon hesitated in the doorway, overcome with bashfulness! He should go! Flights would be cheaper today and less crowded! He needed to get back to Little Rock where he belonged! While he hesitated, his phone jangled! A Colorado area code; he didn't recognize the number! But the jangle had roused the patient, and he flushed with embarrassment!

She fumbled for the button to raise the head of her bed, "Shannon; was it? Wow! I guess~I~owe my life~"

He shrugged, grinning sheepishly, "That's the way I see it, I saved your life so now you owe it to me!"

Big brown eyes drifted shut, and then opened as she struggled to answer, "Yes, that's what we were taught in Sunday School! Since Jesus rescued us from our sins, we owe our lives to Him! You're-you're a-born-again-Christian-aren't you? My life already belongs to Jesus!"

"Yeah, mine, too," he blurted, "But I still want to get married-well-you know-someday-"

'Dumb, Shannon,' he castigated himself! "Well, I just wanted to check on you, that they got you settled into a room! I'm tiring you-"

"Please stay!"

"Really?"

A weak smile that still brought no wash of color to ashen features! "Really! Don't sound so surprised! Although, I may have an ulterior motive for wanting-company-" Tears sprang to her eyes! "I've never known terror like that! And even now, it's hard to-grasp-the fact-that-I'm safe!"

She was so beautiful that he was tongue-tied, and he'd already uttered some boners he wished he could un-utter!

Trent paced the Anderson's driveway, giddy relief giving way to acute frustration! Steb Hanson's army of Medicare recipients had freed the Vaughn girl; although not before she suffered extreme trauma! His guys in conjunction with Cowan and Atcheson, had secured the immediate crime scene and transported the girl to Durango for medical treatment! Even now, he hoped they had chosen the best option! He swiped furtively at tears, hoping the small hospital's staff was proficient enough to reattach a severed toe!

But Johnson had once again evaded capture! Trent was still torn between spending the remainder of Christmas in Dallas with his family, and hurrying to Colorado, once again! He scoffed at himself! Not like his numerous trips there accomplished much! Must look like more government waste! Trips with no tangible results!

And Bailey, crowing about how stupid Hardy Johnson was! Johnson killing his own troops for the slightest challenges to his leadership, and running out of gas in his pickup while fleeing! True, he wasn't the genius of Noë Keller, his predecessor, but he had managed to thwart Forestry Law

Enforcement guys for nearly two years! What he lacked in mental acuity, he made up for in pure ruthlessness, and a certain cunning!

And the toe! Trent shuddered! That answered questions about other victims whose remains reflected the same MO! With all his heart he wished Faulkner would bring Alexandra home until they could eliminate the threat to her!

His phone buzzed! Sonia demanding where he had disappeared to, and telling him dinner was ready! Squaring his shoulders, he marched back toward the imposing edifice! Time to put on his Merry Christmas mask and act like everything was fine and dandy! At least Ellis Vaughn was safe!

⚜ ⚜

Alexandra fixed toast with peanut butter and offered Leisel the same! This was dinner, following a lunch of microwave mac n cheese! Well, she had given most of her staff, including the chow hall cooks, Christmas Day off-still no word from Doug! She tried to thrust concern aside! He just got so engrossed in what he did! After a jar of baby food and a bottle for Angelique, she situated them once again in the new building and lost herself in her new piano! Caressing the keys as she sang:

And the star reigns its fire
While the beautiful sing,
For the manger of Bethlehem
Cradles a king!

Applause startled her as she ended the carol! There stood Doug and Jim Bailey!

She sprang upward to embrace Doug and wish him a Merry Christmas, then paused mid-spring, as her welcoming smile faded!

"You're hurt?"

"We're fine! Blood's not from us! The victim's doing okay! I brought Bailey~"

She nodded perceptively, "Because you figured there would be Christmas dinner at the chow hall! I've wished all day that I hadn't given a cook's day off!" She brightened, "Actually, we have a dinner invitation, if you can clean up quick! I didn't want to accept and try to handle the girls alone! Hallie's house is a treasure-trove, doll-house!"

231

Doug nodded, smiling at her with fresh admiration! Angelique was an 'angel' baby in arms! And no threat whatsoever to anyone's treasured possessions! And yet Alexandra never just came out and told him that his kid was atrocious!

"So, the purpose behind moving this modular in, was that your parents were sending a piano?" His tone sounded flat with disappointment! And he was right! They actually needed a lot of other things before they needed the extravagance of the instrument!

"Hurry! We can talk later! I'll phone Hallie~"

⊨ ⊨

"You're sure I'm not wearing you out too much? You probably need some rest~"

Drug-leaden eyelids forced open, "I know I'm monopolizing your whole Christmas! And after all you did~"

"I didn't really do anything! Agent Bransom~told me not~I-I wish~I~ And you'd nearly freed yourself, anyway! But not before~" he couldn't bring himself to say it!

"Before he cut off my toe! I wonder how bad it'll look! My sandal-wearing days may be over! This is silly, but I always kind of thought my feet were my cutest feature!"

He regarded her in silent wonder! Wow! If her feet were the cutest thing about her, they must really be something! She was gorgeous!

"How did you know where to send searchers? This is a huge area up here, remote and intimidating!"

He nodded slowly, "True, but the Senior Citizen Brigade members are all from around here and familiar with the area! I figured out the mine/tunnel system~because the grocery store featured the same book you were looking at in the square! I photographed the diagrams and emailed them to Mr. Morrison, and the rancher that owned the parcel where that vertical shaft exits, knew right where it was! He had actually hired my cousin's company to drill there this past summer! Right down through the shaft and on down into bedrock! But he tries to keep the opening covered to prevent accidents to livestock! He didn't know those thugs were using it as one of their rabbit holes!"

She nodded, forcing back a yawn! "Tell me about your family and friends! What were they drilling for? All the precious metals are mined out~"

CHAPTER 24: FRUSTRATED

Shannon rose as a flurry of activity in the corridor broke the serenity of watching Ellis sleep! The arrival of her family!

He extended his hand, aware that he looked like a train-wreck! "Shannon O'Shaughnessy! She'll be glad you guys are here! She's so traumatized that she's kept asking me to stay; she doesn't want to be alone yet!"

His voice barely came out! True, he was emotionally drained! And exhausted! But Ellis Vaughn's family was intimidating! Pinpoint black eyes beneath heavy dark brows held his gaze commandingly! US Navy Captain, all right! And her four brothers looked like football linebackers! Also US Navy officers, from what little information he had gotten out of her!

"Hello, Shannon; did you say?" an older, more heavy-set version of Ellis stepped forward!

The Captain laughed! "Mr. O'Shaughnessy, meet my wife, Darlene! The true commandant of the Vaughn family! Thank you for what you've done to aid our daughter!"

The Captain turned from the speechless hero as his wife roused their daughter!"

"Wow!" Ellis' voice soft as her gaze traveled around the circle of faces, "You didn't all have to come!"

⇥ ⇤

Hallie Pritchard squeezed Alexandra and the girls as they made their way out into the cold night air!

"Come back again, soon, Dear! Thank you for phoning and coming over! You brightened our Christmas immeasurably! I'm sorry Shannon was unable to come! I liked him immediately!"

Alexandra smiled! That was Hallie! She liked everyone! Well, anyone even half-way decent!

"Thank you for sharing your beautiful home and your Christmas dinner, and for all the gifts! I wish Shannon could have come, too! I guess he was worried that Hardy Johnson would try to make a move on his victim again! That's-that's incomprehensible-cutting off-her-why would anyone do that?"

"Depravity of mankind!" Russell Pritchard answered in a gruff growl! "We wish he would make another move on her! Because we're ready! Sadly, something tipped him off that Miss Vaughn had escaped, so none of them returned to the mine complex! Our guys retrieved a couple of dead guys down in there, and evidence! As well as evidence from the impounded pickup truck!"

Hallie's lovely countenance crinkled! "You must all be very careful up there! We know you're eager to have your mine be a success-Well, we'll let you go! It's cold out here for me to stand and lecture you!"

"Thank you, Mrs. Pritchard!" Doug answered appreciatively, "Thank you for your concern! If we don't get the woods cleared soon, of this element-" he broke off! He needed an opportunity to talk to Alexandra-but his worry deepened each day! And cutting off a toe had only been the beginning of Johnson's wicked plans for Ellis Vaughn! And he had a real vendetta against Alexandra!

≒ ≓ "

"Do you think everyone had a good Christmas? And liked their gifts?" Mallory's troubled gaze met David's!

"I think they did! There were just a lot of extenuating circumstances that created an undercurrent of tension!"

Her frown deepened, "Then it wasn't just my imagination? Was it because of Alexandra? I begged her to come-"

He sighed, "Indirectly! It's mostly the tension, I think, of the ongoing manhunt for Hardy Johnson! Trent Morrison is frustrated as can be! And I think Faulkner realizes that, and sympathizes! But his issue is Alexandra's safety! So, he's tried to take measures of his own!" He shrugged, "I'm

234

telling you, that I'm for people in law enforcement~but I don't leave your safety and that of the kids in their hands alone! Too many bad guys with evil agendas, and too few good law enforcement people! He quoted a verse they both used often:

> *A prudent man forseeth the evil, and hideth himself: but the simple pass on and are punished. Proverbs 22:3*

"That's a fabulous verse, repeated twice word for word, in the book of Proverbs! And it has thousands of other possible applications! Also the *Home Interiors* founder, Mary Crowley, used to say, *If it's to be, it's up to me!*"

Mallory nodded agreement! "Personal responsibility and not waiting around for someone else to come solve your problems~"

"Right, and then blaming 'them' for where we end up! Just so you know, I had a fantastic Christmas! I love the new saddle and boots! Strictly class! But~more than that, I love our phenomenal life! The kids are just cuter and more fun~with every day that passes! Seeing their eyes sparkle, and hearing them laugh~and you!"

She flushed, and he reached for her! "The kids had a great Christmas, mercifully oblivious to tension and worries of the adults!" He massaged a faint worry line from her forehead with a gentle finger! "You care about people so much, that you want to fix everything for them!" His eyes sought hers, "It's too big of a job, Erin!"

⊰ ⊱

"I guess I should be going, then!" Shannon reached for his jacket and retrieved an empty soda can, making an awkward exit from Ellis' bedside! No acknowledgement of his mumbling departure, and he escaped! So Captain Vaughn was a highly esteemed vascular surgeon! Consequently, his immediate demand was to view his daughter's reattached appendage! Shannon didn't want to see it, but he felt a strange emptiness as he emerged onto the street!

Beautiful, but way out-classing him! He needed to move on, glad for what little assistance he had provided to her rescuers! Placing the rent car into gear, he headed toward the small regional airport! If he couldn't get a connection to Denver and then Little Rock, he could drive to Grand Junction which provided better carrier and destination options!

His spirits soared when a ticket agent informed him that getting out standby on any carrier from any western slope airport, would be impossible in the post-Christmas rush!

He tossed his keys into the air and caught them, 'Why not return to Silverton, then?'

⊨ ⊫

Alexandra was amazed that Doug pulled his boots off, turned on the gas fireplace, and sank into a recliner! She bent and plugged in a cord that brought the Christmas tree to life! The girls were both asleep; they usually fell asleep in the car! And usually, she was relieved to move them into their cribs without waking them! But it was still Christmas! Howbeit an odd one! Starting Christmas music playing, she wakened the drowsy Leisel and pulled her pack n play nearer the tree and the warmth of the fireplace! Glowing, she started her new single serving coffee maker-first with a hot chocolate, and then with coffees for Doug and herself!

A nostalgic smile as she presented the toddler with a resplendent Christmas angel cookie! No need to guess where the hostess, Hallie, had ordered that from! Beth Sander's website, where Beth filled orders for Diana's elegant seasonal Christmas business!

Cradling Angelique, she lowered herself to the floor between Doug's recliner and the pile of gifts under the tree! Carefully, she handed the first gift to Leisel! Carefully, because the child was protective of her space! Fearfully so! Doing the wrong thing could precipitate a tantrum-or genuine panic-who could tell? She proffered it to dimpled little hands that drew back.

"Here Leisel, this is a Christmas present! From Daddy and Mommy! Tear the paper! You tear the paper to get the present that's inside!"

A scowl and the child scuttled to the opposite end of her enclosure!

"Okay, watch Daddy open his!"

Doug's response wasn't too much better than his daughter's, "Look, Alexandra; I-uh-don't have-"

"I know! You just bought my rings! And I love them! This isn't actually that much of a gift! Would you just-so she can-get the idea-?"

With a sudden resonant laugh that dispelled the ghosts of worry, he ripped the paper, to hold up a, heavy, flannel, plaid shirt!

"I love it! Wow! That's really nice! Doesn't help my guilt trip any! Did you take money from your mining account to get-"

She strove for a stern look, "Don't kid yourself, Douglas Hunter! I may love you, but-" She laughed! "No, I withdrew the tithe amounts and money for the brake job! Which, that's actually a mine expense, anyway! I use my car for mining business! So, I gave my tithe, and God gave me the desire of my heart! Something I wouldn't even admit to myself-"

"Oh, yeah, a piano! You could use Abby's!"

She laughed; it didn't matter that Doug didn't get it! Because she had a Heavenly Father Who was true to His Word! And Who understood the impossible logistics of her getting to Durango and back, and actually having time to practice! When Abby wasn't there teaching her lessons! And besides that! Her new instrument was a Steinway!

"And look at all these gift cards from my family and the Pritchards!" She was overwhelmed by God's faithful provision since her tithe given in trembling faith! "They're amazing! Maybe we can go up to Grand Junction and shop the after-Christmas sales! Wal-Mart, we can get groceries and toiletries, but maybe a couple of little outfits for Angelique? She's growing so fast and I want to dress her up for when my mom comes-" Tears sprang to her eyes! Doug had no idea the longing in her heart to dress her baby up cute! But God cared! And He had done something tangible about it, too!

One of Leisel's strange little gurgles caught her attention!

She smiled! "Yeah, that's right, Baby, tear the paper! Rip! Tear! See what you got!"

☜ ☞

Ellis bit into her lip, stifling a moan! It wasn't always easy being a military kid! And the only girl in a family of tough, teasing brothers!

Captain Vaughn straightened with a relieved sigh! Tiny neat stitches and a pinkening second metatarsal showed that good surgeons were on call on Christmas day, even out here in the boondocks! He harrumphed, forcing his tough persona to cover emotions!

"Good! Looks like you're gonna make it! I'll fly out in the morning for San Diego, but Mother will stay until you can come home! I'm hoping your brothers don't all go AWOL hunting for the guy who did this! But they're Vaughns! I'm sure they'll be making this man wish he'd never been born~before their emergency leave ends! Use the pain med! It's what it's there for!"

"Yes, Sir!" A wan smile! He was tough, but she had never doubted his devotion to her! Her brothers accused her of being the spoiled 'Daddy's girl!' She basked in it! Although she had no intentions of going home with her mother, she knew from long experience not to argue! Why bother? When she had devised so many other means of getting her way!

Speaking of getting her own way, she wondered curiously where Shannon had gone!

⚔ ⚔

Shannon shivered as he approached the empty house in the Silverton historical district! It was beyond needing a facelift! He'd flipped enough houses to know this would be a labor of love with no hope of recuperating the expenses! He frowned! Ellis Vaughn seemed irrevocably drawn to it! He tried to shake off the temptation to own it as bait for reeling her in! That was before she had fallen into the hands of Johnson and his cohorts! By now, she was probably just eager to get back East! And not care if she ever saw Silverton, Colorado again!

He shivered again! The north wind, bitingly cold! But something eerie, too! He laughed at himself! There was no such thing as haunted houses! Even in a practically ghost town!

Frozen to the spot, he finally pulled his phone from his pocket and snapped a picture! Then, spinning away, he took off at a brisk trot for the lights of the main street!

⚔ ⚔

Trent was amazed at his own confidence in sending the Vaughns from his victim's hospital room! His work persona, as opposed to his natural reticence! He needed her statement, and when the Captain attempted to sit in, a pleading look from the girl made him extra-firm!

Once the Captain disappeared, she broke into terrified sobs and the story came out in explosive phrases between hiccups!

238

Steeling himself to passive expression, he wrote as the story unfolded, without interrupting to ask for details! Further clarity would come later, but for now, he needed this raw version!

She broke off to ask, "Where did Shannon go?"

He frowned, not totally certain why it mattered, especially at the moment!

"He saw him!" Fearful whisper of indefinite pronouns!

"Okay, take it easy! Who saw who-uh-er-whom-"

"Shannon! Saw the-um-Mr.-make the-grab-"

"Mr. Johnson," Trent clarified! "You can refer to him as the kidnapper or the perpetrator! Where was Shannon?"

"Just coming out of the mercantile! I didn't know it then, but he had noticed me for a while! When he realized how absorbed I was in the books I'd purchased, he went in and leafed through them! He was coming out when-he-saw me stand up and walk-with-uh- the kidnapper-" Her voice dropped to such a soft timbre that he could barely hear, "To his truck! When the pickup-swung around-the headlights-pinned him-he was kind of turned away by then, to-act like-he-uh-didn't notice anything!"

"You think Shannon's in danger?"

"I hope not! Because of me!"

Trent's frown deepened! "If he is in trouble, it isn't because of you! It's the criminals that makes trouble-"

Her eyes blazed into his and then dropped guiltily! "But, I wasn't an innocent bystander! I was here at the invitation of a couple of business associates!"

"I'm aware! Atcheson and Cowan! To help them track Johnson down with your sophisticated equipment! And the book you purchased mesmerized you because it diagrammed the abandoned mine shafts in the county! Giving you a great place to start your search grids! It embarrasses me that I've been so determined to apprehend these guys by pure force of will alone! Proud of my division's working hard, although not working as smart as they might! And so proud of keeping my budget under control, that I don't requisition-state of the art equipment-when I should!"

She nodded, soberly, emotions momentarily quelled, "You do remind me of my father!"

Figuring that wasn't necessarily a compliment, he cleared his throat and proceeded! "So, Johnson had you in his pickup, and it was parked on the street facing west; he swung around to head east, and-did he notice Shannon?"

"Yes, Sir! He swore at me! And asked me who that was- and when I told him I didn't know, he swore worse-and he called someone to-tell them that-I created-a-problem-and to go take care of-it- He-had me-by the hair-and he was hurting me-while he-promised he wouldn't-hurt me-if I'd behave-I thought about-trying to open-the door-and jump-out-but he-my-hair- It hurt! And I was afraid! And then he stopped and this huge guy got in-"

Trent steeled himself against tears that wanted to surface! If he were in an interrogation room, this is when he would excuse himself with a pretext of something coming up! As it was, he pressed onward, knowing the girl's parents were barely beyond earshot, longing to be with her, to comfort her, to learn the details they were only guessing at!

He couldn't help being impressed with her determination and resourcefulness! Well so terror-filled at what Johnson's intentions for her were! She had decided she was going to escape or die trying! Rather than falling prey to them upon their return!

"So, Johnson shot two of his own guys dead down there?" Trent clarifying the tearful details! Seasoned in criminal investigations, these details still gave him chills! "Just for looking at you wrong?"

She shuddered. "They had some 'mission' to fulfill, first! Johnson told them all, 'First things first'! They had 'Orders from headquarters' that they'd be in a lot of trouble-and once they had accomplished their assignment, they could come back and give me all the time I deserved!" She dug the heels of her hands into red-rimmed eyes to quell additional tears!

Trent's numb brain tried to absorb the new details! 'Orders from headquarters'? Why had he assumed Keller's death had left Johnson at the top of the organizational chart? Maybe Keller hadn't even been at the top of the dog pile! Who issued orders? From where? And, why? The broadening scope of the investigation left him nearly physically ill! Keller and then Johnson had both been merely pawns? How could he have missed it? How could Hunter-

He rose, "I'm going to go get another cup of coffee? May I bring you anything?"

She shook her head energetically, "No, Sir! I'm fine! What about Shannon?"

He nodded slowly, "You're right! I'll check on him and then I need to disseminate this new information to my agents! Listen, I know I've worn you out; write down anything additional~"

"You haven't worn me out, Special Agent! And I've barely gotten started!"

"Okay then, give me fifteen minutes to update my guys and contact O'Shaughnessy! I'll give you a sit rep on him when I return! You're sure~"

"You can bring me a black coffee! Fifteen minutes!" Expressive eyes smoldered.

≒ ≓

Alexandra was hardly surprised when Doug pulled his socks and boots on following yet another call from Trent Morrison!

He turned apologetic eyes her direction, but she was already moving into gear! "I'll make a thermos of coffee, and Hallie's leftover turkey will make a couple of great sandwiches! You guys are closing in on them, Doug!" She kissed him long and hard, "But, please be careful!"

"Yeah, you, too! Bolt the doors and keep your pistol handy!"

She nodded agreement, "Believe me, I do! I'll be glad when Mr. Porter can finally start next week!"

Doug's startled countenance changed back to a mask, but Alexandra noticed and laughed. "I know, you're worried about what Trent Morrison thinks about it! He already called him and laid down ground rules! That Mr. Porter and the other security guys can run protective details for me and the girls, and provide security to the mine and ore transports; but they can't go out and beat the woods for the bad guys!"

CHAPTER 25:   DISASTER

Dropping his truck key into his pocket, Doug walked around to get Alexandra's door, still teasing her that she insisted he make a 'phony' first impression on her mother, by opening the door for her!

Her retort died in her throat as she sensed a whizzing sound~

Doug dropped limply, the laughing light in his eyes extinguished in a moment of time! Before one horrified scream could escape her throat, another chilling *whish*, and she was pushed backwards against the truck, sliding to the ground, staring in horror as bright crimson stained the snow! Blood bubbled around the wicked-looking arrow, and she tried to reach for Doug!

Commotion, as skiers at last took in the magnitude of the nearly noiseless assaults! Fleeting impressions tried to register in Alexandra's shock-numbed brain! Knowing Doug was gone, she willed herself to reach him! The babies~her father flying down the front steps of the ski lodge, pistol in hand~They were going to kill him, too! And then she would never find forgiveness from her siblings~

Then, her mother was beside her~but her apology and plea for forgiveness wouldn't come! Muteness, as she attempted to look past the barrier that was her mother to see Doug's form sprawled there!

Why couldn't she talk? Why couldn't she scream, "Daddy! No! Come back!"? Why couldn't she get the words out that both babies were sleeping in the back seat?

A blanket descended to cover Doug and then another materialized around her! Maybe she was dead, too! It was all so fast! And so surreal!

More confusion and a chopper's racket split the chill air as the craft lowered and medical personnel ran toward her! When her mother yielded her care to the medical team, her voice was still frozen up-somewhere beyond the cavern of her writhing belly! She wanted to beg her mother to stay with her, but she had surrendered that right forever!

She watched shocked, as a medic bent to retrieve something and place it beside her on the stretcher!

"We'll try to save the arm, Ma'am!" His words whispered to Diana!

Diana's whisper in return, "Just save her life!"

⊣ ⊢ "

"NO!" A frenzied screech at last issued from parched throat! "No, no! Oh, dear God; no, please-Oh-Doug! Oh No! God, please don't-" Alexandra forced herself upright, despite searing pain in her right shoulder-a worry flitted through her numbed psyche-that she had fought her way back as a violinist and pianist-to lose an arm! Served her right! For defying the Lord when her parents had taught her-

Commotion in the hallway and Janni stood there, staring at her strangely! "Are you okay? I heard you scream-"

"So did we-" Abby and Jared's blanched faces appeared beyond Janni! "Did you see something? Are they out there?"

Confusion gave way to tears, and Alexandra shook uncontrollably! "I-I-guess I-was just-I thought they killed-Doug-It was-all-so-horrifyingly real-"

CHAPTER 26: FORGIVENESS

Diana braced herself, trying to be prepared for anything! At least, after this, she would know! Not knowing what was going on with her firstborn had been hard to deal with! Even with all of the caviar and other solaces!

Jeremiah fidgeted! He figured this trip was about Alexandra! It sure wasn't about skiing! Leaving a Tulsa blanketed with snow, he was shocked at boulder-strewn, brown slopes dotted with a few pitiful patches of dirty snow!

⚜ ⚜

Alexandra patted on powder! She was an emotional wreck, and her swollen, blotchy eyes refused to surrender to the effects of cosmetics!

"You look great!" Doug's valiant efforts to reassure her brought a wan smile! She was so glad he was okay! The vividness of the nightmare caused her to shudder uncontrollably!

"Thanks, but you're a terrible liar!"

He winked at her, "I take umbrage at being called any kind of a liar!" His warm hand covered her clammy one, "Hey, it's gonna be okay! A couple of hours and you'll know~one way or the other~We'll be okay! We're~we're our own family now!"

He fished in the pocket of his new shirt! "I have something for you! Call it a late Christmas present!"

Her startled eyes met his as she unfolded a piece of paper, "A check from the government to replace your personal items?"

Smiling eyes held hers, "Yeah, as usual with the government, it was so slow, I forgot about it! Wh~why don't you tithe on it~and then use the rest for whatever you've been wanting?"

She blinked rapidly, not wanting a fresh deluge of tears to ruin the most recently applied coat of mascara! But there were two significant victories here! Well, three! He had referred to their little foursome as a family, he had decided to at least tithe for the moment, and he seemed to be realizing her need for personal mad money!

Smiling eyes turned serious, "There's a catch to it, though, Baby~"

She nodded, unfazed, "You want me to go home with my family until all these guys are apprehended? I think you're right!" Tears welled up again! "But, you have to promise me, Douglas Hunter, that you'll be careful!"

He was startled not to get her usual argument!

She explained, "Well, we've hit the end of the silver streak, and as long as all the crazies are out there, I can't go out and try to track if there's a fracture and slippage! It's just, that Leisel seems to be adjusting a little~to her new normal~My parents are so perfect, and so are my brothers and sisters~I~I'm not sure I can deal with her~before~such an audience~"

"Oh, you have brothers and sisters?"

She flushed. "Yeah, none of them were in the 'accident'!" Her having deceived him early on was still a point of contention between them.

"How many do you have?"

"Three brothers, three sisters! I'm~uh~the oldest There would have been more of us, but my mom miscarried several times! I was afraid through my whole pregnancy, that I'd lose Angelique! Have I ever told you thank you for delivering her successfully?"

"Beginner's luck, I guess! I don't plan on ever doing it again! And you did everything! I just caught her~the rest is kind of~a blur~"

She nodded, anxious gaze wrinkling her forehead, "I was so scared that Brad was right behind me, and that he'd shoot us~both~"

⚔ ⚔

"You're sure this is a good idea?" David didn't ordinarily question Mallory's judgment, but he thought she should quit worrying so much about the Faulkners and Alexandra, always trying to fix everything!

Her agonized expression was his answer! "Well, we need to visit Dr. and Mrs. Allen and check on our alpaca! The book of Proverbs does say to, '*look well to your herds*'!

He shrugged, 'Good enough point, but since it was too early in the season for shearing, and there was no cause for alarm~the timing seemed obviously to be about Alexandra's having spent Christmas alone'!

When the gate attendant announced pre-boarding for families with children, they began assembling kids and carry-ons!

"There isn't even any snow for pretending we came to ski," he whispered as he settled into the reserved bulkhead seat!

She made a mischievous face, "Would you please relax? We're a couple of grown-ups who can do what we want! There are literally millions of things in Colorado to draw me there, as a Geologist!"

⚜ ⚜

A sob tore from Diana and she was on her feet, launched toward the timid foursome entering the lodge! Daniel rose, watching anxiously, for any response from Alexandra! And then, she was in her mother's arms, sobbing and struggling incoherently to deliver a practiced speech!

"Mom, I'm sorry we're~late~actually~I'm sorry for~everything! I don't~deserve~ forgive~ness ~but~I miss every~one~so~much! I love you, Mom! Oh, Mom~this is Doug~Doug~my~mother, Diana!"

Diana placed a tender kiss on her daughter's cheek before acknowledging the introduction! The scenario was so different than she expected, that her natural aplomb nearly forsook her, leaving her stammering! "Oh~you look so~beautiful~Hello, Doug, pleased~to~to meet you~Who~who's this?"

She made a move toward the security blanket covering Leisel's head, and Doug swung away involuntarily!

Alexandra stepped in, grasping Angelique in her infant carrier from him! "S~sorry, Mom! Leisel gets panicky~in new places~with~new~people~And, this is~um ~Angelique~"

Daniel held his breath! A shock, he was sure, for Diana to assimilate! Still heartbroken about further attempts at childbearing, sudden grandmother-hood was bound to be a jolt to her psyche! He assumed that in all of her worrying, this possibility hadn't entered her mind!

At last, un-rooted from his spot, he reached her side, shook Doug's hand, hugged Al, and got Angelique, carrier and all to the table!

✠ ✠

And I saw a great white throne, and him that sat on it, from whose face the earth and heaven fled away; and there was found no place for them.

And I saw the dead, small and great stand before God; and the books were opened: and another book was opened, which is the book of life: and the dead were judged out of those things which were written in the book according to their works. Revelation 20:11&12

Cowan lay so still, that an occasional blink was the only indication he was alive! Atcheson gave grudging credit! Plenty to divide the two men, but for the moment, they were bonded once more by a mission that bridged their differences!

Today was Johnson's day to meet his Maker! Well, as the expression went! Both men knew enough Bible doctrine, to realize that ending the felon's life would send him to eternal torment! His meeting with his Maker was actually an appointment he wouldn't make until the Great White Throne Judgment, scheduled at the end of the seven year Tribulation and Millennial Reign of Christ on earth! But, all in due time! Hardy Johnson wouldn't be amputating any more toes, torturing any more victims!

Atcheson's brows drew together in concentration! His screen lit up with crouched figures spotted by a spy drone using infrared capabilities He counted eleven, wondering absently how the suspect could shoot two of his own guys dead and immediately muster replacements!

"Scan out!" he ordered softly! "Make sure the woods aren't full of any others!"

The enlarged field of vision indeed indicated more figures! Marked with digital smiley faces! He shook his head! Friendlies!

"Friendlies closing!" a soft whisper to Cowan! "Let's get her done before they approach close enough to become collateral damage!"

"On five!"

✠ ✠

Daniel sent a pointed look at Jeremiah, who ribbed Cassandra, to step on Xavier's toe, spreading the message around the table to smile a welcome! Or do something besides stare like they were under alien invasion!

"Who is that?" Elysia's stage whisper to Ryan!

"Duh! It's Al, our big sister! Where have you been?" a much more subdued whisper in response!

"Oh, yeah," But a puzzled countenance showed that the youngest was searching her memory bank! "So, the little kid, and the baby? Are they sisters, too?"

Ryan's response was to slap his forehead in annoyance! He wasn't sure who they were, but wasn't about to admit it!

⚔ ⚔

Trent Morrison sighed in relief! Shannon was safe! Scared and fleeing from Silverton, he had stopped in Durango to withdraw cash from his Little Rock bank! No one could tell if he was acting of his own volition! Then, after filling the rent car's tank and buying a stash of groceries, he disappeared!

"Okay, thanks for your call, Shay!" Trent laughed in relief! "Yeah, I can get him sprung! Although he may be safest there for the moment! The picture he sent me~yeah~I see why he headed for the tall timbers! It's actually a miracle that he got away! But Johnson's resources are spread thin between Ellis Vaughn, Alexandra, and Shannon! And Johnson's such an idiot he shoots his own soldiers!"

Trent rose and paced, pausing before a huge wall map! He traced Shannon's route through Silverton, Durango, southeastern Utah, into northeastern Arizona! Avoiding interstates and toll roads where he might be documented~evidently running for Mexico! Not the smartest with the crime rampant along the country's southern border! An Arizona highway patrolman had pulled him over because the rent car was considered stolen outside of Colorado and Utah!

His mind traveled to Shannon's photo of the 'haunted house' in the historical district of town! Upon enlarging and enhancing the image staring from the dormer window, the search for Johnson refocused and clarified!

Maybe today would be the day! And all of his victims and fugitives would be safer once more!

The desk phone rang! But before he could reach it an explosion rocked the building!

⚑ ⚑

Ward Atcheson didn't pause to take in the neat control of the blast area! There could still be damage to some of the carefully restored houses farther along the street! Broken windows, if not injuries from flying glass! His plan wasn't to stick around and take heat for the operation! He felt like the ends justified the means!

Michael Cowan, with a grin and disrespectful salute slid from his vantage point, and slunk off in the opposite direction, the detonator and all other incriminating evidence stowed away in his backpack! The two men had differing exfil plans!

⚑ ⚑

Rob Addington automatically hit the ground as it rumbled; flames and smoke shot upwards from the site ahead of them! When there were no secondary explosions, he gained his feet, advancing at a cautious, but rapid lope! Keenly aware that his followers were not following him, he advanced anyway! He hardly blamed them for exercising caution; he wasn't entertaining any death wishes himself! Nearing the site, he paused behind an outcropping of boulders and focused his field glasses!

He frowned as he noticed one survivor of the blast! 'H-mm-m Head guy, evidently leading from the rear! Figured! Lining up with his many other unsavory character traits!'

He spun, making a gesture for silence to the agents catching up! He motioned one survivor, and mouthed, "Johnson! Armed with wicked-looking crossbow-He seems pretty disoriented! Let's move!"

⚑ ⚑

Hallie Pritchard stared around in surprise at a muted roar, followed by teacups rattling and pictures on the wall going askew! "My goodness, gracious; what now?"

⚑ ⚑

"Thank you for calling me!" Ellis expressed her appreciation again before disconnecting!

Her daddy's stern eyebrows rushed together when she didn't immediately explain the call to him! She was twenty-three, and on her own! Although, his posturing usually managed to make her feel like a naughty five-year-old! And her independence was coming at a cost she hadn't figured on! She smiled mysteriously! 'Shannon was in a safe place'!

⚔ ⚔

Disconnecting from notifying Ellis Vaughn of Shannon's whereabouts, Trent paused when another number immediately appeared on his screen!

"You okay, Addington?" He demanded of the Southeastern Division head! "What-blew up?"

"We couldn't be better! We have Johnson in custody! There was a tunnel that branched from a main shaft and came up underneath the empty house! Someone blew it! Pretty sophisticated! The house across the street doesn't even have any broken windows! The force was directional up the tunnel! Somehow they had eyes on Johnson and his band of anarchists-to know when they were approaching! If we had been fifteen minutes ahead-"

"Okay, so everyone died-except-?"

"Yeah, except for the fearless leader! Bringing up the rear! He's in bad shape, though! At first, I thought it just rang his bell-"

Addington's voice died away and Trent heard confusing and conflicting voices!

"Okay, Trent, make that-no survivors! We're transporting Johnson's body-"

⚔ ⚔

Doug couldn't remember ever feeling so miserably out of place! 'No wonder Alexandra's mother made her so nervous!' His thoughts wandering, 'Not that Diana wasn't a real nice lady, because she was-b-but-like her wedding set! He didn't know Diamonds came that big! Alexandra's seemed to shrink in size every time he looked! And he was still in hock for them!

"Where are you from, Doug?" The politely interested question brought him into the conversation!

"Michigan, mostly!"

250

"He served in Afghanistan!" Alexandra's voice inserting itself on his behalf! "He was an MP! He always wanted to be in police work of some kind!"

He nodded mutely, wishing he was out involved in a fresh operation to apprehend Johnson and his goons! Against his wishes, Trent had recruited Addington to come in and lead the raid! Trent wanted him to do this family thing for Alexandra, while at the same time, keeping his eyes open for threats to her!

He was just acutely embarrassed! He didn't look right! He didn't know how to conduct himself appropriately, and his kid was a screwball! No wonder Alexandra voiced such apprehension about going home with them and trying to deal with her kids, surrounded by perfect people! But, she had agreed to go, and he needed that to happen-

CHAPTER 27: LEISEL

"You made an offer on it?" Ellis's voice would scarcely come! She had talked to guys all her life! Her brothers and their friends, classmates, several guys she'd dated! Ward and Michael! Usually they were easier than girl-bonding! But Shannon left her stammering, her skin flushing delicately! "Uh-do you think-you can-rescind your offer?"

He laughed, probably too loudly, "Well, I'm not sure I want to! I'll still own the lot and it really needed to be razed-and rebuilt-from the ground up!"

"Will that be economically feasible?" She tried to sound cool and knowledgeable as she fanned desperately, trying to come across calmer than she felt!

Shannon considered! "Probably not! And if the Narrow Gauge ever stops running, what's left of the town might go away! Even though Johnson's gone, praise the Lord, you probably never want to see the house again, where he holed up!"

She laughed, "Shannon O'Shaughnessy, did you just show me your hand? Let me know if you're ever in for a game of poker!"

He processed her remark in confusion! He had made yet another blunder! His real estate dealings shouldn't hinge on her; and if they did, he wasn't sure he was ready for her to be aware- "Uh!-I don't gamble," he hedged piously!

Another ripple of laughter, "That's good! 'Cuz you'd be awful at it! Why do you care whether I ever want to see the house again? It would really need to be according to the historical society specs, wouldn't it?"

He hesitated, humiliated at his unintended candor. At last, "You're right! And building from the ground up with such strict guidelines would be a project beyond my level of expertise! I guess I should hurry and try to undue my hasty damage! Glad you're doing okay!"

෴ ෴

A household full of emotional, crying females made Doug ready to head for the hills! Almost too bad that Hardy Johnson and followers no longer presented a threat! Well, he was relieved beyond measure about it, but now he had no pressing reason to escape from a situation he was clueless about!

Alexandra was beside herself and eager to get the babies to sleep! Sadly, between their unusual outing and sensing her tension, they refused to cooperate! She tried not to bug Doug too much about helping her more, but she wished he would do something!

"Okay, just try to calm down!" He was afraid to render an opinion, figuring whatever he said would be the wrong thing and make her worse! "I didn't think it went that bad! Your dad and mom were both pretty nice! Now your mother knows you married Brad, he shot himself, you have his daughter, and we're married! I was a widower with my grandma supposedly raising my baby!" He scowled. "Every single time I called her, she told me to come get her, because she couldn't do it! I should have listened to her! I just gave her my pep talk that she was surely doing fine, and let things rock on! Your parents seemed to handle it pretty well, I thought!"

Alexandra raked flaxen locks of hair from her face with both hands. "Yeah, I know!" Sniffling, she continued as she reached for a tissue! "I guess I've been such a basket case about everything! Between Hardy Johnson being after us, and worrying about facing my mom and asking her forgiveness~now that they're both over, I guess~my nerves~" She trembled and a fresh deluge started! Forcing her voice to be stronger she continued, "All my brothers and sisters just stared at us like we were Martians!"

"Well, they're kids! They probably didn't have a clue what to do! You didn't try really hard to engage any of them, either~"

She started to protest, but decided against it. "Yeah, I owed them all an apology, too! But since they don't know all the details, I know my Dad wouldn't have liked it! You know, putting a load on them, to clear my conscience!"

"We did leave abruptly, too! They all came a long ways, to have us~"

253

"I know, but there didn't seem to be much choice! When she gets like that! I guess I should just be really, really thankful that now I don't have to move home with them!"

"Maybe I need to start spanking her! She seems to be getting worse~"

"Well, actually, I've felt like she's getting better! And, I felt sorry for her today~because~really~she just doesn't undertand~"

"When your dad was here before he told us she understands a lot more than we realize~"

"Yes, but put yourself in her shoes!" The tears dried and gray eyes lit with excitement!

"I can't! They're too small!"

She swatted at him playfully! "Okay~duh~but consider this! Your grandmother and her little house were all she knew! And then one day, your cousin picks her up, gets on an airplane with her~and here she's been! Leisel must have had a bond with your grandmother, whether it was mutual, or not! Imagine how confusing it must be to lose the only person you know and love and be dropped down into a strange new world!"

"Well, she's so little~"

"Exactly, why she hasn't been able to figure out that this is what is~so adjust! And we haven't tried to explain it to her! You know, when she just does that babbling thing, that gets on Janni's and my nerves~'gaamaaamaa, gaamaamaa, gaamaamaa'! She wants Grandma!"

Doug shrugged mutely, "Well, Grandma doesn't want her back!"

"I know! I don't want her to go back! But it makes sense now, why she went to pieces when Daddy introduced my mom to her as, 'Grandma'!"

Doug considered the possibility as he replayed the afternoon's drama in his mind! "Maybe you're right! When your dad said the word, she snapped her head around~she was still looking~for~my grandmother~but still,~I'm sure she has it~lots better~here~"

Well, probably, but that first bond is strong~she may think your grandmother died! What do you think about calling her and letting Leisel facetime~"

"You really think that's a good idea?"

She sighed tiredly, "I have no idea!"

彐 彑

"How's the pain level?"

Ellis jumped! Lost in reverie, she hadn't noticed her father's approach! "It's okay!" She forced a smile past tears! "And Shannon O'Shaughnessy is okay! No thanks to me! He actually saved me twice! It was a picture he took, that helped the Forestry agents to finally eliminate the problem for good!"

"Hmmm! About that! Kind of strange tactics! To blow people to kingdom come!"

She bit her lip diffidently, "Well, it worked!"

Another 'Hmmph', and he studied her closely! "If your pain's okay, why were you crying?"

"Well, it hurts some, and everything was just so terrifying~"

He nodded slowly, "That it was! We all had a terrible scare! Ellis~" His voice broke, uncharacteristically for him! "I can't stand what happened to you~even though~I know~how much worse~"

She nodded through tears of her own, "I know, Daddy! But thanks for saying it! You and mom are the greatest! About going home with her, though~"

"You're of age, Ellis! You don't have to do anything you don't want to do! I must admit, that with the threat to you eliminated, I'm less anxious about you! Call me old fashioned~"

She braced herself; usually conversations prefaced with that weren't good~

"Your call didn't go too well, did it? I've never thought that young ladies should call young men!"

She flushed! Nothing new there!

"But since he was instrumental in your rescue, I understood that you wanted to thank him!"

"Yes, Sir!"

His piercing gaze pinned her, "Ellis, you are such a treasure! I hope you haven't given your heart away~to someone~that doesn't~reciprocate~! I want you to be treasured as highly by the man I give you away to, as you are by your mother and me!"

Tears flowed as her gaze locked with his! His expressing his feelings was so different, and his candor brought a measure of wellbeing. Still, she didn't know how to explain the weird conversation with Shannon!

⊱ ⊰

Alexandra pulled herself together as her phone indicated a call from Kayla Hamilton!

"Keep an eye on the girls while I take this!" She disappeared into the bedroom and closed the door!

The attorney taking charge of the conversation, "Hey, I heard the news about Hardy Johnson! I'll bet that's a relief! That's not the reason for my call, though! I know it's getting kind of late! But good news! The Maxwell hunting lodge in Canada is now Angelique's! The bad news is that there are some taxes in arrears, and it's in serious need of repairs and maintenance!"

A disturbed sigh was the only response!

"Well, it's worth a small fortune! It'll mostly be keeping it ready to show for the right buyer! You're the estate executor until she comes of age!"

"Okay, Kayla! Thanks so much for your hard work and the good news! I'm excited! Can't wait to break the news to her! Just, send me your bill~"

The attorney laughed, "Okay, I will! Have a good night!"

＊ ＊

Jay Vincent checked his wife's emails, as he did frequently!

She smiled from across the room, "Anything of interest, Jay? Or is it all spam?"

He smiled in return, although, Sophia was legally blind! Still, she could pick up amazing nuances just from his tone of voice!

He gasped in astonishment, "Here's a strange bit of information! The lodge in Canada~"

She tensed, "What about it, Jay?"

He frowned as he finished reading the news brief! "Hmm-mm, it's been involved in legal wrangling amongst the Stephen Maxwell estate, the US Treasury, the Canadian Treasury Department, and a baby, Angelique Maxwell! And the baby won out over all contenders! Hmmm, no wonder! Kayla Hamilton's her attorney!"

Sophia's delighted laughter sparkled! "Smart baby! It's always best to hire competent legal counsel! I wonder, if I should try to sue again, if I might entice Ms. Hamilton to represent me!"

Jay hesitated! Each suit where Sophie was defeated, seemed to suck the life out of her! Held for years in human slavery, her eyesight taken by a cosmetic surgeon's attempting the delicate eye procedure~ her suits brought against the responsible parties brought little victory and gratification! True, Kayla Hamilton possessed a formidable reputation, but~

Sophia frowned, "I'm not considering anything immediate! But certainly in a nation so proud of women's rights, the legal system seems still to be very much, a man's world! I've never truly been seen as a victim, by anyone~even~often, female jurors want to see me continue to be crucified~ And although we try to make the stealing of my vision a key rallying point, they stole far more from me than that!"

He moved toward her, "Yes, they did unspeakable things, and yet, they can only steal your human dignity if you cede it to them!"

"Yes, you are quite right, Jay! I have you instead of my eyesight, and I treasure you more dearly than I would my vision, should it ever be restored! God has been so kind to us~"

"He has, and He is the righteous judge! Nothing escapes His notice! One day, all wrongs will be righted! Sophia, you do know who the baby is, who now has ownership!"

She frowned and pushed him away playfully, "Of course I do, Jay Vincent! I lost my vision, not my mind! From what I understand of Alexandra's relationship with Brad Maxwell, she and her child should receive far more~"

"We did pay her hospital bills~"

"Yes, Jay; what's your point?"

"Well, do you suppose Alexandra wants a Canadian hunting lodge? To keep up?"

"Well, if she doesn't she can sell it~"

"Yes, right~"

She shuddered, "Surely, Jay, you don't wish to own such a place~"

"Well, if we owned it, we could invite whoever we wish onto the property! You know, they wouldn't have to have 'probable cause' and get a search warrant~if we owned it and invited Agents Bransom and Dawson to tear it apart in search of evidence!"

"Evidence of what, Jay?"

"Sophia, evidence that it was a major stopover for human traffickers and their victims!"

She gasped, "So, you don't think it's just a random~lodge, where Silas Remington's body~" She paused, confused and overwhelmed with Jay's inferrence~

"Well, I did, until the puzzle pieces kind of came together! The Maxwells and Coakleys were close friends in a social circle~Robert and Bobby Saxon, Mel Oberson! I find it amazing that in the few brief stories there were about Remington's death and lodge connection, that it never came out that the Maxwell family owned the lodge!"

She sat, blinking back tears, as she considered the immensity of her husband's words! At length, "Jay, please telephone Ms. Hamilton to approach Alexandra about our purchasing Angelique's lodge!"

≒ ⊨

Darlene Vaughn pulled anxiously on her husband's sleeve! He turned from the ticket agent, trying to mask his annoyance!

"She looks terrible, Cal! Maybe we should check her back into the hospital! At least, let's postpone flying out for a day or two!"

His gaze traveled to his pallid daughter and back to Darlene's ravaged countenance. Darlene was a trooper, and he was just now starting to appreciate the fact! With a husband and four sons in the military, in and out of combat zones, she was probably the bravest of them all! Still, their little baby girl was a different story!

"I think the sun and surf will do her good! She's okay! No fever~antibiotics done! Now she just needs time and a change of scenery! She's been through even more emotionally than she has physically! Maybe the Hickam Chief of Psychiatry can see her, or give us some pointers!"

She sighed; his mind seemed made up!

≒ ⊨

Shannon was the first passenger at the gate! Puddle jumper flight from Flagstaff Pullam to Durango-La Plata County Airport! With the demise of Hardy Johnson and his tribe of anarchists, Trent had okayed his release from protective custody! His grandmother's attorney, Bostonian Lawrence Freeman, was working out the details for paying the fine and returning the rent car! Shannon might have to return for a court appearance, but the danger threat and his fleeing for his life, should resonate with the court and get him some leniency! For now, he just wanted to reach Ellis and apologize for his crazy phone conversation! He still didn't have it worked out in his mind, exactly what to say! But if he could sit across from her and read her expression~He wiped sweaty palms on the knees of his jeans, then wished he hadn't! 'Shannon, you idiot!'

Settled into a seat designed for midgets, he resumed his train of thought! He was legally bound to carry through on his offer for the crater where the house had sat! Another totally dumb decision on his part! His offer could have been contingent upon having an inspection done, but he was such a smart aleck! He knew it was in bad shape! Why pay for an inspection? Well, now it was in worse shape! And he was the proud owner!

'Why would a beautiful girl like Ellis~'

⊣ ⊢

Checked in with the gate, Captain Vaughn moved to join wife and daughter! "Okay, so far the flight to Denver's on time! It's actually supposed to snow in Denver this afternoon! Hope our flight on to Oahu isn't delayed!"

Darlene nodded nervous agreement! Cal was probably right about what was best! He usually was!

"Let's get some breakfast! There isn't much choice here! Maybe we can at least get orange juice!"

"I'll just wait here! Don't get me anything! My stomach~" Ellis' voice uncharacteristically weak and lifeless!

"Okay, Sprite, then! You need to keep the fluids going, Ellis!" The voice that brooked no argument!

She nodded numbly as tears rolled down her cheeks!

Returning with coffees, a boxed juice drink and granola bars from vending, he pressed the juice into her hands! "Just easy sips! We don't want you vomiting!"

"Yeah, these flights across the Rockies in small jets~" She clamped her lips tight at the thought!

"I want to stay here!"

"Why?" Captain Vaughn was totally nonplussed! "Your job with Cowan and Atcheson dried up! Your equipment is packed on the truck and headed home! Some time, relaxing at the beach~"

Tears rolled, "I don't like the beach! I like it here in the mountains! And although, you may hate snow, I love it! Why can't I be me?"

He frowned, totally nonplused! "I do let you be you! Who else would you be?" Always the pragmatist! "There's hardly any snow here, either! And if there were, I don't want you trying to ski~with that~toe~"

She cried harder!

⊰ ⊱

Alice McKay crossed the intersection carefully at the signal, wary of icy spots! Entering the warmth of a long-established, favorite down-town deli, she looked around for her friend! Spotting her at a booth toward the back, she pushed through the gathering crowd to join her.

"Hi, Liz, sorry to be late! The buses don't quite run the same as they used to! And it's gotten scarier! I may take a cab home!" She paused enjoying Liz's startled expression!

"What you selling?" The long-lost friend growing suspicious of the sudden invitation! "You bottle the Fountain of Youth or something? Maylou made it sound like you were nearly-well-not doing so well! Like raising Douglas didn't almost kill you off, he stuck you with his brat, then, too?"

"Yeah, basically!" She looked up as long-time staffer approached the table! Most customers had to wait their turn in line, but Louis had looked after the City Hall ladies for years!

He did a double-take! "Wow! Alice?" He hugged her, then held her at arm's length to study her delightedly! "Lookin' good, Girl! Whatever you're doin'! Bring you the same as you always~"

"Absolutely!" the two women's voices in unison!

Perplexed, Alice responded to her phone! Doug's number!

"Hello, Dougie?" Her defenses going up, she was immediately suspicious again of Niqui Whitmore's actions on her behalf~

"No, Ma'am! Doug's asleep! This is Alexandra, his wife!"

"Okay, Alexandra, nice to meet you! I saw on the news that my grandson is a hero!"

"Really, it made the news up there? Yes, Ma'am! Of course he's been my hero for a couple of years! He's my Sir Galahad! Listen, I'm sure you're busy, but, would you mind talking to Leisel for a minute? Maybe even do Facetime, so she can see you?"

"Listen, I'm just telling you! I-I can't-I-I-just couldn't-do it-any more~"

"What? Take her back? I don't want you to! She's part of our family-but-we-just kind of figured out-that she is lonely for you~ One moment, you were all she had, and all she's ever known-and then

260

suddenly,-her whole-world-changed- We love her very much-but-i-it seems like she's lonely-for you-or maybe-worried-she doesn't really talk-But we think-she understands-a-lot-that goes on! We think that what she does babble, is trying to-ask for-you-If you can please just punch the icon on your phone-"

CHAPTER 28:   SECURITY

Alexandra tried to calm Leisel following the Facetime session with her great-grandmother!

"Gaamaamaa loves you a lot, still, but she's in too poor health to take care of such a sweet little livewire! Maybe we can take a trip so we can visit with her; but you could tell she's doing okay?"

A barely perceptible nod as the agonized screaming lessened!

"But even more important than Gaamaamaa's inability to care for you any longer, was the fact that Daddy and Mommy want you here with us! Daddy had a hard time finishing his Army discharge and training for his job and getting a house for us! But he was doing all of it so he could get his little Leisel with him!"

Silence at last as the child's face registered perplexity! She seemed to be trying to understand!

"I know that you and Gaamaamaa love each other, and that's okay! But Daddy and Mommy love you lots too!" she attempted a hug, meeting with the usual resistance! "That's okay if you're not a huggy-bear~ Are you hungry?"

That question always met with an emphatic nod!

"Okay, well we're going to load up and go meet Grandpa at *The Farmer's Wife*! Do you know where that is? They have yummy breakfast all day! You can get a waffle!"

A nod preceded the familiar babble, "Gaamaamaa, Gaamaamaa, Gaamaamaa, Gam~"

❧   ❦

Shannon gulped in confusion as Ellis' father answered her phone, "Oh, Captain Vaughn, how are you, Sir?"

"I'm fine, thank you; and you?" A definite cool clip to the Captain's tone sent fresh waves of alarm!

"Is-is Ellis-okay-?" Shannon could hardly find his voice, and dread crowded into already worried thoughts!

"As well as can be expected! She's been through a great deal-" Cal Vaughn cut his rebuke off, deciding not to vent his anger at the moment-

Shannon wasn't sure what to say! Ellis was hard enough to talk to! Helped him make a total idiot of himself! Consequently, carrying on a conversation with her formidable father seemed totally inadvisable!

"I apologize for bothering you, Captain Vaughn! Is there a better time for me to-"

"Actually, Mr. O'Shaughnessy, I see her returning to our gate now-"

"Oh! Y'all are going someplace?"

"Here's my daughter now!"

Ellis' voice, a gasp of surprise, "Shannon! Did you get out of jail?"

The Captain frowned at Darlene, not knowing about Shannon's arrest, and taking note of sudden life and vigor infusing his listless child!

Darlene smiled sweetly and shrugged! It was bound to happen to one of their five, sooner or later! But the youngest first, and Daddy's girl at that? She hoped that Shannon was determined !

※　※

"Hi, Gaampaa and Gaamaa!" Leisel broke free from Alexandra, approaching Daniel and Diana with a strange new confidence!

Daniel recovered himself and rose to greet the little one! "You wanna get in the high chair?"

Alexandra scoffed! "Since when do you guys give kids a choice about what they're supposed to do?"

"Yeah," Ryan chimed up! "Since when?"

"Ryan, don't get any ideas!" Diana's mildly spoken rebuke! She reached for Angelique's carrier, unstrapping the baby with skilled hands before snuggling her tenderly!

Daniel watched rage chase the happiness from Leisel's face! Evidently very jealous of attention to the baby

He pulled her onto his knee! "Is that your baby sister? She's nice! Do you help out?"

After a few second's consideration, she shook her head no!

⇥ ⇤

"Just a second, Shannon!" Ellis shot her parents a pointed look but the Captain tapped his watch and pointed toward the boarding gate!

Ellis shook her head, determinedly! "I'm not going," she mouthed! When they refused to move out of earshot, she rose clumsily, trying to get her crutches under her!

While she tried to resume her conversation with Shannon, the gate attendant announced boarding for the flight!

"You-you're going to Hawaii?" Shannon heard the announcement clearly, and defeat threatened him! If he was going to close on a house and rebuild it to the required specs, he couldn't afford another thing! No way could he follow her to Hawaii, even if she wanted him to!

"No, I'm seeing my folks off!" She grinned at them across the gate area as they took their place in the line for first class boarding! "I'm not a huge fan of surf and sun! I love it here! Where are you?"

"I'm at ground transportation waiting for a rent car!"

"Right here? In Durango? So, what happened about your offer on the house?"

He chuckled mirthlessly, "I was kinda hoping you wouldn't ask! I'm now the proud owner of a gaping hole in the ground!"

"Well, look on the bright side! It may be brim full of precious metals!" She laughed, "But if not, you'll have to build it back! Did you want out of the offer?"

"Well, at least the decision would have been mine if I hadn't been so cocky! The realtor, of course, knew it had real issues! And he suggested I have it inspected! I'm such a know-it-all that I thought, 'Well, I knew how bad shape it's in; why waste money~'

"Well, there was no way for you to know it was going sky high! Have you heard anything about that agent, Rob Addington?"

"No, what happened to him? I thought he was the leader of the pack that finally apprehended Johnson!"

"Well, yeah, but then Johnson died in custody! I thought the agent might be in trouble for making a bad call, cuffing him instead of getting him medical attention~"

"Hmmm; hadn't thought of that! Hope not! I for one, am so glad the guy's dead that I could tap dance on his grave! If he even has anyone to bury him! So, after your folks leave, what's~I mean~you can't drive yet~"

"Uh! I'm not sure they're leaving~" humor filled her voice as she carried on a wordless argument! Her dad motioning her to come get in line, and her emphatic, head-shaking refusal!

"Where did she get this stubborn streak?" the Captain demanded!

Darlene smiled blandly, "I haven't the faintest idea, Cal! But if we're not taking her for sun and relaxation, is there a need for us to go? You know that with your airline perks, you can change the tickets and use them any time without even an extra charge!"

He frowned, hating to admit defeat! "What on earth are they talking about?"

"Well, you go ahead on, and call me when you arrive safely! I believe I'll stay too, and keep an eye on her!"

"She's so bull-headed, she'll run over the top of you! Like she always does! I better stay, too! Besides, I need to keep an eye on that toe!"

⊰ ⊱

Alexandra laughed until she cried! It was like the gulf between herself and her family had vanished, leaving a stronger and more mature bond than ever! While her dad tended to Leisel and her mother made over Angelique, she laughed with her siblings about nearly-forgotten incidents, made hilarious by Jeremiah's recounting of them, with plenty of charades and reenactment!

"I'd like to go back and find the place where we all hid out that summer!" Her wistful voice and dreamy eyes caught Daniel's attention!

"Well, that was definitely an epoch in the Faulkner family history! It would have been totally idyllic," he directed his comment to Cassandra specifically. "Except that your mother and I were like our hearts had been cut out when you left!"

Jeremiah couldn't resist being his mischievous self, "We, on the other hand, did not miss you at all! You were a total pain back then!"

Cassandra made a face, and to her chagrin, Leisel mimicked her! 'Great! Like it wasn't enough pressure to be a role model to younger brothers and sisters; but now for little nieces, too!'

"Well, while you were all on an endless picnic, the early days with Lilly were no picnic at all! She was so mean! I mean, I thought I wanted to go with her, but I was five~"

Jeremiah shrugged heartlessly as he resumed the memories with Alexandra! "We fished, and we played in the stream, and we hiked up and down the stream-bed!"

Alexandra nodded eagerly, remembering, "Wish I'd been a Geologist then! No telling what was out there for gems and minerals!"

Jeremiah shrugged, "Well, Dad's a Geologist, and he didn't notice riches untold!"

"Yeah, but his radar's set on oil!" She grinned happily at her dad, "Which, hasn't been so bad!"

"I wish Doug could have joined us again~" Diana's blue eyes reinforcing the sincerity in her voice!

"Yes, Ma'am, but he's back to work! Think he hated missing the action of finally ending Hardy Johnson's reign of terror! He was relieved, though, that he wasn't the one to have apprehended Johnson when he heard he died in custody! There'll be a prolonged investigation into Rob Addington's decision!"

"That's almost a crime in itself! Law enforcement seems to be facing more and more problems carrying out their responsibilities~"

"Well, I agree, kind of, except that law enforcement personnel can't act with impunity, either! All of the investigations prevent the US from becoming a police state! Thoughts of possible consequences do make an officer think twice! Which is both good and bad~if they hesitate and it's the wrong call~ I worry about Doug, but he wouldn't be happy doing anything else!"

"You're going ahead with your security plan to start Robert Porter on your payroll this week, I hope!" Daniel's gaze held his firstborn's!

She laid her loaded fork down to respond, "Well, I did kind of commit to him! So, I haven't been able to think of a graceful way out~ When I started the process, it didn't seem possible~that the anarchists would ever~"

You're right, Al; there isn't a way out! Even with this current gang disrupted, you're still at risk living out there alone with Doug gone so much!"

"Well, I'm never there alone," she argued!

"Meaning you have the mine employees and chow hall staff! They're not trained to defend you, your mine, and the ore! You're still a target,

Alexandra, and although you feel like you can't afford the security staff right now, the truth is you can't afford not to go ahead!"

"Penny-wise and pound-foolish," as Mallory so often quotes! "But that's easy for her to say~"

"It really isn't," Diana interrupted! "Like you, she and David walk by faith and run their businesses the same way! I think they're as nervous to spend and start up expensive projects as you are!"

Amazement swept across beautiful features! "Really? I thought they just have lots and lots of money!"

Daniel laughed, "People think we do, too! Except for Brad and his grandfather who declared us below poverty level! You have money, Al! And saving is an admirable thing~"

She nodded slowly, "Unless I hoard it and don't grow!"

He nodded, "Nothing's static, Al! Even when businesses just want to maintain, and not grow, they begin losing market! You're either purposely trying to move forward, or you'll fall back! Remember, there was a reward out for you! I'm not positive Johnson's death cancelled it!"

⛄ ⛄

"I guess your dad doesn't like me much~"

Ellis shrugged, sending a dazzlingly beautiful smile!

"Well, he didn't want me to call you the other night!" She flushed, "I don't want to be a brazen woman, either, which was his concern! But, you risked your life to help me out, and when my family came, you slipped away! And you were still in danger~because of me! I told my dad it would be the worst manners not to thank a man~who~"

He flushed, "And then, I tripped all over myself, and it seemed the only way out was ending the call~before I said anything even dumber~ But I know it was rude for me to end the call when you were the one who phoned me! Is that the issue~"

"Mostly!" If you weren't even interested in me enough to let me finish the call, he forbad me making a fool of myself~I thought you might call right back and tell me what the realtor said~"

"Well, I would have, but I was dumb there, too!"

"Shannon, you're not dumb! Would you please quit using the word in reference to yourself? What, are you fishing for compliments? 'Oh, Shannon, you're so bright and clever'!"

He laughed, "Yes! Say that again!"

"No! You say it!"

"What? Tell you I'm bright and clever? That would be, 'Blowing my own horn'!"

Her serious eyes met his, "But what you say is important! The things you say about yourself and to yourself, help determine who you are! You should say it! Maybe not to people, but when you write your goals, and when you're alone!"

He grinned as he blushed at the well-meant rebuke, "What, are you a big self-help seminar attendee?"

"No, Shannon Ryland O'Shaughnessy! All of those gurus get followings and make fortunes by teaching Biblical principles! Because they're absolute, and they work! I read my Bible for myself! And it says that we get what we say, so our words should be chosen carefully! Read Numbers 14:28 where God gave the Israelites what they repeatedly said, and the words of Jesus in Mark 11, verse 23! You need to grasp how important each word uttered is!"

He sighed, "You're probably right! I'll take that under advisement then!"

⊨ ⊨

"Why do you wear so many rings?" Sally Allen's tone to Mallory, nearly belligerent!

"Because God gave me so many fingers!" Mallory kept her tone good-natured and humorous and her response brought a chuckle from Dr. Allen!

"Jesus requires that His disciples deny themselves," Sally persisted!

David intervened, speaking softly, "Yes, Ma'am, but what actually did He mean? What are we supposed to deny ourselves? Anything that hinders us from following and serving Him! We really think His main meaning was that we deny our rights to ourselves, doing as we please, especially as embracing the world system and sinful behavior! Drinking and partying, living in excess and rioting, like there's no tomorrow! Let alone an eternity to consider! What we do, we do as unto the Lord!"

Sally's eyes were still fastened on Mallory's beautiful, and jewel encrusted hands! "You don't consider that, 'excess'? There are so many impoverished people, and so many who have never heard~"

Again David responded, "Well, you are right about that! And what we do charitably, we usually try to do without fanfare! 'Give our alms in secret so that the God who sees us in secret can reward us openly', according to Matthew 6:4! We give to the church where we're members in Dallas and give equally to my dad's church in Arkansas where we both grew up! Beyond double tithing, we have missions' commitments at both churches! We create jobs and help other companies start up! We both work earnestly at living for the Lord and one another, and we try to be honest and faithful! It's hard to judge peoples' hearts when you don't know them~ We can't tell whether people have what they have because they're living for themselves, cheating and stealing~or if they have what they have because God rewards them for prayer-closet praying and giving in ways that are for His eyes only!"

⚔ ⚔

On the drive back to the mine, with both girls asleep, Alexandra phoned Bob Porter to firm up his arrival and be sure he was still on board! She felt happy and relaxed as she disconnected and let her mind wander to the family bond she had felt all afternoon! She had a lot to learn! It was still a good thing to have her father's wise advice! She prayed for the finances to stretch for what she had committed to Mr. Porter! She frowned when the phone interrupted her reverie! Then did a double-take! Kayla Hamilton!

"Good afternoon, Kayla! How can I help you?"

A light laugh, "You help me by keeping me on retainer! I have more good news! At least, it seems so to me! I've been approached by a proxy for a couple wanting to purchase the lodge!"

Alexandra gasped, not sure exactly what that meant! But if it seemed good to the attorney~

"Well, the property actually belongs to Angelique! Maybe I should hang onto it!"

"Of course, it's your decision! But it is a great distance away! Maintenance and insurance, as well as property taxes, are certainly important considerations! Your baby's a long way from taking possession and deciding to reside in Canada! You have a purchaser willing to pay top dollar~"

"Why a proxy? Why does the prospective purchaser need to be anonymous?"

"Not sure! What difference does it make, if their money spends? Or invests, as you're concerned about your daughter's future!"

"Well, I'm hardly investment savvy, but I thought real estate was always one of the safest bets!"

"I think again, it depends upon the property! There aren't always buyers chomping at the bit-believe me-"

"Okay, Kayla, thanks, but I think I'll take my chances! If I have stuff that's easily liquidated, it tends to get away-"

With a sigh indicating her disagreement, the attorney disconnected, and Alexandra tried to put the conversation out of her mind! 'Never second-guess your decision,' she reminded herself! Still, the nagging worry wouldn't go away, that she should ask her parents' opinion!

Miraculously the girls stayed asleep while she transferred them to their beds! Realizing getting them back to sleep at bedtime after long, late naps, she opted to get her Bible and allow them to sleep!

"Lord, I hope I didn't offend Kayla when she wants to help! She does amazing things for me that she usually makes a lot more money on! If she does have a fee for herself brokered into the deal-"

Her phone buzzed softly and she grabbed it, afraid it still might disturb the babies!

"Hello, Sophia?"

"No, Alexandra; it's Jay! I called on my wife's phone! We're the couple who made the offer! It was a good offer-"

Alexandra stalled to cover her confusion-

"Why the proxy?" He addressed her stated excuse! "Your attorney informed us that was one of your concerns!"

"We-ell! Mostly, I want something of Brad's to support his daughter-and it seems less solvent-"

"Alexandra, listen to me, please, you must sell us the lodge-"

"Why-must I? Listen, I never thanked y'all for bailing us out with the hospital bills! That was an amazing blessing! I should probably just deed the lodge to you and we might call it even!"

"No! No! That was our foundation, and it's a separate entity! We have reason to believe that the lodge was a haven for criminals in the black market organ and human trafficking rackets! Stephen Maxwell was close buddies with both Mel Oberson and Ted Coakley! Remember the Danay Livingston case when the Norman's intervened and helped rescue her?"

"Yes, Sir; I remember what little I was aware of! My parents tried to shelter us from a lot of the scary things happening in the world!"

"Well, little Danay was abducted from her home in Dallas! The Feds assumed she would be smuggled out through Mexico~as was often the case! Jennifer Mo'a'aloa was taken through Mexico! But then she was grabbed in southern Arizona, so Mexico ~anyway~ Sophia wants to purchase the lodge because then she can invite both Canadian law enforcement and the FBI in, to take as much time as they want~learning what all transpired there! The proxy isn't because we don't want you to know that we're the buyers! We don't want the Syndicate to know we are! We're certain an agent representing some of them will also be making an offer! In order to hide the truth forever, and perhaps continue conducting business as usual! Sophia was disheartened at your declining our offer, but I thought I should call and explain! We don't want to be in a bidding war with~them~"

"Well, I have an idea! Rather than y'all having to purchase it, I'll just invite the Feds and whoever~ I certainly won't demand a search warrant!"

"Please, Alexandra~"

"Why won't that work?"

"Jay strove for patience! "Because you can't necessarily afford to have the place razed to the ground, should that be necessary in uncovering the heinousness of their actions! Sophia doesn't care! If they have to tear down every stone and timber! If they must plow up every acre! If they must cut every slab of concrete~"

Alexandra laughed suddenly! She had just been in the process of seeking God's direction! "Okay, Jay! Thank you for clarifying the situation for me! I'll call Kayla back~"

"No, our agent will handle all details from here~" The line went dead!

⚔ ⚔

Shannon steadied Ellis on her crutches as they circled the crater where the historic home had stood!

"I don't see any huge nuggets~" her bright deduction!

"If there were huge ones everywhere, visible to the naked eye, I'm pretty sure the historical preservation society would nix our mining the lot!" Shannon blushed deeply! "I mean, my mining the lot!" It seemed he couldn't help seeing her in every aspect of his future!

This time, she had no laughing rejoinder! "I liked how you said it the first time!" Her voice was so soft, he wasn't sure he heard her correctly!

"I've never met anyone like you before, Shannon! You're an amazing man! You're probably more down on yourself than you should be, but at least you aren't a swaggering know-it-all!"

"Thank you, I guess! You're the most beautiful-but you aren't just beautiful on the exterior! You have real depth of character! Meeting your family, I can see why! My father-"

"Was a felon! My dad checked! What-what made-such-a difference-How did you meet the Lord?"

"Well, believe it or not, my dad and his bunch of tough buddies were all my heroes! Then, after my dad and mom divorced, my mother-died-in-a car crash! My brother, Shay, and my maternal grandmother, didn't think it was an accident! That my dad and his friends arranged the wreck-"

She stood leaning on her crutches with empathetic tears coursing down her cheeks as he continued!

"When my Uncle Patrick died in a little town in Arkansas, Shay and my grandmother went out for the will! Grandmother wanted to fight for his remains, and have him reinterred in Boston! Instead, she and Shay heard the Gospel for the first time! They both got saved! Then, I overheard my dad and one of his friends arranging a hit on Mallory and my Aunt Suzanne, because suddenly, there was an estate! The will was a bigger deal than anyone guessed! It was crazy, but I ran from my dad and tried to get to Murfreesboro to warn them- It took me a while to wise up enough to receive the Lord! I'm close to my brother and grandmother, but I got really close to my Aunt Suzanne! Even though Uncle Patrick hadn't been gone long, she married Erik Bransom, the FBI agent! They keep in touch with me! Get after me if I miss church-" He broke off with a self-conscious laugh! "I guess I still see myself as the son of a felon rather than an associate of an incredible group of friends and support!"

"I guess it's up to me to help you get past some stuff!"

CHAPTER 29: BLESSED

Even though Alexandra was the lowest on clothes she'd ever been in her life, she felt overdressed for the small Silverton church! Well, her family always seemed overdressed at the large Honey Grove Baptist in Tulsa! Alexandra knew Kendra Meeker would make a catty remark! She tried not to mind when Doug appeared in the new flannel shirt and jeans! Something else for her prayer list! She scrubbed the girls' hands and faces and changed them into cute outfits, compliments of Hallie's generous gift cards! Leisel always desperately fought Alexandra's attempting to tame her thick, luxurious hair! To Alexandra's surprise, Doug intervened!

"Hey!"

Leisel jumped, but so did Alexandra!

"You stop being that way! Mama's trying to make you look pretty! I want you to stop throwing these fits!"

Shock gave way to a little face puckering into a wounded look, but Doug ignored it, "Hold still! Put your hands down!"

By the time they arrived at church, the new style had been obliterated! Doug shook the cute bow in Leisel's line of vision! "This was naughty!" He shoved it back into place! "Leave it alone! You're getting a spanking when we get home!"

⊰ ⊱

"Explain again why Hawaii was a bad idea!" Cal sought Darlene's agreement as they approached the dead little town of Silverton! Gray day, gray peaks, a desolate-looking, nearly deserted little hamlet! "This is the most dismal

273

place I've ever been-well-within the US," he amended! "Afghanistan and Iraq are worse of course!"

"Well, obviously, Shannon O'Shaughnessy is the main attraction for her here!"

"I was afraid you'd say something like that-"

She laughed, "Get over it! It's inevitable that the love bug bite one of the kids at some point in time! Maybe the boys'll figure it out-"

He shot her his sternest look, and she laughed, "Shannon really saved her life, you know! But he's a sharp guy! He's a good Christian, and they both seem mutually gone on each other! I mean-I know she's your little girl-"

He smiled suddenly, "Yeah, the local old people got there just in time! It's not the first time Steb Hanson's followers have stepped into situations and made a critical difference!" Emotion he was unaccustomed to resonated in his voice! "She was so terrified and desperate to escape, that she started climbing one of the vertical shafts! She was so weak and shocky-losing blood-she couldn't climb any higher! She was up about thirty-five feet, she judged, of the seventy-five-they got a rope around her and pulled her to safety-because Shannon sent out the alarm-if she had passed out-and fallen-"

Darlene blinked rapidly, fighting tears at the pain and terror inflicted on her child! "Don't get me started crying! There's the church! At least it looks bright and inviting!"

⚔ ⚔

To Alexandra's surprise, Kendra wasn't there! She smiled as the youthful pastor, Andy McGuire, raced forward offering his characteristically friendly handshake! "Great to see you guys!" He directed his attention to Alexandra, "Could I ask a favor? Would you mind playing the piano for a couple of congregational songs?"

He told her the page numbers, and she agreed readily, "Would you like me to do a prelude, too, and an offertory?"

He flushed bashfully, "Well, I hate to impose-I mean, I really hate to ask-but-"

"It's okay! I love playing!"

⚔ ⚔

"I was wrong to say anything, wasn't I?" Sally Allen met her husband's gaze as they worked on the *Grace* financial documents together!

"A soft sigh, "Well, their grazing fee for their alpaca is what's keeping our heads above water! Fortunately, they didn't seem offended!" He paused before clearing his throat nervously and continuing, "I guess I've never valued and appreciated enough, your willingness to forego all of that and serve humbly by my side! You're still a very beautiful woman! I've been more rabid in the determination to shun everything-for Christ's sake, than you have been! David and Mallory have taught me a lesson, though, about judging! I too, thought that they lived and breathed for money only, and the things it buys! Because looking at them, and all their trappings, that's how it appears to be! It's true, though, the more a person has, the more ability they have to help further the kingdom! They've caused me to reevaluate so many of the things I've clung to!"

"The weapons!"

He laughed at the disapproval still tinging her voice! "Yes, because it's inconsistent for us not to be armed, and then rely on law enforcement that is! The way society is going, some of the good guys need weapons, too! I'm tending to rally around those hanging onto our Constitutional right to bear arms! The founding fathers knew that was the only way America could stay free of tyrants!"

Her jaw dropped in shock!

⚔ ⚔

"Oh, no! Your parents are here!" Panic in both Shannon's voice and expression!

"Well, that's good, isn't it? I thought you wanted to talk to my father!"

"I thought I did, too! But, I guess I was wrong!"

She shook her head smilingly, and his heart lurched! Beautiful! He had faced the wrath of Hardy Johnson to rescue her-surely he could summon courage to speak to Captain Vaughn! "There's not a good place up here for me to talk to him! The only restaurants are closed already!"

She tilted her face up to him, her nearness making him dizzy, "How about at our house?"

He considered the suggestion before laughing, "Our hole in the ground, you mean?"

⚔ ⚔

Mallory held Amelia's hand firmly as David studied the building site! She frowned as he paused next to a bare-branched hardwood!

"This explains why Johnson used this place! One of the side dormer windows opened adjacent to this tree! The attic provided the highest vantage point in town, with the exception of maybe one of the church steeples! Climbing higher in the tree, and with powerful field glasses, he might have had surveillance on the mine!" Mallory frowned, both at the thought, and at David's seeming intention to climb the tree!

He grinned impishly, "I'll be careful! I've climbed trees all my life!"

Her concern deepened! Not in the past five or six years! And he had suffered a serious head injury from which she wasn't convinced he was totally recovered!

"Can I try?" Amelia's face shone with wonder as she watched her daddy ascend up and up!

"Better not! This is why we have the treehouse!"

"We haven't been there for a long time~"

Mallory was accustomed to arguing with her first born! It had really only been a couple of months, which to her, seemed like yesterday! The time probably did seem long to Amelia!

"Da`vid!"~Her familiar stress on the second syllable of his name ended in a startled, and terrified screech as an avalanche of snow descended in a frigid rush from tree tops!

Regaining solid ground, he laughed at her panic! His dark eyes stood out, though, in skin almost as white as the snow covering his hair and shoulders! "What can I say? You were right, again!"

"David Anderson, you are so crazy!"

⚔ ⚔

Alexandra peered through the peephole, summoned by a timid knock! No one there! Then she laughed at herself, opening the door a crack! As she thought! Amelia and Avery Anderson!

"Hi, girls! What can I do for you?"

"Can Leisel come out and play with us?"

Alexandra considered! The little girls were bundled up warmly and beautifully! She didn't want Leisel to get sick, and her Leisel had little experience playing with other children, or being outside in wide open spaces!

"Thanks, maybe another time!"

"Mama said we could ask! She's out looking at rocks, and she's keeping an eye on us!"

It was true, that Amelia always had an answer, but she was absolutely beautiful in lively teal hat and scarf that matched earnest blue eyes, lending extra appeal to the plea!

"Okay, Alexandra capitulated, "We can give it a try! Come on in while I put her coat and boots on her!"

"We can't come in! Can we wait on your steps?"

੩ ਇ

Trent Morrison disconnected from a long conversation with Doug Hunter! With the chilling reports regarding Hardy Johnson and his numerous murders, no one was accusing Rob Addington of any wrong-doing regarding his death in custody! If Johnson had family members to file a wrongful death suit, none had come forward yet, to claim his remains!

Still, Trent needed to conduct a guideline review with all of the division heads for future cases!

He rifled a stack of folders on the corner of his desk! Unsolved murders of young women, now solved, with the criminal's hideous taking of a trophy toe from each victim! He shuddered at details he wished he didn't know! Being rid of such a fiend made it hard for him to retain any angst toward Cowan and Atcheson! Even their blowing of a historic home owned by Shannon O'Shaughnessy wasn't raising any questions! They had gotten the job done, however unceremonious their methods! And the aged, Gingerbread-trimmed structure was beyond repair! Even before the blast!

He opened the top file! Shannon's photo taken of the 'Haunt' inhabiting the aged structure! Enlargement and enhancement showed Johnson's glowering face beneath a dew rag! A dew rag with a cleaning company's logo on it- the logo for Summer O'Connell Prescott's maid service! Enraged at Ellis Vaughn's escape from him, Johnson had come upon a remote ranch house where Summer was cleaning, alone!

Trent reread the report! A miracle that Summer, with her rough childhood, had learned to be mean and resourceful! An education standing her in good stead for evading the felon and surviving a day and a night in rugged wilderness!

Rising, he left his office, galloped down the flights of stairs, and hit a frigid blast as he exited the building! Maybe the blast would clear cobwebs!

"Lord, there's so much more to this! I need the key that unlocks the whole mystery!"

Shivering, he made a wide U-turn in the deserted sidewalk, berating himself for not being tough enough to go on to a nearby coffee stand! Maureen could brew a fresh pot!

"You went outside without your coat?" she demanded as he reentered, radiating cold!

"Yeah, Mom, I did," he retorted evenly! "Start a fresh pot of coffee? Did I miss any calls?"

"One! Jason Hewitt from the forensics lab called you!" she rose as she handed him the message from the ubiqiuitous pink pad!

"Well, they took long enough! But maybe they found something!"

She frowned as she changed out the coffee packet, "Aren't they all dead?"

Trent sighed, "Don't I wish! These people have a membership in the hundreds, if not thousands! They range along the loony spectrum from passing as normal to extreme wackos like Johnson! I wish I could find one piece of electronics: phone, laptop, or something to give me a thread to pull!"

In his office with a fresh hot, cup of coffee, he returned the call! "Whatcha got, Jason? Tell me you~"

"Well, the problem is we have too much! It's quite the~job~to sort~through~so much data~"

"Well, praise the Lord we're in the computer age~"

A fellow Christian, Hewitt laughed, "I'm telling you the system is slow, analyzing so many blood types and matching it to victims~"

Trent's stomach squeezed and he set the coffee aside, "Are you talking about from the truck alone?"

"Yeah, so we have a number of mysteries to unravel! And way underneath the driver's seat, and hidden in the springs, we found a *Hide a key*!"

Trent's hopes soared, "Tell me there's a key in it!"

"Okay, there's a key in it," the lab guy intoned obediently!

Trent liked the guy, but this was a time to be serious, "Okay, was there really?"

"Yeah, real as rain! It appears to be for a safety deposit box! So here's another long and involved search–it doesn't match any of the banks in Johnson's neck of the woods! And we have a program, that–uh–helps; but do you have any idea how many banks and savings and loans there are in this country? Or in Colorado, alone?"

On a sudden hunch, "Okay, see if it matches anything in Fort Collins, or any of the little towns in the northeast of the state!"

Hewitt was puzzled, 'If Johnson haunted the southwestern corner of the state, why look for banks in the northeastern quadrant?'

Without explaining, Trent ordered, "Let me know as soon as you find something!" He disconnected as the tech spluttered!

꒰ ꒱

Hello, Dr. Allen! It's an honor to speak with you at last! I keep hearing amazing things about *Grace*!

"Thank you, Dr. Anderson! Your words are kind, but–do you mind if Mrs. Allen joins us–well–I'm sorry–!"

John Anderson's deep laugh boomed! "Well, to set the record straight, I'm not a doctor! And I'd be delighted to visit with your wife as well! My call is in reference to the problems you're bound to encounter with making doctrinal changes!"

A sigh as the Allens traded glances! "Yes, Sir; Alexandra got us thinking!"

John Anderson barely covered his surprise at the revelation! He had assumed that David and Mallory were responsible for straightening the couple out!

"How so?" he managed weakly!

"Well, Alexandra and Sally were talking about why Christians should never marry unbelievers, and Alexandra asked her, with our beliefs about being in and out of grace, how anyone could be certain they were married to a believer?"

"Okay, I guess there's a valid point there! Also, I guess you've changed your stance personally, on passivism!"

"Well, we're opposed to war and violence!"

Paula Rae Wallace

Anderson laughed, "Aren't we all? And we're opposed to divorce and remarriage~ but~then~real life~happens! There has to be a stance that's firm, but realistic! If your current board dislikes the changes you're initiating, maybe we can work something out, purchase the property from them! You can appoint a new board~"

"Well, they won't like my shift, and I haven't made any announcements, although I've started feeling deceitful~but we don't have any money! We're still barely keeping the doors open, even with the generous grazing fees your son is paying us! There's tuition and some donations through the denomination! I haven't known what to do! Your call is timely, that's certain!"

⊰ ⊱

"You're twenty minutes late!" Alexandra hated to confront Janni, but her father had fussed at her about being too lax as a boss!

"My hair wouldn't cooperate!"

"I'm sorry it wouldn't! But I need to be able to count on you! Brenna Prescott's head geologist is arriving in Durango shortly, and now I'll have to step on it!"

"Well, you didn't tell me you were meeting a flight!"

"Because it's none of your business! I said be here at eight-thirty! It's your start time five days a week! If you can't do it, turn in your resignation!"

Janni looked shocked, knowing Alexandra depended on her for help with both girls, but Leisel, especially!

"They're still asleep! Get them up and dress and feed them! Unless the flight's delayed I'll be back by noon!"

⊰ ⊱

Trent grabbed his extension!

"How'd you know," came Jason's awed question! "You don't happen to have the scoop on Johnson's other victims, too; do you?"

"No! Ft. Collins, then? Courier the key to me! Stat!"

⊰ ⊱

Remembering her promise to Doug about speeding, Alexandra obediently observed the speed limit! She tried to be a woman of her word! But

280

her driving was tough for her to take seriously! She complied because Doug knew all of the local law enforcement people, and they tattled to him! Consequently, Malik and Sheena Owens were waiting when she pulled up!

"Good morning!" She popped her trunk lid and greeted them as Sheena hopped into the passenger seat and Malik folded his long legs into the back! "I can't tell you how glad I am that y'all are here! Equipment moved on site yesterday, so maybe you can start this afternoon?"

She met the geologist's gaze in her rear view mirror!

"Yes, Ma'am! I'm rarin' to go! It's amazing how the weather's held for you! But now I think we better make hay while the sun shines!"

"My thoughts, exactly!" Alexandra turned her attention to Sheena, "You look gorgeous!"

She beamed! "Thank you! Your mother's an amazing designer!"

Alexandra smiled~ouwardly! Inwardly, she still mourned the ruin of most of the Panda coordinates~and her mother hadn't offered her anything else new, even with the restored relationship!

"We'll reach the mine in time to have lunch in the chow hall! Then, I'll help settle you in while Malik gets to work! It's such a relief that it's finally safe to go up there! Hardy Johnson and company are finally out of the way, and my new security people are amazing! You can meet my mining engineer at lunch, too! I'll let him know the plan's still a go!"

⊨ ⊨

"Bingo!" Trent's soft but triumphant exclamation as he and another agent opened the safety deposit box! Trent wasn't surprised at all, but Wilson whistled in amazement!

"Do you think those are real?"

"I don't know why they wouldn't be! You don't need a safety deposit box for fakes!" Even as Trent spoke, he rued the fact that Wilson was new and largely untested! It still remained to be seen if his housecleaning had been a wise move or a total catastrophe!

For being such a perverted freak, Johnson's cache of documents and valuables showed an amazing attention to detail! Trent halted the grudging credit, remembering the atrocious old pickup truck and every other detail gleaned about the old nutcase! No way! This must be Keller's work! That made more sense!

꒳ ꒳

Alexandra's eyes shone! Her father's wisdom was absolutely amazing! Although she read through the wisdom-rich book of Proverbs every other month, his years of experience gave her practical tips! 'Yes, Janni was in love! And, yes, she was a treasure who brought a lot to the table! Still, it was time for her to get in or get out; to get on or get off! Alexandra Hunter was moving forward! She was taking a new dynamic with Leisel, too! Kindness and sympathy for the child's bewilderment were one thing, but being tyrannized by a two year old? Enough!'

She watched, satisfied, as Malik and Jared left together in Jared's truck! Hopefully, Malik could trace the silver vein, or find another! As usual, signing a contract that cost her money nearly made her physically sick! But she was only one woman! And she couldn't do it all! 'Penny-wise and pound-foolish', she reminded herself!

꒳ ꒳

To Trent's amazement, he finally got called on the carpet-for, 'Taking excessive trips to Colorado when there were forty-nine other states and numerous US territories under his jurisdiction'! Evidently his law enforcement victory in the San Juan National Forest hadn't shown up on the Undersecretary of Agriculture's radar!

Trent patiently explained!

"Yeah, Morrison, I get that!" Came the impatient rejoinder! "But you didn't have to fly back out there just to see the contents of a safety deposit box! Any of the agents could have followed the lead provided by our lab, and sent you an inventory of the contents!"

Trent chafed at the inaccurate assessment! The lab hadn't put the clues together! He had! And he had made the correct guess to check out the Fort Collins area! Why? Because there were diamond deposits up there on the Colorado-Wyoming state line! And his supposition that there would be valuable gemstones in the safety deposit box, had made him loathe to send in new agents he didn't trust yet! Diamonds were such a huge temptation! Easy to palm and conceal! And nearly valuable enough to make the risk worthwhile!

Disconnecting, he shook off the rebuke! At least they weren't calling for an investigation of Addington and Johnson's custody-death; yet, anyway! And there were no questions about having blown up a residence-inside of a city limit-maybe he should be glad DC didn't pay much attention to details! If they didn't give him enough credit, on the flip side, they weren't placing too much blame! He grinned to himself! Another example that Romans 8:28 was an important dynamic in his life! God did make things work out for him!

For the first time, he considered the answer to his prayer for a 'key' to 'unlock' his investigation nationwide! Although, he had meant a key, figuratively, the lab techs had located a literal Key! Thanks to that, he was now on the trail of other organization members from Ft. Collins, Colorado to Laramie, Wyoming, as well as the Superstition Mountains in northern Arizona!

※ ※

"I can't find a dress! Maybe we'll have to push the date back!"

Shannon tried to empathize, at the same time wondering why Ellis would want to delay their marriage! All because of a dress she would only wear once, and that for just a few hours!

"Well, I have a friend who's a designer! Maybe she can help!" Even as he spoke, he realized he didn't know Diana Faulkner well enough to seek favors! Maybe he could get his grandmother to ask her! Or get his brother Shay, to ask his grandmother, to ask Diana-

Wishing he hadn't gone there, he tried another tack, "Have you tried any of the bridal shops?"

The question was so crazy that she burst into gales of laughter! "Why didn't I think of that? Yes, Shannon! Every bridal shop and department on the East coast! Tell me more about your designer-friend!"

"You-you've tried New York City-then-"

"Yes, Shannon O'Shaughnessy! It's on the East Coast! We started there! Who is your designer friend? Has she ever designed wedding gowns?"

"Well, her name's Diana Faulkner! I'm pretty sure she designed Mallory Anderson's! Mallory's my cousin!"

"Really!" The distress left her voice! "I've heard of Mrs. Faulkner! Give me her number and I'll call and see what she says! I didn't know you knew her!"

"Well, yeah, you know Alexandra Hunter?"

"Hardy Johnson's other quarry! Yes, what about her?"

"Well, Diana Faulkner is Alexandra's mother!"

"Really? Okay, give me the number!"

"Maybe I should call~"

"Shannon!"

⚑ ⚐

Alexandra didn't remember the simple chow hall fare having ever tasted so wonderful before! She even downed a second helping! Maybe her general state of euphoria made even her taste buds happy! She studied again the photo array before her!

"Malik, you're amazing!"

The young geologist smiled broadly under the lavish praise, thrilled with himself for having accomplished his assignment! Alexandra was happy, which meant that his boss Brenna Prescott, would be happy, too! And Sheena glowed with pride in him!

"Well, the drill designs get more and more efficient," he insisted modestly! "And the good Lord stuck all the valuable resources in the ground in the first place!"

"Yes, He did," Alexandra agreed eagerly!" But four feet! That's a lot of earth movement! I'm so happy that the vein widens; I hope now it goes way deep in, without disappearing again!"

"Yeah, do you agree that everything happened as a result of the great flood of Noah?"

"Well, it was certainly cataclysmic, and there's evidence of it in the Geological record if you study it with an open mind! Whether that's what moved the silver vein four feet to the right~"

"Yeah, good point, Mrs. Hunter! We tend to think of the earth as being static, but~"

CHAPTER 30: ONSLAUGHT

Boom! Windows rattled and the earth trembled! Terror showed in Leisel's brow eyes, and Angelique's little features puckered in alarm!

"It's okay, Babies! That music's sweeter to my ears than Seraphs' songs," Alexandra comforted. Finally, the sound of money hitting the bank! Well, dynamite, first, and then money hitting the bank! She explained, "The dynamite blast broke lots of big rocks away, and now they'll load them into the ore haulers! There will be more loud booms, so don't be afraid; okay?"

"Okay!" The calm response wouldn't have been such a shock, except that aside from 'Gaa-maamaa, it was Leisel's first attempt at talking!

✠ ✠

Trent whistled in astonishment as data hit his laptop! These creepy guys with the double lives lived well-behind their more respectable personas! Very well! Aerial reconnaissance of isolated and elegant estates seemed incongruous, with the mountain-man-hicks as viewed from his vantage point!

"Hmm, so much for the old adage that crime doesn't pay!"

He felt a certain smug satisfaction that the entrepreneurs behind their high walls were about to get a wakeup call! More high walls awaited them! In the Federal Prison system!

Contents in the safety deposit box had led to raids, which scored computer data and pointed to more suspects! Like dominoes, people who had considered themselves untouchable, were falling in the chain reaction!

Concerned about the wealth of natural resources funding the underground, anti-government activities, his mind went to the notorious problem encountered a few decades earlier, African Blood Diamonds! Could the same thing happen in the good ole US of A? Not totally out of the realm of possibilities! Rugged terrain and glittering prospects for riches~these guys were savvy survivalists, and ruthless!

☙ ❧

Diana emitted a shriek, causing Daniel to respond in alarm!

She met his terrified brown eyes with satisfaction in her blue ones! "Sorry! It's just that~" She waved a computer printout as she choked up, unable to continue!

Less alarmed, but still puzzled, he took the paper and scanned down the report! "An order from Al! Honey, please just fill the order! I'll pay~"

"Well~yeah~no problem~but if she needs something~why doesn't she~just~"

He shrugged, not sure himself! "I think it's a combination of things! She's still eaten up by guilt, she's trying to be grown and make it on her own, and she's still partially bought into Brad's story, that we're broke!"

"What?"

"Oh, sorry Honey; maybe that's another thing I still haven't filled you in on! When Brad first showed an interest in Al, Stephen googled us and our businesses! Compared to their standard of wealth, we're paupers! At some point in time, Brad convinced our daughter that we're wage-slaves and practically broke!"

"Oka-a-y, but, why would she order the silk Mt. Huangshan crewneck sweater? It certainly seems ill-fated! First, she returned it to me unopened! Then, the second time, I thought she got it, but what she wore to meet us must have been four years old~"

"Um-m-m~"

Her eyes snapped, "Let me guess! There's still something else you haven't filled me in on~"

"Yeah~about the sweater~she wore it to a Forestry Department banquet, and something strange happened! Another attempt at kidnapping her~she broke the guy's nose and~he bled all over her~"

She sank down, dazed, "What else haven't you told me?"

"Well, Trent was at the banquet, of course, and he recognized~it's a long story~and I never got all the details! But Erik put Al and Janni and the babies into FBI protective custody! Trent was so spooked that he gathered his family and went to Egypt to help Cline! Then Matt found an artifact on a dive, but they didn't report it! The whole Morrison family nearly got thrown into prison in Cairo! And the guy whose nose Al broke, tests positive for AIDS, but Al and Janni and the girls tested Negative! It's a good thing you didn't know! It saved you a lot of worry!"

⚎ ⚎

"Hello, this is Alexandra!" She tried to sound casual as she took Trent Morrison's call! He still made her nervous! "How can I help you, Mr. Morrison?"

"How much do you know about the Colorado/Wyoming diamond deposits?"

"Uhh! Absolutely nothing! Why?"

"Well, I don't know much about it, except that it seems like these anti-government goons may be using them to fund their cause, at least in part!"

Alexandra was confused, not sure what Doug's top boss was fishing for! Not Trout, obviously!

He continued earnestly, "I'm not even sure what I thought you could tell me! But since you're a Geologist~"

"Yes, Sir, and since my sister, Cassandra, is in tight with the head of the Israeli Diamond Counsel~"

He laughed, "Yes, I've had my run-in with Lilly Cowan! I'm not sure if she's a player~"

"Wherever there are diamonds, Lilly's a player! Of that you may be sure! Of course, as you know, that's rugged country! Hardly any population! And the anarchists are survivalists and stealth! It's not out of the realm of possibilities that they're finding diamonds, or any of a vast array of other valuable resources! Even Nanci Burnside found diamonds! There on the Poudre River where the Anderson's cabin burned! If she could find them, probably about anyone could~"

"That's right! Did she say someone kept stealing them from her?"

"Mmm-mm, that's funny! Because she was stealing them! But, yes, Sir; I guess they kept disappearing! That was probably someone acting at Lilly's behest! To stabilize Diamond prices, Lilly doesn't want the whole world to know about new discoveries! I guess! Because Mallory cooperates with her so completely, Lilly had no use for Nanci stealing diamonds belonging to Mallory!"

There was a long silence before Trent plunged in, "Have you ever had the desire to go up there and have a look around? From a Geological standpoint?"

She considered all the implications of the question! She was interested in her Silver mine, as well as alluvial Gold and Platinum nuggets! Honestly, the diamond-bearing area had never captivated her–until now! She laughed, "Well, I haven't! Now, you've piqued my curiosity! But Doug wouldn't like it! Neither would my dad! And most importantly, neither would Lilly! I'm pretty sure her relationship with Cassandra doesn't give me any free passes!"

"Well, this anti-government group had a stash of diamonds in a safety deposit box! I don't want my forests to become like Africa, where diamonds purchase guns and power for the bad guys!"

Alexandra listened sympathetically! That explained why Michael Cowan paired up with Ward Atcheson to come root out Hardy Johnson!

She responded, "Well, I understand your concern! But I'm pretty sure that won't happen! Thanks for your call, but I can't go! I just got that crowd rooted out of here so I can function! I don't want to go where they're still thick as thieves, and I might pose a new threat to their operation! You could ask my dad, but I don't think he'll cross Lilly, either!"

᳀ ᳁

"You're sick!" Diana Faulkner dropped the end of the tape measure dangling around her neck, to meet the beautiful, expressive, brown eyes of the bride-to-be!

"Ellis didn't try to mask her frustration, "I thought you were a dress designer!" Still the damage was done! Her parents both frowned at the remark and Diana continued, "You're hotter than a six-shooter! There isn't infection–in that toe?"

Captain Vaughn intervened, "I just checked and re-bandaged it," he gave his wrist watch an important glance, "not three hours ago!"

Frowning with concern, Diana touched the glands in the Ellis's neck! She jerked free!

"I'm fine! Could we please just get on with the wedding dress? Time is closing in~"

"You're rushing for Valentine's Day! Why?" Diana could show equal toughness!

"It's romantic!"

"To a fifteen year old," Diana shot back! "What are your colors? Red? Or pink?"

"Okay, really, Mrs. Faulkner," Darlene's moderate tone from years of settling disputes among five lively kids, "We've already reserved the chapel at Annapolis and started the invitation process! Seriously, can you~help~us with the wedding dress? Will it take forever? Is that your problem with the date Shannon and Ellis have chosen?"

"Once we agree on a sketch, two weeks, tops, for manufacture and delivery! The issue isn't with the time-frame on the gown! Do you have everything you need for the Bridal party? Bridesmaids? Flower girl? Have you found your dress, Darlene?"

Captain Vaughn sighed, "That is a lot to think about and line up in the short amount of time! Do you do bridesmaids' dresses and the other?"

"I can, but, you have a sick little girl here!" She turned again to the seething girl, "Where do you hurt? Throat, ears?" As she spoke, she rummaged for a thermometer!

"I'm fine! Right now I have cramps that make me want to scream! If you could finish the measurements, I'd like to lie down~"

Diana nodded sympathetically, "We should do this when you feel better!" Her professional gaze traveled from the flushed young woman to the Captain, and back!

"You know, she could have a hot appendix! And between the antibiotics and pain meds for the toe~they could mask the severity~"

⚜ ⚜

"Why did you call Alexandra, of all people?" Erik Bransom's voice sounded crankier than normal!

"Because she's in Colorado, and she's a Geologist! And I want to know if my anti-government forces are stealing rough diamonds to fund their cause, of overthrowing the government! You don't think it's a legitimate concern?"

Erik's laconic laugh! "No, not really! Either your imagination's running away with you, or you're scrounging for reasons to talk to her! You know there's some gossip~"

Fury shot through Trent! "I'm aware of that! I can't help what people think! I have a job to do!"

Erik's ire rose in response, "Well, you have an army of agents! If you can't get it done through them~Alexandra's right! There's no cause for her to purposely stir up issues with these guys! The environs of her mine are finally reasonably safe for her! She's not the person for you to look to for help!"

"Why don't you think this is a cause for concern? Look what happened in Africa!"

"It could be, at some point in time, I suppose: right behind 'Gray Goo' and the possibility of an errant electron in the Superconducting Super-collider starting a chain reaction to incinerate the world~"

Trent chuckled, regaining his equilibrium somewhat! He was aware of the possible doomsday scenarios Erik referenced! Still, he needed to drive his point home, "Forty sizeable, uncut diamonds in that safety deposit box! The estimated value is nearly a million dollars!"

Erik laughed again, "There you go! That's the reason Alexandra doesn't want to involve herself, and why she was sure Daniel wouldn't either! The Israeli Diamond Council and Lilly Cowan! If they weren't aware of this situation before, I'm sure they are now! They'll handle it!"

"They're foreign operatives! It's against the law~"

"Right," Erik agreed, "I don't think they worry about that too much~"

⊨ ⊨

Shannon's heart dropped into his work boots! "Okay, slow down; slow down, Babe! I can't understand~"

Tears sprang to his eyes as he caught the gist of emotional babbling!

"Right now? You can't~wait~until I can~get there?"

"Uhn-unh, I'm prepped, and they've given me something to relax~I begged for a chance to call and hear~um, Shannon, will you~pray for me?"

The line clicked dead as he said, 'Amen'!

⊨ ⊨

290

Puzzlement crossed Alexandra's features as she pulled up at her gate and hit the remote! A package next to the mail box! She had skipped the cost of express shipping when she placed her clothing order with *DiaMal, Incorporated*! Really fast, and it was larger than her expected package! She debated leaving it there! Probably it was something for the mine, ordered by Jared! She frowned; she hadn't authorized any purchases!

To her delight, the return label said *DiaMal*! Getting the girls and all their paraphernalia unloaded from the car, she tore into the box eagerly! Then gasped in wonder! The most darling woolen knit dress fit her like a charm! Great with the solid gray coat which hadn't been destroyed! An identical sweater replaced the beloved, but ruined one! A large square silk scarf which featured the Panda and Mt. Huangshan motif, slim gray suede high heeled boots hitting just below the knee, and slouchy shoulder bag! Instead of an invoice, there was a letter from her parents telling her they loved her-and Doug and the girls!"

⊰ ⊱

Trent sat at his desk, studying the phone! Although Erik's observation had infuriated him at first, now he flushed with shame! What was his problem? Why had it made sense to him, initially, to phone Alexandra Hunter? Because there were diamonds in the safety deposit box? And then, she was the only Geologist in the entire state of Colorado, that he was aware of? Erik was right! If some of his agents engaged in idle gossip about him, the last thing he wanted to do was add credibility to their accusations! Did he have a 'thing' for Alexandra? He honestly didn't think he did! His original disdain for her had given way to respect-grudging as it was at first-He had sons older than she was! And he loved Sonia!

As usual, the walls of his office advanced on him! He forced them to recede, choosing neither to run for the local coffee shop, nor book a flight to any of his districts! The diamonds falling into the hands of men who would use the gemstones' tremendous value in proportion to size, to build their incredibly wicked empires, was indeed, a credible threat! Alexandra Hunter couldn't help him! He didn't plan to leave his job in the hands of foreign operatives, either! This was his fight, and he planned to fight it! He phoned an acquaintance, the Associate Director, Energy and Minerals, and Environmental Health, with the USGS under the Department of the

Interior! Leaving a message with a secretary, he took a black Sharpie and began outlining a plan!

Surprisingly, the official returned his call within fifteen minutes! Ted Henderson, who seemed immediately personable! After the prerequisite pleasantries, Trent quickly outlined his concern!

"I realize I'm requesting a lot of extremely valuable data! I have qualms about requesting it! Further qualms about who to trust and share it with, within my Department! My wife's a huge fan of diamond jewelry; I may have to keep my concerns from her!"

"Well, Mr–is it okay if I call you, Trent?"

"Actually, I'd prefer it–"

"Okay, Trent; are you sure you aren't making a mountain out of a molehill? I'm not sure there's that much of value out there! The mining companies have gone broke–"

"I understand that! But I see a huge difference between owning and operating a viable mine with all overhead and expenses, and trespassers who are prospecting illegally! If I would drive out there, could you give me a few minutes of your time?"

"I'd love to visit with you, although I'm not making any promises about giving you what you're asking! Actually, I'm leaving a few minutes early today! A friend of our family's daughter just underwent an emergency appendectomy at Bethesda! I can take the train into the city in the morning! How about a breakfast meeting?" he named a prestigious downtown DC hotel favorited by key Washington personalities!

"Ordinarily, I would jump at that, but, I'm thinking something lower key?"

Silence, and then a chuckle, "Good point! How about your office at say, eight-thirty?"

᚛ ᚜

Captain Cal Vaughn hovered over his daughter in recovery! Vital signs were good! So was her color! Miraculous in view of the diseased organ–he fought raw emotion! There were staff members around that he didn't plan to 'lose it' in front of! Not that he knew any of them, or vice versa!

Lashes fluttered open and closed heavily! A few seconds later, a more successful try! A wince of pain and cracked lips parted, "Mmm-mm, where's–"

"You're in the recovery room! That was a nasty appendix! It's very fortunate-that Shannon's designer-friend-arrived-"

"I was-he was praying-" Her eyes drifted closed again, and she struggled with an inward torment for a few seconds before sleep once more overtook her!"

He slipped out to find Darlene and reassure her.

❈ ❈

"Hello, Dr. Allen!" delight filled Alexandra's voice at the unexpected contact, before the horrible possibility struck her that the call might be bad news! "Is-is Mrs. Allen okay?"

"She's never been better! We have exciting news! I should apologize for not keeping you in the loop! Things have advanced rather rapidly, though!"

She sank onto a kitchen stool, relieved, but not sure why they felt they owed it to her to keep her, 'in the loop'!

"What do you mean, things have advanced-"

"Well, young lady, you have stood our theology on our ear! Well, the Holy Spirit has-through your influence!"

"Oh, that's good, I guess!"

"You sound as confused as we felt, at first! We realized that we had been in error, but parents have sent their children to *Grace* in good faith that we would build the children's lives on their framework! I guess you are acquainted with Pastor John Anderson-"

Alexandra cringed guiltily before answering, "Yes, Sir! He's a really good man! He's-uh-friends with my dad-wh-what about him?"

"Well, *The John Anderson Ministry* has paid for legal help in our exiting from the denomination to become a separate and independent entity! Everything has been very peaceful and Christ-honoring! Two very strict families are bringing their children home, but most have sent their young ones to us on Sally's and my reputation! And with some Bible students from the area who have been studying on line, -well, Dr., I mean, Pastor Anderson, has heartily endorsed that they enroll and study on campus!"

Alexandra laughed in delight, even as tears sprang up, "Wow, that is all really good news! I can't tell you how happy-well, this area really needs y'all's influence! I pray for the school all the time; for the needs to be met-"

293

A lighthearted laugh, "Is that so? Well, we wanted to invite you to be on the Executive Board, even before I knew you cared enough that you've been praying~"

Confusion as Alexandra processed, "Did you run that past John Anderson?"

Dr. Allen's voice came more softly and infinitely tender. "I did not! Unless there's reason for *Anderson Ministries* to suspect us of wrongdoing, our college is autonomous! After so much heavy handed oversight, we feel let out of prison! We know you made a mistake once, that you've been sorry over!" A gentle laugh, "You do still believe in the Doctrine of Eternal Security of the Believer; do you not?"

Her turn to laugh, "Yes, I do! Through everything, I haven't doubted my salvation! Well, the chastisement, for one thing~" she quoted softly:

Hebrews 12:5&6 And ye have forgotten the exhortation which speaketh unto you as unto children, My son, despise not thou the chastening of the Lord, nor faint when thou art rebuked of him:

For whom the Lord loveth he chasteneth, and scourgeth every son whom he receiveth.

She paused after quoting two verses of the passage, and he continued with verse 11:

Now no chastening for the present seemeth to be joyous, but grievous: nevertheless afterward it yieldeth the peaceable fruit of righteousness unto them that are exercised thereby.

We've been impressed with you and your walk since that day we first met you! An exceptionally talented musician, and don't give us that stuff about your father and sister! We're sure they're something~ because you say so! And you're the one with the vibrant testimony in the community! We haven't invited you frivolously! We've seen your patience through testing and chastening! Now we have other calls to make! Can you accept the position now, or do you need time~

"I'm honored! Thank you!"

Tears slid from the fringe of luxurious lashes! Ellis was thrilled to see Shannon! But they couldn't afford his trip! One thing she had been less than forthcoming to her parents about was her fiancé's finances! Which had been in good shape, until he saw her, and consequently bought the house she had fallen in love with! Which was now a gaping hole! So much expense in dirt work alone!

"We have to push the date back now," she whispered! "I can't believe this happened."

He scooted nearer and nodded seriously, "It would have been much worse, though, if Diana hadn't insisted! Why didn't you tell anyone-"

Soft ingenuous eyes met his, "I had no idea! I don't have a particularly high tolerance to pain! Mrs. Faulkner thought the pain meds I've been on-have masked my symptoms! I-I guess I wasn't very nice-and she already had the most adorable sketch! I wish-" she paused as she winced- "I wish I could show it to you, but you're not allowed-to see it-ahead-"

Darlene found a table and watched Cal as he stopped to pay for their cafeteria selections! Maybe too austere looking to be handsome, he possessed a commanding presence! Although he wasn't in uniform, she could tell staff took him for an officer!

Once seated, he covered her hand with his for a brief blessing! A rare laugh erupted, I feel like shouting and dancing all over the place; kind of a holy Pentecostal fit!" That announcement followed by sudden deluge of tears!

"How could I have missed that? And with taking care of her toe, and shopping for a dress, I've been with her more than I ever have!"

Darlene sat dunking her tea bag absent mindedly! "Well, I wasn't sure what to make of Shannon's designer friend! I thought she would probably be a slightly bohemian college student trying to get a leg up-Needless to say, I was shocked to see such a beautiful woman, so put-together!"

"Mmmm; I didn't even think about the persona! I just hoped it would be the answer for a suitable wedding dress! I agreed with Ellis when she didn't like such low necklines and bare tops! But when I suggested 'sewing in a piece of something', she went to pieces!"

Darlene agreed, "She's always had her own definite opinions on things! You're lucky this has been your first try at shopping with her- Since she was three-"

He chuckled warmly, "Doubtless I've never given you the credit you deserve-all of the things, big and small, that you've covered so I could serve-"

She considered! In the past few months, he had begun to get an appreciation for her! Over the course of their married lives, however, he had been something else! Since Ellis' abduction and injury, they seemed more on the same page than ever! She rallied to the present, "We've always been proud of you and what you do!"

"You've believed in me, and you instilled it into the kids! I don't deserve you! Some of the things-And I don't deserve-We-We've nearly lost her twice-within the past month! If the Lord wants my attention, He has is!"

⊰ ⊱

Ted Henderson paused in the doorway of the hospital room! Although there was a sizeable crowd of visitors, he didn't see either Cal or Darlene!

"Hello, Mr. Henderson!" Ellis voice sounded exhausted, "My parents went to grab a bite to eat! Mr. Henderson, meet my fiancé, Shannon O'Shaughnessy, his cousin, Mallory Anderson, and her husband, David! You know Todd and Josh," she indicated two of her brothers!

At the invitation Henderson crowded in, even as he voiced concern for her seeming exhaustion!

David moved toward the exit with a significant glance at his wife, "We should go!"

She laughed, "I'm sure you're right, but-" she turned shining eyes on the newcomer, "You're with the USGS, aren't you? You're over minerals? I'm a Geologist and you're one of my idols!"

Totally taken by surprise at the shy admission, Henderson extended his hand, "Your name again?"

"Mallory Anderson! I know you must be really good at what you do, and I've been impressed with the stand you've taken-"

He shrugged, pleased, "Well, when you work for the Federal Government, there's a tightrope-"

"We know," David's entry into the conversation. 'Being wise as a serpent, and harmless as a dove'! That's sad though, in a country that one time-well, I won't get started, but-"

Mallory laughed, "David's dad's a preacher, and he isn't called to preach! But if he gets started, he isn't too bad!"

"Okay, call me slow, but this is coming together now!" Henderson extended his hand to Shannon! "So, you're O'Shaughnessy, and your cousin~ Didn't recognize her by her married name! Mallory O'Shaughnessy! The young lady who wrote an open letter challenging the esteemed Dr. Phelps Hensley~"

Mallory flushed, "Yes, my main motive for marrying David was to change my name and try to lose the connection to that fiasco! That, and the name, Anderson, moved me up search engines!"

David caught her and planted a solid kiss, "The main thing is that you married me! I figured you had dubious motives; you usually do!"

"Wow, Ellis you've attracted a crowd!" Cal's voice carried above the others. "We met Trent and Sonia Morrison on the elevator! They heard~" his voice died away as he noticed Henderson! "Hey, Ted, thanks for coming! Trent, Sonia; Ted Henderson, one of the deacons of our church, and all round good guy! Ted, Trent's forestry law enforcement personnel helped rescue Ellis, out in Colorado~"

"Shannon was the one, though, that knew~" Ellis' eyes were riveted on Shannon's as she credited him again with being her hero!

岂 岂

BOOM! Alexandra jumped a mile and Angelique shrieked with terror!

"Don't be scared! Them's up breaking rocks loose!"

Alexandra's eyes widened in amazement as she stared at Leisel's stolidly matter-of-fact expression!

"You talked! You understood what I told you the other day, and you remembered! I wish Daddy was here! Will you say something for him when he comes home?"

A somber negative head shake was her answer!

CHAPTER 31: GEMSTONES

Trent and Sonia sat facing Ted Henderson and David and Mallory in a quiet corner of a superb steak place! It was an odd arrangement, and Sonia sensed Trent's determination! David drummed on the tablecloth and didn't even make his characteristic grab for bread when the server placed it!

Once their orders were placed, Mallory spoke softly, "You're both right! Mr. Henderson is correct that no mining corporation has retrieved diamonds profitably from the Larimer County finds! And Trent, you're right, that the forest hooligans with too much time on their hands, can find enough to fund mayhem! The problem is that the country up there is too rough and undeveloped! The reason it's undeveloped is because developing it would be a nightmare! If you get the maps you've requested, there isn't enough man power to patrol the acres and acres to prevent theft!"

Trent frowned, not sure how Mallory was aware of the scheduled meeting between himself and Henderson, and the nature of the meeting. He credited Alexandra Hunter for spreading his confidence! And maybe Mallory was wrong; maybe his guys patrolling up there occasionally would be a deterrent to gemstone theft! He had to do something! He wasn't an all or nothing kind of guy! He did what he could; even if it wasn't the best! You could delay action forever waiting for just the perfect time and circumstances! Sighing, he stabbed into his salad!

Henderson followed suit before quizzing, "Why is this of interest to you? You're in the private exploration sector, are you not?"

Mallory nodded, noting that the man's previous warmth toward her was chilling, "Yes, Sir, I am! But that's not my purpose for interposing myself into your meeting! My being here might even appear as a conflict of interest! David and I did try to check it out up there a few years back! Not an easy task, especially as we were trying to keep our mission somewhat stealth-"

Trent released his fork, and it clinked against the china, "Let me guess! Alexandra didn't tell you about the stones in the safety deposit box! This is about Lilly Cowan!"

Mallory met his gaze, and he gave in first!

"Alexandra tried to warn you!"

"I don't sit on my hands and hope that foreign operatives will do my job for me! Illegally, I might add!"

Mallory shrugged as she responded, "I get that! Erik wrestles with the same dilemma! But you aren't in a position to spend a huge part of your budget looking like you're about protecting diamond deposits! Your law enforcement is to protect people-"

"Right, but a fortune in diamonds in the wrong hands, and we're talking people who will be hurt! On a grand scale! These are the guys who blew up Federal facilities-"

Ted spoke up, "Why are we sitting in a corner booth talking about 'foreign operatives'? If you know anything that's going on like that, you need to blow the whistle! What are you talking about? The Chinese?"

"No, not the Chinese!" Trent's voice a sigh, "And Mallory isn't endorsing treason! She's just been put into a position of cooperating with Israel, where her Arkansas diamonds are concerned!"

Mallory nodded, weighing her words carefully, "Usually US interests and Israeli interests are pretty parallel! We don't always share intel with them, if it compromises what we're doing, and they do what they need to do! If we seem to be protecting diamonds, it will seem frivolous, another waste of government money! But protecting them, and thereby stabilizing prices, is a high priority with them! I'm saying you should let them do what they do! You can't stop them! I think your find in the safety deposit box caught them sleeping! But, I'm pretty sure it won't happen again!"

≒ ⊨

Cal and Darlene Vaughn greeted Daniel Faulkner deferentially! It was true, that they had been terse with Diana! Had she decided to bring backup? Someone to champion her? Faulkner was intimidating, and Captain Cal Vaughn wasn't easily intimidated!

Diana's breezy voice broke the tension, "What a relief that our little bride-to-be is on the mend, once again! Now maybe I can finish taking measurements and get her dress ordered! You said that pushing the date into March worked better for everyone all the way around! I shouldn't have said what I did about Valentine's Day!"

Cal and Daniel loaded luggage into the back of the Caddy SUV and they were on the freeway before the conversation resumed. Darlene elaborated, "There was a snafu with whoever scheduled the first date at the chapel! One of her best friends, Allison DeLong, got bumped in the misunderstanding! She had already phoned Ellis in a rage, claiming that with Cal's outranking her father, he had pulled strings~"

"Which, I couldn't do that if I wanted~and for Ellis, I usually want her to have what she wants~" He laughed, "But not guilty as charged!"

He turned sober, "Mrs. Faulkner, our family owes you an apology! That appendix was so bad~no one on the surgical team had ever seen one that bad, that hadn't ruptured! Your being here was~timely~! Dr. Mann apologized for kind of doing a hack job, but with the pressure~"

"Mmmm, going to be a bad scar, then? She's already worried about how her foot's going to end up looking~" Diana, sympathetic to the girl's vanity!

"Yeah, she keeps saying Shannon's going to change his mind about her!" Cal met their gazes in the rearview mirror, "I don't think it's sunk in with her yet, what close calls she's had!"

※ ※

Erik ran his magnifying glass over a grainy black and white image for the umpteenth time! Pictures of the dynamite theft Doug Hunter had recovered from security cameras trained on Alexandra's explosives shack! Images of three men! Dressed head to toe in the protective gear they had invented for themselves! He grinned, though. True to Trent's observation, the gear had the proverbial Achilles Heel, in that the culprits sported whatever footwear they owned! Not positively conclusive, but two of the images linked to guys killed in the blast, Hardy Johnson and one of his lieutenants! It was hard to tell, but it looked like the third guy, not only seemed stand-offish in the photo from the other two, but wore expensive-looking wing-tips! Kind of an incongruous note! On a hunch, he emailed the photo to Jay and Sophia Vincent! Although, Sophia was blind, their adopted son, Brandon, might recognize the third man!

'Why would an outsider have been involved in the dynamite heist?'

He was surprised when his phone rang, practically instantaneously with his hitting the send button! He answered eagerly, "Hey, Jay, did the picture mean anything to any of you?"

"Well, it didn't to me! Brandon's been down in Arizona spending a few days with his Grandpa Vincent! I haven't had time to describe the picture to Sophia yet! I called because we're really excited! Sophia's been trying to purchase a property that Angelique Maxwell inherited from the Maxwell estate! It's crazy, because there's been a lot of crazy legal wrangling to stop the sale, and Alexandra's gotten forty astronomical offers trying to outbid Sophie! We closed this morning, and it's ours! We wanted to invite you to be the first one to come look it over!"

"Well, that's real nice-uh-maybe, sometime-where is it?"

"Manitoba!"

"Canada?"

"That's right! A bit of an odd coincidence that it's the exact site where the body of Silas Remington, the headmaster of Sophia's private school, was found! Guess the Mounties have yet to solve the murder mystery! Our recently acquired lodge lies between Lake Winnepeg and Cedar Lake! We thought you might be interested in looking it over!"

"Wow! Interesting! Have you extended the same invitation to the Canadian authorities?" As Jay's meaning sank in, Erik Bransom longed to jump at the invitation!

"American kids were held there, as a type of clearing house, before they were sent along to other centers in Europe and the Far East! Doesn't that give you some jurisdiction? And it's our lodge now; we're inviting you! Listen, Agent, we don't know who we can trust up in Canada!"

Erik answered carefully, "I understand that, and I'm not familiar personally with any of the authorities up there! I need to check with my superior, Jed Dawson! He's the only one I'll include in the information loop! If we break Canadian laws, it might nix our chances of nailing culprits, even if we can prove their guilt! While I'm doing that and getting back to you, describe the picture to your wife!"

⌐ ¬

Lilly Cowan rose from a stool in the window of a popular London luncheon chain, "Ah, Mallory, Darling, you look more radiant and stunning than ever! Hello, David!"

Mallory embraced Lilly warmly before teasing, "Come on, Lilly, you know David looks radiant and stunning, too!"

She harrumphed, enjoying her game of shunning him, "If you think so, Dear, that's all that matters! Commendable job with the Misters Morrison and Henderson the other evening!"

Mallory nodded at the compliment, "Thank you, Dear Lilly! I have the most astonishing news to convey to you!"

Lilly arched a brow, ready for the pending accusation! "News? Really? Do tell!"

"Yes, Lilly; forty very nice rough diamonds disappeared from the Forestry Law Enforcement Division's evidence room!"

"Really! How tragic! You Americans can be so careless! I'm afraid that diamonds are terribly easy to make off with! One of the, oh so charming, things about them! I hope Mr. Morrison won't be in too much trouble!"

"Lilly?"

Lilly's eyes widened in feigned innocence as a bejeweled hand with blood red nails clasped across her heart, "Surely, you can't be-I haven't been to the United States in ages and ages-"

Mallory grinned and sighed at the incorrigible Lilly, "Well, I guess that exonerates you then! Do you mind if I see your passport?"

Lilly pretended to pout, "I left it at home! I didn't know I was to be accused of a crime, for which I would be forced to prove my absolute innocence! Where are your adorable children?"

David spoke up, "We left them at the hotel with my sister! We didn't know you think they're adorable-"

Lilly made a face, "Well, as children go-"

※ ※

"You're home early!" Alexandra swung the door wide for Doug and his armload of gear! "You'll never guess what happened-" she paused in confusion at the expression on his face, "Maybe you should share your news first-"

He shrugged his way past her-evidently not feeling communicative! It occurred more and more often! He was home little, and then he was a growly-bear!

302

"Just put your dirty clothes on the kitchen floor! I'll sort and wash them first!" Even as she spoke she regretted procrastinating with laundry for herself and the girls. They were dangerously low on clean stuff! "Should-should I start a pot of coffee?"

"Not for me! I'm hittin' the rack!"

⚎ ⚎

Daniel and Diana were on a mission! Seemingly hitting every musical instrument dealer in central Boston!

"We should try pawn shops," Diana's suggestion as they paused to rest and grab a coffee!

"Nah! Honey, you're too elegant to hit the seamy side! You never know if you're buying stolen goods-"

She laughed, "You look the refined gentleman, yourself, but we've combed Oklahoma City, Tulsa, and now Boston! Look, there's one, and the neighborhood still looks respectable! If you don't find what you want, we can try Dallas! I'd like to see Herb and Linda! It's been an age! With being so concerned for Alexandra, I've allowed some important relationships to slide!"

He patted her hand in sympathetic apology! After his being so careful to guard his daughter's confidences, she had assumed he blabbed it against her wishes anyway! Consequently, every remark she had made to Diana during the Colorado visit had begun with, 'Did Daddy tell you...?'

Sometimes dealing with women-make that, usually-dealing with women was confusing! When they swore you to secrecy, they really meant go ahead and tell! It would be helpful if they ever said what they meant; eliminate all of the wrong guesses that they then got mad about!

"Okay, we can try that one! Then by the time we catch a cab back to the Vaughn's, they should have Ellis home and you can finish your measurements! Di, you really are incredible! If you hadn't insisted you were right, that little gal's appendix would have ruptured! She could have died, but even if not, she's been through so much-" He cleared his throat and strove for a lighter tone, "I'm praying we find a lovely violin right across the street! So even if we don't have to go to Dallas to shop for one, you should plan to go and see Herb and Linda! They are really crucial to what you-er-we-have going on."

She sparkled at the idea! It always pleased her when Daniel took ownership with her for *DiaMal*, which, she had started as a passionate hobby to supply her own charming style with high quality and luxurious designs!

The match between Linda Campbell, Mallory's spinster aunt, and the master jewelry designer, Herb Carlton, was attributable to Mallory! Another of her amazing accomplishments! Thanks to Herb's creative genius, the *DiaMal* designs sometimes offered fabulous matching jewelry suites! So the businesses complemented and interrelated, doing cooperative advertising through web sites and glossy catalog distribution, in addition to *DiaMal's* reps situated strategically around the country!

᪸ ᪷

Alexandra's eyes stung with tears as she shoved her hands into unbelievably nasty pockets in search of items designed for the sole purpose of ruining entire loads of laundry! Ball point pen, chap stick, gum, Kleenex wads! Great! His cell phone! Tempted to go through it for clues to his irritability, she resisted! Not enough time, for one thing! And if he had an interest on the side, she wasn't sure she could handle it! Placing it on the counter, she started a load and brewed a cup of coffee!

He clattered in beside her and rinsed a dirty mug to make a cup for himself!

"Sorry for the way the place looks~" she began!

He glanced sideways at her, "Every time I come home, I'm surprised you're still here!"

She bit into her lower lip, but her hand still trembled as she lifted her mug, "Why? Where would you think I'd be?"

"I don't know! I can't figure out why you haven't left me!"

Annoyed she responded, "Why would I leave? This is my mine!"

He laughed suddenly at the realization, "Okay, then, why haven't I come back and found all my stuff out by the gate with the code changed?"

She leaned back against the counter, mug cradled in both hands, her characteristic hand warmer! She sighed sadly from the depths of her being, "I love you, Doug! We~all do! I~know~that your work demands~a lot of time~and energy; Do~do you just~stay away~on purpose~until all your clothes are dirty? I mean, I don't mind~"

To her horror, he began to weep!

"Doug, wh~what's going on? Did you get fired? Whatever~do~you~is~there~ someone else?"

His head shot up and his eyes met hers, profoundly shocked, "Someone else? Good grief, no! Is~have you~thought~?"

"I haven't known what to think, Doug!"

"Well, I've thought~I~was just someone~there! For you to grab onto~when you lost Brad!"

Tears rolled unchecked down pallid cheeks, "You were! You were there for me! My rock in the~storm! You~you delivered Angelique~when you~had to figure~he'd kill~both of~us! I grabbed onto you~to keep~from being sucked under~but I love you~for all of that~! I know we made a quick decision! It has my parents baffled,~but I've~I've never regretted~" She set her jaw solidly as she asked, "Have you?"

"What regretted marrying you? No! Not that! But regret my life~before~sticking you~to~look after~my warped kid! 'Cause I'm clueless~to deal with her! It's like~you have everything to bring to the table~and I'm bankrupt!"

"You mean financially?"

He dropped his head into his hands, moaning. "I mean every way! I was kinda tryin' to hang in there; real proud of getting you your rings! The payment's behind, and then when I met the rest of your family, your mother~"

"Well, Mom likes you, Doug!"

"Yeah, she's just nice! I'm pretty sure she doesn't like me for you!"

"Well, I disagree, but it doesn't matter! I love you, Doug! I want to be with you! I want us to be a couple, and not be shut out~I love my rings, Doug! I love that you sacrificed to surprise me with them! My mom had some eye-popping jewelry on; she always does! From my dad, but then, it's just the way God has worked things out for our family! She has that jewelry to wear, but it's either owned by the jeweler's corporation or by her company, *DiaMal*! It comes more at cost, and then, it's business expensed! I guess that's the reason that Stephan Maxwell thought we put on a good show; but we're not among the super-rich! God honors my parents because they live for Him!

Um~I tithed on some of my money, and then Hallie gave us all those gift cards! When I wasn't expecting them! So, then I tried it again, and Malik Owens located the vein of ore in under four hours! The mine is producing again! And it's just a miracle~the drought! I know it's going to hurt, but for now, it's boosting me along in an amazing way! And, then another thing; Dr. Allen called me, and they've changed their theology, which should have created a nightmare within the denomination! But the denominational leaders were relieved to cut the school loose because it was a financial drain! And now *John Anderson Ministries* is helping them get a new doctrinal statement and reincorporate! Some of the students' parents put them at *Grace,* more because of their high regard for the Allens, than for the religious tenets! So they aren't losing their student body, and Pastor Anderson is recommending the college to local Christians! Dr. Allen invited me to be on the advisory board! And I'm not stuck with Leisel! She's an adorable part of our family! She's part of you, Doug! And she said a sentence! And not just a sentence, but something that showed me she remembered and understood something I told her!"

"Well, that's all good news! I guess-you're so gorgeous-and with your privileged background! You have no idea how hard it is for me to believe someone like you could actually care anything about somebody like me!"

She blushed, "Actually, I liked you from the start! But, I was just stuck in this emotional thought groove, that since I'd done what-I did-with Brad- I mean, looking back, it was crazy! That I felt the only way to right that wrong, was to marry him! And then that night at Burger King! I figured you thought he was an idiot for the way he, 'Asked me if I wanted to marry him, or not?' I don't think he really wanted to marry me, but he didn't want me sitting there talking to you, either! Like, he didn't want me, but he didn't want anyone else to have me! I felt like I deserved his total lack of respect for me-" She broke off!

He considered before responding, "Yeah, I was stupid that night! I guess this seemingly peaceful mountain splendor lulled me, after the constant vigilance in Afghanistan! Brad had the drop on me, because he was carrying, and my weapon was in my truck! The last time that's happened! If you didn't actually save my life by going with him, you at least averted a nasty scene! I was prepared to deal with him had he rounded that curve behind you the night Angelique-"

She nodded, eager to continue through the opened door of communication," Well, it was a relief that you believed in me about the explosives' theft! I knew it should be a federal investigation, and if Sheriff Cassidy had listened to me, well, maybe those two Forestry Service buildings wouldn't have been blown up!"

He frowned before rising to brew another cup! "Interesting that that should come up! The film from that security camera still had me stymied! Two of the images matched to a couple of the deceased bad guys, but the other guy dead-ended me! I forwarded it to that FBI Special Agent, Erik Bransom! Have you ever heard of this woman, Jennifer? With a Hawaiian-sounding last name?"

"Jennifer Mo'a'loa? Yeah, how does she connect to my dynamite shack?"

"She doesn't; she connects to the third guy in the security photo! She insists it's this Mel Oberson character-"

Alexandra's features registered immediate distress! "Mel Oberson! Was right here? On my mine property? Th-that's kind of hard-to-believe! Thought he usually left the dirty work to his minions so he has deniability! So far, it's worked for him! But if Jennifer's right-" Tears welled up, "And she probably is-that would explain why the sheriff seemed so antsy to arrest me-"

"Well, Trent Morrison asked the FBI to look into Sheriff Cassidy; I guess he's an all right kind of guy-" Doug was troubled!

"But that's how this human trafficking ring works! They target people that can perform key favors they need, lure them into questionable activities, and then blackmail them for the favor! Usually performing one favor doesn't satisfy the group, and their victims get sucked in deeper and deeper! It was a jet owned by Mel Oberson that was used when Mallory and Amelia were abducted! And if Mel Oberson came here personally to steal my dynamite and frame me for it, he wanted the sheriff to arrest me and turn me over to him! That means that they're still actively after me, and I'm not safe just because Hardy Johnson has been taken out of the equation!"

Rather than dealing with the scope of her fears, he changed the subject, "I haven't told you the worst news!"

"What can be worse than having a criminal organization after me to sell me into slavery?"

"You won't believe it!"

"Try me, Doug!"

"Well, we can't begin to figure out how it happened, but you know those diamonds? That Agent Morrison retrieved from that safety deposit box in Ft. Collins? They were in the evidence locker! Not just some Podunk Holler PD's evidence locker, but a Federal one!"

"Let me guess!" The sarcasm she usually tried to curb sprang to the surface, "They disappeared! All forty of them! And unless I miss my guess every photo and document pertaining to them has disappeared too!"

An aggrieved Doug, "Well, I doubt that! We haven't gotten that far! Forestry Law Enforcement has a secure system! So removing Trent's files would be even harder than removing the actual stones! I mean, that evidence bunker is state-of-the-art! There's no evidence that the security system was tampered with, and yet~"

Alexandra laughed, "And yet, the diamonds are gone! My guess is that the Israeli Diamond Council is involved! I thought David and Mallory met with Trent~um~er~Mr. Morrison!"

Doug was nonplussed, "Well, that's one theory! I mean, he's beside himself! He's never had evidence disappear! And this is such an important investigation!"

Alexandra shrugged, "Well, you can still unravel the organization, and although the diamonds are gone, probably never to be seen in this hemisphere again, you now know that's what provides much of the criminal enterprise funding! All of the places where their numbers seem the strongest are also where there are valuable mineral deposits of one sort or another! For instance, Idaho's nickname, *The Gem State*!! Idaho's a battleground for anti-government groups, and the Federal government owns and manages a larger percentage of its land area, than any of the other fifty states! Remember the Federal showdown at Ruby Ridge? Since these groups excel at survival, meaning they know each root and berry, is it unlikely they wouldn't be trained to recognize mineral sources? Keep finding these guys and raiding their possessions! Of anything of value that could fund them! As long as you don't make too much of an issue of diamonds~well, like Mallory said, 'you can trust the Israelis to guard their interests'!"

CHAPTER 32: INVESTIGATION

Erik Bransom personally oversaw every aspect of the Canadian lodge investigation! Amazing that Mel Oberson was once again center-stage as a prominent suspect! Erik admitted to the Lord how discouraged he had been when Oberson had beaten all of the previous charges and walked free!

"Romans 8:28 is right once again! All things do work together for good! Oberson's gotten so cocky and confident that he's been careless! You know, Lord, that justice doesn't always prevail as it should! But we have a lot more on this guy now, that's rock solid evidence!"

And the amount of cooperation from the Canadian authorities seemed ideal, too! Interested enough in the case to provide chain of evidence for the many findings, but burdened enough with their own caseloads, that they didn't take over!

As was often the case, his jubilation was short-lived; his euphoria collapsed like a pin-pricked balloon! Oberson was conveniently out of the country: both out of Canada and the US! Seemed he was gone to some obscure Eastern European nation! His travel destination alone, should put another nail into his legal coffin-provided he didn't stay permanently and plead for asylum!

Nasty, dirt-poor place that would serve him right to be stuck in! Except the low standard of living would enable him to really live there as a king! And cross over the border and back! Doing his dirty business as usual!

〜 〜

Alexandra met Mallory at DFW Airport where they located their gate for a flight to Boise! The on-time status seemed 'iffy'!

"How crazy am I," Alexandra laughed good-naturedly, "To leave my producing silver mine and amazingly mild winter weather in Colorado, for this wild-eyed venture?"

Mallory nodded, "Still, we can get the lay of the land! I've been excited since you called me! Maybe we can stake some claims, and get some groundwork laid before spring!"

Alexandra gulped, horrified that Mallory seemed ready to act immediately, while she was suddenly unsure why she was even making the trip! She didn't have the money Mallory had! A fact that she was trying to move beyond! That Mallory was better at everything she was good at; Mallory had more money; Mallory! Mallory! Mallory!

"I'm surprised that David agreed to this; Doug isn't real crazy about it!"

"Well, I brought all four kids; he was hard-pressed to turn down a deal like that! Of course he drilled me on our security protocols! We're not the only ones excited! Janni and Melodye are glad to get together for a chance to visit!"

Alexandra forced a smile! "Yeah, hope that works! Sometimes it's hard to get Janni to focus!"

Mallory laughed, "Same concern here! I mean Melodye does a good job, but she's not the mom! She helps a lot with nuts and bolts, but I still always feel the responsibility! I wouldn't have it any other way! But there is more to parenting than meets the eye!" With that said, she returned to the gate where David's sisters watched the six kids! Addressing Melodye, "Okay, I'll watch the baby and the stuff while you take the girls to the ladies' room! Looks as if we might depart on schedule!"

⚜ ⚜

Ellis and her mother met Diana at her hotel suite near Boston, Logan! The dresses were in, and Ellis was nervous! Just because Mrs. Faulkner could draw beautiful fashion illustrations~if this was a bust~ Well no telling what they owed for her three trips in, and for her efforts! If her products were a fiasco, there was little time for Plan B! Well, actually, Plan B was sewing 'something' in the voids of ready-to-wear Bridal gowns!

Diana swung the door wide at the first timid rap! "Come on in? How's the patient? You still look a little peaked! Darlene, great to see you again!"

Elllis stared in wonder at the garment rack and sheet spread on the floor! Even though the suite appeared immaculate, Mrs. Faulkner wasn't taking any chances on soiling the hem of the pristine gown!

Tears welled up as color infused the bride, "Wow! It's gorgeous! Even better than the illustration!"

Diana nodded, concerned, herself, "Well looking good on the hangar is one thing! The way it fits is the acid test!"

Darlene gasped in wonder as the luxurious and charming dress slid into place!

"It's perfect!" Ellis whispered softly!

Frowning and reaching for a pin cushion, Diana grasped some of the fabric, "You've lost weight; not a total shock in view of what you've been through!" She paused, meeting Ellis gaze in the mirror! "You really need to try to gain a little bit back! I'm not going to recommend any alterations right now! We can do it the last few days if you don't gain~"

"She'll gain it back," Darlene assured! "She had no appetite for the first week after she came home, but we're about to get our old Ellis back! The one who could always keep pace with her brothers and not gain an ounce! That is positively the most stunning wedding gown I've ever seen! I wish Cal weren't out of the country!"

Diana smiled, pleased with her creation and the compliment on it! It was adorable; of course, Ellis was the cutest thing, ever!

So, the bride had liked the asymmetrical look of one long sleeve and one bared shoulder! Except! Ellis didn't want her shoulder bare! So, where that basic style ordinarily bared the left shoulder completely, Diana had placed a sheer strap and covered the shoulder with a lavishly elegant self-fabric bow! The slender gown of silk satin topped with silk tulle, hugged her form gracefully before falling to a chapel length train! A smaller-scaled bow secured her hair on the opposite side from the shoulder bow, in lieu of a bridal veil!

And the bridesmaid's dresses were also to die for! In keeping with the style of the wedding dress, they featured asymmetrical bodices, but instead of a bow covering the sleeveless shoulder, Diana had designed a single large silk flower atop self-fabric strap! Creamy ivory satin fell to a border print of riotous tropical flowers, the over-layer of ivory tulle subduing the vivacious blooms ever so slightly!

Ellis gasped at the gorgeous array, "Now I see why a Valentines' Day theme with red struck you as being hoaky!"

"Well, too ordinary, at any rate! You're such an extraordinarily lovely young lady!"

Ellis beamed at the praise, before fingering each of the gowns. "This is amazing! Which one is whose?"

"Well, the one with the yellow flower is your sister-in-law-to-be, Emma's; the teal is Shannon's cousin, Mallory's; the hot pink is for Alexandra, the lime for Cassandra, and the orchid for your friend, Allison"

Darlene laughed, "You've not just supplied dresses, but a wedding party! Sadly, Ellis doesn't have many girlfriends who have stood the test of time!"

Ellis blushed as she laughed. "It's true; if I tried to hang out with any of the girls I knew they were just ga-ga over my brothers! Made me so mad! I'd want to go do something, and they wanted to watch football or play pool-to get noticed by either my brothers or their friends! But I really like all of these girls; well all of Shannon's friends! This is all beautiful, but I wish I could just marry him and be done with it!"

Diana smiled understanding, "The date's bearing down; it'll come!" She pulled a glossy paper from her attache, "Look at the shoes!"

Ellis tried to keep her jaw from dropping, but the strappy sandals, color-coordinated to each girl's dress were adorable: a pair each, of yellow, teal, hot pink, lime, and orchid! "I suppose you know everyone's shoe size-"

"Another advantage of my picking your bridal party; The Rivera's in Spain, who manufacture the shoes, have lasts for everyone but Miss DeLong!"

Darlene gazed at the items longingly, wondering if Diana Faulkner had any tricks up her sleeve for a Mother-of-the-bride! She flushed at the thought! She needed to hold on! They didn't have a clue yet, as to how much they already owed the talented designer! She and Cal weren't made out of money! And they had lived long enough to be sure the adage was true about its not growing on trees!

"I'm hungry! Should we order up some brunch or go downstairs to the restaurant? Let's go down!" Diana's upbeat voice still retained a slight, charming accent, from her growing up years in Africa where the English held a definite British-inflection.

Mallory moved swiftly to a tall, muscular man with red beard and faded plaid jacket! Dag Swenson stood in the Boise terminal, holding the ubiquitous sign, announcing, 'Anderson party'!

"Mallory greeted him and he came back with, 'The Cowboys won'! Which incidentally happened to be the fact, but was also the code.

Quickly, she introduced Alexandra, Janni, and Melodye; they fell into step behind him as he headed to baggage claim and ground transportation! He scratched his head in perplexity as the women claimed piece after piece of luggage! This was something David had failed to mention! But, the money was good and the gals were pretty, but down to earth! Might be one of the pleasantest weeks he'd put in in quite some time! Once he commandeered a moving van for all their stuff!

⊰ ⊱

Caroline Hillman thanked the airline security guy and with a grin, pressed Bransom's button to share the update!

"Yeah, Hillman, what?"

She was accustomed to the gruff voice presenting a tough façade over heart of gold!

"Oberson just booked a ticket home," breathless with jubilation! "We must have pulled it off!"

Erik considered carefully! Prior to Sophia's purchase of the lodge, there were a lot of interested parties desperate to acquire the property! However, the real estate agent had assured them that with lodges of that size, buyers were usually few and far between! There were now actually ongoing investigations into the lives of every one of the would-be purchasers! Providing some surprising new leads and mountains of evidence! Although the FBI and Canadian authorities had tried to be stealth, posing as delivery personnel and remodeling crews, he couldn't believe Mel Oberson would just skate into Memphis on a commercial flight! Memphis was interesting, though!

Hairs stood up along his arms and sudden tears sprang from the core of his being! Memphis, Tennessee! One of the terminals along which the traffickers operated! Where, following Mallory and Amelia's abductions a few years previously, a private jet-from east Texas to Mem-"

"Erik, are you still there?" Hillman's puzzled reminder!

"I am! Hillman, you have to track down private intermediate sized jets~"

She dreaded the scope of the assignment about to hit her, but Erik was right, "Check on all private, medium sized, mid-range jets bought by Oberson, but through some unknown pyramid of shell corporations!"

A cackling laugh, "Sounds like you're on to me, Hillman! Maybe something will stand out through the sheer convolution of ownership!"

"Yeah, maybe," her voice held little hope! It was just that it seemed like there were more people trying to hide stuff~who could even make a guess at the stuff going on in the world? Covert stuff, deadly and underhanded~She brightened! Maybe they could put a stop to more culprits than just Oberson and company!

Erik was right! Oberson undoubtedly was returning to the US, but the fare purchase was a decoy to throw law enforcement off! By the time that flight arrived, he would already be back in the US! Attempting to evade arrest!

⊣ ⊢

"These are nice!" Alexandra's enthusiastic observation!

Mallory nodded whole-hearted agreement and Dag relaxed! His camp was hardly the Taj Mahal, and the four women looked like a bunch of divas used to first class establishments!

"Chow's five to seven! Be there in that time frame or wait 'til breakfast!"

"Don't worry; we're already getting hungry! Why don't you scram so we can change and get some exploration in before sundown?"

Alexandra's voice, teasing but firm!

Mallory was shocked by her transformation! In a good way!

Twenty minutes later, they headed out on ATV's, following the latest terrain map with GPS coordinates for an unstaked area!

On site, Mallory drank in the scenery and the prospects eagerly! Already convinced it was a great claim before arriving to view it personally, her eagerness was over the top! And this exploration was even with the blessings of Diamond council magnate, Lilly Cowan! Mallory could look for any gemstones, with the exception of diamonds! And if it happened that she found a source of the forbidden~that was fine, too, as long as she announced it only to Lilly! She felt like a bird freed from its cage! With her wings clipped from most Geological exploration, her new agreement was liberating! Pulling on work gloves and grasping a spade and screen, she moved quickly toward the creek which ran along one side of the claim!

A couple of hefty whacks broke through a thin covering of ice, and she spotted gravel that looked promising! To her amazement, Alexandra waded in next to her, pan in hand! After the confinement of the flight and the three hours to the camp, the physical exertion in the frigid air felt good! All the kids, under the watchful eyes of their nannies, played tag, laughing and cavorting happily!

Mallory was almost disappointed, "Well, I've seen enough-"

Eyes alight, Alexandra nodded agreement! "So, are you calling David to file the claim?"

Mallory shrugged as her gaze traveled upstream toward an interesting looking formation, "What do you think about slinging a drill in here first thing in the morning?"

"Is that on this claim?"

Mallory sighed, "Actually, no! Which proves the old adage, that the grass really is greener on the other side of the fence! Or the wealth is more concentrated on the next claim over!"

Alexandra laughed, then her expression clouded with puzzlement!

"Okay, breathe! I'm not planning on trying any claim-jumping, if that's what you're worried about-"

"Well, I didn't really think-"

Mallory sighed, "My one-time gate-hopping offense still follows me! This entire area is great, but that claim seems to be the most promising out here, It's been staked a long time! With nothing being done on it! Arkansas law stipulates-but, this isn't Arkansas!"

"So, where are you thinking to drill?"

Mallory indicated the one spot on the open claim nearest the formation across the boundary! We stake this one first thing in the morning, then we drill! If the logs show what I'm thinking, then, depending-we might pursue buying this out from the current claim-holder!"

Alexandra nodded, less certainly! For their being partners in this venture, Mallory was certainly taking the lead! Of course, she had more experience, as well as more cash to lay out, and more clout in the exploration and mining businesses

Although Alexandra's Colorado silver mine was finally bringing in a steady cash flow, she hated to risk it on something less certain! She turned to study the rock face again, and as she did so, the sinking sun burst through a pin prick in leaden wintry clouds!

Raising her hand in an exuberant high-five, she chortled, "Oh, yeah! Let's do it!"

⚞ ⚟

Special Agent Caroline Hillman refilled her coffee and sank into the broken chair at her desk! Maybe she should spring for a replacement, herself! The requisition process was a tedious one! For the moment, she did neither, suddenly caught up with the significance of the thick file before her! Why did so many organizations use such convoluted paperwork for purchase or lease of private aircraft? The obvious answer astounded her! There were that many people who had a lot of wealth at their disposal who were up to no good!

In a move the FBI seldom made, she put in a call to Mike Behr at Treasury! Although, he didn't take her call immediately, it was only a few moments before he returned her call!

"Good evening, Agent Hillman,"

"Thanks for returning my call!" She was frankly taken aback by his prompt courtesy. Not exactly the norm between agencies.

"Yeah, thought your message said something about illegally owned and operated private aircraft! Rumors like that always have me licking my chops! Problem is, you have to solve the crimes before we can move in and seize assets!"

"Well, if I can get some IRS information on some of these corporations, I might be able to solve the crimes; so you can grab the toys! I'm sending a thick dossier! If you can help me out at all~"

⚞ ⚟

Alexandra paced as she talked to Doug by sat. phone! To help thaw her frozen feet, for one thing!

Doug wasn't sure whether to be pleased with her revelation or not! Finding a promising looking claim was good news, but if it brought the wrong people out of the woodwork, sniffing around~

"Okay, Babe, give me those names again~"

"I'm sure it's just my over-active imagination~"

316

"Their names; just in case it isn't~" He pulled his pencil free to scribble in his ever-present notebook, "Eddie Henderson and Bud Newcomb? They're hands there at Swenson's camp? Tell me again, their reaction; the things that started your alarm bells jangling~"

"That's the thing! Now that it's over~I'm pretty sure~well~ Mallory announced bringing in a drill tomorrow and Swenson kind of laughed her off! You know, like she's real cute, but she doesn't know what she's talking about! I mean, Mr. Swenson seems legit! He's real nice, he just isn't used to dealing with women and kids!"

Doug smothered a laugh; he knew the feeling! Although probably wisest not to say so! He wondered how Leisel was doing, but the weird reaction of Swenson's workers came first!

"Okay," Alexandra ordered her thoughts. She needed to present them clearly to Doug, and let him be the judge of whether something was fishy! She lowered her voice! "The creek gravels were encouraging! We tucked the promising-looking gemstones into our packs and returned to our cabins! It's freezing cold, and it was getting dark! At chow, which was yummy blackened trout and fried potatoes, Mr. Swenson asked us how things were going! Mallory doesn't just get all exuberant; she's been at this for a while! She just said things looked promising enough to bring in a drill! That's when the two guys did their look exchanging thingy! My dad was right! It is disconcerting! Then, Mr. Swenson told Mallory that local drillers are always in high demand, and with this being springtime~she'd be lucky to drill by next year!"

"You're heading home, then?" Hope surged in Doug's voice!

"Well, no; not yet! David's flying in with the drill and crew! And this was just the first site! I think Mallory plans to do a lot more prospecting! This state is~"

He laughed, "Okay, you can't blame me for hoping! Keep an eye on those two, and don't let your weapon out of your sight! Oh, I nearly forgot; you have an official-looking letter; looks like a check, but it might be one of those 'gotcha ads'! Has a real postmark though!"

"Well, if it's where you are, open it and tell me what it is! Then I need to get the girls bathed and put to bed! You~you~wouldn't believe Leisel!"

"Causing problems?"

Alexandra laughed, "Succumbing to peer pressure already! Actually of a good nature! Amelia can get real bossy, but Leisel's so taken with kids to play with~well Amelia wasn't mean to her about not being potty trained, but she did ask her why! I think it's going to be a real breakthrough! An answer to prayer, for sure!"

"Okay, that's great news! I had to go out to my truck to find the letter! You sitting down?"

A laugh, "No, Douglas; I'm pacing to keep from freezing! I'm glad Mr. Swenson informed us it's spring! What~"

"A check made out to you from the Justice Department! Twenty-five thousand dollars bounty for taking out Noë Keller!"

Her screech of delight echoed through the silent woods, and nearly made Doug drop his phone!

꾸 ꃔ

Shannon fought panic! Rebuilding the Victorian gingerbread dream home seemed more out of the question every day! His money was literally down the rat hole! And although David had taken a look at it, Shannon hadn't heard anything from him or Mallory! The only other thing he owned was a small, older home in Hope, Arkansas! A home that reflected his first awkward effort to buy low and remodel! It had been fine for him to operate from! He wasn't eager to bring Ellis to it, and carry her across the sagging threshold! Thoughts of his lovely fiancée took him from peaks of delight to pits of despair! Although sorry for her appendectomy and pushed back wedding date, he needed the time reprieve! To come up with a plan! The problem; no plans seemed to be occurring to him!

꾸 ꃔ

An all-out effort succeeded in nailing Mel Oberson at a local airfield twenty-five miles west of Memphis, Tennessee! Obviously assuming himself too smart to ever be apprehended, he carried a laptop laden with incriminating emails and other evidence! Oberson's arrest was particularly gratifying to Hillman, Bransom, and Dawson! And as curiosity-piquing as some of the convoluted jet ownership was to the Feds, part of the rationale was secrecy from competition, as much as any illicit activities!

But as the investigation into Mel Oberson and his associates swung open in ever widening circles, attention was once more focused on a skilled cosmetic surgeon, Darius Warrington; a former sheriff, Roberson, in Arizona; and Oberson! Oscar Malevitch was deceased, and Bransom was convinced, by a tip from a Boston homeless man, that Otto, his identical twin was, too! Undersecretary Ted Coakley, Stephan Maxwell, Robert Saxon, and son, Bobby! Whatever money these scum earned at the expense of their victims, they hadn't lived their lives out to enjoy it!

To his immense joy, many of the rescued victims were springing back from their horrors, living victorious lives far beyond what he would ever have imagined they could!

Issuing the usual precaution against suicide attempts or jail cell attacks, he headed out for the night!

⊰ ⊱

Alexandra couldn't sleep! Even though the girls had drifted off immediately and the cabin had grown cozy! Well, plenty to think about! Finally getting the reward money was a good thing; although, mention of Noë Keller brought hideous images flashing back through the video player of her mind! And thinking about that night, brought Brad's unwelcomed image back, too, in a fresh new way! How overjoyed she had been at his heroic rescue of her!

The excitement of finding a rich enough gravel deposit to merit drilling thrilled her, too, although, she wasn't certain what her obligation financially would be! At least the reward money-well-less tithe, of course!

She rose resolutely! Grasping her phone and pistol, she pulled a heavy parka on over her gown! Pulling on a thick pair of work socks, she moved out softly to a broad front porch! The scene was eerily beautiful! Sinister, naked trees stretched their arms toward the sliver of moon, sighing mournfully in the breeze! To her right was an empty cabin, and to her left, the one Mallory and her kids and Melodye slept in! She shivered! Not surprisingly! The temperature was forecast to dip below zero! Thrusting her hands into the deep jacket pockets to protect her tingling fingers, she didn't leave them there to absorb the warmth!

⊰ ⊱

In Boise, David finished arrangements for the drilling and answered some emails! Not feeling particularly sleepy, he hit the sack anyway! Morning would come quickly, and the drillers with the rig in possession were scheduled to meet him for the transport to site!

He was just drifting off when an alert on his cell phone brought him up out of it, terror gripping him!

☙ ❧

Doug watched big lazy flakes of snow drift down past the office window in the first major snowstorm of the year! This late in the season, maybe there wouldn't be enough accumulation to shut down the silver mine! His mind returned to his conversation with his wife earlier in the evening! Was her imagination over-active, at the reaction of a couple of Swenson's hired hands? He was beginning to regret his decision to let her go! Like a couple of cabins full of beautiful women and helpless little kids, wouldn't make them enough of a target; they had discovered and retrieved handfuls of valuable gemstones! As he bowed his head to utter another prayer for their safety, his screeching phone brought him to his feet like a cannon shot!

☙ ❧

BAM! Bam! Bam!

Mallory came up out of a deep sleep and grabbed her gun simultaneously! Surely Alexandra wasn't in trouble! She paused in the darkness, confused as to what her course of action should be! Of course, the kids all shrieked in terror!

As she stood, shaking, and fumbling for an additional clip, her phone practically jumped off the table as it vibrated and screeched a distress alarm! Alexandra was in trouble, all right!

☙ ❧

Alexandra lowered her weapon and listened intently, aware of commotion cycling up from Mallory's cabin! Afraid for her friend, she slipped across the porch railing at the end nearest the empty cabin! She knew it with clarity! She had heard a vehicle, laboring up the steep incline leading to the camp! An odd thing, in the middle of the night, and with lights off!

The biting cold forgotten, she crossed the shadowy area between the cabins, moving to the rear of the neighboring one, straining to see into dense underbrush! Odd, that whoever she had shot at, hadn't come forward, hands up, to explain what they were doing~

That was her answer! Whoever it was, it wasn't a neighborhood watch group!

Flattening herself against the back of the far cabin, she made her way to the end! A sharp blast of air from the north hit her, sucking at what little air was in her burning lungs! Bracing against the piercing wind, she stepped from the protection of the corner, pistol trained ahead of her!

Crunching boots on gravel as the hunter realized the tables were turned on him! Making the cover of his vehicle, he swung in as it picked up speed down the hill!

Alexandra watched, satisfied! So, there were at least two of them! One driving, the other moving in on foot to case the situation out!

CHAPTER 33: VOWS

Ellis frowned as she reread an email! Of course her business had suffered during her absence! Once the wedding was behind her, and with hopefully no further health crises, maybe she could devote herself to it again! Shannon continued to keep the honeymoon destination top secret! Hopefully, she wouldn't be too out of pocket! She laughed at herself, longing to be married to her hero! Since he was so perfect, and they had seemed to understand one another from the first, she never questioned if he would understand her need to keep her fledgling corporation!

She shot an email back to the disgruntled customer, offering a full refund for her services! Of course she couldn't really afford the loss! But she could less afford to lose a valuable customer, and her reputation!

Grabbing a bottle of water from the refrigerator she pulled her bike free from its mounting on the wall of the four-car garage! A new bicycle, courtesy of her oldest brother, Joshua! She wasn't sure what had become of her old one, left behind in Silverton! She shivered, memories of the fateful attack on her, unbidden and unwelcome!

※ ※

"Someone was trespassing on my property, Tim! Threatening, or at the least, alarming my guests!"

"Well, he bled out! Your 'guest' may have been a little trigger happy!" Sheriff Tim Black's retort, "She admitted having an over-active imagination!"

Dag spread huge hands in a frustrated gesture, "Which, the later events of the night bore out–that she wasn't imagining things! Anyone with any sense around here knows that trespassing in the middle of the night, lights off, is pretty much asking to get shot at!"

"Well, she could have fired a warning shot into the air!"

"She coulda, but would you have? Muzzle flash shows your position then, making you a real target! Then maybe Mrs. Hunter would have been the one to bleed out! Why don't you run along and question your suspect further?"

"Well, he's a little overwrought! His buddy just died in his arms!"

"Probably because they didn't go seek medical attention! And why would they not do that?"

⚞ ⚟

Mallory calmed Alexandra down to the best of her ability! The kids were back asleep, and Alexandra had assured Doug there was no reason for him to come!

"I'll start some coffee! I'm pretty sure I can't get back to sleep before the drill rig arrives! I'm glad David's coming!"

Alexandra's wide eyes were troubled, "Yeah, me too! I hope they don't pull the plug on us! This is amazing! I-I didn't feel like I had any choice-but-to shoot!"

"I agree, and so does Mr. Swenson! He never has any trouble out here! His guys swear they haven't left the bunkhouse, but he figures one of them must have made a phone call! You did what you had to do! I mean, we don't go out looking for people to kill! They come at us! And then, we're basket cases over it!"

She frowned when her phone buzzed an early morning call! Kerry Larson, her brother-in-law, and also her attorney!

She moved to the other room, afraid the call was a warning that Alexandra was being arrested! To her relief and delight, he was calling to inform her that the elderly claimholder of the adjacent claim was interested in assigning it!

⚞ ⚟

Dag Swenson scowled reflectively as he released powerful field glasses to fall against his down jacket! The county sheriff's department was still conducting their investigation, and the drill rig pounded noisily on the

323

mineral claim adjoining his land! Now he had done his homework! Too late, though!

His thoughts traveled to his two hastily accessed corporate bios! Accessed too late! Mallory Erin O'Shaughnessy Anderson! And Alexandra Marie Faulkner Hunter! Looking like fashion models, they were actually well-respected Geologists! And, when they first contacted him, they were straightforward about their plans!

Since he could always use the between-seasons-revenue, he had eagerly rented two of his units! Just women and a bunch of kids! Let 'em search for gemstones! That was like looking for a needle in a haystack, even though Idaho's nickname was, The Gem State He would pocket a thousand dollars, and they'd be on their way, disappointed!

His pale blue eyes stung! From the brutal north wind, he assured himself! The Anderson/Hunter plans bode no good for his business! The activity and relentless racket would make wildlife scarce! He counted on the different hunting seasons; especially deer and duck! But there were pheasants-wild turkeys, boar! And fishing! Well, used to be! He suddenly worried that Sheriff Tim Black would try to link him to the nighttime incursion on his property! It would have been in his best interests, if the women had been scared off! He wasn't party to it! Mostly because he was too dumb to have seen the ramifications!

※ ※

Cade Holman met his wife Catrina for lunch, his jubilation tough to hide!

Without waiting for the server to bring their beverages, he plunged ahead with his news!

Cat's brow shot up, revealing smug satisfaction!

"So, no gold or silver, at all! Not even traces?"

"Yep! Nothing in the sample but nutrient-rich soil! Might make a good worm farm!" They enjoyed a laugh and a meal before returning to their chemical analysis company!

Cade kissed her at the door to the executive offices, ready to head to the labs, "Are there any new invoices? We're about caught up with everything-Do you suppose that the Anderson's business has fallen off?"

Cat laughed, "Well, Mallory told her mom, and her mom told my mom, who told Daddy, that they're doing better than ever! They've even gone up to Idaho to prospect around! Have we gotten-" She broke off to resort some previously sorted documents~ "That's odd, that we're not starting to get delivery on the Idaho samples!"

⊣ ⊢

Shannon read a new email and sighed in consternation! From *Holman, Corporation*, informing him that the soil sample from his Silverton property tested negative for the presence of valuable minerals! There was even a tacky suggestion that he might consider starting a Night Crawler business!

He wasn't positive, but it didn't sound economically viable! Not sure what else to do, he flopped in the middle of his bed with his Bible!

"Lord, I can use some help, here!"

⊣ ⊢

Dag took in the scene in his chow hall with a forced aplomb! So much for feeding women and children! Not that they hadn't put groceries away! And with the dearth of any nearby eateries, they had taken away 'snacks' for their kids, for later! Now, the sheriff and deputies, as well as the drilling operators had depleted the lunch round!

'What difference did it make? He was ruined anyway!' He thought glumly about the age-old tale of the Bedouin whose camel had begged to get his nose inside the tent door, to be protected from a Haboob (fierce wind and sand storm)! Sympathetic, the Bedouin agreed! Moral of the story was that the camel took over the tent, leaving the guy out in the sand and grit! Shocking how one event could bring such catastrophic results!

He forced a grin as David and Mallory Anderson entered together, "There's plenty of coffee and other beverages! Sorry the chow ran out!"

"Not a problem! Coffee sounds great! You got a minute?"

"Guess I got all afternoon!" the answer more of a sigh than anything!

"Hey sorry, we went through your supplies! We didn't have any provision made for feeding our crew, and everything's so far away! Just bill us for the extra provisions!"

Anderson seemed like a decent guy. Swenson shrugged, "Gladly! I'll go draw up an invoice~"

David shifted, "Well, before you take off, this is an amazing operation! How long have you been out here?"

325

Dag paused, "Thanks! I've enjoyed it! My uncle actually started it in the eighties! It was farther from Boise then; the city crawls ever nearer! Time for me to sell out and move on!"

David nearly dropped the heavy ceramic coffee mug! "You serious?"

The resort owner shrugged angrily, "Tell me what other options I have now! This is the perfect time for your discovery and mining set-up! Another year or two, this will be inside the city limits or one of these suburban havens! Gated community! The law of eminent domain can't force out a profitable mine! I wouldn't stand a chance against it!"

David prayed for wisdom to proceed with caution, "So, you've seen the 'Handwriting on the wall', so to speak?"

A mirthless chuckle, "So to speak! I counted on a little more time!"

⚔ ⚔

Diana was everywhere at once! Ellis' gown fit her like a dream, and the bridal party all oohed and ahed as they dressed in the sumptuous gowns! She hurried; the swells of the organ prelude were the cue for everyone to assume their places! She paused, mid-stride before scurrying in search of Daniel!

"Hey, Honey!" Noticing the alarmed expression on her face, he questioned, "Everything okay? Someone rip their hem out~"

"Shannon looks awful! I saw him heading into the groom's chamber! You need to go tell him to sit down with his head between his knees! Or he's going to faint!"

He shot her a desperate look before complying! Her area of expertise! Not his! Still, he heeded her plea!

"Hey, Shannon! Jitters?"

Tormented eyes met his from stark pallor! Faulkner didn't need a nursing degree to see that the bridegroom was in trouble!

"Diana said you need to sit down and put your head between your knees! Hey, it's gonna be okay! She seems like a great girl!"

"Oh, yes, Sir! That's not it~uh~do you know~anything about~worm~farms?"

Daniel frowned, "Can't really say that I do! Sit down!" He shoved a chair behind him and he plopped heavily! "Okay, now put your head between your knees! Take deep breaths!"

⊰ ⊱

Dag signed closing papers and left the title company, whistling happily! 'Wow! Talk about things working out!' He gained the Jeep and hopped in! Grimacing as he ground the gears, he headed her up toward his newly acquired acreage!

'Nice folk, the Andersons!' Well, he guessed they were! The thing of it was, that the deal was mutually beneficial for their and his operations! Maybe they weren't really that nice! One of those coincidences, where his former hunting resort would provide the *DaMal, Corporation* with infrastructure for their new mining operation, and he could relocate somewhere more remote!

Even as he considered the serendipitous 'coincidence', he was forced to admit something he kept trying to run from! That only God-

⊰ ⊱

Captain Cal Vaughn frowned, again uncertain whether Diana Faulkner was a blessing or not! True, she had caught Ellis' symptoms in time to prevent her appendix' bursting! But now, she had honed in on Shannon; and the prelude was playing, the clock was ticking!

"I told you to have him put his head down! Not take deep breaths! Now he's hyperventilating!"

Daniel bit his lip to keep from retorting!

"I need to find a bag to put over his head!" with that, she raced away!

⊰ ⊱

As Mallory took her spot as Matron of Honor, she made eye-contact with Shannon! He looked as awful as Diana had described! Or maybe a little worse! The Faulkners had thought Shannon was totally off his rocker mumbling about starting a worm farm!

Forcing her ire aside, she smiled as Shannon's little niece made her way down the aisle, daintily dropping rose petals on the white runner! Then her heart swelled with pride as the junior bride, Amelia, came toward her! Mallory smiled at her! Against David's grumbling wishes, who didn't want their first born to be a junior bride-or ever even a bride at all! He reveled in being her 'boyfriend'!

Then as Amelia arrived at her spot, a breathless hush filled the space!

As the amazing and historical organ swelled with Wagner's *Wedding March*, a glowing Ellis stepped forward on her father's arm! Gorgeous, gorgeous sights and sounds!

Mallory stole another peek at Shannon, relieved to see that his gaze, riveted on his bride, seemed to have chased his panic away! She fought tears at her part in ruining his wedding day! Not that she had been aware of it! Cade and Cat Holman were going to get an ear full from her, before she even moved to the reception!

The uniformed chaplain's voice intoned hypnotically, "Repeat after me, 'I Shannon Donald O' Shaughnessy take thee, Ellis Marie Vaughn, to be my partner'-"

Shannon's expression registered shock before he rephrased, "I, Shannon Donald O'Shaughnessy take thee Ellis Marie Vaughn, to be my wedded wife-"

The chaplain harrumphed with disapproval before continuing-

With gaze steady, Ellis spoke firmly, "I, Ellis Marie Vaughn, take thee, Shannon Donald O'Shaughnessy, to be my wedded husband!"

Then the vows took a real detour, with nothing said about poverty and wealth, sickness and health, till death do us part-

Dazed, Shannon took his bride into his arms, and kissed her lingeringly, "Till death do us part," he whispered against her ear!

≒　≓

"Are you planning to eat your cake?" Not usually a fan of wedding cake, Trent eyed Sonia's slice greedily!

"At least part of it!" She shielded it playfully as she placed it at her setting! "It's nice to know that Diana can do it all, including wedding coordination! Wish I could get her to put Michael and Gina's together!"

Trent frowned. He liked his son's fiancée, Gina Clark, but her family didn't have money! He was in no position to take on any additional expense beyond what the groom's family traditionally did! He was pretty sure Diana had never heard of the word, 'budget'! He hoped Sonia wasn't thinking they could put on a shindig like this!

"Did you know Alexandra shot and killed someone else?" Her gaze both curious and troubled as she sliced into the fluffy confection before her!

"Yeah, I heard the same thing!" Though he knew the details she was fishing for, he added nothing further!

"Where was Bob Porter? Or Doug and David? Do you think they should have been out there like that? Just Mallory and Alexandra and the kids! I guess the Anderson girls were there as nannies~"

Trent sighed, "Why are you asking what I think? You know how old-fashioned I am! I guess I'm conflicted! That wives and mothers should want to stay home and have their kids on a schedule; maybe bake cookies for entertainment and a sense of accomplishment! But in the US, I think we should all be safe, even if we don't stay home! You know the goal of my job is to keep everyone safe who enters the national forests and grasslands! That includes families, lone females, little kids!"

"Were they on Federal land?"

"No! Private, and I don't know where Bob is or what he's doing! I assumed he's running security at Alexandra's Colorado mine, and not actually her personal body guard! Why are we talking about this instead of what people are wearing?"

She shrugged, "Did you hear that Terri filed? And the divorce isn't final, but she's engaged?"

Tears stung his eyes at the stunning revelation! He felt pain for his former buddy; but maybe God would still heal the family! He hadn't ever liked Terri and her incessant whining; nothing, nothing ever good enough! Maybe Bob could meet someone easier to get along with~he didn't know!

"Well, I've always been grateful for you! Your steadfast love, even when making ends meet was tough~"

She flushed, "Well, we did try to leave you that one time~"

He winced at the memory! "The worst few months of my life, thanks to Lilly Cowan! Mallory seems to think Lilly is behind my diamonds disappearing from evidence! Makes me madder than mad! That any other government thinks we can't take care of our business, and they have to 'help' us out! But I have no desire to cross the vindictive Mrs. Cowan again!"

"She's gotten saved!"

He shrugged, "Good news for her; I'm not counting on any measure of Christian charity should I cross her again!"

Sonia shrugged slightly as she remembered, "I guess I should have trusted you more, but~"

"Well, you did trust me, and you put up with me when things were precarious! Lilly's vengeance was certainly vicious, and convincing to you! Trying to make things look like I was chasing Mallory! Was she even eighteen at the time? Speaking of Mallory, I've been watching for her~"

"Mmm, she went back to the bridal chamber to make a phone call! She was crying and seemed really upset~giving someone an earful!"

⊰ ⊱

"Strictly class wedding!" Admiral Wesley O'Bannion paused to speak an additional word to Cal and Darlene! "I love a string quartet! Where'd you meet Daniel Faulkner?"

Cal rose to converse with his commanding officer, "Thank you for coming, Sir; Mrs. O'Bannion! It's kind of a convoluted story! Ellis hated every wedding dress she tried on from here up to Maine! So, Shannon told her he has a friend who's a designer~to the rescue, Mrs. Daniel Faulkner! Literally to the rescue, because when she started to measure Ellis for the dress, she noticed the fever, and deduced appendix! She has a degree in nursing and keeps her license current!"

Darlene chimed in, "Yes, so she made the drawing for Ellis' gown, which was an immediate hit with 'Miss Impossible to Please'! Then offered to help with gowns for the wedding party! She designed the wedding cake too, in the tropical theme! All of the beautiful table linens are courtesy of Shannon's grandmother! The flowers from Mrs. Anderson's mother, Suzanne Bransom! We haven't been hit with the cost yet! Then Mr. Faulkner offered to provide the string quartet!"

"Kind of a fiasco about the vows," Admiral O'Bannion frowned. "I mean I know rehearsals never actually involve repeating the vows, but there should have been a consensus about them before the ceremony!"

"Chaplain Moore already apologized! He tries not to use vows that are actually vows~because he assumes none of the couples really mean them~ He actually quoted Scriptures to Darlene about how it's better not to vow, than to make vows and not keep them!" He paused, "I thought the kids were cute amending them to the more traditional!"

"Well, a very elegant event came together! This is far lovelier than Commander Helms' daughter's, last fall! And they slapped down a hundred grand!" With that, Rose O'Bannion placed a jeweled hand on the admiral's arm, and they drifted away!

The Captain shot Darlene a desperate glance, and she bridled, "You've left it totally up to me, Calvin! You know I'm not good at confronting and saying, 'No'! Evidently, you aren't either, or each time you've asked me how much we're up to, and I've said, 'I don't know', you haven't called to check either!"

"Yeah, you're right! Shopping dresses put me in sticker shock! Some of them were going for seven to fifteen grand–and she still didn't like any of them! And I'm sure custom designed will set me back more than the off-the-rack! It's a good thing we only have one girl!" He smiled suddenly, "Whatever we owe, we'll pay! Mrs. O'Bannion was right! Mrs. Faulkner has put together a dream wedding!" He sighed heavily, "Now I hope it leads to a happy life for Ellis!"

CHAPTER 34: BLESSED

Alexandra nodded gratitude as a white gloved server placed plates! Doug was actually conversing with some of the male wedding guests! From her spot at the wedding party table, she gazed around contentedly! Yes, doubtless, her dad and mom had planned to give her a comparable wedding! She felt regret for disappointing them, but that was all! Two quick court house weddings; the second one, to Doug, had more than compensated for the disastrous first one! All the hoopla seemed superfluous in retrospect! She turned her attention to the string quartet as they began the first movement of a Haydn composition! When her father winked at her, she smiled! Then amusement changed to alarm as he indicated she come take his instrument! Her self-confidence took a dive out the window; she flushed as she refused!

Doug slid into place next to her! "Go on! I'll guard your plate for you!"

She smiled, "Unlike you, that's the last of my concerns!"

"True, but you can trust me not to eat mine and yours, too! Go on; you can do it!"

"I haven't even practiced–"

"You always practice! If it isn't on the piano, it's your violin!"

She sighed, "You don't understand–"

He leaned in and his whisper against her ear tickled, "I understand more than you think I do!"

With a giggle she pulled away to meet his gaze, and he continued, "I know you think I'm tone-deaf and don't know what I'm talking about! So your dad and sister are pros; don't sell yourself so short–"

Ellis moved gracefully, greeting guests with sincere interest and giving liberal hugs! Shannon beamed at her, his panic forgotten in the emotion of the moment! Finally, he intervened, "Okay, that's enough! You're starting to limp!"

She smiled triumphantly, "At least I made it this long! The Rivera's custom fit these slippers to support my toe and accommodate the swelling! I'm still far from wearing sandals. Daddy's afraid I might still lose it!" She stiffened her bewitchingly twitching lip, and he planted a gentle kiss!

"We'll keep praying about it!" Even as he spoke he fought the fear that threatened to sweep over him and bury him forever! 'More surgery-she needed to be on his health insurance-marriage, even to such an absolute charmer, was serious'!

⚎ ⚎

Mallory joined the wedding party in time to hear the end of a Richard Strauss selection! To her amazement, Alexandra played first violin! Sounded good; she looked around for Daniel and saw him visiting with the Admiral and Captain and Mrs. Vaughn! Alexandra was doing an amazing job!

David slid in next to her, "Did you get Cat and Cade dealt with?"

"Do you have a problem with that? They practically ruined Shannon's wedding with their tacky and ill-timed announcement! Diana said that Shannon was trying to postpone, right before the ceremony! In the groom's chamber!"

"Maybe we should talk about it later!" He knew she wouldn't like that, but he didn't agree, and he didn't want to further wreck the wedding by arguing with her!

⚎ ⚎

"Did you find out how much we owe?" Darlene's anxious whisper as the meal commenced! "Ellis does look beautiful and so happy!"

"You won't believe what Faulkner wants in return for his wife's services!" The Captain tried to convey stern worry, but she knew him too well!

"I'm guessing far less than a hundred grand?"

⚎ ⚎

Doug held Angelique, and Alexandra clasped Leisel's hand as the child blew enthusiastic bubbles after the scurrying bride and groom!

Doug's rich laugh was sympathetic, "Go back in before you freeze!"

Glad for the offer, Alexandra held out her hands to take the baby!

"I've got her! She's bundled warm! Go tell your dad and mom and everyone goodbye!"

"I'll hurry!"

"Take your time! Our flight doesn't leave until late! We'll be in when the bubbles run out!"

Alexandra laughed and dashed toward the imposing doors!

≒ ⊱

"Beautiful job with everything, Mother!" Alexandra practically clung to Diana, then released her suddenly to pirouette in the charming dress! "Usually, I hate bridesmaid dresses, but I'm hoping for an event to wear this again!" She paused, sensing a gulf still between them, but not sure how to cross it!

Her dad appeared before she found a way! "Great job on the violin, Al!" Not worried about a chasm, he pulled her close and kissed the crown of her head! "Really great job!"

She flushed, "Thanks, but I think it's that violin! What a rich tone-what-uh-happened to your other one? That you got in Honolulu?"

"Nothing! I play it all the time! The one I handed you isn't mine!"

She sighed at his attempt to be mysterious, but he continued, unabashed, "Your mother and I found the instrument in question at a pawn shop! We nearly got it really cheap, but you remember that old song about *The Auctioneer?*"

She laughed, "You couldn't resist trying it out; and of course, between the resonance of the violin and the touch of the master's hand, it sounded so good that the price shot up! Is it Zave's? He's really good; isn't he?"

His warm eyes met hers, "He really is! I mean, as the family hammer, he sometimes sounds heavy-handed-" He broke off to laugh, "He's getting there!" His expression turned doubtful as he changed the subject, "I hope you don't mind, but I changed your flight out from tonight, until tomorrow night-"

She checked herself from listing a series of protests! It could all wait! A couple of phone calls could rearrange her pressing chores!

"That sounds great! I hope you guys can make room for of us!"

"Yeah, we thought of that! We have a room reserved on the floor below us! I guess the janitor is ready to turn out the lights! Don't leave your violin here!"

She emitted an exuberant screech as tears sprang up!

⚓ ⚓

"Okay, can we finish the conversation now?" Mallory's expressive eyes sought David's! "Just so you know, we might as well have finished the fight when we started it! Because between my distress at Shannon's predicament and your being mad at me, I was pretty distracted to be a good wedding guest! And I already know what you were thinking!"

'Yeah? Well, I'm sure I overreacted, but~" he hardly knew how to proceed!

"Well, have I been wrong? Being upset with Cat and Cade for spreading information that their Confidential Disclosure Agreements forbid?"

He sighed! They got along so well together, and he hated being at odds with her, "Well, in fairness, the way the CDA's are worded, the main thrust seems to be not disseminating information that will hurt our businesses or help our rivals! Telling Shannon that his soil sample seems best-suited for worm-farming, while ill-advised, doesn't seem to be anything we can fire or sue over!"

"No, but it proved what I've been telling you!"

He laughed, but it wasn't his normal, tickled giggle, "It did, but your 'sting' was so convoluted! Switching Shannon's sample with your Arkansas worm-farm dirt, and misleading them~"

She flushed, "Well, I didn't exactly mislead them~I mean~well~kinda~but the whole purpose was to see if they'd keep the information close to their chests or blab it~"

He shook his head, "You're so mad at them for, 'practically ruining Shannon's wedding day', when you're actually the one who set the dominoes up!"

Color shot up her cheeks, "Oh, that isn't fair!"

"Well, I'm not saying you intended things to play out as they did, but the truth of the matter is, that you, as the head of this thing, had a responsibility to warn them! Just a 'Hey, I know this document sounds

335

like it only protects the really profound data, but be careful about sharing any information!"

"So, do you not agree with me, that we need to rewrite the CDA's and make them more specific?"

"Come on, Mallory, you know I'm on the same page with you about everything! But the CDA's are standard! Changing them at the moment is reactionary against Cade and Cat and makes the change look like, 'The Holman Rule'! It singles them out to be embarrassed, and we can't afford to lose what they provide!"

"Yeah, we can!"

A frustrated sigh, "Yes, we can if we have to! But let's hope we don't have to! They're great people, Mallory! Come on, one slip-up shouldn't crucify them! And they aren't the only ones getting lackadaisical! We need to get back to periodical training and retraining seminars! That way it refreshes all of us about our goals and objectives and the best ways of reaching them, without singling anyone out as the corporate buffoon!"

She stared at him in horror! "There isn't time for that, David! Or money!" She ticked off a long list of responsibilities staring her in the face!

"I know! I hear you! But we're being like the lumber jack that doesn't stop to sharpen his tools because he has such a quota of lumber to fill!"

⚐ ⚑

Daniel hit his button to disconnect with more force than necessary! He supposed David had a good point, but it didn't seem like there would be any good time to hold a seminar in the foreseeable future! His mentioning it to Diana only brought a worried frown! He made his way into his office and started a slide series he hadn't viewed in months; maybe more than a year! Well, with their worry about Alexandra-

He scoffed at himself! An excuse he had leaned on for too long! And Al was doing fine! He sat quietly, making a point of concentrating on each familiar photo as it cycled through! Tears sprang up, but he made no attempt to either quell them or mop them away!

It was a strange experience: like he had stepped outside of himself and was watching the significant events of his life in disconnected awe! What a blessed man that man was; to have what he had, to visit the destinations visible in the backgrounds! To have a beautiful wife whose expressive blue eyes beamed approval of her attractive mate! To view a procession of baby pictures and church dedications of each subsequent infant! To see Christmases past and birthday parties, one after another! He smiled at pictures taken the weekend he and Diana had assumed guardianship of Mallory Erin O'Shaughnessy! A sudden imposition of perfect blue sky day, filled with only a high wire and group of sparrows as the shot's subject matter!

He paused the show to dwell on the significance of Diana's photo, taken the day they had taken Mallory and joined the Andersons to ride rapids or simply float on the Little Missouri River above Murfreesboro, Arkansas!

Was the day they gained Mallory actually the day they had started to lose Alexandra? Looking back, he could see some bumps in the road that he and Diana had missed in the crush of life! Alexandra was becoming an accomplished pianist–and then there was Mallory–who was better! Who was outstanding at everything she put her hand to! There was Mallory partnering with Diana in the fledgling garment manufacture and design business, creating *DiaMal, Corporation*! Mallory who needed them and was just so easy to love! While Al had grown thornier and more distant! Yeah, harder to love; at least harder to express love to! From the vantage point of the present, he could see his beautiful and elegant child scornfully freeing herself from his hugs, making him feel the idiot for trying! With a sigh, he realized that he should have given her more, rather than backing off!

With the display paused, he punched in a number! Al answered immediately!

"Hey, what you up to?"

"Laundry! And practicing on my new violin in between switching loads out! I love it! It sounds a-mazing! And the Allens have asked me to come down to Grace this afternoon at three! I'm not sure what that's about! And Mom made it look so fun putting Ellis Vaughn's wedding together, that I advertised locally to be a wedding coordinator, and I've gotten about ten calls! I have a wedding a month scheduled taking me into next year! I don't want to try more than that until I see how it goes!"

He laughed, "Wow; you've been busy! You're making me worn out listening to you! David called about doing an employee seminar! The fact that no one wants to bother with it is a sure sign we all need to! We're all like the Bible says about working like fiends without taking time to sharpen our axes!"

"Well, count me in! I've tried to teach some of the business stuff I remember to Jared, but he acts like I'm a dumb blond; and since he's just a mining engineer, why bother with any etiquette? Well, actually, I wish Doug could hear some of it, too! It's really foreign to him! I mean, he's such a great guy~"

Daniel laughed, "He is; we're so glad you have someone who appreciates you; but we can all use some sharpening up!"

⊰ ⊱

Shannon regarded Ellis covertly! Marriage was proving interesting, and challenging! In spite of her desperate efforts to shake off Hardy Johnson and her ordeal, he was still alive and well in her head!

Shannon's head hurt and every muscle ached with exhaustion! At least, for the moment, he was back in her world!

"Okay, I didn't call my dad to come get me!"

Shannon wanted to believe anything, but the facts bothered him, "Well, you were packed by the time he got to the hotel~"

"Yeah, Shannon, I know! I knew he was coming after me, but~I actually called to talk to my mom! I mean, I thought she answered all my questions, until~I just wanted to ask her~And she's supposed to be home on weekday mornings, and my dad isn't~"

"Yeah, you told me all that; it's okay~uh~I just felt a little dumb, not knowing you were calling either one of them, and his showing up~and then you just left with him!"

She dropped her gaze and gave an adorable puppy an extra squeeze before meeting his eyes again!

"I know, Shannon! It just doesn't seem fair to you to put up with me while I sort things out! I thought that~and so when my dad answered instead of mom, I knew she'd left him! And that he'd need me! I walked away because I really felt like you'd be better off without me~"

He sighed wearily, "Well, from now on, get my input on how I'll be better off! I love you~"

"But, you were having second thoughts, too! Josh told me, before the wedding~"

"Not second thoughts about you, Ellis! Just about the timing! I got~er~some~ disturbing financial~reports~"

338

The oven timer interrupted his confession, and she jumped up, placing the puppy carefully into her chair!

"These smell great! I'm starved!"

He nodded! An odd and interrupted honeymoon! He watched as she used a dishtowel to pull a couple of frozen meat pies from a small antiquated oven in her office kitchenette! "I'll leave the other two in to keep them warm!" Turning the knob to off, she pulled a couple of mismatched forks from her desk drawer!

"He laughed, "Here's to one of life's greatest meals!"

She sniffed at his assessment! "I like these! I'm glad they were on sale!"

He shrugged, exhausted; then laughed as the puppy dropped clumsily to the floor to dance eagerly at their feet!

"Oh, poor little baby," Ellis crooned! She laughed, "He knows good stuff when he smells it! Oh, Shannon; I love him! I'm naming him Peppy! Do~um~you just want to stand up and eat at the counter?"

"Yeah; that's fine! You need to sit, though! You've really put your toe through it~"

She complied, limping gingerly to her desk! With the pie before her and the pastry pulled open, she watched steam escape and blew delicately on a forkful!

"Okay, you were saying, before we were interrupted by the buzzer~"

Shannon flushed! He had barely gotten his nerves steeled for making his confession! With the interruption, he was back to square one! He stirred in the pie; "I'm not sure what difference it makes if you're moving back home to help your dad~"

"Well, I can't move back home! He won't let me keep Peppy!"

Shannon was at a loss! "Well, what are you going to do, then?"

She stared around her with pride, "Live here, I guess! It may be humble, but it's home! I got a lot of work done, but I'm buried! If I have to have another surgery~"

❧ ❧

Without so much as a word of argument with Mallory, David changed their flight reservations! He felt like he had things pressing at home, and knew she did, too! But her concern for her cousin took precedence!

"Okay, you remember that they are on their honeymoon! Which probably means they don't want friends, and/or relatives looking them up! What if they've already left on a flight to Bora Bora or someplace?

She grinned, "Yeah, we'd sure hate to trail them to some place like that!"

"Yeah, but since Melodye has all four of our kids, the prospect of that would delight her even less! And although she does a great job with them, I figure my dad and mom are interfering with her system!

"They haven't left the area, David! Shannon's too broke, and although the situation isn't as dire as Cat and Cade told him, it's certainly not rosy! Do you suppose there's some property insurance that he hasn't thought about?"

David started the engine on the rental vehicle, "I doubt it, because he didn't bank finance! He just sank all his cash-but it might be worth asking him about! Lending institutions demand insurance, and prudence suggests it-but-"

"He isn't just that savvy, to automatically insure," she finished.

☙ ❧

Ellis jumped with a start and Peppy yelped at a loud banging on the front door! Her startled eyes met Shannon's! "What could anyone possibly want with us at this hour?"

Holding a shushing finger to his lips, he handed her the wiggling Peppy! As she tried to quiet the yipping, Shannon freed his pistol and moved toward the door!

"Turn the light out," she whispered!

☙ ❧

"Hey, we found you, first guess!" Mallory's tone triumphant as Shannon turned the key and moved to unset the burglar alarm! "What smells so yummy?"

"Pot pies; there's one left over that we didn't eat! Want it? It's probably not very warm by now, but there's a microwave-"

"Dibs!" Mallory figured David would want it! He was always starved! "I haven't had one of those-" she teared up suddenly, "since Daddy died!"

Shannon laughed, "Okay kids, don't fight over it! We have eight more in the freezer! When I went to that little store"-he pointed- "to pick up some puppy food, the pies were on special! For some reason, they appealed!"

Mallory nodded knowingly, 'Yes, and no! They weren't bad, and they could be a mainstay for people with scrimpy budgets! Probably a sale price on the already inexpensive items-'

"How late's the store open?" David didn't wait for an answer, but sprinted away!

Shannon frowned after him, "I just said we have eight more in the freezer-"

Mallory laughed, "Yeah, but you didn't mention if ice cream was on sale, too! David's a grocery store junkie!"

Shannon presented the cold pie; one side, seriously black! "Here's the pie; you'll have to wash one of the forks in the sink! What brings you guys to our door in the middle of the night?"

Mallory rubbed one of the two forks under tepid water, and sinking to the floor, did the silent blessing before digging in!

Ellis viewed Shannon's elegant cousin with a mixture of horror and admiration! Horror at being caught like this! But admiration of her digging into the cold dish without disdainfully looking around for a chair!

"Darling puppy!" Mallory's smile dazzled, "I think he wants down! Is it okay if I share with him?"

"Uh-I'm not sure how people food might affect him! We're starting him out on puppy food! He'll jump all over you! Shannon got him for me-for his wedding gift to me!"

Mallory laughed, "Great job, Shann!" She tried to slam the door on a sudden nostalgic memory! Of David's wedding gift to her, Zakkar! A beautiful little white Arabian mare!

"So, what's his name?"

"Peppy!" In unison!

David unloaded his arms full of groceries on the counter in the small break room! Shannon helped stash ice cream into the freezer of the small refrigerator!

"I started the oven preheating to bake a couple more pies; I guess y'all are hanging around that long?"

David paused, "Sorry Man, I tried to tell Mallory you're on your honeymoon! It's just-she's so worried about you-"

Shannon flushed! "I'm the one who kept bugging Holman! He tried to explain that he reports to Mallory only, and then she passes the information along! But I knew that she and Alexandra were up in Idaho, with a lot more on her mind than my soil sample-did-uh-she put a bunch of money into my account?"

David's eyes widened, "I don't think so! We burned through a lot of cash rushing into the Idaho gem-mining! It looks encouraging, but at the moment, we're kinda cash poor! I think if she had bombed money down on you, she would have told me! And it would have appeased her conscience and concerns enough that we wouldn't have hunted you down in the middle of the night!" He stopped, considering, "How much money you talking about? Maybe we can catch a flight home in the morning!"

CHAPTER 35: EXPANSION

A frustrated Ellis pressed the control on the electric wheelchair and maneuvered carefully into place at a coffee house! "Really, all of this for one little tender toe! I hate being a wimp!"

"Yeah, been there! Done that!" Mallory's response! "But the doctor said absolutely keep it elevated and stay off of it, if you want to save it! After all you've been through, why not baby it a little longer?"

Ellis nodded agreement, fighting tears! She hated whining, and Mallory's loan of the chair was kind beyond words! Very expensive, and when she was done with it, it would be donated to someone seriously in need of it!

"So, to change the subject, are you seriously interested in repping our fashion line?"

Ellis met Mallory's hopeful gaze steadily, "At this point in time, I'm not sure what I'm interested, in! Don't get me wrong! The designs are gorgeous! Maybe in a month or so, if Mrs. Faulkner is serious, you can send me the particulars of what all's involved!"

"Okay, but trust me, she's serious, or she wouldn't have made the offer!"

"Actually, I think she made it to my dad about my mom! Which, no wonder my mom was suspicious! She's the farthest thing from a fashionista you could get! And then, I think my dad scrambled it up even more! He thought Mrs. Faulkner said the value of the dresses, material, labor, the wedding coordination, cake, and string quartet-would probably be about twenty thousand! But that the Faulkners would write it off in exchange for my mom's being their model! Mallory, you saw my mom! I mean, I love her, but~ My dad should have just pulled out his checkbook and settled up! Since he didn't, I'll pay for it!"

Mallory's expression showed genuine astonishment, "I'm not sure what your mom was worried about! We're a Christian company! We don't ask anything~you know~weird~or off the wall~I mean, why pay twenty-thousand dollars out of pocket when you don't have to? But you're right! I doubt Diana would have made it sound so much like extortion!"

She looked up as Shannon approached with their coffees!

"I really wish David had let me help him," Shannon's worried voice brought a smile from Mallory! David didn't want help; especially not from Shannon, who considered himself an expert in remodels! Actually in five years of investing and fixing up properties, Shannon was only a little better than terrible, and broke!

"Yeah, he appreciated the offer, but he thought you should come along and keep an eye on us two girls!"

"Okay; I'm worse at that than I am at building!"

"Yeah, what exactly happened?" Mallory's eyes widened as she sipped her beverage!

"Well, it's a long story and a series of events! I'm not sure where to start," Ellis's voice was tentative! "I guess my dad and mom got in a fight about my mom and repping the *DiaMal* designs! Dad thought she was being silly: what was there to lose? Free clothes and the major cost of my wedding would go away! You cannot possibly imagine my mom's low self-esteem; which hasn't been helped by my father's lifetime of philandering! But I don't blame my mom for being skeptical; about being a fashion model, I mean!"

Mallory listened sympathetically, "Well, believe me, Diana and I have learned some things by trial and error! Whereas youthful and beautiful women show the designs off to greatest advantage, people don't stop them on the street or grocery store lines to ask where they shop for clothes! Too intimidating, I guess!"

Ellis studied Mallory, who looked elegant in matching yellow wool coat and dress! "Yeah, probably so," she agreed!

"Diana used to have practically a prejudice against women who didn't stay pencil-thin! Well, you know your sister-in-law, Emma? I've known Emma's dad and mom since I was in grade school! I always loved her mom, Beth! I never thought much about her being overweight! It was just who she was, and she always made the most delicious goodies! My mom was

Roger's secretary back then, too, and she used to bring Beth's treats home to Daddy and me! Beth just has this warm and radiant personality; but she got caught into valuing her self-worth by her girth-"

Ellis fought tears, "Yes, but my father made it worse for my mom, always demeaning her-I always felt like she planned to leave him as soon as we were all grown-but I'm twenty-six and I thought she was resigned to her life! Even after my dad finally accepted Christ, he was drawn to a militant style pastor and church! He's never grown Christ-like! Just judgmental of everyone else-well-listen to me! I'm passing judgment! If he's changed, it may be too little too late! Anyway, I'm sorry; you were telling me about Beth Sanders?"

"Hey, no problem! Yeah, Diana and I finally had an intervention with Beth because her weight issue was poisoning everyone around her! People loved her; but then, she got so withdrawn and 'poor me' that Roger and her kids started pulling away in return! It was wearisome, always trying to compliment her and make her feel good about herself! And the feeling good never lasted and she was back being miserable and making sure everyone else was too! We convinced her to be happy, 'in the skin she was in', and that her knowledge of food and entertainment were her key to finding herself! So she started this blog and it took off like wildfire! Diana asked me if I thought Beth would plug our lines, and I suggested designing for Beth! So, now her blog credits her wardrobe to *DiaMal, Corporation*! Which, of course, has created stellar results! But Beth is just such a big personality and warm-hearted person, that people do stop her to talk to her! And women with weight issues that have a hard time shopping for quality apparel, stop her to demand, 'Where did you get that'? Your mom seemed the same way! Just a nice motherly lady that people could relate to! I doubt Diana explained all of that to your dad to tell your mom!"

Ellis met Shannon's gaze, and he entered the narrative, "So, yesterday morning, Ellis needed to talk to her mother-"

Mallory nodded knowingly! "About the marriage thing-yeah, I called Diana with a hundred questions- My mom always had too much tendency to tell stuff no one wants told! But-uh-your mom wasn't there, and you got your father, instead-?"

Ellis nodded, "So then between not having anyone to answer my questions, and finding out Mom had left, I went to pieces! Daddy thought Shannon and I-so he came and got me-"

345

"And, I didn't even know she was making calls, or that we had a problem, until Captain Vaughn was beating on the door to out suite~" Shannon's voice quavered!

"She just paraded out, pulling her bag, without even looking at me~ I~uh~asked if I could call her later, and she just asked me, 'about what'?"

Ellis wiped at tears, "So, I was having doubts about Shannon! Well, my brothers told me he was chickening out~before the wedding~and I thought, 'maybe we're not meant to be'! So, anyway, when Daddy got me home, he didn't even take my suitcase upstairs for me! My oldest brother, Todd, was there, and they were down in the den drinking together! It's so crazy; my dad always asks prayer for Todd to find Christ~and then when Daddy could show him how to rely on the Lord in difficult times, he just calls him over~to drink~"

Mallory nodded sympathetically, almost unable to relate to the narrative~

Shannon cut into the story, "In the meantime, I packed up and checked out of the hotel! No use staying~and spending my honeymoon alone! I was on my way to return the rent car when the breeder called to tell me I could come get the puppy! Well, I kind of figured that was no use, but when I tried to back out, he threatened to call his attorney~so I went out and picked him up! Well, actually, I had found Ellis's phone when I was checking out!

"Well, I felt caged up in my room," back to Ellis's side of the saga, "So I told Daddy I was going for a bike ride~at which he swore at me because of my toe! I promised to be careful, and took off! Not realizing I didn't have my phone!"

"Well, the puppy was really cute, so I thought, maybe if I take her phone to her, and she sees him~"

Mallory laughed, "Well, he is adorable~so go on~"

"Well, no one answered the door, so I was just driving around~aimlessly~and I couldn't call her because I had her phone with me~"

"Well, I went to a park near my house where I've gone all my life~but not since my toe~" She paused to dab at frustrated tears! "Well, my dad was right! I didn't make it far, and then, suddenly, there were these two guys looming over me! I mean, it's a nice park in a nice neighborhood, middle of the day~and there wasn't another soul around~And, I needed help~which it was obvious they weren't going to provide!

"I caught sight of her as they were trying to push her into their car!" Shannon's face reflected terror, remembering! "So, my gun was unloaded in my suitcase-because I was considering flying home! So, I pull over, and I'm trying to call 911 and get my gun-"

"And Peppy got out!" Joy infused Ellis' countenance at every mention of her new puppy, "and he came bounding toward me, yelping for all he was worth! I mean, he's a tiny little baby-"

Mallory laughed in spite of the drama! "Don't try to tell me that he rescued you!"

"That's exactly what we're telling you!" Shannon again! "So he sinks his little puppy teeth into the hooligan's designer jeans hem, and he's pulling and growling, not inflicting much pain or strength-and the guy pulls out a gun-and he's trying to shoot him, but Peppy was pulling at him and ripping the jeans-and somehow the guy shot himself in the other foot-! Bad too! So, his buddy pulls him into the car and they peel out!"

"I thought Peppy was hurt; he had so much blood and stuff on him! But when we got him cleaned up, he didn't even get a scratch! Except he lost a couple of teeth-I love him so much! I've wanted a puppy all my life! Except that I forgot I did, when I actually got out on my own!"

☙ ❧

Alexandra sent a terse code to Janni to lock down with the girls as she made a move for her gun! Whoever had just passed through her gate must be aware that Jared and all the miners were up at the mine! Holding her weapon behind her, she advanced, then paused, fighting dizziness and a ringing in her ears! This couldn't be happening!

☙ ❧

"Hello, Mr. Morrison," Mallory's expression registered surprise as Trent approached their table! "Are you here for coffee, or were you looking for me?"

"I'm looking for the O'Shaughnessys! Mr. Vaughn informed me that Ellis might be at her place pf business! David was there working and he sent me here!"

Shannon extended his hand for a handshake, "Why were you looking for us?"

"Were you guys involved in a crime?"

Shannon looked horrified, "No, Sir! What kind~"

"Well, they kind of were," Mallory corrected! "Not in committing one, but as victims! But it wasn't in the forest; was it, Shannon?"

Trent frowned! "No, a city park, but did it not occur to you to wait for the police?"

"Will we be in trouble for making the 911 call?" Ellis' brow crinkled with worry. "We were seriously in trouble, but then the one guy shot himself! They took off, and so did we, in the opposite direction! Maybe~um~we were afraid our new puppy might get impounded~"

※ ※

"Hey~hey~take it easy with that thing!" Profanity and a nervous chuckle from Stanley Hayward Maxwell! "I heard you were fast on the draw! And that you shoot people dead, too!"

Alexandra didn't waver! "In that case, you were decidedly unwise to trick your way onto my property! Turn it around, and I'll allow your egress! Myrna, you turn yours around, too! I'm kind of surprised that you helped~"

"Well, Stan and I are back together now, since Stephen died! We~uh~wondered if we could see our grandbaby!"

"You should have phoned before you came so far! And the trick of Stan following you through the gate isn't exactly endearing!

Stan made the mistake of cracking his car door open!

Alexandra's response was to shoot out a tire! "I said, get off my property! As it is, one tire can be a fixed!" She aimed toward the other front tire, and he backed slowly into a turn!

"I can contact my attorney, you know~" was his parting warning!

※ ※

Trent listened attentively to Shannon's repetition of the park incident! He had heard about the fiasco from Maddie, who saw it on social media! The police were searching for the gunshot victim, wondering who carried a gun with armor-piercing rounds! Which, not surprisingly had shattered his foot beyond repair!

348

"Well, the only thing you really did wrong, and it isn't illegal, was not alerting the authorities to the situation! Men cruising the park trying to abduct female victims, and who seem a little eager to fire on law enforcement personnel, are serious cause for concern! There's no telling where they might be by now!"

"And-and-they might have succeeded in kidnapping someone else, because of me-" Ellis voice dropped to a guilty whisper!

"Well, they have to find medical help! Of course the police are contacting hospitals and urgent care clinics! They need to get the story out on the mainstream news! The emergency call Shannon made from your cell phone tracked back to it! What else can you tell me about them?"

Trent listened in amazement to detail after detail! "You know what? You really need to go in and give the PD that statement! The only thing they should do about your dog is give him a medal!"

⚓ ⚓

"Thanks for stopping by to check!" David watched the aluminum-framed door swing slowly closed behind a city inspector, suddenly regretting repairing the stop! He was nearly finished with a quick facelift to the office suite when the guy had stopped by to make sure the remodel wasn't extensive enough to require a permit! It wasn't! And then, deflated by that, he had proceeded to warn that according to zoning, no one could live in the commercial space!

Now he needed to access the local code to determine the difference between Shannon and Ellis' 'staying here', as opposed to, 'living here'!

He was pleased! His signature loft bed rose above seating arrangement and coffee table, framing the lower space attractively! A large flat screen and comfortable furniture, in lieu of the only chair, the broken office chair at Ellis' desk! A chaise lounge he had rescued from a discard pile along the street was his biggest pride! With the nasty stuffing replaced, and upholstery to compliment drapes and bed coverings, it looked amazing! A twelve by fourteen area rug pulled the small living space together!

He called Mallory, "Hey, I'm hungry! What do you say to meeting me somewhere for dinner, and then we can bring them back and show them my handiwork!"

"Great plan! Why did you tell Trent Morrison where to find us?"

"Because he asked me! Why? Are y'all fugitives from the law?"

"Not exactly, but we are at the police department; we've been here forever! Ellis keeps telling everyone of every rank the same details over and over! At least, they don't seem to think the puppy is any threat to public safety! Is he doing okay?"

David laughed, "Yeah, cute as everything! Hey, do they seem to be doing okay?"

Mallory lowered her voice, "I hope so! I'm not a shrink, but I'm thinking Ellis definitely has PTSS from her kidnapping by Hardy Johnson! I'm pretty sure she loves Shannon! Her mom's leaving is about one thing too many for her! Hey, good news! Looks like we're about to get cut loose! Where do you want to meet? I'm suddenly starved, too!"

⚒ ⚒

Doug headed toward the mine! Usually, nothing shook Alexandra! Which was perfect! He wasn't sure he could handle marriage to someone overly needy! Still, it was nice that she needed him occasionally! His forehead wrinkled in concern; was she trigger happy? She had relayed the story to him in a fairly coherent and calm manner, but now he thought of some details he'd like to clear up!

The guy threatening to hire a lawyer wasn't a good thing! Maybe if Alexandra hadn't panicked- a soft answer did help turn away wrath! And he could tell that she was disappointed in Myrna's actions!

⚒ ⚒

Trent looked up in surprise at the figure suddenly looming in his office door! Maureen appeared behind a livid Mike Behr, looking apologetic for being unable to stop him!

"It's okay, Maureen! Just brew fresh coffee and bring us a couple of cups when it's done! Mike, do you take anything in yours?"

"No coffee! This isn't a social call!"

Trent didn't sense his normal alarm at the ill-reputed Treasury honcho's sudden appearance! "I'll still take a cup when it's done! And a donut if any are left!" He named an enticing brand, "Sure you don't want to mix business with pleasure, Behr? It's the DC modus operandi!"

"Well, okay! But I still want some answers from you!"

With the tray set on his desk, and the door closed, Trent leaned forward! "I'm sure you do want answers! Knock yourself out getting them! Fill me in when you're done!"

"Who had access to those diamonds in evidence besides you?"

Trent raised an eyebrow, "I'm sure you know the answer to that better than I do! And I'm sure you were licking your chops to sell them at one of your government auctions! But, I didn't take them! Because I'm not smart enough to do it, or stupid enough to try!"

"A substantial cash deposit showed up mysteriously in your newly-wed couple's bank account? Roughly the value of said evidence?"

Trent sighed, "That's what I understand! But I don't think either of them could have breached security and then sold them on the black market in such a short period of time! And then depositing the cash into their own, on-shore account, would be dumb!"

"Criminals have done dumber things! And maybe those two kids had help!"

Trent laughed off the innuendo, "You think maybe the puppy was involved? If so, he's quite the plucky little accomplice!"

"Did the Israelis have anything to do with the diamond's disappearing?"

Trent's best poker face, "Israelis? Why would they be involved? They can't operate on US soil! It's against the law! The theory that Peppy the puppy did it is more credible! Which, if you're really interested, you could launch an investigation! Let me know if you find anything out!"

Behr chewed a wad of donut slowly before answering, "They keep hitting walls!"

⚔ ⚔

"What do you want me to do, Mrs. Hunter? Get a restraining order? If they only wanted to see their granddaughter~"

Alexandra maintained her composure! She had never liked the local attorney, Ray Meeker, very much! For the money she was paying, she wanted counsel on her options! If she knew what needed to be done, she wouldn't be sitting here! And he was a poignant reminder to her of her friend, Norma, now deceased!

"Honestly, Mr. Meeker, I don't know! That's why I'm here! If they wanted to meet Angelique, I would have been amenable to it! Brad's mother has held a soft spot in my heart! I felt like Brad's treatment of me was a reflection of Stephen's treating of women, and Stan's treatment of Myrna! I thought it was Myrna who sent me the modest wedding ring set! A very kind gesture in view of her small and hard earned income! I was shocked that she was party to Stan's sneakiness! But the Maxwell men are manipulators, and if he's returned to take her back, maybe she does whatever he wants!"

Her lip quivered suddenly, "I'm willing to share my daughter, Mr. Meeker! I want her to have grandparents in her life! But if they think I'll give her up, they are in for the fight of their lives! I won't stop at flattening a tire!"

⊣ ⊢

Shannon pulled pizzas from the oven! This week's sale item at the little grocery! Placing a couple of cans of soda, he went in search of his bride! Finding her among her contraptions, he studied her lovely concentration before interrupting, "Are you hungry?"

She started and then laughed, "As a matter of fact, something smells amazing! Help me up?" she reached a manicured hand toward him, and he pulled her to her feet! To his amazement, she nestled against him before hopping to the motorized chair!

He scooped the dog into her lap and preceded her to the front of the building!

"Can you take enough of a break to watch something?" He reached for the remote as he asked.

Her eyes alight, she shook her head negatively! "No, can we talk instead? Although it is incredible to have such a nice television and this place fixed up so cute! And comfortable!"

He met her gaze, "Yeah, David and Mallory are pretty incredible!"

She flushed at the winsome twinge of envy in his voice, "Yes, they are! And I would never have met them, or any of this fantastic new group of friends, if I hadn't met you! You're the one who's incredible! Shannon, I'm~uh~I'm sorry!" She clamped down on her trembling lip as she struggled for composure! "So, let's bless the pizza and eat!"

⊣ ⊢

Mallory and Melodye managed to board the flight for Boise with all four kids and their truckload of gear! From her queasiness, she wondered if there might be a new member joining the family! The amazing thing about it, though, was that Amelia was getting big enough to be a huge help, and Avery was gaining some independence! She missed David, but he had gone ahead to do his wonders for getting Dag resituated at his new and more remote property!

Everything looked encouraging! She wanted to get on site and dig in, but life kept handing her interruptions! Well, first, stopping the operation to go to Shannon's wedding! Not that she would have missed it for anything! And now, Jeff and Juliet were finally getting married! All part of the fabric of life! And the people in her life needed to have priority over the plans in her life! Although her plans made her pulses race with excitement!

When the kids fell asleep, she moved to an empty seat to gaze out the window! Wow! Incredible to think of the technology available in Ellis's equipment! Developed by the military, but now declassified, she was on the cutting edge of development for civilian use!

'No boundaries!' Her thoughts charged giddily ahead! 'No private property, no Federal or State lands! No gates and fences!' She cringed in embarrassment! 'No trespassing!'

The flight attendant at her side brought her back to earth; well at least back down to the plane's thirty-five thousand foot altitude! Of course all of those rosy prospects depended on her ability, combined with Ellis's, to break ground (no pun intended), in a new way of interpreting data! It should work! She tried to chase away the doubts she had discredited in convincing Ellis to join her efforts! Strange how her stomach was suddenly uneasy! She tried a tiny sip of the proffered Sprite!

⫷ ⫸

"As one grandfather to another, you went about it all wrong!" Daniel's attempt at lightness with Stan Maxwell!

"Well, didn't you have to ambush her, yourself?" came the swift response!

Daniel laughed, "Yeah, yeah, you're right! So, did you actually contact your attorney?"

"The only attorney I'm familiar with at all, is French! I'm pretty sure I want nothing to do with the legal counsel my late father relied upon!"

353

Daniel felt a deep sense of relief! Maybe he could rescue a relationship! "Well, your appearance made my daughter skittish! She was actually leaving Colorado for a week or two anyway! Why don't you and Myrna fly into Salt Lake City and meet Diana and me? We would love to get acquainted with you!"

Stan sought Myrna's approval and she nodded hesitantly!

"Okay, Faulkner, seems you're calling the shots! Just find out when and where!"

After noting down the appropriate airport hotel, he disconnected and met Myrna's troubled gaze!

"Sorry for messing it up again!"

She shrugged, not sure what to say! He gazed into the faded eyes which had once been alight and full of fun! What he had missed out on! Maybe a life with her wouldn't have been easy! But it hadn't been, anyway! He could hardly blame his father for where he was! His own poor decisions were heavier on his shoulders than anything he could place blame for! Now he felt more of a broken down wreck than she was! An idea struck him suddenly! Why not?

"You know, we could fly to Vegas, get married, and then back to Salt Lake to meet the Faulkners!" He paused, "If you would be willing to give me another chance, that is!"

No tears sprang up! Probably her tears were long since spent! She just looked at him, as though trying to plumb his depths, see what he was conniving now!

He was tired! He couldn't remember what his thinking had been! That he could stay in Europe, do his own thing, and then assume his role as father, whenever he chose to pick that mantle up! What women had he been in 'relationships' with, since Myrna that had amounted to anything more than time passed? What a life wasted! And yet, he had expected his ex to jump at her chance–She didn't care about him! She wanted to be in Brad's life! And since that couldn't happen, she wanted to be in his daughter's! He had little to offer her! Owning a winery in France was like owning a computer startup company in the Silicon Valley! And yes, California was another wine region, creating more fierce competition! So, he had sold out, and with the modest amount, returned to the States!

Lilly Cowan stomped angrily around her lavish London flat! Mallory! Just when she thought she had the lively entrepreneur on her page-What was to be done? Whenever Lilly was at home in Israel, she resorted to Caesarea on the Mediterranean Coast to deal with difficulties! Now, she just felt caged! She stomped again, before pausing beside her phone! Why did nothing do any good? She should stop and read her Bible! It usually brought calm when life was a turmoil around her! Before she could settle into a spot with it, her phone made her jump!

"Hi, Lilly! This is Mallory! I figure you know what I'm doing before I've decided what I'm doing, but I figured I should still call you with a heads up! Several of us are going together into a gemstone mining enterprise in Idaho! Just letting you know, that we're not looking for diamonds, so you can relax! It's always hard for me to know exactly what to say to you, because you don't want me to find more diamonds, but you have great disrespect for any of the other gemstones!"

"Yes, Mallory! I am aware that you are in Idaho! And yet I am also aware of your very clever ploy!"

Mallory sighed, "I guess you lost me, Lilly! What 'clever ploy' are you talking about? I'm pretty sure I'm not clever enough to fool you about anything! Consequently, I don't try!"

"Well, although you and your friends are in Idaho, I'm aware of a small plane that took off from the Mena, Arkansas airport with Ellis Vaughn's equipment on board!"

"Well, yeah, Lilly! To take readings at the Crater of Diamonds and the surrounding area! I'm not looking for diamonds that you and I both know are there!"

Lilly sank onto the deep sofa, "Then, pray tell, my dear; what are you looking for?"

"Okay, what Ellis and I are trying to do is pretty ground-breaking, I think! Not trying to use a pun! This new technology from the military is available now to civilians! Archeologists have started using it a little, to tell where the earth has been disturbed, and excavate historical sites! I thought maybe I could use it to look beneath overburden, and read Geological differences! So, if I can see how the Arkansas lamporolite pipes appear on the screen, I can interpret similar data other places!"

Lilly considered the implication of Mallory's words! "Well, you're certainly biting off a big mouthful!"

Mallory laughed, "Daunting all right, Lilly! But, hey, I've gotta start somewhere! At least for now, I'm only interested in the thirty percent of the earth's surface not covered by water!"

"Oh, not such a huge job, then!"

Mallory laughed, relieved Lilly could see the bigger picture than diamonds and threats to Israel!

"Right, so as we do the scans from the air, and we see rock formations, we can get permits to drill, to validate our findings!" Her voice infused with wonder! "Lilly, you wouldn't believe the perspective on things~"

"No, I'm sure! Quite ambitious, dear Mallory! But you have never lacked for ambition! And thank you for your very good talk with Mr. Trent Morrison!

⊱ ⊰

Alexandra raised her gaze from the pages of her Bible to drink in the astounding contrast between blazing sunrise hues and the whiteness blanketing the lodge! Apart from the occasional crackle of the fire, her little cabin was silent! Even though tears blurred her vision as she returned her focus to the beloved verse before her, she spoke it softly from memory:

> *I Corinthians 2:9 But as it is written, Eye hath not seen, nor ear heard, neither have entered into the heart of man, the things which God hath prepared for them that love him.*

Mallory! How often had she chosen to resent her, rather than embracing her as the gift she was? Seeing her as a rival for her every area of expertise! For the love and attention of her parents; in the musical arena; in looks, style, and beauty! For popularity, but also spiritually! Envying what Mallory had quietly and faithfully nurtured; her walk with the Lord!

Mallory's expanding her attention beyond the Colorado silver mine to Idaho and beyond was exhilarating beyond words!

But it wasn't until she had experienced motherhood that Alexandra recognized the capacity parents have for love! That she could better understand her dad's insistence, that Mallory nor anyone else, could ever take her place in their hearts~although, Mallory had carved out a space of her own! Angelique's position with her was unassailable, and yet she loved

Leisel, too! As part of Doug! As an integral part of their new reality! As a precious little personage in her own right!

"Call me slow to catch on, Lord, but Mallory and her synergy-it really is something else!"

CHAPTER 36: JUSTICE

Trent sat absent-mindedly twiddling a pencil between his fingers! He hated to admit it, but Mallory was right! All the people with interests in the diamond industry were better prepared to safeguard them than he was! There was an industry within itself to prevent pilfering of the valuable little Carbon chunks! He guessed he was mostly humiliated professionally about the loss from Federal evidence! But, if Lilly Cowan had been the one behind spiriting them away, and in her own definition of justice, thought if only fair that Ellis, as the latest victim of the vigilante, should receive proceeds from the sale-

He rose and paced! Not sure why he wrestled with it! There was plenty within his sphere that he could do something about! Still, Mallory's reminder haunted him! Of the thin line delineating the good guys from the bad guys! And finding a fortune in anything could erase that line in a blink! Not surprisingly, she still felt a lot of animosity toward Rob Addington! And his dereliction of duty that delayed David's receiving emergency medical attention! The four months of suffering she had endured at David's bedside! Not knowing if he would ever regain consciousness! And if he did-whether he would be her same David?

The problem wasn't Addington! The problem was the before mentioned thin line-and how could he judge a man and determine which ones were beyond price? He scoffed at himself! Probably, there weren't many! He trusted Doug Hunter! Surely all of his national forests and grasslands were laden with undiscovered treasures! For his sake, best left undiscovered! Hey, if Lilly Cowan wanted to downplay the fact that there were diamonds in the US, he could help her with the subterfuge! Let his guys concentrate on solving crimes in their jurisdictions, unaware of natural resources inches beneath their feet!

He rubbed the tense muscles in the back of his neck as he closed an imaginary folder in his mind!

⊣ ⊢

Stan didn't have much money from the sale of his winery in Provence! And his balance kept dwindling! A Las Vegas wedding wasn't cheap! Well, a ring set was definitely in order, and although the cost was moderate, there was also the license, the wedding chapel, and a payment to the minister.

"Why are we going to Salt Lake? We don't have any guarantees that after we meet with Mr. and Mrs. Faulkner, that Alexandra will let us see the baby!"

Her tone still accused him for the folly of following her onto the mine property!

He sighed, "You're right, of course! But I see no other avenue! I don't have money for attorneys and court costs!"

She chewed her lip nervously! "Alexandra doesn't deserve that kind of hassle! And I don't want to take the baby! I'm in no condition or position to raise a little one! I-I just want to be~"

He finished the sentence, "In her life!" He sank into a sofa in the hotel lobby! "Attorneys and law suits and threats! Those are the only methods I ever heard for dealing with problems! I wanted to be different from~my father~finally~ Once I realized he'd never have any use for me, no matter what!"

Myrna smiled numbly, "Yeah, sorry you had to find that out! He~uh~wrecked everything~with everybody~Well, no use going back through all of that again!" She twisted the new rings uncomfortably, not sure in retrospect what she had gotten into!

"I'm going to go check with the desk if the room's available for tonight, too! Rooms are cheaper here than they will be in Salt Lake! Rates are lower here, to lure people to come gamble! Their odds are in favor of recouping their room charge losses in the casinos! Once I take care of that, we need to go shop!"

⊣ ⊢

The repurposed lodge/mine burst with activity! And people! With chow hall experience, Alexandra stepped in to double the grocery order! Then, not sure why, she phoned Delia O'Shaughnessy to order table linens! The property boasted commercial laundry units for keeping up with sheets and towels! Why not add table linens too? Maybe she wouldn't use linens at breakfast and lunch, but in the evenings she could dress things up! She contemplated ordering pretty, but durable china or stoneware, but decided to run that past Mallory! Maybe she had overstepped with the table cloths and napkins!

She paused to call Diana again, "Hi, Mom, I hope I'm not driving you crazy~"

"Whoa~that won't happen! After not hearing from you, this is like an oasis~anyway~what can I do for you?" She was delighted to have the wall torn down and didn't want to start rebuilding it by heaping guilt on Alexandra's fragile shoulders!

"Walk me through again, how Mardy did the baked egg casserole! If you have time!"

"I always have time, and that's a delicious but simple dish! I guess I should give you a heads up that Mr. and Mrs. Maxwell contacted us! We're meeting with them in a few minutes~just to get acquainted," she added hastily at Alexandra's silence!

Alexandra's laughter lilted! "Thank you! Try to talk them out of suing me! I~uh~guess I overreacted!"

Diana's tone turned sharp! "No, you didn't! In view of all that's gone on! Remember, your dad doesn't want you to second guess yourself in retrospect! If you or the kids feel threatened in any way~ How's Idaho?"

"Mom! You wouldn't believe! I wish you and daddy could come see it! All the kids would love it, too!"

"Well, thank you for the invitation, because we're meeting the Maxwells here in Salt Lake this afternoon; then we're flying to Boise tonight!"

A screech of joy followed by a sudden caution! "I hope you brought warm clothing! And your ski stuff! There's been snow here this winter!"

⚞ ⚟

Dag, Shannon and David stood back, viewing their work crew's pads for modular buildings! With a quick phone conversation, three helicopters appeared above trees on a high ridge opposite the new camp! A company rep alit from the smaller of the three craft, directing the other pilot where to winch down its load! The third chopper set down, and a work force swarmed out, to tie the modular down and complete its setup! With daylight fading, a second building appeared, accompanied by the steady beat of the rotor!

Shannon watched in awe as David signed off for the units and the chopper trio lifted away! Ten minutes later, their leased chopper set down to pick them up! He thrilled at the thought of seeing Ellis and her spoiled little puppy! He wasn't sure who she loved best, but for the moment, there was no sense pushing the issue!

⚸ ⚸

"That was sad!" Diana addressing Daniel as they settled into the first class cabin for the short hop up to Boise!

Daniel's warm brown eyes stood out in his handsome features, "You've got that right! I would be that guy, if God hadn't intervened in sending me you! My life wasted! If I'd had kids I probably wouldn't have known them, cared about them! We knew Brad better than he did!"

Tears clouded her vision, "Yes, and we knew little good about him, due to his lack of proper rearing! I resented Stan's suggestion that Alexandra might have shot him! I resent having anyone consider her trigger happy! It's a good thing she's-" she halted in frustration and he laughed.

"I couldn't agree more! Brad-uh-was planning to kill her! That was his reason for showing up there-I guess he dosed himself with PCP's so he could go through with it! If he hadn't accidently tasered himself-that's what gave her the opportunity to flee!"

"I wish you hadn't told me that now, when I have to hold myself together!"

He looked miserable! "That's why I told you now!"

⚸ ⚸

"Well, I can get a job!" Myrna's assurances back in the coach section as Stan stewed about finances!

He stared at her, "Waiting tables?"

She shrugged, bitter, "It pays the bills!"

"If you don't have many bills!"

361

"Do-do you-are you heavily in-debt-"

He leaned back tiredly in the seat, "Actually, no! But I need to find something to invest in before my money all gets away! Order me a Seagrams when they start serving, and wake me up when it comes!"

⊰ ⊱

"Okay, thanks, Hunter! Great job! Why don't you get down to Denver and catch this flight? I haven't had an oversight visit to the Challis National Forest in a couple of years! The flight's vouchered, and I'm guessing you can find a place to stay?"

Doug laughed, "Yeah, maybe; if she hasn't thrown me out! I'm not sure why she puts up with me and my craziness!"

Unsure how to respond exactly, Morrison suggested buying flowers!

Agent Hunter responded quickly, "Great idea! That's cheaper than renting a room!"

Trent disconnected with a laugh! Hunter was right about that! He dialed a florist, himself!

⊰ ⊱

Daniel and Diana took in the frenetic scene in wonder as they led their children and Stan and Myrna Maxwell toward what seemed like the office area!

"No wonder Al loves this! Between the beauty and the action!" Daniel pulled his top coat around him more tightly as a gust caught at it! "And it's a Geologist's version of heaven!"

Alexandra dashed to meet them, then stopped short as she caught sight of Stan and Myrna! She recovered her composure, "Please come in where it's warm! Have you eaten?"

"On the plane," Diana responded!

"So, in other words, we've snacked!" Jeremiah stepped forward and offered a hug!

Daniel laughed! Although first class meals were okay, the portions were small! And with the short flight-

"Hurry in! Chow line's still open! Hi, Myrna! I'm just about to put her to bed! Maybe in the morning?"

362

"Oh-uh-yeah-sure-" The woman felt awkward! Since separating from Stan, her life had taken a decline from the elegant! Now the Faulkners left her gasping for air! Stan wasn't saying anything and he reeked of Seagrams, thanks to turbulence!

Fires burned cheerily from heavy planked fireplaces, and the blend of wood smoke with the chow tantalized!

"Better load up your plate, Stan," Daniel encouraged! "They may close the line before we can get seconds! Looks like we made it in just under the wire!"

Alexandra noticed her dad's skill in making people feel comfortable! His people skills were second to none! Well, maybe to Mallory's! It was hard to remember, but she thought Mallory possessed the gift, even before exposure to her dad! For Alexandra, it was still a learning curve!

Evidently thinking about Mallory conjured her up, because she materialized to hug Diana and speak to all the kids before extending that friendly handshake to Stan and Myrna!

Taking a hearty scoop of bubbling Shepherd's Pie, she sought a place where she could visit with the new arrivals! Which, she was a draw to people, and it seemed like she was swarmed!

Diana watched, intrigued by the scenario! At last she addressed Daniel. "She needs an organizational chart! She can't eat for trying to address everything from running the generator to why there isn't more meat in the pie!"

Daniel nodded, "Chain of command! You're right! Like Jethro's advice to Moses in the wilderness! If you let people eat up your time, they will! I'll find David tomorrow and see if we can bring organization to the chaos! Still, for the short time, what's been done is amazing!"

⊰ ⊱

Erik Bransom filed a folder carefully into his attaché! Darius Warrington's realization that Sharon Saxon was telling all in an attempt to extricate herself from the criminal ring, had him spouting information faster than he could write! Erik felt encouraged! Not that it would ever stop! Not while there was money to be made! But he wouldn't quit! Until every one of them was placed behind bars! He frowned! Not that there weren't problems galore in the nation's penal system! Privately owned jail facilities made more money when they had full occupancy! Consequently, seeing inmates reformed, transformed, kicked free, was not in the interests of their pocket books! But maybe he curbed the activity! He needed to think so!

He sent a text to Nick Moa'a'loa to tell Jennifer, that with Warrington's signed confession, her testimony against him wouldn't be necessary! Not that she had ever agreed to face him in court! But now his conviction without pressuring her, should surely ease her mind!

⚎ ⚎

"Are you doing okay?" Mallory met Alexandra's gaze worriedly! "Are they leaving soon?"

Alexandra laughed, "Actually, I'm fine! They didn't discuss their plans with me, but the only thing they really want is to see Angelique occasionally! Suing for custody or causing me any trouble is the last thing they want! They were-I don't know-like trying to feel-me out-about whether I'll be living here-or Colorado!"

Mallory looked up sharply, "Why?"

A shrug, "I guess they don't have much money! Since they're looking to buy a house and a small business interest in something, I guess being close to Angelique is one of their considerations!" She sighed, "It's like, since both of them lost Brad without ever really knowing him-they can make amends or atonement-"

Mallory's expression turned to lively interest, "Really?"

Alexandra frowned, "Yeah, really! Did you need something?"

"Actually, yes! To talk to you about Jared!"

Alexandra crossed her arms defensively, "What about him?"

"Figured you'd get all possessive of him! Hear me out!"

"I'm listening!"

"Not with an open mind!"

"You can tell that how?"

"Okay, he has the silver mine running like a sewing machine! He's restless anyway!"

"So, that gives you the right to hire him away from me?"

"No! He's beyond capable of maintaining your Colorado mine and getting this going too! It gives him the opportunity to make a lot more money and gain prestige! Takes care of both his boredom and his salary cap! It'll give Abby a change of scenery! We can work out the details and offer him the package!"

Alexandra laughed suddenly! "I'm such a dummy to always hold your motives suspect! Of course, that's brilliant! I've felt like I'm about to lose him anyway~and you're right! It's perfect! Sorry for being a hardhead!"

Mallory nodded slowly, "Now tell me about the Maxwells!"

⇥ ⇤

Trent listened to a report from the Bethesda police department! DNA left at the park had led investigators to an Amos Silva! Really bad dude, violating his parole in ways too numerous to count! The worst violation being that of possessing a pistol! With armor-piercing rounds! Kind of an ironic but divine justice that he shot his own foot off with one of them!

He sighed with relief, that not only had Ellis and Shannon avoided harm, but that the fearless little puppy had survived!

He checked emails! No report yet from Hunter! He grinned! If Hunter hadn't heeded his advice of sending flowers, his having done so was standing him in good regard!

⇥ ⇤

Alexandra couldn't help laughing! Janni was more upset about Myrna Maxwell's appearance than she was!

"Would you relax? In case you haven't noticed, you don't replace a grandma in Angelique's life! You're too young and pretty!"

"Your mom's young and pretty!" Janni quipped back!

"I'll be sure to pass the compliment along! I agree, and it'll make you an extra bunch of points with her! Your job is safe, and Myrna's being here won't make you stuck more with Leisel! And when I'm working, you're the authority, so don't let Myrna try to run over you! And God intended children to have two grandmas; a paternal and a fraternal!"

"Okay, thanks, I guess that clears up my concerns!"

"What do you think about gathering everything up and going skiing? Surely Myrna doesn't ski! She can watch the baby, and we can put Leisel in ski school!"

Alexandra considered, "Not a bad idea! Fun sounding, actually! But I don't trust Myrna that much yet! I'm not sure the ski school is prepared for a toddler like Leisel! The main crunch is that we're doing a lot of organizational meetings today! We'll go soon, though!"

365

🙵 🙷

Stan paused uncertainly at the open office door before tapping lightly!

Mallory Anderson looked up with a welcoming smile, even as she sprang up to extend her hand!

"Good morning, Mr. Maxwell! Do you mind if I call you Stan? Can I get you coffee? I'm getting some! I hope you rested well and that the cabin was okay! That it stayed warm enough?"

Before she could make a move to get the promised coffee, Alexandra appeared with a tray bearing coffee and pastries! She set it on the desk and retreated.

"Yes, Ma'am, the cabin was very nice! Thanks for asking!" Even as he responded cordially enough, she knew his curiosity was piqued about the summons!

With a rippling laugh, "Okay, I'm feeling around in the dark here, but according to all of the information our grapevine could summon about you, you owned your own company?"

He relaxed slightly in response! "I did! Past tense! I'm sure no one would believe me, but I cared about my son! Being an American competing in the French wine industry presented problems, but I thought someday, I'd have something to invite Brad over to see! Uh-to be impressed with! Although, I didn't know Brad as I wished-the news hit-hard-Actually, I lost father and son within a few months' time! The struggle suddenly didn't seem worth it! I sold out at the first offer!"

Mallory nodded sympathetically, "So Myrna mentioned to Alexandra that you're looking for another company to purchase?"

He sighed, "Like I said, I didn't hold out for as much as I probably could have gotten! I have enough proceeds left to buy a fast-food franchise! Which I could probably be successful at! Myrna hoped for us to settle where she could see the grandbaby~"

"Well, franchises are a good bet for someone who has skills managing a business! The reason I'm asking all of this is that we're in need of someone who possesses your managerial skills and business expertise! This isn't a job offer, per se; but we would like to explore the avenue further if you think you might be interested!"

Hope shot through exhausted features, "I might be very interested! I would need to talk to Myrna and check you guys out!"

Mallory didn't flinch! "As you should! I didn't want to offend you by handing you an employment ap, or even requesting a resumé! But if you could provide us with some references and details, we could move this process along!"

⚔ ⚔

Kayla Hamilton was flying higher than the jet carrying her from Grand Junction to Boise! A tip from Mike Behr? Of all the crazy people? He was one she crossed swords with more often than she cared to count! With his tip making her dizzy with the possibilities, she double-checked the story with Trent Morrison before filing a fistful of papers on Alexandra's behalf! The sophisticated ham radio, supposedly invented by the late Noë Keller, was attracting the attention of the Pentagon! With the threat of virtual warfare, the military and Washington-powers-that-be, were aware of the position they would be in regarding comms, should the internet go down! Really? Back to Ham radios? Who would have guessed?

But Keller's invention was upgraded from the days of yore with encryption and other security gizmos she didn't understand! Well, with the criminal deceased, Treasury usually swooped in like a bird of prey to seize anything valuable to replenish their coffers! And the radio design was valuable! Except that Brad Maxwell, on the night Alexandra had shot Keller to death, had claimed the patent rights for her! Hearsay, right? And who cares? But with first Behr, supporting the claim, and then Morrison-There would be high demand for the product once it became available! The money Alexandra might make!

Hence the reason for her flight to Boise! Maybe Alexandra would sign over a percentage of the revenue for fighting for the patent for her!

CHAPTER 37: SALVATION

The lodge, bursting at the seams, with every cabin full, lent an air of excited opportunity! David and Mallory vacated their small cabin to take up temporary residence in the lobby of the main lodge! Mallory didn't mind, loving the activity and potential!

"Why don't you get someone to build one of your signature screens? A big one that hides the cribs and mess from view to the rest of the lobby!"

"Not a bad idea! I'll get one of the guys right on it! I'm thinking that another RV on site might be a good idea! As a matter of fact, maybe we can add a small RV campground into the model!"

She screeched with delight! "David, you are so genius!"

⚐ ⚑

Robert Porter greeted old comrades-in-arms cordially! Sort of a group who had 'blown it' together, they were thrilled to get another shot at a promising career! Although security was up and running at the Colorado facility, it was on the ground floor here! Herding the lively group into the between-meals chow hall, he called them to order!

Jason Edwards raised his hand, "So if this place is going to be open to the public, we have to screen people, but without being too invasive? And there's lots of valuable stuff here?"

Porter's eyes sparkled, "Thanks for boiling it down for me! Basically, that's our assignment!"

James Bailey broke in, "You can't convince Mrs. Hunter to forget about opening the public attraction?"

Porter frowned, "Uh-I haven't tried! What she wants presents challenges, of course! Can we rise to the challenge? We have budget to get what we need, as far as metal detectors, cameras, and other equipment! Fencing is going in as we speak!"

"Why can't these two women be happy to have a gem mine, ban the public from it, and collect the cash?"

Porter did a slow count! He might as well make the job description clear, and if some of them wanted out, give them an out!

"I guess, both ladies are avid Geologists! And they believe what the Bible says about Creation, and they reject evolution-"

A derisive snort!

"If we could keep things civil and respectful! I was asked a question, and I'm answering it! So you'll all know before you decide to stay on or not!"

"If we don't stay, do we still get reimbursed the time and expenses for coming?" Another voice interrupting!

"One question at a time! The ladies plan to share their passion for Geology with the public by maintaining a museum and allowing people to pan for their own gemstones! That's the business model they want, and that's what they've hired me to protect! They hope to keep full occupancy for all the cabins, with fishing as well as the gem hunting! When people phone in reservations, we perform background checks! Much of it will be mundane! Preventative! We wear uniforms provided by the company, and stroll or drive around to make our presence felt! If that's too much of a challenge for any of you, let me know! You can head out with time and expenses reimbursed!"

No one moved!

⊨ ⊫

"Look, Mommy! Is this a piece of candy? It was all dirty on the ground!" Amelia, nose running, and with Peppy zigzagging at her feet, held up a pink thing resembling a *Jolly Rancher*™!

Mallory sprang for it with a jubilant yelp! "Good grief, Baby, where did you find it?"

"I didn't put it in my mouth! You tell me never put stuff in my mouth!"

Dirty evidence around her mouth testified to the opposite, but Mallory let it go! It was hard to tell if it was a swipe of a dirty hand across a runny nose!

Mallory raised the stone in wonder! Gem quality Tourmaline! And Amelia's sharp little eyes! She wasn't sure why she was so stunned! They were in the process of starting a full-fledged mining operation because the gravels were so promising-

She phoned Alexandra and Daniel to come see!

Daniel surveyed it in wonder, turning it over and over in his hands, and finally asking to borrow Mallory's loupe!

He looked up at last to meet the gazes of the two women, "You're sure you want to open up to the public and let Joe Tourist find and walk off with something like this?"

Mallory knew what her feelings were on the subject! Her desire was to see other people experience the same joy and wonder she had just seen in her little girl's eyes! But she was in a partnership with Alexandra! So, although, they had initially agreed on the plan, seeing the beautiful and valuable Tourmaline might cause Alexandra to rethink!

Alexandra cast a questioning gaze at Mallory, who wore a poker face! "Yes, Sir! We do! We have a commercial mining venture! There's no reason to get stingy! It's like the Old Testament says about not gleaning your field, but leaving small bits of the crop behind for the less fortunate!"

Mallory reached for the glowing pink crystal! "What do you guys think about putting this as our first exhibit in the museum?"

Daniel frowned, "Selling it will go a good ways toward funding your startup costs!"

Alexandra held it for the first time! "Yes, Sir, it would! But-but it is museum quality! We want our museum to be a real testament to God's glory!" Her voice, more hushed yet, at the mesmerizing effect of the pink glow, "And I'd say, He's given us a good start!"

彐 㠭

Jared appeared with Abby, as expected, but Alexandra was shocked to see her attorney picking her way across the snowy lot! She moved to meet her, "Here, take my hand! The last thing I need is for you to get hurt and sue me!"

Kayla laughed, "Is this beyond civilization? Or what? I thought Silverton was isolated! But I guess valuable resources don't appear in the middle of cities!"

Alexandra laughed, "If they do, they get built on top of, so they're less likely to be discovered! What in the world brings you here?"

Making the relative safety of the salted steps, the attorney took in the ordered confusion before asking, "Can I talk to you someplace in private?"

Situated in a corner of the empty chow hall, Kayla leaned forward, "Do you remember anything about the radio Noë Keller invented?"

Alexandra flushed slightly, "No, Ma'am! Not really! Brad was blown away by it! He was worried that the bad guys would hold it close! Uh-why?"

Whenever Alexandra felt herself at a disadvantage, the old haughtiness crept in, to cover her inadequacy! Amazingly, that was an asset in dealing with the bold lawyer!

"It looks like we can get the patent rights in your name! If I help you fight for it, I was wondering if I could earn five per cent! But no cash up front for you!" She pulled a sheaf of documents free and spread them on the table, "If you'll sign, I can get right on the filings! We don't want to waste any time and allow anyone else to come forward!"

Alexandra scanned over the papers, "I should ask my dad what he thinks! He's out at the dig site, but as soon as he comes in–"

Kayla puffed out an aggravated breath, "Well, suit yourself, but you make executive decisions every day! Like I said about wasting time–"

⇥ ⇤

Agent Doug Hunter's visit to the local Idaho division of Forestry Law Enforcement wasn't met with hostility! But there wasn't exactly a welcoming mat out either! After swigging down five cups of coffee while he studied recent case reports, he left in search of Alexandra's new mining operation! Hopefully his reception from his wife would be a little less cool!

He turned the wipers on as feathery flakes of snow fell! Pretty area! He notched the heater up and punched buttons for a decent radio station! Giving up, he switched it off, wondering if he should call and give Alexandra a heads up, or just put in an appearance! Following Siri's directions, he veered to the right at a fork, noticing deeper snow and less road maintenance! Well, word was the place was isolated! He remembered his alarm at hearing about the intruder she had shot! An eerie feeling swept over him and he tried to shrug it off! Even as the snowfall increased in intensity and the visibility lessened noticeably, he continued!

A sickening sensation of losing control swept through him as his government car fishtailed! Maneuvering skillfully into the skid, he regained control! Quite a drop off if he hadn't! Even as his knuckles whitened on the steering wheel at the narrow escape, he noticed headlights gaining on him from behind! Easing his hand onto the grip of his service revolver, he crept forward once more!

≒ ⻊

Daniel turned off the weather report, glad for the snug lodging! Finding Diana and the rest of his family, he herded them toward the chow hall! Aroma of garlic and oregano hung deliciously in the air! Lasagna! Usually not his favorite, but an afternoon's exertion in the thin mountain air, and he was suddenly ravening! Though not yet crowded, the room hummed pleasantly with low conversation, chinks of dishes, and typical kitchen sounds! He indicated settling at a long table near one of the fireplaces! Though extremely rustic compared with his usual preferences, he could get used to this!

"Wow! Look at this! Table linens and new china!" Diana's quick approval! "I love the Pandas! I wonder if Alexandra didn't like the ensemble I sent her! She sent it back unopened the first time, and I haven't seen her wearing it since I re-sent it!"

"Um-I think it got ruined! She-uh-was fighting this guy off-and-his blood got all-over it!"

"I see!" Her tone and shocked stare, equally icy! "Is that something you were sworn to secrecy about, too?"

"Uh, I'm not sure! Look, there's David! I'm thinking we're not going to be able to get out in the morning for church! Maybe we should plan to hold our own service!"

"Well, let's pray over our dinner and we can start getting our plates while you talk to him!"

He knew she was struggling to shake off her ire at him! She was such a trooper!

"Sorry," he mumbled before commencing the blessing!

≒ ⻊

Doug let out a long ragged breath of relief, as his car fought its way up a long snowy hill and approached a curve! Before him was a traffic light, a

372

main highway that was mostly cleared, and bright neon announcing a gas station/store! As he pulled into the busy lot, the car that had been behind him turned onto the highway and sped away! Watching as casually as possible, he stomped snow from his boots and entered the business! Coffee out! Coffee in! Siri indicated he was within five miles! On a whim, he picked up a couple of inexpensive items! Now he wished he had listened to Trent about sending flowers!

⚞ ⚟

Alexandra fought tears at Daniel's reprimand! "Five per cent! That's a lot, Al! Why in the world would you let an attorney put pressure on you to sign without getting another opinion?"

"Well, it may come to nothing! And five per cent of nothing isn't that much! And she's the one paying the upfront stuff!"

Daniel reread the contract, "That's not exactly spelled out here! This verges on conflict of interest on her part, to put her hand into your pot! Next time, stall, and let me be in the loop! What were you thinking?"

Al struggled to find her voice, "Well, I was thinking that when I turned loose of some of the gem mining profits to allow the public to pan, and when I agreed to putting the Tourmaline into the museum rather than selling it, that the radio patent coming up like it did, was God's way of blessing me! And that I'll have ninety-five percent of something that wasn't on my radar this morning!"

Daniel sighed, "Well, you're right! But five per cent is still a lot! And your ninety five per cent won't be free and clear!"

She laughed, and the woebegone expression fled! "No, Sir! It never is!"

⚞ ⚟

Trent's desperation made him particularly annoyed at Bob Porter's negativity!

"It's snowing hard out there, and forecast to be a whiteout! It's so bad that the Faulkner/Anderson crowd are planning to stay in and hold their own church service tomorrow!" Porter's excuse sounded lame, even to himself

"That's a reason why you need to get out there; not a valid excuse for not!"

373

"You know; I no longer work for you! Your choice! Not mine"! Bob shot back!

"Look, just because Hunter has been on-scene to help me, is no use for you to resent him! But even if you resent him, as a Christian man, you have a responsibility to help someone in trouble!"

"You said, he said, it might just be his imagination! And if the division guys stationed at Challis have a problem with him, too, which I doubt; they'll only scare him a little!"

"And if that's their intention, it could still get out of hand! If they panic him into driving off a cliff, or heading out afoot in severe conditions-little things can turn into major catastrophes in a hurry! And, he isn't sure that's who's dogging him! You know what? Maybe I'll just call Ray Beecher! What's your take on Ray?"

"Well, he wasn't in DC to get caught in your sting! I've always thought he's okay!"

"It wasn't a sting, Porter, which you know! Every guy made his own choice, and I had no idea why so many agents were absent from the nice banquet that tax payers put out a good sum of cash for! That shouldn't create you a problem with Doug Hunter!"

"Maybe my beef with him has to do with something else!"

"Alexandra?" Trent's voice exploded!

"Why's she your project?"

"She isn't! And I'm pretty sure if she knows Doug's in trouble, she'll agree that you should help!"

"Yeah, maybe! Hunter has a gorgeous wife waiting for him and taking care of his idiot kid twenty-four/seven, and he hardly comes home!"

"Yeah, well Porter, put this in your pipe and smoke it! All of us have been double-stepping, trying to take up the slack for guys not aware that their actions wreaked havoc for everybody!"

᛭ ᛭

Doug stopped to listen once more! Whining wind tore at his clothing and obscured any other sounds that might warn him! He staggered several yards farther before casting his 'survival kit' under a fir tree where a sheltered void was free of deep snow! No sense in trying to push ahead! Heavy clouds that were dumping snow, also blotted out stars by which he might navigate! The world was black and white with a few eerie gray shadows! Beautiful in stark contrast, if he had presence of mind to consider such things! The scanty shelter provided by the stand of trees was far from adequate, but so far he had forged through the icy darkness without injuring himself! Pushing his large frame into the small space, he wasn't sure whether it was good or bad that dislodged snow from the branches above nearly obscured his hiding place! He hoped his pursuers weren't savvy enough to notice the snowless branches above him! He scoffed! Like there wasn't a deep trail through the drifts ending at his hideout!

⫷ ⫸

An astounded Stan went in search of Myrna! "Can you believe we're hired?"

She nodded with a worried frown rather than the jubilation he was hoping for, "Did you have to put all your money up?"

He laughed, "Well, I offered! Believe me, Myrna, this is a better deal than a restaurant franchise! Which that's a great opportunity for anyone willing to do what it takes to be successful! But without investing any of my money, I get stock options as part of my pay package! I mean, our pay package! I can't figure out why they've let us in, in light of our son's actions!"

"I guess they can tell it was all Stephen's fault!"

He reached for her! "No! It's my fault! I should have stood up to my father! For you and my son! I try to let myself off the hook, that 'hey, I was young, inexperienced'~ None of it helps!"

⫷ ⫸

Ray Beecher listened to his superior in shock! "Well, I admit," he responded, "none of us rolled out the red carpet for him! But we cooperated, and then he left! Where did he say he was when he abandoned his vehicle? Did he describe the car that was tailing him? I'm pretty sure none of my guys are involved, but in the outside chance they are, I doubt they'd use their personal vehicles!"

"Gray, Bond-o beater! Old-style sedan! When Hunter was on the paved and cleared road, he poured on some speed to gain distance! Seems the derelict looks of the car are deceptive when it comes to performance!"

375

"Terrible night for Agent Hunter to have been forced to abandon his vehicle! Did you agree with his decision to do that?"

"I trust his instincts! But it's my Forestry service vehicle, so after Hunter, it's my second concern! Sure would hate to see it go to the 'dark side'! Thanks for mustering your guys! Porter and some other guys will meet you at the store on the highway! He knows you're the one giving the orders! Be careful, Ray!"

⚔ ⚔

Alexandra finally prevailed, and both girls were asleep! The plan was for Janni to come over and watch them once she got them down! There was a big corporate planning meeting happening in the lobby, and it was already later than she had anticipated! Grabbing her phone from the charger she noticed a missed call from Doug! And his message filled her with alarm! Rather than changing to business attire for the meeting, she pulled on heavy socks and boots and a down-lined parka!

"You're going to the meeting like that?" Janni spoke without considering! None of her business!

"Yeah, it's snowing to beat the band, and I'm freezing! They should stay asleep! Thanks!"

Slipping out into the snowdrifts she moved quickly to the garage and selected a snowmobile! Fortunately, the fence wasn't completed! And she didn't see any of her security guys! Ordinarily she would have a problem with them not being in evidence, but for this plan, it was fortuitous that they weren't! Turning the key, she took note of the full tank! Water, granola bars, guns and ammo! Then, with another gizmo secured, she eased from the property!

⚔ ⚔

The weird car with its weirder occupants studied the abandoned Forestry Law Enforcement vehicle, gazing around them uneasily, knowing their quarry, undoubtedly armed, might have them in his sights! Although he probably couldn't take out the four of them, none planned on being the sacrificial lamb! Easing back into their own vehicle they proceeded, following the obvious path through deep snow! One of the stalkers lowered

376

a window, easing out a sawed-off shotgun, even as an icy blast obliterated the efforts of the heater!

"Turn the lights off, Dude!"

"Why? He knows we're out here, playin' with 'im! Makes if more fun if he can see us comin'!"

᛭ ᛭

As the snowmobile topped a rise, Alexandra cut the headlight and engine! She figured she was about a mile above the store and a quarter mile off the unmaintained road that led from the highway to the lodge! Pulling out powerful field glasses, she scanned her surroundings! Trying to adjust to the darkness veiled with heavy snowfall, she waited, praying for wisdom and for Doug's safety! At the moment, her personal risk was the farthest thing from her mind! Wind whipping up the rise sculpted the snow bank into crusty but graceful waves! Still, she waited, oblivious to the cold and the passing of time!

᛭ ᛭

"I'm going to tell her to just come on and bring Leisel! She won't make any trouble if she's in the pack 'n play, with a blanket over it!" Daniel was to the door before he finished speaking!

He stared at Janni in shock, refusing to believe it! "She-she's out there alone? Looking for-Doug- Is there a reason why-"

Janni hung her head guiltily! You didn't rat on Alexandra! "Um-well, I called my dad, after she left-so he could-uh-you know-pray- Which, he's praying, but he called Mr.-Morrison! I-I guess they have guys out there now-hunting for both-of them!"

Daniel sank down weakly while he fought panic and gathered his thoughts! "Okay, well, I guess I should go break the news, then call Trent and see if any of us can help!"

᛭ ᛭

Racket shattered the silence as Alexandra throttled the snowmobile up, choosing her course through a low area thick with shadows! Light off, but with plenty of noise to announce her arrival! Leaving the craft idling in the protection of a deep drift, she clambered to where she could once again survey the area with the glasses!

Elation swept her! The four guys were out of their car, easing forward, sprouting an arsenal of weapons, and advancing along a path evidently left by Doug! A path that ended at a stand of pine trees! With a quick mental once-over for the untried weapon she was counting on, she remounted the snowmobile and shot it forward! Racing what she hoped was the right distance, she veered up the drift, speeding toward her startled quarry! As their weapons swung her direction, she pushed on the headlight and focused her own new brand of ammunition in their direction!

It worked! Because they dropped their guns and fell into the snow, holding their ears and screaming! She considered her options; shooting them while they were incapacitated, might put her in a legal jam! But, if she eased off the piercing, high-pitched sound, they would probably go for their guns again! She turned it off, watching coldly! Then, to her relief, Doug approached them, his weapon trained warily! She nearly went limp with relief as he kicked their weapons aside! Grasping a cell phone from the pocket of the leader, he placed a call to Trent!

※ ※

Shannon kissed his wife's soft curls, then tipped her face up toward him to meet her parted lips! "Wow! Never a dull moment! And then to still hold the middle of the night board meeting! I have to tell you, I've been jealous since Alexandra and Mallory hired Stan Maxwell to oversee this place! I was-uh-hoping-they'd-uh-see some executive skills in yours truly!"

"Well, you have them, and I'm glad they have noticed! It's all so amazing, and then to have my equipment in demand, besides! I think Mallory plans to scan the whole world, and in the meantime, Mr. Morrison wants to look for caves and tunnels, or old mine shafts here! These bad guys live in the ground like moles!" She shuddered and the haunted look flashed in her luminous eyes once more!

Shannon tightened his arms, crooning softly, "It's okay! You're safe now!" He laughed suddenly! "What did you think about Mrs. Faulkner's nickname for the dog?"

She clung to him without looking up, "What? Braveheart? He was that! He is that! I'm so glad he didn't get hurt!"

⊰ ⊱

David tried to control annoyance, and focus on the task at hand!

"It's okay," Mallory reassured! "A one-time deal because authorities are requesting people to stay put unless they have an emergency! It doesn't mean you're called to preach or that anyone here wants to pressure you in that direction! Just do a simple salvation message! I'm hoping Stan and Myrna~"

"Whoa! Hold on! No pressure!"

"Really, there isn't; but to do your best! And leave God with the rest!"

"Why can't Daniel do it?"

"He's doing the music, David! If he wanted to preach and do the music, you'd accuse him of trying to be a one-man show!"

David sighed, "I wish he'd recognize me as a musician!"

Mallory laughed, "Don't we all?"

⊰ ⊱

Alexandra greeted newcomer after newcomer! Neighbors, relatively speaking, arriving for the improvised church service! Trent Morrison and Erik Bransom materialized amidst the sea of strangers!

"Thanks for helping look for Doug!"

Trent merely nodded, not happy about her conducting her own search and rescue! She had gotten the job done, again! With relief he had learned that none of the Challis LEI's were behind hassling Hunter! And the four suspects were locked up at the county sheriff's department! He addressed her somberly, "We got the vehicle! Doug can get his personal belongings out before I head out in it!"

She nodded acknowledgement, "You may be in time to grab a little breakfast! You, too, Erik!"

"I may take you up on that! The reason I'm here is because we've finished the search of the Canadian property! We've advised the Coxes on our findings! There's really nothing you want to know about, with the exception, that Brad left some of his journals! I didn't know if you want to look at them~or save them for Angelique~at some point~"

Color rose on fragile features, "No! I don't want to see them at all! Nor would there be any point in my baby~"

"You need some time to think it over?"

She strove for control! "No, Erik; I've had time to think it over! But–you know what–Brad's father and mother are here somewhere! They–they'll probably want–they neither one knew Brad–at all–"

⚐ ⚑

John 3:16 For God so loved the world, that he gave his only begotten Son, that whosoever believeth in him should not perish, but have everlasting life.

Stan moved to the coffee pot, still mopping at his eyes! An emotional day! First, he and Myrna had finally heard the Good News: what all of the 'Saved' talk was about! Followed quickly by an FBI agent who introduced himself as Erik Bransom before handing over a shopping bag full of Brad's recent journals! Just enough time to hand them off to Myrna, before he was in an inquisition about his father's activities, and what he had been aware of!

Nothing for sure; just always a sick feeling of not wanting to know! He remembered Ted Coakley; Robert and Sharon Saxon and Bobby; and some of the social circle, but any connections beyond the Country Club, he was in the dark about! No! He had never visited the lodge in Canada, nor been aware of its existence! Yes, he had been to Canada, but only to Quebec for a wining and dining exhibition among the French population there!

At the end of the interview, it was hard to know who was the most relieved, the agent or him!

⚐ ⚑

Trent found himself butting heads with Porter yet again!

"It's what Alexandra wants to do, and she's my boss now!" Another pointed reminder that he no longer answered to Trent, still resenting the entire situation!

"Okay, I'll talk to her then!" he shoved his chair back and rose, annoyed! Not that he liked to talk to Alexandra! For multitudes of reasons! "Maybe I'll talk to Daniel! But when I finish you're going to look like an idiot for coddling their hair-brained scheme!"

380

"Okay, but make sure you mention that the Andersons are installing state of the art security!"

Trent sank back into the chair! "Bob, listen to me! What's it going to do? Alert you and your guys of an incursion, and then dial up the sheriff's department? Do you know how long their response time is, to get out here? In good weather, bet it's close to an hour! And then, who will respond? One car and a deputy? With his one bullet? What Mallory and Alexandra are talking about is a huge target for the criminal element! Tell them to donate their stones to the Natural History Museum in Boise without making mention of where they found them!"

"The museum in Boise pushes Evolutionism! What about the place in Arkansas where Mallory's from? How do they manage security? Where the public can come hunt their own diamonds?"

"It's a State Park, and it has a host of Park Rangers and other state law enforcement! It isn't as remote as this! The girls' plan here is asking to get someone killed! I understand their excitement and longing to share both their beliefs and good fortune! But your guys are right, and they're about to mutiny if you insist on going ahead!"

"They shouldn't have said anything to you!"

CHAPTER 38: SUCCESS

"Well, I did have a plan!" Doug's woeful words! "It just wasn't a very good one! I'm glad you raced to my rescue!" A woebegone Doug, forced to admit being rescued by his wife! Even though David confided about having been rescued before by Mallory! A couple of times! Hard on a guy's ego, maybe, but better than dying!

Alexandra nodded at his admission before confiding a concern, "What do you think about Bob Porter?"

"You know, he's knowledgeable and capable! You need him! I have to admit Trent made a good point about not luring gangs of armed robbers out here!"

"We aren't trying to lure armed robbers out here!"

"No, but that's who'll show up! I understand that you and Mallory want to give God the glory for the beauties of His creation, and also for the way He blesses those who honor Him! But maybe you should consider what Mallory was telling us at dinner about her dad and the way he hid his valuables!"

"In plain sight?"

"Well, yeah, but not exactly! I mean, you still need all of the security systems, and the personnel! But Trent was right! Don't make a big public deal about the value of the material you're getting! Don't donate to the museum! Just~"

Expressive gray eyes clouded; surrendering their idea wasn't easy! She watched as Leisel extended a windup toy to him! A toy he had picked up at the little grocery the previous evening! Something he had never done before! Chintzy as the toy was, she loved it, and she was forcing Doug to interact with her!

Taking it, he wound it, then watched as she quickly ran it down again! "Let me show you how to wind it–"

☩ ☩

Tears streamed down Ellis' face, threatening to freeze into icy little rivulets, "Mama, I'm not calling to ask you to come back to Daddy! I just need you to come back to me! Please, pick up! Please call me! I love Shannon, but I'm creating a disaster between us–Mom, I-I just need you! I-I guess you thought when you got all of us out of the house, we wouldn't–still–need you– But we all do! Well, me especially– When you gave me 'The Talk' and asked if I had any questions– Well, then I didn't–but, now–I'm so confused–and Shannon tries to be understanding–" Disconnecting in frustration, she limped painfully up the icy hill toward cabins beyond the main lodge!

Trent's heart dropped with such a thunk that he was surprised not to see it beating at his feet on the floorboard of the Forestry Department truck! Ellis Vaughn–Well, Ellis O'Shaughnessy, now–And it was strictly against policy to give any unauthorized person a lift–Not that he was in the habit of offering rides to beautiful young ladies in his personal car! Still, he crunched to a stop beside her!

"Hey, what's going on?"

She swiped guiltily at the flow of tears with a sky blue mitten! "Nothing, Mr. Morrison! I'm fine! Just one of those days when everything makes me cry! Guess you're heading back to DC, huh?"

"Actually, one of the agents in Challis is meeting me in Boise to take the truck back, and my family's flying in for a few days of skiing! Are you sure you don't need some help? It's kind of cold to be out walking; what's the status with the toe?"

"It's a lot better," she fibbed bravely!

"Either that or it's so frostbitten you can't feel it! Let me go borrow a snowmobile and give you a lift!"

"I'm almost where I'm going–"

☩ ☩

I wonder what's going on out there!" Diana paused with a fresh coffee refill to study the discourse between Ellis O'Shaughnessy and Trent Morrison!

"I wonder what she's doing out walking around! I'm not sure anyone's keeping an eye on that toe!"

Daniel's warm brown eyes met hers guiltily, "Well, she walked up here and asked to see you! I told her you were busy!"

She frowned, puzzled! "Well," he defended, "I know none of you ladies like her too much~"

Her frown deepened, "Well, we just noticed she never has much to say to any of us, and she always wades in with you guys when you're talking!"

"Right, so I thought you didn't like her, and I told her you were busy because you were! You were having your devotions and helping get the kids dressed and ready~" He paused in concern as she reached for boots and down parka! When someone was in need of her nursing skills, it didn't matter if she liked them or not!

"Okay, you stay here! I'll go out and help her in! I just thought it was a little early in the morning to pay anyone a call~"

~ ~

Shannon felt like giving up! Just pack and head out, for who cared where? It was just that he cared too much what everyone thought of him! Sinking dejectedly onto the unmade bed, he stroked Peppy absently! "Well, you bought me a little bit of time! At least she adores one of us! I mean~I get it~her being freaked out by~well~maybe I don't entirely~"

~ ~

David and Mallory lingered over breakfast, visiting with Erik! "We just heard about the Forestry Law Enforcement Banquet in DC, and that you just happened to be at that same hotel~" Mallory broke off! None of her business why Erik hung around luxury DC hotels~

His crackling laugh caused him to choke, and he took several swigs of coffee before explaining!

"Well, I didn't just happen to be there! I think it was definitely the Lord's wise planning~that came about through your mother's insatiable curiosity!"

Mallory flushed, "Should I ask you to go on? Or do I not want to know? Is it true that Alexandra nearly got abducted and she and the girls had to move from safe house to safe house?"

Another chuckle! "It is true! Somehow the hotel staff fell down on the job, and Trent ended up asking Doug to help set the ballroom up for the banquet! When Alexandra came to his rescue, she decided live flowers would be a nice touch! So, she called to ask your mother for a wholesale florist contact! Since information on Alexandra had been pretty scant, and I was in the city, she called me and asked me to snoop!"

"On Alexandra-" Mallory was a little flabbergasted!

"Yeah! You're surprised?"

"I guess I thought she was a reformed gossip! At least, I guess I've hoped! And you agreed?"

"Yeah, I try to keep her happy! We didn't know Alexandra had gotten married-the first time-let alone the second, to Trent's guy-! Anyway, there was a football game I wanted to see, and I ended up being able to watch it on a sixty inch in the lobby! That's why I was on the spot when the call girls and their handlers showed up! They caught some of the Forestry personnel who were supposed to attend the banquet! And then, we were able to make a significant number of arrests and put a dent in the illicit operation! But in the excitement and confusion, one of them did get the drop on Alexandra-She got a few licks in herself, and drew plenty of blood! Only to find out that the guy was HIV positive and she was exposed-"

"Is she okay?" David's concern as he entered the exchange!

"Yeah, I guess! It was quite a bit of confusion before we were aware of the danger, and then it took her a while to work out getting tested! Results came back negative!"

Mallory stared, horrified, but dry-eyed, "I'll bet Diana never knew about that!" She paused considering her next question! The last thing she wanted was to sound like her mom! "Did you read any of Brad's journals that you brought her?"

"I didn't! Hillman and Dawson both did! A need to know! How much Brad knew about Stephen's lifestyle and friends and associates! It didn't seem like he was aware, let alone complicit! It's tormented, and rambling-Ambivalent feelings about not just Alexandra, but her whole family and you-"

"Me?" Mallory was shocked!

"Yeah, and Brenna and Gray Prescott! Brad didn't know what to make of Christianity and the Creationist stance! I guess his only reason in befriending the Alvaredo kid was his hope that he could help it all make sense!"

≒ ╞

"You know, I can't say for sure, but maybe she gravitates toward men because she was around brothers all the time! And their friends! And, Diana, you ladies are pretty intimidating!"

Diana pushed the brew button to start another pot of coffee, still aggravated because by the time they managed to get Ellis back into the cabin, she had changed her mind about confiding! Frustrated, she had refused to say anything but apologies for the inconvenience to everyone! She wouldn't even let Diana examine her toe!

"Well, I realize she's still traumatized! But it isn't like she's the only one that's ever been through anything!" Diana surprisingly stout in her opinion!

"Hey, Trent, thanks for stopping by to help her!" Daniel's suddenly changing the subject! "We don't want to hold you up any longer! We know you're meeting your guy! Have fun skiing!"

Trent laughed in spite of the, 'Here's your hat; what's your hurry?' tone to his friend's words! Faulkner was right! He needed to get moving!

≒ ╞

Shannon handed the ticket from the automated check-in to Ellis! Finding a low cost fare from Boise to Dulles hadn't been easy! He didn't even know if she was accustomed to traveling economy! Since he couldn't figure out a plan of action beyond letting her go, he wanted to hang onto as much of the money in their account as possible!

"Okay, let's get a cup of coffee! Maybe you should eat something! Snacks onboard are overpriced and not that good!"

"Shannon, what's the point? I'm not hungry and I drank coffee all morning! You should go! The dog's in the car! Someone will break in and steal him!"

His world spun, careening crazily out of control! How could he let her go? If she cared so much about the dog~why make the choice she was making? He lifted her bag onto the scale for the agent to check~

"I'm sorry, Sir! Your flight's delayed! Storms on the East coast!"

Shannon shrugged, "No one could say anything an hour ago when we booked the flight?"

"We just now got the official word!" She folded the tag around the handle and swung the bag onto the conveyor belt! Turning back to the counter she directed her attention to the next passenger!

✄ ✂

"Did Shannon and Ellis already eat?" Alexandra met Myrna's gaze, perplexed!

"No, Ma'am! They checked out! I think they were going to the city so Mrs. O'Shaughnessy could fly back East! Shame if you ask me! Mr. O'Shaughnessy's an attractive guy, but better'n that, he seems so devoted~"

Alexandra's expressive eyes widened in shock! "Good grief, Myrna, don't tell anyone else that!"

Myrna looked hurt, "Well, you asked! If someone else asks, do you want me to lie?"

"Well, no, not really! It's just that you don't have to tell~ Mallory is going to be so mad~"

"Yeah, isn't she related to Mr. O'Shaughnessy?"

Alexandra nodded slowly! Mallory was protective of her cousins! But more importantly, Ellis was committed in a business endeavor! Surely she wouldn't dare skip on Mallory!

"If anyone asks, just say you're not sure where they are! That's the truth because you don't know if they made it to Boise yet~or~" She scurried away, guilty at coaching a new convert to be~less than forthcoming!

✄ ✂

The mind is its own place, and in itself
Can make a Heaven of Hell, a Hell of Heaven.

Ellis' eyes blazed into Shannon's at the quote! "Is there some reason you're quoting the words of Lucifer to me? Do you even know where that quote came from and its context?"

He leaned forward across his Smoothie cup, "As a matter of fact, I do! Lines 254 and 255 from *Book I* of <u>Paradise Lost</u> by John Milton!"

"I'm surprised you actually know that! The lines are often abused and misused by the prophets of 'Positive Thinking'! I thought maybe you came across it in one of their books. Or S.H.A.M.S as I call them!"

387

"Shams?" he echoed, "I can tell you're dying to fill me in!"

"Self-Help and Actualization Manuals! They're all shams! People buy books on getting rich, and the authors and seminar speakers are the only ones who do!"

Shannon shrugged, 'Why avoid arguing with her now? She was leaving anyway, just as soon as her flight could be airborne-

"Well, at some point in time, people who want to be successful have to quit reading books and attending seminars on the subject, and get busy and get to work at something! Dreaming doesn't make it happen! Well, according to some of them, it does! Visualizing what you want! It doesn't hurt as long as it spurs actions! It's like *Joshua 1:8*

> *This book of the law shall not depart out of thy mouth; but thou shalt meditate therein day and night, that thou mayest observe to {do} according to all that is written therein: for then thou shalt make thy way prosperous, and then thou shalt have good success!*

A lot of people misunderstand it, that reading and meditating bring prosperity and success; but it actually asserts that they have to do-something-based on the tenets of the Bible! But the mind is a powerful thing, and that's why I quoted Milton! I wish you would give me a chance! I can't figure out why going home and cleaning, cooking, and doing laundry for your father, appeals more to you-"

"It doesn't, Shannon, but it's the right thing to do-"

"It isn't! You changed the vows from what the Chaplain wanted you to say! We promised to love each other and be married until death parts us! That's what's right, Ellis! Let me come to Bethesda, too! I'll get my own apartment, and you can stay at *Practical Technologies*! The apartment there is uber-nice now! They even put in a new range and oven so meat pies and frozen pizzas won't have burnt and frozen sides! We can work on our relationship, with no pressure! Let your toe heal, and-the other wounds-"

⇥ ⇤

Erik regretted taking Cal Vaughn's phone call! His thought for doing so, was that possibly the irate man might slip with something! So far, the only thing he had allowed to slip was compound-complex sentences infused with the foulest language Branom had ever heard! And-he had heard plenty! Evidently, 'cussing like a sailor;' ascended up into the officers' ranks! Vaughn was definitely provoked into letting his Christianity slip!

"They showed up with a search warrant, Special Agent! They've gone through every square inch of my home and vehicle! If they show up on base-well, you understand why that simply can't-I didn't kill my wife! I don't know where she is, or why she won't answer Ellis' calls! The problem's with her! You probably didn't notice at Ellis' wedding, but her mother's a couple of bolts shy of a battleship!"

"Well, NCIS will probably handle going through your office and on-base electonics! In fact, they'll probably send my Agents packing! Doesn't matter to me, which agency investigates-"

"There's nothing to investigate! They found Darlene's cell phone here! Why she hasn't gotten any of our calls! Obviously, she didn't want to be tracked down by it! She stole some money out of one of my accounts, but she took it cash! No telling where she's gone! I didn't kill my wife!"

"Maybe not! With a gun or knife, in a physical way! But what about the day to day assaults on her psyche-"

"Don't have a clue what you're talking about, but pretty sure you're in legal limbo on whatever you're getting at!"

"Unless you want NCIS on your doorstep, you better cooperate with some good suggestions of where your wife might have gone! Friends? Relatives? Our finding her alive and well someplace, and quick, might help you keep your career!"

⚔ ⚔

"Shannon! Where did you guys take off to?" Mallory getting straight to the point without pleasantries! "I thought I might see you guys at lunch since you missed breakfast! Is Ellis where I can speak to her?"

"Uh-we're in a discussion! Can she call you later?"

"How much later? Just promise me that she's committed to all we've talked about!"

"Okay, not making promises I can't keep! Her dad needs her at home, so-she's uh-as soon as her flight is cleared to leave-"

"Her flight? To DC? When's she coming back? When's her flight scheduled to leave?"

"An hour ago, but weather-"

"Well, if she's just sitting there with an indefinite weather delay, why can't I talk to her?"

⊰ ⊱

"Hey, Ellis, Baby, how's your toe?" Cal Vaughn's attempt at concern and nonchalance!

"I'm not sure! I'm trying to get home, and then you can decide what to do next!"

"Coming home? Here? We'll talk about that later! I'm calling-uh-do you have any idea where your mother went? I've talked to your brothers; they don't have suggestion one! You were the one closest to her!"

She fought tears! "Not really! The only thing I've thought of is that trip to Hawaii you were ready to take! Maybe she changed the dates when we didn't go then! It was paid for; wasn't it? I've tried and tried to call her! You've treated her so crummy that she won't even answer me!"

"Is that what she's told you?"

"No! Never one word! But I have eyes and ears! Do you need me to come help run the house for you? I'm pretty sure she's never coming back!"

"Hawaii! That's a good idea! I'll see what I can find out! Maybe I'll phone the hotel manager! I thought you wanted to make a home for Shannon! I've hired a woman to come in to help! Were you the one who told the FBI I might have harmed Darlene?"

"No, Sir! Nothing of the sort! Although Mallory's step-father is an agent and he's been here in Iowa this week! Daddy, nothing like that entered my mind! I just thought she took off for Hawaii and didn't blame her! I mean, I think everybody wondered why she wouldn't return any of my calls-if she was okay-you know-because I thought I was close with her, too!" Her voice ended with a wail as tears started!

Cal raised his voice to cut through the hysterics, "Ellis, your mother left her phone here! She hasn't received any of your messages! Why don't you see if you can contact her? Here's the name of the hotel-"

⊰ ⊱

"You're a liar! I should have known when your vows to God didn't mean anything to you, that our deal wouldn't either!"

390

David cringed! He didn't blame Mallory for being disappointed and upset, but she usually toned her rhetoric down before making crucial phone calls!

She turned her back on him as she fought tears!

"Mallory, let me explain!"

"I'm listening!"

Silence from Ellis's end of the line!

Mallory continued her blast, "Yeah, you've been traumatized! We get it! Haven't we all? But you were already 'traumatized' before you committed to the agreements you did! I could see a delay-if something happened-I-I just thought-you could deliver!"

"Well, I can't!" A small, child-like voice that suddenly made Mallory mad at herself for ever thinking she could!

"So, are you out of business? Is your equipment for sale?" Mallory suddenly saw a possible 'silver lining' in the fiasco!

"I-I don't know! One of my brothers is kind of interested, and he might not re-up! He's the one who's been working with the GPR and Infrared as the military has developed it!"

Mallory did a slow count to ten! 'Her brother <u>might</u> be interested! He <u>might</u> not re-up'! Those were a lot of <u>might</u>'s to be in limbo over! "Why don't you consider selling us your business? Get with your attorneys and whoever you need to-maybe you should include Shannon-and work out a sales agreement for us to consider! If your brother leaves the military and wants to pursue this as a civilian, we'll definitely consider hiring him in management!"

⊣ ⊢

"Hello, Agent Bransom!"

"Hello, Ellis; what can I do for you?"

"I called to tell you that my mother is in Hawaii and she's okay! I didn't get to talk to her because the person in reception said she took an excursion to Lanai! Maybe if agents over there can check-and you won't have to involve NCIS-"

⊣ ⊢

"Look, I don't think your flight is getting out tonight? The puppy's in the car, and it's cold! Let's go~"

At the mention of her puppy in the cold, Ellis' demeanor changed!

Returning to the vehicle, they were relieved when Peppy seemed unfazed! Evidently his chronic exuberance kept his blood circulating!

Ellis tucked him tenderly into the front of her coat, crooning crazy endearments that made Shannon question whether the purchase was a good idea! Shaking his head in bewilderment he quoted softly:

How do I love thee?
Let me count the ways!

Quoting the *Sonnet from the Portuguese #44* by Elizabeth Barrett Browning from memory!

"Shannon O'Shaughnessy, why do you do things like that to me?"

"Things like what?"

"Quoting my favorite poetry! I love Milton and Browning! Who~who told you~"

He met her gaze, sighing involuntarily, "Nobody! They're my favorites, too! Although, I have a hard time choosing favorites when there were so many greats~"

"Have you ever heard of George Wither?"

He nodded,

"If she be not so to me
What care I how fair she be?"

He paused, flushing, "I do care! I love you, Ellis!"

Her gaze faltered, and when she raised her eyes once more to meet the ardor in his, she spoke slowly, "And I love you, too! I've been thinking about the lines you quoted from <u>Paradise Lost</u>!

The mind is its own place, and in itself
Can make a Heaven of Hell, a Hell of Heaven.

Life is what you make it! What you choose to focus on and prioritize!" She paused with a self-conscious ripple of laughter! "If Satan was cast out of Heaven, with his glory and most of his power gone, and he still decided to use what was left him to the best advantage to oppose God; what should I do, with having the gift of eternal life and all of the power of God available to me? A lot of life is approaching it with the right frame of mind! I've stopped rejoicing in God's goodness to me! I'm letting Satan win in my life by focusing on what happened~can~can~you forgive me?"

⊣ ⊢

"What now?" Mallory's voice trembled with impatience as Amelia entered the front door of the main lodge, howling!

As usual, David shot her a dirty look for her callousness as he dashed toward his overwrought firstborn!

"Aaaahhh~ahhh~uh! I~smashed my~finger!"

"Okay, let Daddy see! Let me kiss it! Kisses make~ Okay~turn loose! Let me see! Let's run it under~"

"Noooo!" a shrill shriek! "That makes it hurt more!"

"Okay, Amelia! Calm down! Let Daddy help you!" Mallory's voice, firm but sympathetic! "How did it get smashed?"

Mumbling tearful gibberish that made little sense!

"Okay, let me get my boots on, and you can show me!" She pulled them on as she spoke, following a still sobbing Amelia toward the creek!

"Right here!" She patted a place on a boulder and Mallory followed the little, smashed, pointing finger! To her amazement, there was another jaw-droppingly beautiful Tourmaline!

"Okay, how did that mash your finger?" Totally perplexed while wondering at the source of the gem!

"Right like this!" Amelia grabbed a large stone as she demonstrated! "This is another one of them pretty rocks, but it's kinda ugly here!" She pointed as her earnest blue eyes met Mallory's! "So, I was trying to break off that part!" Even as she explained, seeing the wounded digit reminded her that it hurt! Tears flowed harder!

Mallory gathered her into her arms, amazed at her little second-generation rock-hound, and proud of her!

"Okay, Baby, look at this green part with the light shining through it! The green end's really pretty, too!"

Amelia wiped at her nose with the heel of her hand, leaving a dirty smudge! "Yeah, I don't like it! I think the red's pretty! I'm gonna break it~I'll just watch out~for my fingers~better!"

Mallory pulled the ever-present tissue from her pocket, parroting her mother's words she swore she'd never use, "Don't wipe your nose with your hand! And I'm really sorry you hit your finger!" She kissed it tenderly, "But I'm glad you didn't break the crystal! It's actually called a Watermelon Tourmaline, because the red and green come together like watermelon and the rind! It's very valuable, Baby! Where did you find it?"

Amelia's face set obstinately, "I don't like the green parts of watermelon! And I don't like the green end on my rock!"

"Okay, Amelia, listen to me! If you just smash this with a rock, you'll ruin both parts! There are rock saws and better ways to do it! They have safety-devices to protect fingers, and they don't ruin the whole thing! I like breaking rocks up, to see what's inside! But, you have to wear safety goggles to protect your eyes from flying rock chips! Where did you get this? Let's look for more together! Maybe we can find another one that's only red!"

CHAPTER 39:   ELEGANCE

Mallory stared amazed at the pegmatite glittering with crystals! Nearly forgetting her own admonitions about safety precautions, she found a stick with which to poke the matrix in an attempt to free one of them! She paused, suddenly alarmed as a delivery truck screeched to a halt at the lodge! There was nothing on order that she was aware of! Alexandra's security personnel were spread too thin between her Colorado mine and this new venture! Trent and Erik had both left! Stick still in hand she watched nervously as the truck labored on the snow before gaining traction and heading back the way it had come! She was suddenly convinced that Trent was right about not bringing scores and scores of un-vetted members of the public!

"Mommy!" Amelia's voice seemed to shatter the stillness like a rifle shot!

"Sh-hh-h!" Mallory's soft warning accompanied by a finger to her lip!

Amelia was torn between obeying and her pleas for Mallory to keep digging with her!

Frozen with terror and indecision, Mallory stood rooted to the spot! Deja vu, and an uncanny memory of a morning past at their Arizona property~ Perspiration trickled despite the cold!

⛊ ⛊

Trent skied blacks with Michael and Matt, enjoying the crisp frigid air and chance to bond; an exhilarating activity! With mixed feelings about Michael's fast-approaching wedding date, he decided to concentrate on the present!

"One more run from the top; then let's go find mom and the girls and get some lunch," he suggested!

"I'll be more than ready," Michael agreed, and Matt nodded enthusiastic agreement!

"This cold mountain air makes me hungry! And it is cold air! I'll be ready for a bowl of hot chili and a table by the fireplace!"

Trent shivered involuntarily! The temperature was dropping, and then with a pause in their exertion~ "Okay, well let's be careful! No use risking getting hurt!"

⊰ ⊱

Mallory hesitated just inside the back door, wishing the stick she gripped was her pistol, and that Amelia could keep her hysterics under wraps! She thought she recognized the whooshing of the commercial dishwasher and an animated movie from the plasma in the lobby, before an annoying ringing in her ears obliterated identifiable sound! Of all the worst times for a recurrence of the tinnitus! Shaking her head in an effort to halt the din, she once more cautioned Amelia to stay still!

"Mallory!" David's voice made her jump as he slammed in through the back door! "What are you doing? I couldn't find you, and I was getting worried! Are you okay?"

She grasped at him unsteadily as she nodded numbly, "Yeah; are you?"

"Yeah, we're okay! Here, sit down! What happened? Are your ears bothering you again?"

She sank down gratefully, then dropped her head into both hands, sobbing and shaking!

He waited, perplexed! Then his perplexity deepened as Amelia reached for him and her tears broke free!

"It's nothing," Mallory gasped at last! "She just got scared because I did! The-the delivery-van-and then~I thought~"

"That someone absconded with me and the other kids? No, it was actually a valid delivery, but I thought the same thing! We need to secure this place, pronto! Hey, it's okay! Are-are your ears acting up again?"

She rested against him as the shakes subsided, "Wha-what did they deliver?"

"I thought you'd never ask! Come and see!"

❧ ❧

The ski patrol was on the verge of starting a search by the time Trent and his sons skied up to the lodge! Caked on snow crumbled off as they released their bindings! Stomping snow from boots and pulling off hats and mittens, they made their way to the restaurant!

"Trent!" Sonia's complexion was nearly as white as her fur-trimmed parka! "I-I was starting to worry–"

"So were we! The wind just picked up and there was a whiteout! We've been picking our way down, nearly on hands and knees! A medic wants to check us over for frostbite! Order us some chili and burgers; will you? We'll hurry! We're hungry!"

❧ ❧

Alexandra watched in relief as the Morrison family reunited! "You knew Trent would be okay; didn't you?"

Doug sighed, "Well, he knows survival! Still, you never know! Yes! I admire the man, but I was getting worried, too! I'm pretty sure skiing's done for today! I'll take the girls and put them down for naps! I feel one coming on, myself!"

"You sure?" She was afraid she might burst the bubble of Doug's sudden interest in parenting! "They don't always go down easily, just because they act tired!"

"I can handle it! I've been watching the pro for months! Why don't you go have a coffee with your mom and sister?"

❧ ❧

Mallory stared, dazzled and speechless, "Oh! Oh! David!"

He laughed his crazy exuberant giggle, "You like it?"

"Do I like it? It's absolutely-well-you know I love the Leprechauns-but-uh– (She referenced a gorgeous suite of jewelry.) It isn't my birthday, or our anniversary!"

He chortled again, "Why I figured I could surprise you! I didn't mean to make you nearly drop dead with fright!"

Mallory fingered the exquisite jewelry with awe, "This is~" her being speechless with wonder further delighted him!

"Herb did a good job!" His stating the obvious brought a chuckle from Mallory!

"He outdid himself, David! And that's saying something!"

"Here, why don't you try it on?"

She extended her hand while he secured a glowing bracelet of profuse poppies! Mainly crafted of Fire Opal and Sapphires that blended from yellow to orange to deep cherry! No gems could have lent themselves more perfectly to the chosen theme! Leaves and stems peeked around in Emerald, Peridot, and Chrome Diopside! The black centers of the blossoms were either black Spinel or black diamonds; she couldn't tell for sure!

His dark eyes penetrated hers as he secured an Omega necklace pinpricked with the colors, which supported a lavish coordinating bouquet slide!

"Are you worried that you might send a bad message by wearing poppies?"

"It's beautiful, David! It takes my breath away!"

He giggled again! "You didn't answer the question! Don't forget, I know you better than anyone else on this earth!"

Concern clouded her radiant countenance, "Well, I was wondering if this is the same kind of poppy they make drugs from!"

He laughed, "Gotcha! Yes, they are! But they are so vibrant and beautiful! God promised that He would clothe us better than He clothed the flowers, if we trust Him and put Him first! An abundant field of these beautiful blossoms should make us high on Him, just for the visual sensation! And although opiate drugs are commonly abused, that's just what the devil does with things that are intrinsically good! Opiates relieve a lot of pain and suffering! Or they create a lot! Depending on if they're used or abused!"

He stood back, admiring the glow against the throbbing pulse of her creamy throat! "Gorgeous! Now that my package arrived, we can head out, too!"

She moved in front of a mirror atop the mantle to admire the gift, "Where to?"

With the SUV packed for departure, David secured Amelia in her car seat! "How's the finger?" he questioned sympathetically. He kissed it tenderly, pretty sure the little nail was going to turn black before falling off!

"I'm having a bad day," her tearful voice affected him like he couldn't believe!

"Yeah, I guess! You smacked it hard!"

She nodded so soberly that he could hardly suppress a smile! "But that's not why I'm having such a bad day!"

"No? What else?"

Tears flowed again and she raised both expressive little hands in a shrug, "Everybody just lefted!"

"Well, yeah; everyone was finished with their business! We're last to leave because I had to wait on the delivery of Mommy's jewelry! What do you think about it?"

"I never ever had such a fun time! And~" She broke off, giving way to her grief!

"Yeah, with Leisel, and Elyssia, and Ryan~"

"And the puppy! We was having so much fun! And playing in the snow and hunting them red candy diamonds!"

"Okay, well listen, stop crying! We're the last ones to leave here, but we're all going skiing together!"

⚑ ⚑

"Jared asked me how finely we want the screens set for sorting gems!" Alexandra's question to Mallory!

"I'm glad you called! What are your thoughts on that?" Mallory's mind was pretty well made up, but since this venture was cooperative with Alexandra, and Jared was her find, she decided to proceed with caution!

"Well, sometimes he annoys me because I think he looks for what's easy more than what's best over-all! There's such a trend to set tiny stones into pavé that I'm reluctant to discard anything that might be of value! Or is it more expensive than it's worth? To polish the small ones?"

"I couldn't agree with you more! Even if we have to send them to India where cottage industries polish them! I should call Uncle Herb to be certain! I mean, he's buying them somewhere! And so are Samuel and Davis Hall, and their students~it's an expanding dynamic! I've gotten out of touch by missing gem shows! After the staff training next month, maybe we should plan to attend a show!"

"Sounds like a great idea! Do you suppose it's too late to rent a booth to market our stones that way, too?"

"I hope not, because that's a genius idea! We're on the road, so we should be able to get half-day tickets and get some skiing in today! Just before we left, Amelia showed me a gorgeous tourmaline pocket! She calls them 'Red Candy Diamonds'!

Alexandra laughed, "Well hurry and get here; Leisel's been practically inconsolable!"

⚔ ⚔

"We'll watch the kids in ski school," Janni's insistence to Alexandra and Mallory!

"We have a lot of catching up to do! That way you guys can ski! You can't go on blacks today though, because the wind's strong up there, and it's white-out!"

David's disappointment at the black runs' being temporarily shut down gave way to an amazed acknowledgement that God knew best! Skiing at a more relaxed pace with his wife and Doug and Alexandra, was amazing! Maybe five year old Amelia was onto something, valuing relationships and grieving at being separated!

"Let's go in for coffee and check on how our nannies are making it! Maybe we should relieve them! There's night skiing!"

"So, are you going to show me the jewelry?" Diana's eyes danced with anticipation as she greeted them! "Why don't you come over to our condo? I'll start some coffee!"

⚔ ⚔

Once the kids trooped out to night ski, Trent and Sonia sat in the lodge watching soft colors stain the sky, reflecting on glistening drifts! The entire resort took on a fairy-tale appearance as shimmering points of light illuminated the trails!

Trent was happy sitting by the fire with Sonia! He had experienced enough for one day! With their youthful exuberance, Michael and Matt failed to grasp the gravity of their close call!

400

"Isn't that Mallory's cousin and his new wife?"

Trent looked over his shoulder in response to Sonia's question. Since Shannon and Ellis had spotted him, he motioned for them to join them! Of course Sonia wasn't in the loop, but Trent was surprised they were still together! He rose courteously, and moved to get more chairs! Since he usually opened with questions about the toe, he changed his approach: "Where's the puppy?"

"With Amelia! Melodye offered to watch him while we get a bite to eat! As soon as we're done, she and Janni are going to ski awhile! Have you guys been out?"

"We have! Well, Sonia hasn't given it a shot yet! The boys and I were the last ones off," he named a black run! "The ski patrol was ready to mount a search! That was enough for me today, but the kids are out now!"

⚔ ⚔

David and Daniel exchanged stunned glances as Mallory shot past them, head held high, complexion splotched by emotions!

"You about ready to leave for Yellowstone?" Tense voice aimed at David and brooking no contradiction!

He fell into step next to her, speaking softly, "Well-well-did she have you an outfit? To go with the new jewelry?"

"Yeah, it's beautiful! Of course! You know Diana! I think I need to get a load of clothes out of the dry-"

David blocked her escape, confused! Their condo didn't have a dryer! Probably a huge mistake with a houseful of babies and toddlers- He was aware of Daniel's having taken the scene in with consternation! It was true that he and Mallory had discussed a visit to Yellowstone, a really happening place to a Geologist-but at the end of the few days skiing!

"Did she like your new jewelry?"

Her eyes blazed into his as a huge tear plopped down onto the front of her sweater!

⚔ ⚔

"Come in!" Diana's voice from behind the closed bedroom door!

Daniel pushed it open, peering in cautiously! Diana stood with Mallory's new ensemble crumpled around her, sketchbook still in hand?"

401

"Back to the drawing board? She didn't like it? What jewelry?" He was so shocked that nothing made sense! Mallory always liked Diana's designs~

When Alexandra dropped her gaze, sidling guiltily past him, he demanded, "What on earth is going on?"

An exasperated sigh from Al, "Nothing! I need to go make sure Doug got the girls in bed!"

Frowning, he watched her exit!

"Would you please tell me~"

Diana's eyes suddenly welled with tears as she gathered the brilliant silk ensemble to return to its hanger! Her hands trembled, "I would be glad to tell you, but~uh~I'm not sure~myself~"

"It's Al? Did she say something? To hurt Mallory's feelings? I thought they were getting along the best they ever have~"

"Alexandra had dropped in to visit when Mallory came to try on the outfit!" As she spoke she opened a case to reveal the exquisite jewelry! "Mallory loved the suit!" Her hand brushed the exquisite garments in wonder! "But she liked the print in the lining so much, that she was asking about~" She extended her sketch pad toward him as the easiest way to explain what Mallory was asking for additionally! "Our minds were just popping with ideas! We have so much fun with it all!"

Confusion showed on every handsome feature, "I guess you're getting to the point then, because Mallory didn't appear to have been having fun~"

"I don't understand it!" Diana's attempts at composure were failing her! "We were laughing and talking about utilizing the print, and we both looked over at Alexandra, to see what she thought! And~and she was just glaring at Mallory! With the most malevolent expression~"

᷁ ᷃

Too savvy to ask her if she was sure, David listened sympathetically! And it probably was true! Alexandra could be the queen of snotty looks!

"Please let's just leave tonight! We can see Yellowstone and then stop and ski on the way back!

"Okay, Mallory, I'm thinking! This skiing jaunt was kind of our idea! Then we were the last ones to get here! Let's just try to get some rest, and maybe in the morning~"

Tears still flowed as she nodded grudging assent! Mallory Erin O'Shaughnessy Anderson had never been one to run away! But the sheer murderous envy in Alexandra's expression wasn't easy to wipe from her memory! And Diana had been equally staggered And Diana was already walking on eggshells, longing for her relationship with Alexandra to normalize! Mallory guessed she was part of the problem! And she hadn't meant to be!

⚞ ⚟

"What's going on with you, Al?"

Daniel's eyes blazed into his firstborn's until she squirmed!

"Nothing!"

"That's a lie! I'm tired of it! Why don't you level with both of us? You've basically walked on your mom's heart like it's nothing for a couple of years! She sent you her designs, and you returned the box unopened! That's fine! But then you turn into a beast because Mallory loves her and respects her! I'm tired of you staring daggers at people!"

"Well, Mom just always makes over Adam! And that's fine! But she could at least show a little interest in Angelique!"

"Myrna showed up! And since she missed out on Brad's life; your mother relinquished the grandmother thing temporarily to her! Your mom just likes babies, in case you never noticed! And don't blame your mother for any of your actions! Blame me! If you have to blame someone! Have I gotten through to you? How quick can you get your apologies made?"

"It wasn't that big of a deal!"

Daniel sprang from the desk chair and was in her face! "The look on your face was purely murderous! It shook both Mallory and your mother to the cores of their beings! Al, you've killed people! Do you have a problem determining who your friends are, and who the enemy is?"

A look of horrified shock crossed her face before her countenance finally crumpled, "No, Sir!" Tears broke free, "It's just that–I was visiting with Mom–and then–here she comes! With her little treasure chest brimming with jewels! And it was like I wasn't even there–any more–"

"Al! That's all in your mind! You're listening to the lies of Satan! First, he deceived you into doing wrong, and now he's not letting you forgive yourself and get past it! In a roomful of Mallory's, you're the one who's our child! Your mother's child! The mother that you sent into a severe Caviar addiction, by the way! If you're jealous of Mallory with her treasure box full of jewels, you aren't the only one! I–at least confess it–as a sin–and

403

then I try to stay under the honey-bucket! Okay, think about this; you love Jeremiah and all your brothers and sisters; don't you?"

"Yes, Sir!"

"You even love them a whole, whole lot?"

"I know, I've been a terrible example!"

He sighed in pain at her self-incrimination, "I'm not going there with this, so don't you either! I'm trying to make the point that you can love your siblings deeply-but do you love Angelique more?"

She swatted at tears, "Of course!"

"Your mother's no different! I'm thankful for what Mallory means to her life, but you're her child, Alexandra! Your mother has never treated you like you're not there! If you drew into yourself and got all huffy because Mallory came to try on the outfit, it's because of the house of cards you built in your own mind! Your mother would never purposely make you jealous!"

一 匕

Mallory threw herself into bedtime and interacting with her kids with abandon! Then, when they were at last asleep, she phoned her mother and talked to her for a long time!

David extended his arms and she rested against him, "Is your mom doing okay?"

"I think so!"

"Did she just talk gardening?"

"Well, mostly she was digging dirt, let's say! When she quit pumping me for information and started talking flowers it was a relief! I was worried that she might be jealous, too, of my friendship with Diana-but-I'm pretty sure not-" she sighed!

"Well, that's the thing, though! People can act like they don't care, when they're dying inside! Speaking of-when did you last talk to Lilly?"

"Well, I've been busy, and I always end up getting yelled at! If I act like I'm looking for diamonds, she goes berserk; and then when I focus on something else, that's not right either!"

He kissed her lingeringly, "If you could see yourself like others do, you would know how much they depend on an approving nod from you! Call her and talk a few minutes, and then come right back here!"

She met his deep eyes, "Good plan! Don't go away!"

彐 㠯

Daniel sat for long moments after Alexandra's footsteps died away! Sometimes he thought she was doing great, and at other times, he despaired! Mallory was a force! And since the day of her entrance into the Faulkner family dynamic, nothing had been the same! He sighed! With her attractive appearance, he had received ribbing and innuendos that he might be more than just a guardian! Something, he had worked hard to avoid! The New Testament commanded Christians to abstain from even the appearance of evil! Maybe Alexandra had heard whispers, or wondered about his deportment! Blessedly, Diana had been a trooper, allowing the guardianship to happen, even after the rocky, early days of their marriage! His heart ached for his struggling eldest, whatever had caused her to choose the path that she had chosen, and the many obstacles toward coming back! He was torn between going up to the bedroom to make sure Diana's equilibrium was restored, and calling David! Instead of doing either, he dropped to his knees!

CHAPTER 40: SYNERGY

Pastor Andy McGuire's heart soared as the little church filled up, humming with life and warmth! Although the long-timers looked askance at the newcomers, he figured he could meld them into a congregation! Well, the newcomers were in and out! Not because of lack of Christian commitment, but because they had far-flung business ventures! He continued to stand in the back greeting people as Alexandra Hunter started the prelude with a lively selection! He blinked rapidly as he sensed the presence of the Holy Spirit in a tangible way!

He breathed a prayer of thanks! The Lord was already at work solving the problem of the gap between worshippers! At Shannon and Ellis O'Shaughnessy's entrance, a number of older members of the long-timers' group, surged toward them in a wave! He grinned inwardly as he took his chair on the small platform! That's right! They were the mobilized army who had actually rescued Ellis from the vertical shaft where she had frenziedly tried to escape the clutches of Hardy Johnson! Tears streamed down his cheeks as he witnessed the emotional reunion!

⇥ ⇤

Alexandra took note of Janni's happiness at seeing Jacob again! While David's other sister seemed glum at having left a budding friendship with Dag in Idaho! Still, it was a happy clan that overflowed the café for Sunday lunch! Happy for the moment! The kids were undoubtedly going to go to pieces as everyone went their separate ways again! She smiled to herself; mostly they would miss little Peppy Braveheart! He was an adorable breed, and Ellis was good natured at the rough and tumble play of all the kids!

"He's going to be very bored and lonely when it's only Shannon and me again," she lamented!

Daniel took it all in, relieved! Amazingly, everyone seemed to be friends again, on the best of terms! Ellis' decision to overcome her phobia and stay with Shannon, which in turn made her eager to continue high-tech-equipment exploration with Mallory, was a major miracle! And, although he hadn't forced the situation, when Al sensed a good moment, she had mended the fence with Mallory! They needed each other! Well, Al needed Mallory more than Mallory needed her, but Mallory was wise enough to recognize what Al brought to the table! His gaze traveled to soaring, snow crowned peaks, drinking in enough to last him as he returned to Tulsa!

"Tulsa's better than DC!" Morrison's voice at his elbow startled him!

With a laugh, "I guess you're right! Trying to fill my tank, though, with the beauty until I get back! Must be nice working for the National Forests!"

Trent laughed, "Doesn't life have an odd way of working out differently than you envisioned it? That was my dream! Getting an assignment in one of the forests, with maybe a small, occasional promotion! Sonia would have gone nuts in a cabin in the woods, though! I guess I'm where the Lord wants me, because aside from a bump or two in the road, my job has stayed secure! Even through Administration changes and different Cabinet Secretary appointments!"

"Yeah, that is a wonder! I was~uh~wondering if you and Sonia could join Diana and me~ Um~what would you think of Jeremiah talking to Megan?"

A startled Trent stammered, "About what?"

Daniel masked aggravation, "I don't know! Whatever kids find to talk about!"

⊰ ⊱

Trent paused as his family turned ear protectors back in! No use in denying facts! His family needed to own pistols and be well-trained with them! Even as he waited in the popular gun range, he noticed a distinct bad vibe! Law enforcement from five states frequented the popular shooting range! It wouldn't be surprising if Kittrick's pals hung around here! As well as weapons enthusiasts not necessarily on the side of the law!

He smiled brightly at his wife and kids, "Ready to load up?"

Still, a guy he didn't know hailed him in the parking lot!

"Hey, what can I do for you?"

The beefy guy grinned sheepishly, "Well, we caught the guy who blew his foot off, along with three other gangbangers! We already notified Mrs. O'Shaughnessy! She's willing to testify, but all of them broke and ratted one another out for the best plea deals!"

"Man, that's good news!" Trent felt a genuine sense of relief! "Great work!"

The officer beamed at the praise, somehow reminding him of Doug Hunter, "Thank you, Sir! That means a lot!"

Trent was shocked at the response! Why did his praise matter? The reward was removing some seriously bad dudes from circulation! "Have a good evening!" Gaining the driver's seat, he couldn't close the door because the compliment-starved cop didn't seem cognizant of his personal space! "Is there something else?" He wasn't alarmed so much as growing aggravated at the guy's sticking to him like Velcro™!

"Well, Sir-uh-just curious! Are you taking applications for the Forestry Service Law Enforcement positions?"

"Always! Go on line and fill out the application!" Usually saying that was a deterrent to people who expected him to hire them on the spot!

"Really! That's all I have to do?"

"It's a good starting place!" He pulled a business card from his visor! "This is the web site to access the ap! Don't call me, though!" Even as he issued the order he remembered getting a call from Doug Hunter, a probationary agent, who didn't know who else in the entire department to turn to!

When the star-struck cop finally ambled away, Sonia broke into gales of laughter!

"What's funny?" Madeleine's voice from behind her sounded aggrieved!

"He was just so-needy-"

"I thought he was cute! I like it that he admires Daddy so much!"

Trent shook his head sadly! It was lonely being a good guy in departments that should be all good guys!

He shivered involuntarily as he took note of a knot of men next to an older model pickup truck! Something about them-

"Brace yourselves!"

"Mama!" Ellis flew out the door and skimmed across the snowy yard as her mother pulled up at the curb!

"Ellis! You look so pretty! Your limp's almost gone?"

Darlene's complexion was a little pasty; driving mountains, and in sketchy weather conditions, besides, wasn't her long suit!

"I'll help you with your stuff! Please stay with us!"

"No! I don't want to fit the mold of the classic mother-in-law with Shannon! Moving in when you've not been married a month! Your dad reserved me a room! If you have some coffee made, though~"

She laughed at the antics of the puppy Ellis had told her so much about! "So, that's the little mutt that fended off gangsters until Shannon could come to your rescue again? Wow! Ellis! This is really nice! The fire feels good!"

Ellis shrugged! The fireplace was more decorative than functional! And the new double-wide was sufficient for the present! It perched above a pristine little valley where a new, state-of-the-art gold mine was emerging! An operation Shannon would run for David and Mallory! Several lots below were being offered as sites for custom homes, the first of which was to be hers and Shannon's; state-of-the-art modern, built with the whimsical exterior charm of the Victorians in Silverton!

"Sit down! I'll pour us some coffee! I bought a couple of slices of lemon meringue pie from the diner! It's the best there is short of yours! And, no, you're not on a diet! You're here so we can have fun!"

Darlene's protests died away at sight of the gleaming, frothy confection!

⋊ ⋉

David grinned as he set the kids free from the confinement of car seats!

Amelia took off at a gallop, "Look, there's new Crias, and here's all our fun stuff! And our toys we haven't played with in a long time are in the house, too! I've really missed this house!" She led her troop of little sisters to a small playground and miniature cabin! "Look at this place! It needs a good sweeping!" She went to work on it with an imaginary broom and they followed her example!

"I'll keep an eye on 'em, if you want to start doing laundry~"

Mallory forced a stern response, "Flip you for it! It's beautiful out! The snow was gorgeous but~ You're right! We're out of clean clothes; spring fever, or no!" She paused only long enough to admire the darling little additions to the Alpaca herd!

⊰ ⊱

Doug unloaded the car slowly! A long day driving with sun glaring on gleaming snow! He was glad to be back! He paused to wave as Jared and Abby pulled beyond to their place!

Alexandra appeared in the back door, "Let's get something to eat before the chow hall stops serving! We don't have much for groceries if we miss the main meal! I'll help unpack later~"

"Great idea! I didn't think I was hungry after grazing on snacks all afternoon~but the idea of going without until morning doesn't appeal! Here, let me carry her! She's getting heavy!"

Settling Angelique on his hip, he held out his opposite hand to Leisel! Alexandra struggled with sudden emotion as they burst through the chow hall door! Were they actually melded into a family?

⊰ ⊱

Diana spoke to Daniel as they finished lunch together in the Sullivan Building Bistro, "Well, we have reps for my lines in new geographical areas! It certainly wasn't easy!"

He nodded seriously, "When we have all of the enterprises humming along on all cylinders, so to speak, the devil doesn't like it! I guess I need to write myself a note that the more passionately Al wants something, the more indifferent she acts about it!!"

Diana nodded as her eyes snapped! "That is true, but she needs to work on being more honest! That's been mostly counter-productive for her, and then, by extension, to all of us! One person out of sync can hurt the whole! That's why I'm really excited about holding the training seminar next week!"

He placed his credit card on the ticket and nodded, "Yeah, we actually let things ride way too long! It's time to tighten the ship back up! Speaking of ships, I'm glad Darlene decided to give Captain Vaughn one more shot! And so happy that Ellis and her mom are both reps!"

With the tab settled, he rose, blocking her way as she moved toward the door, "Do you have time to come up to the office so I can show you something?"

410

"Sure! What?"

"It's a surprise! You'll see!"

⚗ ⚗

Shannon finished a lecture on English Literature and paused to phone Ellis!

"How'd it go? I prayed for you!"

He laughed, "Thanks! That must be the reason it went okay! Have you and your mom been catching up?"

He waved good-bye to Dr. Allen as he pulled his coat on and exited onto the street! Snow was falling! Hard! He interrupted her response, "There goes a snow plow! I'm gonna get right behind it! As a Bostonian, I'm used to driving on lots of snow! I'm not used to steep drop-offs on either side of the road, though! Did I ever tell you about Shay and Emma's car trip up the Andes?"

"No! Is he still mad at us?"

"Well, let's say sometimes he has a hard time letting things go! The last time he saw mother's rings, they were on her finger, just before they closed the casket! I think he jumped to the conclusion that I robbed her grave later, or something!"

He skidded several yards beyond a stop sign, and since there was no oncoming traffic, he eased in behind the lumbering piece of highway equipment! The drive would be slow! He continued his narrative! "Grandmother had to explain to him that funeral homes customarily return jewelry and valuables to the family prior to interment! My dad hardly had anything-at the end-the fact that he hadn't hocked the wedding set-well-it made me hope he wasn't responsible for her death-"

"Well, let's give him the benefit of the doubt!"

"Yeah, that's a good idea! Grandmother thought maybe we should have the rings redesigned! Something more modern and up-to-date!"

"No, Shannon! I love them the way they are! They're traditional!"

"Well, Herbert Carlton will be at the meetings next week-"

"Hmmm, maybe something to consider in the future!" She laughed at his astounded silence! "Yeah, I was never much of a jewelry person before! But, being around your grandmother, and Mallory, and Mrs. Faulkner-my eyes have been enlightened!"

⊰ ⊱

Diana waited, her curiosity piqued more than ever as Daniel fumbled at unlocking the door to his private office! He never bothered locking it when they went to lunch! There were always people around!

"Close your eyes!"

She giggled in delight, "Aren't you the mystery man?"

"Yes, and no peeking!" Pulling the door open, he nudged her forward! "No peeking! No cheating, Diana Marie Prescott Faulkner!"

Placing a hand firmly over her eyes to insure compliance, he maneuvered her in front of his desk!

"Okay! Open!"

⊰ ⊱

Alexandra listened to Sally Allen's updates with delight! "That's fantastic!"

She was pleased at *Grace's* growth and success, and appreciated the warm bond of friendship with Sally! And she was flattered that the Allens worried about her opinions, especially in regards to hiring Shannon! Alexandra felt it was fortuitous for everyone involved! Shannon and Ellis's fortunes were improving on a daily basis! His being Dean of the English department was a fit! With Tom Haynes taking oversight of the course development and creating the audio-visuals, Shannon didn't have to be on campus full-time! He would earn royalties from Haynes's corporation every time they were used in on-line education courses! World-wide!

"Do you suppose that there's any way we could lure you back on staff? I know how busy you are~"

A warning flashed in Alexandra's mind! "Don't try to play it cool! You've been dying for this! At the same moment, a viable means of expanding her income occurred to her!

"Sally, there is nothing in this world that I would love more! You're right about the time element! What do you think~"

Sally hopped onto the barreling idea, "About your recording the curriculum? Great idea! You make more money than just our modest salary, Mr. Haynes makes money, and a course becomes available for on-line students around the globe! You will put in appearances on campus occasionally, though?"

412

"I'm absolutely thrilled at the prospect~"

Sally continued tentatively, "Could you come down tomorrow~and~um~bring your family? Maybe take dinner with us? The girls have really been missing you!"

"Well, you can count on me and my daughters! I'll have to check with Doug if he can get free! Thank you, so much, Sally!"

⊰ ⊱

Diana's hands flew to her face and she gasped with delight! "Oh! Oh my! Who~what?"

Daniel stood grinning with delight! Happy to have pulled off the coup and relishing the moment!

"Okay, in case you fear that your position as designer is in jeopardy, Mallory tricked you into designing your own ensemble! Trust me, none of the rest of us have the capability!"

She nodded! It made sense now, why Mallory had asked for additional pieces to her 'Poppies' design! It was unlike Mallory to ask for anything extra, but the strangeness of that request had been superseded by Alexandra's unexpected attitude!

"So, once the drawings were done, of course your factory employees have your size, and they took it and ran with it! And~of course, Herb~"

She stared at the lavish array in speechless wonder! No detail overlooked! And she loved butterflies!

Tanzanite! A lovely, lovely gemstone rapidly being depleted! Herb must have accumulated every piece still in circulation! She studied the heavy ring in amazement! A heavy gold setting held a ten carat; emerald cut Tanzanite, further embellished by decorative prongs: a small jeweled butterfly hovered at the upper right corner and a diminutive Lilly of the Valley rested at the bottom left! The bracelet repeated the border print of the silk Dupioni suit! A line of intermingled green-toned, baguette-cut gemstones formed the base line across which a pavéd flower garden flowed! Intricate Pansies, Daisies, Bachelor's Buttons, Mini Carnations, Cosmos, Daffodils, and Tulips sparkled, tipped occasionally by hovering butterflies! The Omega slide featured a centered *Blue Moro Butterfly* shimmering in deep tones of Blue Diamonds, Sapphires, and Tanzanite, surround by a lavish bouquet of sparkling blossoms!

😅 😅

Doug wasn't one to participate in water cooler gossip, but he caught an alarming snatch of conversation! Hurrying to his Forestry Service issued SUV, he phoned Alexandra for confirmation!

"What?" It was news to her! "They were in a wreck that hospitalized all of them? I haven't heard anything! Maybe my dad has~Want me to call and check?"

Before she could place the call, her phone jingled an incoming call from Mallory.

"Hi, Mallory; how can I help you? Have you heard anything about the Morrisons being in a bad wreck?"

"Yes, it's what I'm calling you about! They were all more shaken than hurt, but they were in danger~or Mr. Morrison felt they were! I trust his sense about it! They were leaving from a gun range~and a Bethesda policeman he knew, through Ellis's close call, stopped him to ask about applying to Forestry law enforcement! That delay caused him to notice alarming activity where the parking lot empties onto the county road! A street lamp was out, and it was mostly shadows around dark cars!

Then, a couple of guys jumped in front of the Morrison's van and simultaneously a beater pickup pulled forward to block the exit! Mr. Morrison plowed through all of it! One of the men was thrown five hundred feet, and he's in critical condition! Another one has multiple fractures in both legs! The Morrisons all claimed to be hurt, in order to be transported to a hospital, away from the sketchy scene! Here's the deal, though! Mr. Morrison might be in legal trouble, which won't help his job!"

Alexandra listened wide-eyed to the narrative! "Okay, thanks! I need to call Doug back and tell him! Do my parents know yet? That's a bunch of prayer requests, for sure! The Morrisons didn't get hurt, though?"

"Just some bumps and scrapes! Erik called me! The only witnesses were the cop who had been talking to Mr. Morrison, and the ones who were part of the scheme~whatever it was~So there are two totally different versions of what happened!"

😅 😅

Diana pirouetted giddily in front of the three way mirror in her design salon! Daniel laughed from the doorway! "So, I guess this means you like everything?"

She flew into his arms and turned bewitchingly beautiful face up towards him!

He kissed her lingeringly, "You are so incredibly beautiful, Diana! Where would I be, if it hadn't been for God placing you into my life when He did? You grow more beautiful to me with every day that passes!" His serious eyes searched hers, "I know becoming a Grandmother hit you like a bolt out of the blue! Since we didn't know that Alexandra was married, we certainly didn't realize that she had a baby! There's usually a chance to adjust to the idea~"

She shrugged, caught! It was a struggle for her she wished she could deny!

"I know how much you've wanted more children! How it's been tough~miscarrying~ And, you are still within the childbearing time frame~"

"I guess, if you average in Sarah!" She tried to laugh it off!

"Well, speak for yourself! I'm not as old as Abraham was! Aging is tough for me to think about, too! Especially in our culture of youth and beauty! The time will come when we don't look like Ken and Barbie~"

She chuckled, "You don't think it has?"

His eyes alight, he considered, "Well, I think we look like a maturing Ken and Barbie~so~no~the time hasn't come yet!"

He held her away to study the charming costume and her winsome expression as he quoted softly:

She maketh herself coverings of tapestry; her clothing is silk and purple.

Her husband is known in the gates, when he sitteth among the elders of the land.

She maketh fine linen and selleth it; and delivereth girdles unto the merchant.

Strength and honor are her clothing; and she shall rejoice in time to come.

She openeth her mouth with wisdom; and in her tongue is the law of kindness.

She looketh well to the ways of her household, and eateth not the bread of idleness.

Her children arise up, and call her blessed; her husband also, and he praiseth her.

Many daughters have done virtuously, but thou excellest them all.

Favour is deceitful, and beauty is vain: but a woman that feareth the LORD, she shall be praised.

Give her of the fruit of her hands; and let her own works praise her in the gates.

What an incredible woman you are, Diana! What an incredible life God has blessed us with! Are you going to wear this for the opening sessions of the training seminars next week?"

She nodded as her expression clouded, "Maybe we should pray for the Morrisons again! I can't imagine everyone getting together, and them not being a part-"

※ ※

Alexandra felt she might burst with happiness! Doug had taken time off on purpose to go with her to *Grace* for dinner with Dr. and Mrs. Allen! And he affirmed his pride in her for initially having landed the teaching position!

"And then there's the chance of expanding my income, who knows how high-through the virtual arena?" She bubbled, and he sobered.

"Only problem with it, is bringing the old boyfriend back into your life!"

She beamed at him! "Wow, a lot of water under my bridge since that juvenile infatuation! I'm not sure there will be any reason for me to interact with Tommy, and Mr. Haynes is okay with the way things turned out, because Mrs. Haynes never liked me too much! Well, I acted like a brat in

Paris and nearly ruined a fabulous trip for everyone! Uh-I guess I've never worked too hard at being likeable!"

Doug laughed as his hand covered hers, "Well, you did shoot me down!"

She flushed, "Well, after what happened with Brad, I felt like the whole world knew what I'd done! I thought, you probably thought, I-"

"I just thought you were the most beautiful girl I'd ever seen! And I was too dumb to realize you were so far out of my league!"

She shot him a sideways glance, "Well, we got off to a strange start, but I'm so grateful for how things have worked out-

⊰ ⊱

"You are certain, Michael?"

"Why do you always question every report I bring you? Of course, I am certain! I like it less than you do, but that's how things are!"

Lilly Cowan, Israeli Diamond Council Director, paced, her habitual limp more in evidence than ever-

Michael laughed harshly! "The solution should be more than obvious to you! A plan whereby you might, 'Kill two birds with one stone', to quote an oft-used expression! Perhaps accomplish more than two goals-with one operation!

She frowned! "Ah, so you reference getting the Morrison family to Israel until his legal issues are resolved!"

He clapped sarcastically as she grasped what he intimated! She gave voice to the benefits, "Goal two would be resurrecting the group's interest in the true Exodus route our people historically followed! I have been most distressed by their abandoning of it! And part three would be bringing in new tourists who have never yet visited our land!"

Her eyes glittered, "Who would fund it?"

"You and your council, of course!"

She gasped, "Do you know the size group we're talking about?"

"Within an error margin of twenty or thirty either way! Yes, a major cost, but what might it reap in benefits? Maybe unequivocal proof that Moses and the Israelite slaves crossed the Red Sea at the Strait of Tiran? Leading to a Mount Sinai in present day Saudi Arabia! That is of inestimable value! And most of the guests you would be hosting are fabulously wealthy! Surely they will boost our economy by what they'll spend, especially

417

freed from the expenses of travel and lodging! And don't forget Mallory's cooperation with you in agreeing to produce such a low Diamond quota and keep silent about the scope of US deposits!"

⚏ ⚏

"What? Lilly, are you kidding me?" Mallory came up with a screech of amazed delight, her aggravation at the interruption of her Red Sox story forgotten! "You–you're offering to host–our entire–do you know how many of us–Okay, I'm sure you do! If anyone does her homework, it's you! Okay, well, I'll need to get a memo out to everyone to make sure their passports are current– At Eilat? Oh, yes, Ma'am, perfect! Wow, I haven't been able to figure out why on earth we couldn't get the details to come together– Thank you, Lilly! This is so ex–ciiii–tinggg!"

CHAPTER 41: CONTENTMENT

Let your conversation be without covetousness; and be content with such things as ye have: for he hath said, I will never leave thee, nor forsake thee.

Hebrews 13:5

Alexandra watched happily as Doug located studs and hung a stunning oil painting above the credenza in her mine office! An oil painting from the magical brush of Risa Perkins she had yearned for since her arrival in Southwestern Colorado! And purchased for her sacrificially by her students at *Grace*! He stood back to survey his handiwork!

"You know, every would-be artist that comes through here tries to paint Mt. Sneffels-well, you know I'm no art connoisieur-but this really captures a mood-"

"It does! And I never told a soul how much I wanted it! And then it got sold-and I had no idea the girls had watched me that first day I met them- The Lord truly does give you the desires of your heart, when you delight in Him and put Him first! And as much as I've longed for the painting, the love of the Allens and the girls in the student body, means far more!"

Smiling understanding, he reached for Angelique, who clapped with delight and stretched her arms to him in return!

Tears sparkled on long lashes! Doug taking ownership of their foursome as his family was a special answer to prayer, too! With no real father roles in his family background, he was feeling his way! In the meantime, Alexandra continued to nurture Leisel's skype sessions with Alice McKay, his grandmother!

"Do you mind if we load our trays and eat dinner in the Annex?"

Alexandra's face registered surprise; she enjoyed the camaraderie of the chow hall, but if taciturn Doug had decided to communicate~

After several minutes of silence, "Doug, was there something~"

Oh~uh~yeah~ Well, first of all, the charges were dropped on Agent Morrison! Although there wasn't video of the actual wreck, cameras inside the gun range showed the conspirators targeting Trent and his family with conversation and even some mocking charades! The instigators ended up wanting the whole incident to go away, even more than the Morrisons did! Meanwhile, even though they dropped the charges and the law suits, they've come to the attention of their various departments! Some of them have their activities under investigation! Careers, benefits, retirement on the line!"

"Well, that is a relief! I've been concerned that if he lost his job~where would that leave us?"

She took note of his injured expression, "I'm sorry, Doug! I like the Morrisons a lot! But I can't help it, when I hear news, I always analyze, 'How might this affect me'?'

"Well, I think everyone's that way! I didn't want my job in jeopardy, or even to work in Forestry Law Enforcement with a different man at the helm! I still can't wrap my head around the fact that I just got back from Israel! Whenever people would try to talk to me about foreign travel~well~ my mind was pretty closed~"

She smiled, "But you had a good point about how much there is to see here at home! I'm trying not to be jealous that David and Mallory did Yellowstone! Talk about happening, Geologically! Yellowstone is! And Israel was fantastic, and all of the sessions!"

He brightened, "No kidding! That was a lot to absorb!" His brow furrowed, "All of that business training~I never had a clue! Your father was right! All of those principles are from the Bible! The world makes a killing using them, and most Christians! Well, we fail to use the light the Lord gives us! So~are you okay~with your mother? When you were so upset after Christmas, about seeing her, I thought she must be a real Attila the Hun!"

Alexandra laughed ruefully, "Most of the time she isn't! But if she catches you giving her a dirty look~" She fought sudden tears despite her attempt at levity! "And everything I thought I was so right about~I was jumping to conclusions! Mom was backing away from Angelique to give Myrna some bonding time! And Adam is adorable! All of Mallory's kids are! And Mallory and my mom are close friends! They have been from day one~"

"Which doesn't change your standing with her in the least! It never has; you're the one who's pushed people away!"

"I know!" Her gaze faltered, "It's true that what I want the most, I act the most indifferent about! It isn't being real~or honest~but it's a really hard habit to change! My parents know this Christian psychologist~

Doug moved closer and pulled her into his arms! "I love you, Alexandra! You are amazing; and dealing with miners and businessmen, that icy façade stands you in good stead! I think that with having three mines to get up and running, and with Abby back, and with the training from those sessions, Jared's going to be okay!"

"Mmmm-hmmm, and I'm relieved for Shannon and Ellis! There wasn't a significant amount of gold in the sample from the blast site, but there were significant placer deposits that my Aunt Brenna's staff geologist tracked above town! Shannon's oversight of that operation, along with his teaching income from Tom Haynes and *Grace,* will dig him out of his financial hole!"

"Yeah, and the house is coming along! An exact replica of the turn of the century Victorian Ellis fell in love with~" He paused, "So our income has risen too!"

She nodded, "Yes; that it has! Praises be to God! I'm glad I started tithing when I did!"

He bounced Angelique absent-mindedly as he considered, "Do your parents and the Andersons really tithe? Call me a man of little faith, but I can't figure out how they have what they do, by giving it away!"

"Okay, 'Man of little faith', yes they really do! I'm not sure David and Mallory give double, but they tithe to their church in Dallas and give a lot to his dad's church in Murfreesboro! And my parents have been tithers for as long as I remember! Everything they taught in those sessions, Doug, they do themselves! And they're testaments to the fact that the principles work!"

He flushed and desperation flashed in his eyes! "Okay, that's not exactly where I was trying to take this conversation!"

She smiled happily, glad for his attempts at communication! Although, he had been the one to bring up the tithing issue! "I'm sorry! Where was it supposed to go?"

"Well, I was talking about Shannon and Ellis's house, and our increased revenue~and I wondered if you want to build a bigger house~ I mean the modular here has been great~maybe I'm talking too much money~"

She regarded him narrowly, "So, that's what you want to discuss? Building a bigger house?"

"Mmm-hhmmm," he kissed her hard! "So we can have more room~to build~our ~family!"

ted in the United States
Bookmasters